D1797614

Eulogy for Love

Steve Dowson

Copyright © Steve Dowson, 2024

All Rights Reserved

This novel is a work of fiction and any resemblance to actual persons living or dead is purely coincidental.

This book is subject to the condition that no part of this book is to be reproduced, transmitted in any form or means; electronic or mechanical, stored in a retrieval system, photocopied, recorded, scanned, or otherwise. Any of these actions require the proper written permission of the author.

ISBN

978-1-0687136-1-3

Published by Steve Dowson 2024

And since life ends and laughter,
And leaves fall and tears dry,
Who shall call love immortal,
When all that is must die?

Ernest Dowson

"To His Mistress"

Prologue

It was in those last weeks, watching Kat as she slept, that I decided I would write her story. Not, I should tell you, because I thought she was a remarkable woman—or not, at any rate, an unusually remarkable woman. She hadn't fought in a war, or broken a glass ceiling, or pioneered life-saving medicines. She was not a celebrity or a politician, and she hadn't raised millions for charity.

I might take a risk and suggest she knew a love that, in the depths of its joy and its awful misery, was a harsh gift that few of us will know. But who's to say? Look at the faces you see on the street, especially the faces of women. Better still, when you are waiting at the traffic lights, look in your mirror at the woman in the car behind you. She might be preening herself, getting her hair and face ready for a day at the office, or for a meeting with a friend or lover. She might be talking with a companion beside her, or on the phone. But if she's alone, she'll most likely be staring ahead, her face oddly expressionless. What hides behind the dulled eyes of these women? What invisible loves, what losses, what injustices? And who is to judge whether their love, or their suffering, has been exceptional?

In those first months of 2014, I was watching Kat approach her death—that most unexceptional of all human experiences. We were in a room in an English country hospital, remnant of healthcare in a less industrialised era. It was solidly built, with thick walls and tall ceilings, its back against woodland. If the doctors had realised that she would last so long, they might have moved her to a hospice; but she lingered from February until April. In the first weeks they left the door open. Staff often came in to check pressures, ask for menu choices, peer at drips. I would pop in and out, bringing magazines and other supplies, and news of happenings in the world, as if it were only a matter of time before it would be her world again.

Later, in the last weeks, they knew that Kat needed to concentrate on her dying, and they closed the door. She and I were set apart, hearing little of hospital life beyond the murmur of voices, the rumbling of trolleys. In March a pair of blackbirds came to nest in a hedge against the wall outside. Their wings would rustle the leaves, and flicker the sunlight that fell down on us from the high windows.

Mark would sometimes visit for a short time, early in the evening. I aimed to leave before he arrived. He came straight from work, smartly suited, his bespoke shoes tapping as he neared Kat's room. He liked to use his brief visits to fuss, to ask questions about the meals or changes in medication. He did this because he thought it was how a husband should act when his wife was dying, and because he could not bring himself to sit and hold her hand.

The children visited once each weekend. Mark had declared that more frequent visits would be too wearying for their mother. Instead, the children stayed at home in the care of the woman he had brought in to act as housekeeper and nanny.

Often, in those last weeks, Kat and I were alone. I would sit at the bedside holding her hand, feeling how thin the skin had become, how loosely it slid across the bones and sinews. She mostly slept, by that stage—usually motionless on her back, her colourful bandana bright against the white hospital pillows. I felt as if I were on the banks of a river, watching over her as she readied to drift downstream to an unknowable sea.

There was a period in between. At that stage, she often lay awake but deep inside her own thoughts. Sometimes she would stir to tell me some small pleasing memory, or to fret over a trivial domestic concern. She might suddenly lift her head and speak in alarm: *Has someone remembered Rachel has her piano lesson today?*

Far worse things troubled her mind. She was full of regret for the wasted years with Mark, for her cowardly refusal to be true to herself. Most of all she was tortured by the thought that she would no longer be able to protect her children. They were going to be left in the custody of the husband she feared and despised, and her death was an excuse she could not allow herself.

I am well-placed to tell this story. I was Kat's intimate friend, her confidante and confessor. A second authoritative source would confirm and augment what Kat had told me. Where I have added anything more, it is only varnish to bind the bright pigments.

And me? I am irrelevant for the moment, a distraction. I'll introduce myself when the time comes.

PART 1

When the game began between them for a jest,
He played king and she played queen to match the best;
Laughter soft as tears, and tears that turned to laughter,
These were things she sought for years and sorrowed
after.

Algernon Charles Swinburne
'Stage Love'

Chapter 1

'Daddy.'
'Daddy!'
'Daddiee!'

David was standing at the sink, rinsing pots and staring out of the window. A lock of neglected sandy hair fell onto his forehead. He had changed out of the t-shirt and old jeans he had worn all day, replacing them with a collared shirt and newer jeans. In those days—at the start of his forties—he was sparely built, and the jeans hung a little loosely.

It was early February in 1998, and the twin's eighth birthday. It was also a Thursday, which meant that the double birthday party would have to wait until the weekend. Today was to be marked only by unwrapping gifts before school, and a meal out at teatime. The time was nearly six. David had already allowed the girls two lots of snacks, but they were becoming restless and contrary.

'Daddiee!'

It was Lauren. Though Hannah and Lauren were twins, Lauren was usually the spokeswoman. David turned to look at them where they sat together at the kitchen table, the empty snack bowl in front of them.

'Daddy, do we *have* to go to Pizza Express?'
'What's wrong with Pizza Express?'
'We don't like pizza.'

'You did yesterday. And every day before that, as far as I remember.'

'But we don't like it today.'

The phone rang, and David picked the cordless receiver off the wall hook to answer. It was Helen. 'Love, sorry, I'm running late. Meeting went on longer than planned and I've got a couple of things to sort before I leave. Could you head on to the restaurant and I'll see you there?'

It wasn't a request. 'OK. See you there. Please try not to be too long.'

'Great, thanks. Bye.' Then: 'Oh, David . . .?'

He put the phone back to his ear. 'Yes?'

'Which restaurant did we decide?'

'Pizza Express. The one in the middle of town.'

David replaced the phone and turned to the twins. 'OK, you two. Time to get ready. Toilet please, and shoes. Mum will meet us there.'

They arrived at the restaurant half an hour later. David got the twins settled, coaxed them into liking pizza again, talked them out of choosing the worst of the fizzy drinks, and alerted the staff that they should make at least the customary fuss over diners with birthdays, in particular the special dessert with sparklers on top. He wanted to ask for double desserts, double sparklers, and double fuss, but didn't have the courage. Helen arrived when the pizzas had been served, pressured the waiter to hurry her own order, and then sat back to distance herself from the family as they ate. She had lately acquired a mobile phone, paid for by her employers, and put it on the table. When it rang she mouthed *sorry* to David, and went outside to talk and smoke a cigarette.

Another birthday group reached the sparklers stage, and everyone was expected to sing Happy Birthday to a little girl who was too young to understand. David detested the consumerist production line. The twins became impatient for their turn.

The meal concluded well. The twins were persuaded to wait until their mother had finished eating. The restaurant staff, charmed, made double birthday fuss and brought double special desserts and sparklers. The other diners sang half-heartedly. The girls grinned in the white fizzing light, and jiggled their thin bodies with pleasure.

Once home, David supervised Lauren and Hannah through their bedtime chores, and then Helen came up to read their bedtime story. They had bunk beds and, at story time, Lauren always came down from the top bunk and squeezed in next to Hannah. David left them to it, and went downstairs to the living room. He turned on the TV but sat thinking about the familiar pattern of the evening, wondering what to do about it.

Helen joined him a few minutes later, choosing to perch on the arm of a sofa. It was a signal she did not intend to stay. David sensed she was about to conduct a review, as if she were still in the office. She did the same with her staff after a book launch, he felt sure.

'I think that went well, don't you? Restaurant people did us proud, I thought. Girls certainly left happy.'

David contemplated saying nothing in reply—it had, after all, been a verdict and not a question—but decided to risk a comment.

'It would have been even nicer if you'd got home earlier and made it a proper family event,' he said, only glancing at her.

'Of course it would,' Helen answered, her voice hardening, 'but it's the kind of job where things come up sometimes, and I have no choice but to deal with them. That's the way it is. You know that.'

'But it's hardly *sometimes*. It's practically all the time, and it leaves me having to fill in the gaps. Like half term next week, when you're offering to help one afternoon, and I'm doing the rest.'

'So what would you have me do? Stop working?'

'I'm not asking you to stop working . . .'

Helen interrupted him. 'Pleased to hear that! We'd all be in a mess without my salary.'

'For goodness sake, Helen, I'm just asking for a little re-balancing. I mean changing the balance in your life, just slightly, in favour of us as a family. And shifting a bit in the balance of responsibility between the two of us. I have work pressures too, y'know! It's all very well you buggering off to work every day. Just because I'm the one who works from home, it shouldn't mean I have to pick up responsibility for all the childcare.'

'Well, yeah, but that's the way it is. You have the flexibility. I earn the money.'

It was true, but there was no need to say it. Helen, senior partner, was pulling rank.

'Anyway, I'm off to bed,' Helen announced, standing up.

David remained on his own. He knew Helen would soon be sitting in bed in an old t-shirt to keep her shoulders warm, and browsing women's magazines—the thin weekly ones, the kind she unaccountably liked. She would pick out the romantic short stories, and the articles about *How to relight the passion in your sex life*, or *Ten ways to please your man*. She wouldn't thank David for interrupting.

His resentment over the unfair burden of domestic tasks had been growing for some time but, now it had been mentioned, it became a sore place they couldn't help but pick. Next morning, as Helen stood in the hall preparing to leave—a cigarette already in her hand to light as soon as she made it to the car—he asked her to try to get back earlier. 'I'll try,' she answered gruffly, 'but I can't promise.'

After that it didn't need to be said. Each morning the request hung unspoken in the air, and every evening it became a silent rebuke when she arrived home late. At the weekend, tired after the twin's party, they bickered again. David complained about having his working hours taken up by the need to do domestic tasks. Helen suggested finding a cleaner. David pointed out that this would still leave his worktime hemmed between the school runs. The potential answers to this problem—an au pair, an after-school club, a neighbour to help out—had all been discussed and dismissed before.

They struggled through the extra childcare demands of half-term week. At the end of it, on the Saturday, Helen offered to take the twins into town so that David could spend a few hours working. She would walk them in, and find somewhere for lunch, and in that way give him a few good hours of peace.

David and Helen Barber lived in a tall house at the end of a short Georgian terrace. They had bought it before the twins arrived, a time when there was more money and optimism. A previous owner had built a workshop at the far end of the garden. It was little more than a man-shed, but it was large and solidly built from breezeblocks. They had been able to find the funds to improve the insulation and flooring, run in electricity and water supplies, and put plaster on the walls. The only extravagance had been to replace one end wall with glass. Back then, David had liked to describe himself as an artist, and a studio with a high, north-facing window seemed to affirm that identity. More than that, it symbolised the hope they shared for a future that would bring a life of contentment, security, and success in their professional fields. There was a place for children in this vision—children who were amusing and appreciative, and who might be heard, unobtrusively laughing and playing games in the house while their parents engaged with friends in cultured conversations.

The vision cracked and broke in the years that followed. The twins brought a double dose of parenthood that included moments of happiness but drove out intimacy, culture, and all but the most tolerant friends. Meanwhile, financial pressures forced David to respond to the demands of the marketplace. It wasn't too painful to restyle himself as illustrator rather than artist, as it still allowed him to imagine the upmarket children's titles with his name below the author's. But that didn't happen either. He had to settle for commissions to provide line drawings in obscure publications, office manuals and company calendars, often briefed to leaven amateurish copy with a little humour or 'personality'. The colour had gone out of his work.

Helen discovered that where babies were concerned, she had the hips but not the inclination. She used the need for income as a justification to return quickly to the more rewarding world of work. She, at least, was still having success, steadily ascending the management levels. However, the higher she went, the more her days were taken up with dull corporate meetings and office politics, and every day she returned home feeling stressed.

That Saturday afternoon, when Helen came back from town, she walked down the path to find David in his studio, and leaned across the doorway.

'Kids on their own in the house so can't stay long, but I think I may have found the answer.'

David sat back from the tilted board of his drawing table and looked at her with a frown.

'You know,' she went on, 'your problem with not getting enough time for your work.' David noted the way it was *his* problem. 'Stopped and chatted with a neighbour, and she says she knows this girl who's looking for work. Well, young woman—early twenties, I think. Lives locally. Been looking after her dying mum. Now her mum's gone, she's planning to start uni this autumn. Needs something to do in the meantime, and might be willing . . . you know . . . to give us some help on a daily basis.'

David was still frowning. 'Could we afford that?'

Helen had plainly decided this was going to be the solution. 'Well, we wouldn't have to pay her much per hour. In terms of the job market she's not much better than a school leaver. And not an attractive proposition to other employers when she's going to leave after a few months.'

'Doesn't really help us much either, as a long-term solution,' David commented, reluctant to be pressured, 'but I can see it's worth taking further.'

***

Helen took on the task of recruiting this young woman, magnanimously working to resolve a difficulty she considered to be David's problem. She followed up the contact details the neighbour had given her, and arranged for the young woman to visit the next Saturday morning, when all the family could meet her. And it was Helen who, when the day came, cleared away the remnants of breakfast from the kitchen table so that they could use it to sit and talk with their guest. The twins were playing upstairs. David retreated to his garden studio until Helen used the primitive intercom system to call him back to the house.

When he got inside the house, Helen and Kat, as she was introduced, were already sitting at the kitchen table. David had known that Kat was in her early twenties, yet for some

11

reason his mind had conjured up a gangly, gum-chewing teenager. Kat wasn't that at all.

She was sitting at the end of the table, her slim body upright, hands cupped around a mug of coffee on the table, legs crossed tidily at the ankle, her feet in black pumps. Poised, calm, self-possessed. She wore a lightweight black sweatshirt, and leggings that were likewise black. Her hair, in natural curls to her shoulder, was dark, though warmed by touches of auburn. It all could have signalled someone timid and self-effacing, but for two features: the large brown eyes that looked confidently towards David as he walked in, and the vivid scarlet lipstick that delineated her smile.

David sat down at the table while Helen and Kat continued their conversation. He was feeling unsettled. It had crossed his mind that the awkward teenager he had been expecting might have something about her—jiggling breasts perhaps, or long legs and a short skirt—that would provoke difficult feelings. As a right-thinking, middle-class man in his forties, he had readied himself to suppress them. But this Kat, this young woman with quiet presence, called up feelings in him that were far more complex and unexpected.

He tuned into the conversation they were having, noticing that Kat spoke softly and with no distinctive accent. She was explaining that she had chosen to take a year out after leaving school, intending to travel for part of it. While backpacking through Europe she had got to know an American family living in Florence. She earned a little money by helping out with babysitting their seven-year-old boy. The relationship with the family blossomed, and she paused in her travels to live with them as their au pair.

The family was in Florence because the husband and wife were both academics, and temporarily teaching there. When that came to an end, Kat was invited to continue her work for them back in the States. It seemed too good an opportunity to miss. University could wait another year. The news came, a few months later, that her mother had fallen seriously ill, and Kat felt duty bound to return to the UK. Kat nursed her mother through her final illness, watching as the start of two more university years slipped by her.

Her mother had died a few months before, and now Kat was waiting to start university in the autumn. In the meantime, she was spending time with her dad, assisting him with daily living where necessary, but also to make sure he was independent of her by the time she started at university. So part-time local work would suit her very well, she assured Helen and David, especially if there was the flexibility to spend a bit of each day with her father.

The conversation turned to the practical arrangements. To take the load off David, Kat would need either to escort the twins to school, or collect them in the afternoon. And if she could do some domestic duties, such as emptying the dishwasher and putting on some laundry—tasks that seemed to delay David from starting his own working day—then so much the better. Kat thought this entirely practicable.

Helen suggested that she should take Kat upstairs to meet the twins, and David was left on his own at the kitchen table. Helen was obviously enthusiastic about the proposed arrangement, and David had to admit that it could be very helpful. At the same time, he sensed that this young and interesting woman could destabilise the Barber household.

It was a long time since David had felt either loved or desired by Helen. He sometimes wondered whether she had a lover at work, but chose to believe it was work itself that affirmed her. As her career had developed, and his had stalled, she seemed increasingly to despise him. For the sake of the twins, they sustained the fiction of a happy marriage, but in private the arid condition of their relationship was undeniable.

Once a month or so they would fail to avoid going to bed at the same time, and then they would lie side by side in silence. Sometimes, in the darkness, Helen would announce, 'You can fuck me if you want.'

It had come to this, as these things usually do, in small steps through the years. What had once been unthinkable became tolerable, and then eventually incorporated as an ordinary element of married life. Helen also insisted on the custom, once pleasurable, of going out sometimes for a meal together, though they would look across the table at each other and find they had nothing to talk about. She would organise a babysitter so that they could go to the cinema, though they did not like the same kinds of film, and never held hands as they watched, nor shared their opinions afterwards. And, about once a month, she made herself available in bed.

Helen was not a woman who liked to discuss emotional issues. Occasionally she might allow herself a moment of vulnerability to voice some worry about family or work, but always quickly closed the conversation off. For the most part she issued edicts and position statements, rarely permitting follow-up questions. Life was too busy already, she seemed to be indicating. As a consequence, there was never the possibility of a heartfelt dialogue that might have yielded better understanding; never a quarrel that might have led to apologies, kissing, and making up.

Years later, David would look back at this time and see himself as a coward. Certainly, some of it was sheer gutlessness. He didn't like arguments, especially with Helen. But there was also the dreadful sense that it might take only the breath of a raised voice to blow their marriage away. An honest exchange of feelings might have led, not to the kisses and the making up, but to the moment where they would be left staring at each other, knowing there was nothing left, no love to carry them forward. That possibility had to be avoided, whatever the cost.

For these reasons, David chose instead to accommodate her. He guessed that she insisted on these rituals of married life, however miserable they might be, because it helped her to pretend the marriage was healthy. As a body on a hospital bed may be judged alive if it breathes and has a pulse, so Helen might have persuaded herself—or at least tell the world—that all was well at home because they sometimes dined out, saw a film, had sex.

The truth may have been that Helen was just as aware as David that the marriage, regardless of these vital signs, persisted only in a vegetative state. Perhaps she offered him use of her body in the belief that it was he who still clung to the illusions. Perhaps she thought she was giving him everything a man really needs. Then again, David would look back, years later, and suspect—with good reason, moreover—that it was all engineered by Helen to conceal a much larger untruth.

At the time, David thought he was being kind to accept the invitation, much as he hated doing it. Her position in bed when she made it—staring upwards towards the ceiling, or on her side with her back to him—would let him know how he should set about it. He would do it—again, as a kindness—as quickly as possible. After he had performed and withdrawn, he would lie awake in despair.

In daylight hours, his sense of emptiness and failure was eased by the chores and routines of life, and by the small pleasures that he found within them. The twins, with their energy and honesty; perhaps the freshness of dew on the grass as he made his morning passage to the studio; or the distraction of a late-night film on television, watched alone. It was these conjugal incidents, more than anything else, that obliged him to see how far they had fallen.

David had decided long ago that he would endure this life until the twins left home. It was partly a vestige of obligation to marriage vows, but mostly a recognition that, if they separated, Helen would take everything that gave his life meaning and security. The only future without Helen that he could envision was a life in a dingy flat where he would be unable to work, and where he would pass his days in agonies of grief for the loss of his children. So, instead, he quietly counted the passing of each month and year, endured Helen's deprecations and condescensions, and wore the public mask of a happily married man. Moreover, because he knew how deeply he craved a woman who would desire, love, and respect him, he made sure he never met one. As a solitary, home-based worker, he had not found this difficult.

Now, as he sat in the kitchen, Helen was upstairs contriving to introduce a new feminine energy into their household. Kat was young, slim, and pretty in an oddly casual way. She was too young for him, of course, but her youth might make her impressionable. He was sure he could resist the impulses of lust. Seduction by kindness or flattery would be a far greater threat.

At that moment Helen entered the kitchen, alone. She pushed the door closed with her back but put out a hand to stop it shutting entirely.

'I think she's great,' she said in a stage whisper. 'Don't you? She's already down on her hands and knees playing with the twins. Snap her up, I say! Agreed?'

'Get some references, maybe?' David answered, trying to make a contribution to the process.

'Of course,' Helen replied, signalling that he had failed. She went back upstairs to Kat, and David could hear them in conversation. A few minutes later they both came down, the twins trailing behind and grumbling because Kat was leaving so soon. Kat stayed in the hall, and Helen positioned herself in the kitchen doorway so that Kat could hear her explain the plan to David.

Helen was hopeful, she told him, that she could get references by phone within the week. All being well, the arrangement would start the following week. Kat would take the twins to school on Mondays and Fridays, and do an hour or so of housework afterwards. 'So that,' she said loudly, 'will leave you free to get down to the studio by eight-thirty, David, and put in a solid day's work.' On Wednesdays, Kat would collect from school, and stay with the twins until around five. If she had a chance to get some housework done in that period, so much the better. That meant, Helen pointed out, that on Wednesdays David would have a full nine-to-five working day.

David had wanted to be released from the overlapping pressures of work and home, but was now starting to feel he was being banished. What would he do if there was a lull in his work? He nodded gratefully to Helen, once her announcement was completed. Kat barely had time to offer David a farewell smile, and a little token of a wave, before Helen escorted her out. There was another brief chat on the doorstep; then Kat was gone. Helen returned to the kitchen.

She was triumphant. 'Well, I think that's great! You must be pleased, aren't you?'

'Absolutely,' David answered. 'Really good.'

Helen picked up the coffee mugs and stood at the sink to rinse them out, her back to David.

'I, um,' David started, 'I'm just a little surprised that you're OK about her being, well, on her own in the house.'

'I don't see the problem. If she has any queries she can come and find you in the studio.'

'No, I don't mean her *on her own alone* . . .'

There was a pause, then Helen threw back her head and laughed. 'Oh my god, David, you mean *when the two of you are alone!*'

Hands still in the sink, she glanced back at him. 'Well, well, I'm delighted your self-esteem is in such good shape, my dear, that you think a girl like Kat would be interested in a man like you—a man literally twice her age. Really, I'm not going to lose any sleep over that possibility. Face it, David, before you embarrass yourself. In her eyes you're a boring, middle-aged dad.'

She picked up a towel to dry her hands, and turned to face him. 'In any case, there's an even bigger reason why I know you won't be cavorting around the house in carnal pleasures while I'm at work.'

David looked back at her and frowned.

'She's a lesbian.'

David could not hide his surprise. 'Are you sure?'

'They don't all have Doc Marten boots and spikey hair, y'know. I was told by the neighbour who suggested her. Kat doesn't live with her father all the time—she has a lesbian partner. Haven't you heard of lipstick lesbians? Well, you've just met one.'

Chapter 2

On the Monday that Kat started with them, Helen had somehow been able to delay the start to her working day. Kat joined her on the walk to school, and afterwards was briefed on the workings of the domestic equipment and the laundry routine. David, in the studio and trying to use his extra hours productively, heard Helen's car leave at about nine-thirty. Ten minutes later he went over to the house, carrying a mug.

He found Kat walking down the stairs with a basket of laundry. She greeted him with a hint of diffidence. David suspected she was only pretending to be shy and deferential because convention required it. He managed to say hello, standing awkwardly at the foot of the stairs and looking up at her. She was barefoot, he noticed. She wasn't wearing the bright lipstick now, and as a result looked more girlish. Today, instead, the scarlet was on her toenails.

She stopped before reaching the foot of the stairs and looked down. 'Oh yes, sorry. Hope you don't mind me revealing my little pinkies. Much more comfortable around the house.' They both looked at her feet as she wiggled her toes on the edge of the stair.

She looked up at him. He felt unsettled.

'I've just come over to make myself a coffee,' he said. He held up the mug as evidence. 'And to check you're getting on OK. I can do instant for myself in the studio, but in the mornings I like a proper coffee.' He was in Kat's way, so

19

turned around and headed into the kitchen. Kat followed, put the laundry basket on the worktop, and flicked the kettle on. She held out her hand to take the mug from him, but he didn't realise what she was doing, and clung to it.

'Let me have the mug, David. How do you like it?' He still hesitated. 'You're the busy artist, I'm the Mrs Mop,' she continued. 'So let me make it.'

He pulled the cannister of fresh coffee from the fridge, and showed her the cafetière. They both looked at the kettle, waiting for it to boil. 'Actually,' he said, 'I'm not that busy. Not much of the time, at any rate. And these days I can't really call myself an artist. Commercial artist and illustrator, more like.'

Kat poured the water slowly into the cafetière until he signalled her to stop.

'I should add,' he said, 'that I do have busy times, of course, and then it will be wonderful to have the extra hours. But just happens this isn't one of them.'

They waited again while the coffee brewed. Kat poured it into the mug and followed his instructions on adding milk. He enjoyed watching her slim hands.

'I'd best get back to it. You know how to use the intercom?'

Kat nodded. 'But I won't bother you unless I really have to.'

'No—don't worry!' He picked up the mug. 'It can get very quiet over there. An interruption or two would be nice.' All of a sudden, he felt as if he were doing something immoral and perverted: luring a young girl to his studio. He turned quickly and left.

***

Eulogy for Love

On the Wednesday, as agreed, Kat collected the twins from school and took responsibility for them until five. It was an affectation, given the nature of his work, but David liked to sit in his studio with his back to the glass wall, so that northern light fell on the surface of his drawing board. There was, however, a window to his side through which he could look across the grass to the house, and on that day he also left the studio door ajar so that he could hear anyone arriving. At about three-thirty he was relieved to see Kat in the kitchen, and he could hear her talking with the twins. He resisted going to over to them, but after a while they came outside—Lauren in the lead and carrying a child's plastic football. David watched as they began throwing the ball in a muddled but happy mix of *catch* and *piggy in the middle*.

Kat was lovely with them. She played at their level, and shared the same unselfconscious, joyful energy. He listened to her soft voice and laughter as she praised the twins for their well-aimed throws, mock-scolded them when the ball went awry.

In a pause while Hannah went to rescue the ball from a flowerbed, Kat turned unexpectedly and caught David watching. She smiled and gave him a wave in the same way he had seen before: the hand at the level of her chest, palm forward, rocked slightly side to side, just briefly. He smiled back. Sunlight seemed to fall across the garden.

When the girls were tired, the three of them gathered in the studio doorway. 'Shall I get them tea?'

'No, you shouldn't be doing that. Not part of the job description.'

'Really, I don't mind.'

He hesitated. 'Well, maybe you could put the oven on, and I'll be over in a minute.'

After the others had gone inside, he tidied up from the day, and then went over. The twins were still in the kitchen, exuberant and noisy. He put some chicken nuggets and chips in the oven. Kat organised plates and drinks without being asked. He said little, but noticed that he was feeling an unfamiliar sense of contentment. She wasn't criticising or belittling. He had a companion.

By five-thirty, David and Kat were standing together, leaning side-by-side against the kitchen worktop, and chatting to the twins, who were finishing off their meals with yogurts. Then Helen arrived, throwing her keys noisily into the pot on the hall stand where all the keys were kept. David grasped a dishcloth to signal he had been busy, while Kat feigned surprise at the late time, and went to find her shoes. It was wasted on Helen, who began to share her irritation with contractors who had failed to show for a late afternoon meeting.

On Friday it was Kat's turn to take the twins to school, and David was again able to get over to the studio early. At around nine-thirty, his intercom buzzed.

'Shall I bring you some coffee, David?'

He almost declined. 'Thank you, that would be lovely.'

When she arrived at the studio, he asked, 'Didn't you make one for yourself?'

'Yes, it's in the kitchen.'

'Why don't you bring it down? We've hardly talked since you started.'

'I don't want to get in the way of the creative process. Have you got time to stop?'

'If you have, I have.'

Kat went and got her coffee. On her return she held the mug as she stood and gazed around the studio. David's large drawing desk dominated the room. Behind him was a metal cabinet with narrow drawers, a bulky PC on top of it. To his side, an old table with pots of pens. The rest of the room looked more like a neglected storage area, and there was dust on the tiled floor.

'Somehow I'd expected jars of brushes, and tables splattered with dried paints, not computers.'

He laughed. 'Oh, yes, and you thought you'd find me waving a brush and a palette loaded with paints.'

Kat was assessing a battered chaise longue placed against the wall below the window. Its once rich blue upholstery was faded and starting to pull away from the studs. 'Is this OK to sit on? Or is it only for ladies that you're going to paint naked?'

'I don't paint ladies naked.'

'You mean you keep your socks on?'

'Ha ha. Somewhere to put my brushes, you mean? Don't worry, I haven't done life drawings since art college. You're very welcome to sit there. And feel free to keep your clothes on.'

Kat put her coffee on the window ledge and sat down. However, if she sat straight on it, she was facing in the wrong direction. She tried sitting at an angle, so that she was facing David, but then there was no support to keep her back upright, and when she leaned back against the rising end of it, she was leaning too far, and looking down her nose at him. She tried lifting her legs onto the sofa, and then holding herself upright by pointing her knees up and curling her arms around them, but that was unsustainable. David watched, amused, as she stood and dragged the seat around until it was facing him. She sat on it again, but it was too narrow for comfort. In the end, she put her legs up and out along it, supporting herself with an arm across the raised end.

'Damn you, sofa!' she said, laughing. 'I've just been objectified by a piece of furniture! The only way to be on it comfortably is to lie like a whore on a tea break at the brothel.'

'I'm sorry. I could get a chair from the house.'

'No, no. Don't worry.' She smiled broadly at him. 'It'll make sure I don't stay too long. Just as long as we're clear I'm not modelling for you.'

'Shame, you'd make a good reclining Venus.'

'Not sure about that. If you mean Titian's Venus of Urbino, I don't have the plump figure or the small dog. And, for that matter, I'm not really cut out to be an icon of heterosexual love, as I guess you've heard.'

David noted the reference to her sexuality, but it was her knowledge of art that had shocked him. 'Well, you could be a different kind of reclining figure,' he said, testing her. 'Maybe Manet's Olympia?'

'A little closer to my figure, but she really was a tart.'

David beamed. 'In that case, I suggest you stick with Venus. Feel free to modify her looks and appetites.'

'And her clothing, I hope.'

David laughed. 'Yes, adorn yourself as you prefer.'

Kat retrieved her coffee from the window ledge, and then settled back once more on the chaise longue. 'Anyway,' she said, 'if you aren't doing oil paintings, what do you do?'

David explained the wide-ranging demand for illustrations, from books to greeting cards and office manuals. 'Let's suppose you run a business where lots of stock is held in a vast warehouse. There's a real danger of people getting hurt as they're heaving the stuff on and off the shelves, so you think you'd better produce a safety manual. The workers may still get hurt, but you'll be able to show that you took reasonable steps to prevent it.'

Kat nodded.

'So you get some junior manager to write the thing, but then it's just pages of text, which is really, really dull. What's the answer? If you've got any sense, you come to someone like me to make it, y'know, more *fun*.

'Do they tell you what to draw?'

'Sometimes, yes. But the ideas are usually dreadful, so thankfully they often agree a certain number of illustrations but leave me to come up with the ideas.'

'Like what?'

David glanced down at the surface of his drawing board. 'Well, suppose you want to underline the danger of people climbing up the warehouse racks. What would you draw?

'Maybe the racks tilting over on top of someone?'

'That's OK. But a little obvious and po-faced. Our managers like to think of themselves as witty.'

'OK, let me think . . . I've got it! Someone climbing up as if they're climbing a mountain?'

'You mean like a mountaineer? Coils of rope over their shoulder? Belays along their belt?'

'Yes, that's it.' With her free hand, Kat mimed pulling herself upwards, as if climbing hand over hand. 'An ice pick, maybe. And a peaked cap.'

'Excellent idea! And, as finishing touches,' David said, taking over from Kat, 'a silly smile on his face, and a pipe sticking out of his mouth, to suggest that he's being foolishly casual.'

David lifted the paper off his drawing board. 'Kat, I'm pleased to announce that you win this year's prize for Most Promising Newcomer to the dreary world of company manuals.'

He turned the paper round and held it up to show her. Kat saw David's black and white drawing of the mountaineer ascending the warehouse racking.

They talked a little more, and then the mugs were empty.

'Better get back to doing what I'm paid to do,' Kat said, and jumped up. She pushed the chaise longue back to the wall, collected up both mugs, and left, only pausing at the doorway to give her distinctive little wave.

***

On the following Monday, Kat came across to the studio not only with two mugs of coffee, but also two cushions tucked under her arms. She threw them onto the chaise longue and was about to pull it away from the wall, but paused. 'Unless you're too busy?' she queried. David shook his head and smiled, and so she continued to drag the sofa until it faced David as he sat at the gently tilted drawing board. She then drew up her legs onto the sofa and shoved the cushions between her hip and the rising end.

'If I'm going to be a bleedin' reclining Venus,' she said, pushing at the cushions, 'then at least I'd like to be comfortable.' She looked up at him and smiled.

They talked, as they drank the coffee, like old friends. If they disagreed it was only for the pleasure of teasing. Somehow they had already found the certainty that, on all the things that mattered, they were united.

'By the way,' David said, when empty coffee mugs signalled the end of their time, 'what's *Kat*? Short for *Katherine*?'

'Almost right. It's *Kateryna*.' She said the name again slowly, accenting each consonant, playing with it in her mouth. 'Ka-te-ryn-a.' The *e* was strengthened, and there was a gentle tilde on the *n*.

'Yeah, I know,' she said, when he looked surprised. 'Even spelt with a *y*.'

26

Eulogy for Love

'Were your family from another country?'

'There's always been fanciful talk in the family about East European ancestors. But for all practical purposes my parents were British, and working class, and very, very plain. But when the sixties arrived they got seriously into the hippie thing. Not like the middle-class kids who put flowers in their hair at weekends. Nope, my parents bought a Romani caravan and a horse, and spent five years travelling around the country.'

'Good for them! If you're gonna do it, do it properly!'

'That's right. And they really did. My sister was born on the road. But they stopped when my mother fell pregnant with me, and went back to being working class and ordinary.

'They named my sister Anichka—even more exotic. In reality, of course, everyone calls her Annie, which is terribly ordinary. Anyway, please call me Kat.'

'But I like *Kateryna*! It's lovely, and a little bit different.' He frowned at her. 'OK, as far as I'm concerned it's *Kat* for ordinary everyday use, but I claim the right to use *Kateryna* on special occasions.' He did his best to mimic her pronunciation, putting a hand to his mouth and rotating it, as if to curl the sound.

'If you like,' she replied lightly, collecting up the mugs.

From then on, they had their routine. Each Monday and Friday, Kat would visit the studio after she had taken the twins to school and tidied the kitchen. She never stayed long, and worked a few extra minutes to make up the time. David would often continue to draw while she was there. Nothing untoward was done or said between them. They shared information about their lives, but not their intimate feelings about their lives, or any feelings they might have had for each other. Sometimes they discussed politics and cultural issues, but more of the time they gossiped and giggled. David was aware that Kat's visits to the studio, and her brief company on Wednesday afternoons in the house—and indeed Kat herself—had become special to him. His daughters brought joy to his life, but he could still be lonely when he was with them. It was only with Kat that he felt alive.

He did feel a little guilty about it, but could not see a reason. The two of them did nothing wrong, and it did not undermine his roles as husband and father. On the contrary, it made him happier, and that helped him to engage more with his family. Everyone benefited, he told himself.

He wondered whether he felt guilty because Helen did not know about it, which made it seem furtive. With that in mind, he took to dropping it obliquely into conversations with Helen. 'I was chatting to Kat today,' he would say, 'and she told me . . .'. And then he would share some innocuous fact that Kat had mentioned. Helen might feign mild interest, but nothing more. He got bolder: 'Kat brought me some coffee this morning, and she was saying . . .' And, again, he would insert some titbit of information. Still there was nothing more than mild interest from Helen. His chats with Kat were no longer a secret, he reckoned, so his sense of guilt was needless; though, he noticed, not entirely assuaged.

One Friday morning Kat talked about going home for the weekend, and David asked which place that was. 'Well, that's a contentious issue at the moment,' she said, pursing her lips in distaste. 'My daddy wants it to be his house. It's where I grew up, but it's not home to me anymore. I lived there while my mum was dying, and for a while afterwards to get him set up to live on his own. But now I'm trying to make my home with Andi, and Daddy is playing all sorts of games to slow me down.'

Andi, her partner, had been mentioned briefly before.

'I don't think it's the lesbian angle that bothers him,' she went on, 'he just doesn't want me to leave.'

David had not heard her use the word 'lesbian' before.

'So, you've never lived with Andi?'

'No, not full-time, though we've been together—girlfriends—for a couple of years.'

'But . . .' David looked up from his drawing, '. . . you've always been a lesbian? Sorry, is that a stupid question?'

'No, it's not stupid. Ask away! It's not that easy to answer, though. Some women are born lesbian, and grow up knowing it. Andi's like that—she's a proper lesbian. For her, being a lesbian is not merely a sexual preference, it's a political identity. She rejects everything to do with straight sexuality.

'She insists I was born a lesbian but took a while to discover it. And she sometimes gets impatient that I still haven't adopted the full identity.'

Kat shrugged. 'That's all too complicated for me, though. Men are OK socially, but can be such silly creatures. I had the usual fumbles with boys behind the bike sheds, and short relationships with a couple of guys, but none of it impressed me. And then I got seduced by a girl in the sixth form, and that was it. I like the company of women, find them much easier to be with. I like the female body too. The softness, the mysterious folds, the taste of a woman. So for me it's simple. I like the company of women. I like sex with women. End of story.'

Kat was wearing a darker lipstick that day, more claret than scarlet. He looked at her lips and caught himself imagining how she might taste another woman. Then he felt ashamed of himself. He needed to turn the conversation somewhere safer, and for a few minutes they talked about the twins. When a lull came, and the coffee had been finished, Kat stood up to go.

'I'd better get on,' she said, and held out a hand towards David. 'Mug please.'

'Yes,' he said, passing it to her. '*Carpe diem*, and all that.'

'*Quam minimum credula postero*,' Kat answered, as she pushed the sofa back against the wall.

'I'm sorry, what was that?'

She turned back to him. 'It's the second part of the Horace quote, the part that people forget. '*Seize the day, and put the least possible trust in tomorrow*'. Gives it a darker edge, don't you think? A reminder that the days to be seized are not endless.'

'Wow! Yes, you're right. Where did you learn this? In Florence?'

'Yes,' Kat said. 'In Florence. And after that, too.'

She left to walk back to the house, and David stopped working to watch her walk across the garden path.

Chapter 3

Kat's part-time membership of the Barber household was her first encounter with family life since her time as *de facto* au pair with the Millers, the American family she had met in Florence. Inevitably, she made comparisons. The contrasts were not, however, as one might have supposed, because the Millers were not the sort of family that American families are supposed to be. The Millers were not loud, or brash, or ignorant of the rest of the world. On the contrary, they were flawlessly urbane, and identified themselves, at least intellectually, with European culture.

Ben Miller was a professor of classics; his wife, Erin, a lecturer in sociology. They had organised a complex three-way arrangement between the universities of Boston and Florence, and New York University's outpost in Florence, one that provided teaching work for both of them. Ben was also there to undertake collaborative research that autumn with his Italian peers in Florence.

Ben spoke fluent Italian, and had an easy erudition that blended his European sensibilities with American charm. As he approached forty, Ben had put on a little middle age weight, but he still had the strong and expansive physicality so common amongst young American men who once played sports at college. His large hand was always ready to reach forward to a stranger, always matched by a full and honest smile.

Kat first met the Millers in one of Florence's many public art galleries. It was October 1994. She was only two months into the backpacking adventure that she had planned as the highlight of her year after finishing school. Ben and Erin were visiting the gallery with their seven-year-old son, Jacob. While absorbed in a Botticelli of the Madonna and Child, they had failed to notice Jacob wandering away. They were unconcerned at first—Jacob was a sensible boy—but their anxiety rose when the minutes passed. After ten minutes they began searching through the rooms and courtyards. After fifteen, Jacob was found, sitting on a bench and talking contentedly with Kat.

'Jacob didn't know which room you were in,' Kat said, looking up to them with a smile, 'so I thought it would be best to wait until you found us.'

As a gesture of gratitude, Kat was invited to join them for refreshments in the gallery café, a proposal that Jacob enthusiastically supported. It was Kat's hand that he chose to hold as they made their way there. When, over coffees and juices, Kat described living in a hostel and eking out her gap year funds, Ben and Erin immediately saw the value in asking her to provide some baby-sitting. This arrangement worked so well that Kat was soon invited to take one of the spare bedrooms in their rented home in return for some help with Jacob and household chores. Jacob already had an English-speaking tutor to maintain the continuity of his education, and Kat would provide enough extra hours of childcare to relieve the pressure on his busy parents.

Kat moved in four days before Thanksgiving. Deprived of their own families to join them, the Millers compensated by calling in their new Italian colleagues and their families, then plying them with turkey sourced from the Mercato Centrale, and the closest to cranberries and stuffing that could be found in the city. The university had allocated the Millers a dull but generously sized house outside the city, and here they held court from Thanksgiving to the end of the holidays. When she realised what was about to happen, Kat hastened into the city and spent far beyond her backpacker's budget on new clothes. Then she sat at the dining table, and mingled at evening gatherings with these cognoscenti, and marvelled at their elegance and erudition. It was understood that she was expected to support Jacob on these occasions until his bedtime, but he took the social demands in his stride. It was Kat who was often startled and speechless at the splendour of it all.

Erin was, very likely, her husband's intellectual equal, but she did not have Ben's inclination to seize centre stage. She was the perfect match for a professor of classics. A decade younger than Ben, Erin had green eyes and warm blonde hair that she either left to flow in curls down her back, or put in a loose braid that she placed around her shoulder. It could not have been mere chance that her appearance, especially when she was dressed for social occasions, recalled Aphrodite. She quietly graced each event, always seeming to be available for the guest who had been left on their own or with an empty glass.

Ben seemed the model husband. He often told her how lovely she looked, especially at the start of social evenings, and he would unfailingly thank her for making each event a success. The relationship seemed, to Kat, too good to be true; but she no reason to question it. She began to believe that mature heterosexual relationships could remain loving and affirming.

In dinner-table debates, and in more private conversations, Ben had a distinctive way of deploying his erudition. Kat guessed he also used it in formal teaching, but was not sure whether it was a tactic to engage his students, or simply his naturally generous style. His device was to work on the assumption that his listeners were always his equals in knowledge and intellect, and that, as a consequence, he did not need to explain himself fully. He never, it seemed, presumed to tell or teach people, but only to remind them of things they had momentarily forgotten. It might so easily have left his less educated guests feeling excluded, but instead made them feel honoured to be members of a club to which they had no right to belong.

On the third evening of her residence, Kat was one of a dozen people around the long mahogany dining table. Ben, momentarily caught in conversation that had become too serious, looked up from the Italian academics at his end of the table. He lifted his glass, smiled, and toasted his guests jovially with the words, '*Nunc vino pellite curas*!' As he spoke, he looked around the table, taking care to smile at each person. Kat waited for his eyes to reach her, and was delighted by their arrival. It was not important what the Latin meant. It was obviously a toast, and she knew to lift her glass in return. What mattered was that she felt, in the moment of that single smile, that she belonged.

There were some times when Kat felt she had to ask Ben to translate or explain. She discovered, to her relief, that this did not jeopardise her membership of the club. If she queried the meaning of something he spoke in Latin or Greek, he would only chide her for a lapse in memory. 'That?' he would say. 'Oh, but you've forgotten that Marcus Aurelius wrote in Greek, not Latin. One of the many good things he said about how to live well. You know . . ..' and then he would pause while apparently translating in his head. 'Something like: *Do not act as if you were going to live ten thousand years. Death hangs over you. While you live, while it is in your power, be good.*' In these ways, Kat was entranced.

When, after Christmas, Jacob recommenced home schooling with his tutor, Kat had daytimes to spend as she wished. She took the chance to learn and enjoy as much as she could in the city, and her new friends from the Miller social circle were often pleased to accompany her. They acted as her expert guides not only in the art galleries and museums, but also in the shops and restaurants. She listened with equal care to their explanations of the great renaissance paintings and sculptures, and to the way they summoned the waiter. Over the first three months of the new year, Kat had an intensive course in the classics, modern Italian culture, and the Italian language. It was a privilege, and she made the most of it.

Meanwhile, Ben and Erin had started talking about the possibility that Kat might return with them to Boston. She raised no objections. The plan was almost ruined by the slow processes that had to be followed for her to be recognised by US officialdom as a genuine au pair, but in the week before Easter she flew the Atlantic with the Millers, and at their expense.

***

Kat had already realised that the Millers were not a typical academic couple, even by US standards. The full truth became clear on arrival in the States. They had said they lived in Boston, but that was a simplification for the benefit of foreigners. They lived in Wellesley, a wealthy suburb where the houses nestle down driveways and behind trees, as if ironically coy about their grandeur. The Miller residence was an older property than many nearby—a white clapboard house that sprawled itself into decks and annexes, one of them to become Kat's own little home. Though as big as those residences nearby, it did not look so grand. But this was old money, too self-assured to bother with ostentation.

Ben was bringing in the last of the luggage, and Jacob had rushed to be reunited with his bedroom, leaving the two women walking from room to room and opening the curtains. Erin saw Kat gawping, and laughed. 'Yeah, takes some getting used to, I know. Not the sort of lifestyle I was born into.'

'But Ben was?'

'Sure was. Great granddaddy was the industrialist who made the family fortune, and grandfather looked after it well, when his turn came. Ben's daddy did let things down somewhat by becoming a writer, but there's still enough left to keep us all in comfort.'

Ben found them at the back of the house as they were opening up what appeared to be a games room. 'Much as I love Florence,' he said, 'it's very good to be home. Horace was so right: *Caelum non animum mutant qui trans mare currunt.*'

Erin tentatively started to translate. 'The sky not the spirit?'

'That's the one,' Ben said, encouragingly. '*They change their sky, not their soul, who rush across the sea.*'

'I think my soul is pretty confused about where it is right now,' Kat said.

'I bet it is,' Ben said sympathetically, and touched her shoulder, 'but don't you worry—we'll soon have you feeling at home.

***

Eulogy for Love

Ben was right. Although she had loved Florence, and had come to know both the place and the language quite well, it was always too exotic to feel like home. Once she had become familiar with the differences in language and custom, the United States was much more comfortable, especially in this wealthy and refined district. With Easter over, the household settled into the same pattern of life as any western suburban family with children at school, albeit in more opulent fashion than most. Kat's duties were, in the morning, to see the other three breakfasted and away to their weekday commitments, and then to tidy the house. In the evening she would take charge when Jacob returned from school until one of his parents—usually Erin—arrived home. Ben and Erin were scrupulously careful not to exploit her, and paid her more than she needed to cover her everyday needs. Soon she was able to complete the transition of her wardrobe from British backpacker to young, affluent American.

Though she soon found her own social circle, most of its members were busy during the day at school, work, or university studies; and, as a consequence, her days were quiet. Sometimes she went into Boston, but the journey was awkward. She found that there were pleasant woodland areas nearby where she could walk, peaceful places where nature ruled and national culture evanesced. When summer arrived, she often stayed home and lay on a sun lounger on one of the decks, reading books from the Miller library, and developing her tan.

Social life at the Miller home blossomed in the warmer weather. In contrast to the formal occasions in Florence, gatherings seemed to happen organically. Sometimes, as far as Kat could tell, they occurred without warning. People—whole families—would roll up and form spontaneous parties.

The conversations between the adults could, nevertheless, be as academic and arcane as those in Italy.

It was mostly at these gatherings that Kat acquired her social network. She discovered, however, that she fell between the generations. Sometimes she was invited to the homes of Ben and Erin's colleagues, or on excursions with them, and experienced generous American hospitality. Her alternative was to drop a generation to the children of these colleagues, but that placed her amongst high school kids. She would hang out with them in the coffee shops and pizzerias of Wellesley, but found their conversations unengaging, full of teenage preoccupations and gossip about boys she didn't know. It all seemed so very bland, particularly in comparison to Florence. Moreover, Kat was needing intimacy, and knew she would not find it with these children.

On a Saturday afternoon in July, and amongst an impromptu gathering of a dozen people scattered around the garden and deck, Kat found herself talking to a woman she had not met before. Mid-twenties, Kat guessed. Janine worked as an administrator at the university, where Erin had come across her seated at her desk and looking dejected. When Janine explained she had broken up with her husband, Erin had invited her to come over at the weekend. So here she was. Saturdays worked well, Janine explained, as this was when her three-year-old son spent time with her husband and—she added, scowling—with her husband's new girlfriend.

It was apparent that, though used to academics at university, Janine did not generally mix with them socially. Kat guessed that the breakdown of Janine's marriage had also destroyed her self-confidence. Whatever the reason, Janine seemed nervous, and Kat—by this time counted as host, not guest—wanted to help her feel at ease. Janine was, in addition, a small refuge from the heady intellectual conversations happening around them. She was pretty, too. A little overweight, and her blonde hair needed better styling; but still pretty.

Kat noticed a hand scooping up the last of some crudités from a platter on a nearby table. Erin had also noticed, and picked it up to replenish it. 'Erin, let me do that.'

'Would you?' Erin held out the platter. 'Thanks, Kat.'

Kat said, 'No problem,' and rose to take it.

'Hey, I'll come help,' she heard Janine say behind her.

In the shade of the large kitchen, Kat and Janine stood closely side by side at one of the granite worktops, and set to work on a pile of carrots, celery, and dumpy cucumbers.

'I'm trying to live on this stuff at the moment,' Janine said, 'but Jeez, it's not easy.'

'Why's that?'

'Why isn't it easy? Because I like my food too much. Why am I doing it? Because I need to get into shape if I'm going to find another husband.'

'But you've only been separated a couple of months. Surely there's no rush?'

'Worried I'm going to pass my sell-by date. And I want my husband to know that I can be attractive to other men, even if he doesn't want me.' Janine pressed her knife down hard on a carrot, splitting it noisily.

'But don't you see? If you think like that, you're still letting him control you, still worrying about the way he sees you. He doesn't matter anymore.'

Janine nodded. 'I suppose you're right.'

'And for what it's worth, Janine,' Kat ventured, 'I think you're a very attractive woman.'

Janine stopped chopping and turned to look at Kat. 'Do you? Do you really?'

Kat turned to Janine, bringing their faces close together. 'Yes, really, I do,' she said, and reached out to take Janine's hand. Kat thought she was doing it because she felt sorry for her, and wanted to comfort her; but it was not wholly innocent.

They stood in silence, their bodies and faces close. Kat smiled. Then Janine smiled back, as if she had suddenly understood something. Kat found herself letting her eyes flick up and down between Janine's eyes and her mouth. Half consciously, she was signalling: *I want to kiss you.* She sensed that Janine had understood.

It was too risky to kiss there, in the kitchen, but Kat was enjoying the frisson of the resisted desire, and was slow to move away. 'Maybe we could meet again soon,' she said.

'I'd like that,' Janine answered. 'I'd like that very much.'

Janine had to leave a short time later to collect her son. By then they had agreed a plan to meet up the following Saturday lunchtime. They pretended to each other, as they would to the Millers, that they were arranging simply to have lunch together, but they each knew that was not the true intent.

The following Saturday they spent five minutes in Janine's house—the spacious former marital home—feeling awkward. Then they did kiss and, very soon after, they went upstairs to bed and enjoyed each other for three hours. Kat got things she had been missing. Janine discovered pleasures she had not believed possible. Kat knew that, though she liked Janine, what she mainly wanted from her was uncomplicated sex. If Kat had used her a little, she had in return made Janine a gift. Kat had shown her the delights of sexual intimacy that is freed of the judgemental male gaze, that is concerned with mutual pleasure and not obsessed with penetration; and which does not have to hurry down a one-way street that comes abruptly to an unsought end.

Eulogy for Love

Having discovered this different kind of love, Janine was hungry for more, and Kat happily fed her new appetites on most Saturdays through the rest of the summer. Kat was in no doubt that, in the end, Janine would be drawn by the need for conformity and security back into heterosexual marriage. At least, though, the next husband would have to contend with a wife who knew she was worth loving, and knew what it really means to make love.

***

Kat had been impressed in Florence by Ben's loving attitude to Erin. Back in Wellesley, and no longer in a country where ostentatiously romantic gestures are part of the culture, Ben's adoration of his wife was even more conspicuous. There were always lingering kisses if they left separately for work, more kisses on return home, and every time with whispered assurances of devotion. Often, and seemingly for no particular reason, he brought her gifts, and tickets for the theatre or concerts. Kat began to think that it was not so much too good to be true. It was simply too much.

One Saturday morning, Erin and Kat were to go out to do some household shopping, leaving Ben at home with Jacob. Kat had gone ahead to the car where it was parked in the driveway, believing Erin was following her. Several minutes had passed, and Kat had become impatient even before Ben and Erin appeared at the door. There were further delays while they stood together as Ben held Erin's hands, spoke to her lovingly, and kissed her several times. At last, Erin walked towards the car. As she did so, Ben called something out to her. Kat could not make out the words.

Kat was both irritated and curious. 'What was Ben saying?' she asked, as if she were thinking it might have been a request for something extra from the store.

'Oh, it's just something he likes to say. A quote from Virgil's Aeneid. *The goddess is revealed by her step.* Venus is disguised as a huntress, and it's only when Aeneas watches her walk away that he realises who she is.' Erin had paused the car as they reached the end of the driveway, and she looked across at Kat with an embarrassed smile. 'I know, it's very silly. Some people find it cloying, the way he is with me.'

'I think it's lovely,' Kat assured her.

Erin turned the car onto the road. 'The thing is, people don't know the reason. I guess no one has told you, either.' She glanced again at Kat, who looked mystified.

'I'm not Ben's first wife. He was married to Susan. They were young—both in their early twenties. In Ben's memory, Susan was the perfect woman, and they were going to be blissfully in love all their lives. I'm not saying she wasn't lovely, but over the years he's made her mythological.

'They'd only been married about a year. She went out in the car one Sunday morning. Some small errand—like ours now, I guess—and she should have been back home in an hour. But she never did come back. Some young dude, his blood still thinned with alcohol from a drinking session the night before, was coming the other way. He was late for work, driving way too fast. Lost control on a corner and went head-on into Susan. She was dead on arrival.'

'How awful,' Kat said.

'Ben dealt with it by immersing himself in his university work for five years. He only surfaced when we met.'

'So now,' Kat ventured, 'he's frightened that at any moment the same thing might happen with you.'

'Sure, that's part of it. But he's also full of guilt. He was young and very ambitious in those days. Thinks he didn't appreciate Susan the way he should have. Crazy, really—as if that made any difference to her death. He can kiss me a thousand times on the doorstep, but it ain't gonna change anything if some drunk teenager chooses to drive on the wrong side of the road.'

Kat stared out of the window in thought. 'He only recognised the goddess when she had walked away for the last time. Is that it?'

Erin laughed. 'I don't think that was the story Virgil was telling. But, yeah, maybe that does sum it up for Ben. How does the song go? *You don't know what you got 'til it's gone.*'

'But at least you have the benefit of a husband who never lets you doubt he loves you.'

'Well, yeah, he's wonderfully loving. But you can see it's a little weird. I get the loving, but I don't know if it's mine to have. I don't like the thought that I may be getting it only because Susan is unavailable.'

Kat wanted to say, *I'm sure that's not true.* But it seemed trite; and, in any case, they were now parked up at the grocery store.

***

There were warning signs that Kat's life with the Millers was about to come to an end, though it still felt sudden when it happened. Kat had not seen her parents for a year, and it weighed on her conscience. She told herself that they had each other, and could manage perfectly well without her. Then phone calls from her father brought increasingly troubling reports. Her mother had started to undergo strange mood swings, and nothing so simple as depression. She was sometimes angry, even violent. A few weeks later she made herself unwelcome at her weekly social club for using obscene language and starting to take her clothes off. It was when Kat's father, distressed and too embarrassed even to describe it in plain language, indicated that he had to clean his wife after she had used the toilet, that Kat recognised that she had to go home. Much as she wanted to pretend to herself that it was only a temporary return to England, she knew her time with the Millers was ending.

It was a school day, so she said goodbye to Ben and Jacob at home before Erin took her to the airport. Erin found a drop-off space outside Departures, and helped Kat heave out her luggage, a suitcase now added to the backpack she had brought those months before. Erin put her hands over Kat's shoulders, tugging at Kat's hair where it fell behind her ears. 'We're all going to miss you, Kat,' she said. Unable to say more, she mouthed 'Go!' and waved Kat towards the entry doors. Kat touched Erin's cheek, and turned away.

Kat was standing at her seat on the plane, pulling items from her bag that she would need during the flight, when she discovered an unfamiliar book. After she had settled in her seat, she inspected it. It was a copy of the *Meditations* of Marcus Aurelius. There was a note with it, expressing thanks and love from the Millers. Inside, an inscription—in Ben's handwriting, she thought—offered her a quotation from the book:

Adapt yourself to the environment in which your lot has been cast, and show true love to the fellow mortals with whom destiny has surrounded you.

***

Eulogy for Love

Almost exactly a year after she had joined the Millers in Italy, Kat's plane set her back down in England. It was a dark October day, the grey clouds low and oppressive. It would seem to Kat, looking back, that those clouds remained over her for eighteen months, only lifting with her mother's death. If she had known how hard that time would be, she might have turned away; but having started on it, she felt the obligation to see it through to the end.

Her mother had a vicious form of dementia. Loss of memory was the least of it. The deterioration of the brain caused destruction both to her physical and her intellectual faculties. In fact, her physical collapse outran her cognitive disintegration, leading ultimately to the horrifying sense that there was a small fragment of her—the woman she had been—left inside but barely visible, like someone's terrified face glimpsed at the porthole of a sinking ship. Kat's father failed to help at all, mired in his own distress. Nursing assistants were allocated to visit in the last months, but there was only one way in which either Kat or her mother would be released from this hell. It came in autumn 1997.

***

Now released from that grey underworld, Kat was starting to know the Barbers. They were, she was discovering, ordinary, middle-class, English folk, with none of the wealth or glamour of the Millers. David was not an intellectual in Ben's class or style, but he was bright, educated, and with a dry sense of humour. He knew the visual arts as much as Ben knew the classics; and, of the two, David was the one who could create works of his own.

The loveless state of the marriage hung like dust in a house where the windows are never opened. Ben's overstated affection seemed, by comparison, an ozone breeze. What made it most saddening was that Kat found nothing dislikeable in either Helen or David. Neither had committed any crime that deserved punishment, and yet they · had sentenced themselves to live in each other's prison. Kat felt sorry for Helen. She seemed so constantly distracted—by the pressures of work, Kat presumed—that she was not even able to take delight in the children she had made.

As for David, the more she got to know him, the more impatient she felt. It was not that she disliked him. On the contrary, it was because she saw so many likeable qualities that she was impatient. He was kind, and gentle, and perceptive to a degree she had not known in a man before. She found herself lingering at the end of her afternoon duties, watching him with his children—the only time he seemed to come alive. Late one Friday afternoon the four of them had been together at the kitchen table while the twins ate spaghetti. They had shown David drawings they had done at school of a street scene, part of a project about the place where they lived.

'So tell me,' he said, 'what colour are tree trunks?'

'Brown!' they said together, in a tone that suggested their father was stupid. They pointed at their drawings.

'You sure about that?' They nodded and smiled, their lips smudged with ketchup.

'OK. Excuse me, Kat. I'll be back in a mo.'

David went out of the side door into the dusk. A minute later he returned with sawn logs from the store they kept for the wood-burning stove in the front room, and dumped them on the table. Some woodlice fell out. Kat gathered them up and threw them back into the garden.

'Right,' he said, in a sergeant-majorish tone the twins knew to be fake, 'let's see what colours we can find on these.' Then he took them on a tour, pointing to different areas of bark, asking the twins to name the colours: the alternating grooves of grey and silver, interrupted where green moss had become established; the hint of something close to white where the bark had cracked. He also made them see how the full strength of the kitchen light changed the colour, just as sunlight would do.

'Good,' he said, once the twins had understood the point he was making. 'When you've finished your yogurts, we'll see who can do the best drawing of a tree trunk.'

Kat played no part in this, other than to stand and watch, smiling. She left before the new drawings were completed, because she always felt awkward if Helen came home and found her still there. But, when she was tidying the house the following Monday, she saw two new drawings pinned to the kitchen notice board—two interesting studies in the textures and colours of bark, with hardly any brown.

These glimpses of pleasure with his own children, and the sparks of wit she saw when she talked with him in the studio, told her that David could be so much more than he allowed himself to be. That was what made her feel frustrated and impatient. He could have been joyful in his own life. He could have impressed others, in the way that Ben did. Though she knew little of the industry in which David worked, she was convinced that he had the potential to be appreciated much more than he was.

If she had been asked, Kat might have admitted that David was the sort of man who could turn her back to heterosexuality. But no one was asking, and she firmly identified herself as a lesbian in a fulfilling relationship with another woman. She didn't want him for herself. Rather, she wanted him to be fully *himself*. Kat had spent over a year watching her own mother yielding up her humanity, the unique textures and colours of her personality bleached out until all that remained was coarse animal need. But that had been imposed on her by a sadistic disease. David, on the other hand, was choosing to suppress himself. Kat thought it not merely saddening, but immoral. At some barely conscious level, Kat wanted to put him right.

Chapter 4

Easter came that year at the start of April. On a Monday evening, while the twins were watching TV, Helen raised the issue of childcare over the Easter holidays, suddenly only two weeks away. She announced that she had talked to Kat that morning, and got her agreement to provide help two afternoons each week over the holidays in place of her usual routine. The twins could go to Holiday Club each morning, and Helen would only be working four days in both weeks. That would leave David on childcare duties for only two afternoons.

David saw Kat bring the twins back from Holiday Club on the first day of this arrangement, and went over a while later to see how things were going. Kat had brought some rolls of lining paper, and the twins were on the kitchen floor with their crayons, converting a length of it into a magical world for their toys to live in.

'Problem,' Kat said, as she stood with David watching them, 'is that it's not much different from what they've been doing at the play scheme. I'd take them out for a walk somewhere, but it's so chilly today.'

'Cinema, perhaps?'

'Yessssss!' the twins shouted in unison.

Kat laughed. 'Sounds like that's a popular plan. Will you come?'

David pursed his lips, and then shook his head. 'Best not. Shouldn't really abandon my post on my first full day. But I can run you to the cinema.'

His car was a dusty grey hatchback. Good enough to get him to clients' offices when the need arose, though he tended to park it somewhere the clients wouldn't see. The twins, in the back, were in high spirits, excited both about the cinema and about going out with Kat. Kat sat next to David, as ever sitting in a calm, symmetrical pose, knees bent tidily and together, hands in her lap. He wished she would reach out and put her hand on his thigh—not for sexual frisson, but as a sign of the comradeship he felt growing between them.

David had sole care of the twins the following afternoon. It was another disappointingly chilly day, so they stayed at home. But the next day, Wednesday, was sunny in the morning, and a little warmer. He watched for Kat and the twins to come back from the play scheme, then went straight over to the house.

'Let's all go out somewhere for a picnic,' he said, sounding more assertive than he had intended. 'It's hardly summer out there, but by the sounds of it the nicest day we'll get this side of Easter.'

Kat looked at him doubtfully. 'Are you sure? I'm supposed to be here so you can work.'

'Oh, bugger that!'

David went back to the studio for half an hour while Kat made some sandwiches, and then they set off. The twins were again excitable. Kat got them singing songs, loudly, and she had to lean across to David to speak to him.

'You do realise, don't you, that they'll tell Helen about this?'

'Don't worry about it. She really doesn't seem that bothered. I'll explain it to her.'

Eulogy for Love

They drove a few miles to a little-known country park, a group of small hills that rose from the surrounding fields to form a moorland in miniature, complete with sheep. A track allowed cars to drive up to a parking area near the top. There were a few cars already there.

The picnic was postponed until they had had some exercise, and soon they were all playing a game at the top of one of the hillocks. It amounted to a version of tag in which the twins would try to defend the high ground from the adults. David would make a frontal attack that needed attention from both of the girls while Kat tried to sneak from another direction. When Lauren or Hannah managed to tag her, Kat would cry out, hold herself as if she had been run through with a sword, and then fall down melodramatically. Their laughter drew attention from families nearby—the adults puzzled or disapproving, the children silently envious.

When they were tired, they sat down on top of the same hillock to eat the sandwiches. In one direction they could see outwards across miles of fields, while on the other they looked down a few yards to the car park. The day was breezy and a little chilly. Small, fast-moving clouds dropped shifting shadows on the landscape.

The picnic was still unfinished when an ice-cream van pulled into the car park.

'Jeez,' David said, awkwardly holding onto his egg and cucumber sandwich, 'who'd want an ice-cream on a day like this?'

'I could name a couple,' Kat replied, nodding towards the twins, who were focused on a bug in the grass.

Moments later: 'Daddiee! Can we have ice-creams?'

David used his free hand to pull some money from his back pocket. Kat held out her hand to take it. 'Finish your sandwich. I'll get them. You don't want one, then?' David, mouth full, shook his head.

The twins stayed down near the car to eat their ice-creams. Kat came back up, a wrapped confectionary in her hand. She sat down on the grass next to David, and they both watched the twins. David became aware that she had started to eat the ice-cream—some hybrid of an ice-cream and a lolly, a cylinder of cream on a stick. He turned a little more, and saw that she was sucking on it as she slowly, absentmindedly, moved it in and out between her lips.

She looked sideways at him, and then her eyes crinkled in a smile. She drew out the ice-cream.

'Why, Mr Barber! I do believe you were having a naughty thought!' David felt his cheeks flush, though he shook his head feebly. Kat laughed at him affectionately. 'Yes you were!'

Now facing him, she put a finger to her mouth where a thin streak of white ice cream lay on her scarlet lower lip. She looked at him, intently, seriously. Slowly, she wiped away the ice-cream with her finger. Then she held the finger in front of her mouth, and used the tip of her tongue to lick it. Finally, she put the end of the finger in her mouth and sucked on it.

The finger was removed, the serious look gone. She winked at him, and grinned. 'Don't be embarrassed, David. I'm flattered that you can think of me in that way. Enjoy! What's the harm in it? I trust you not to get confused between fantasy and reality.'

David, briefly transfixed, was now working hard to focus on the twins heading back up towards them. 'You seem to be very knowing about male fantasies, considering . . .'

'Considering what? That I'm a lesbian? It's easy to know what men like.'

For a while the four of them sat in a row and chatted innocently. Then they set off back home. Kat had gone, and the tea eaten, by the time Helen returned. She stood in the kitchen holding her briefcase. The twins came and wrapped their arms around her hips.

'Mummy, Mummy, we went for a picnic with Daddy and Kat.'

Helen looked up at David, her raised eyebrow requiring an explanation.

'It was only a little outing to that country park with the sheep. The girls were getting so restless it seemed unfair on Kat to leave her with them. And it was only part of the afternoon.'

It was a carefully rehearsed account. David waited for the response. Helen nodded. 'Oh, OK, good. As long as you can spare the time.' She looked back down at the twins and continued talking to them. Evidently, she saw no need to know more.

***

Helen chose that night to allow David to satisfy his male needs. It was the night of Good Friday. Perhaps it was her idea of a gift at Easter. They were due to leave early the next morning to drive to her parents, where they were spending the weekend, and Helen had gone to bed even earlier than usual. David allowed more than an hour for her to settle, and slid carefully into bed to avoid waking her. She was lying on her side away from him. But she was not asleep.

'You can fuck me if you like.'

He considered declining politely. But he had never turned her down before, and she might start to wonder whether something had changed. Nothing *had* changed, of course—

nothing of any substance—but he would rather she didn't start wondering.

Foreplay was not included in the service that Helen offered, so David put his hand down below the duvet and started to arouse himself. It always helped if he could imagine an erotic scene, and he allowed his mind to cast about for something suitable. His imagination presented him with Kat close to him, facing him. He had his hands under her sweatshirt, pushing the rough material upwards with the back of his wrists as his palms moved inside. Then she was sinking down, sliding out of the sweatshirt as she dropped. David realised his imagination was about to show him Kat kneeling semi-naked in front of him, head at his groin, her mouth sucking in the way it had sucked the ice-cream.

His mind—or at any rate the educated, liberal, feminist-supporting part of his mind—shut the image out. The rest of him was disappointed. As Kat herself might have said: *Where's the harm?* Yet that other part of his mind could not allow it. It was not so much a matter of being mentally unfaithful to Helen. It was out of loyalty to Kat. Even in fantasy he did not want her associated with the sordid real-life scene that he was about to act out with Helen.

Still, the images had their effect. He moved against Helen's back, and she raised her leg enough to allow him in. He entered, performed as quickly as he could; and withdrew. Then he turned away from her, and was overcome with humiliation. He wept, and hoped Helen would think his shudders were the dying spasms of his orgasm.

The erotic images of Kat found a place in the corner of David's mind where, it seemed, the right-thinking David had no authority; and from there they taunted and teased him all through the journey to Helen's parents. He was also discomforted to discover how much he was missing Kat, even though the Easter break was only six days long. From a third place in his psyche, he heard murmurings of guilt.

The spacious semi in South London had seen little change since Helen had left for university. Her parents had reached the stage in life where they were happy for the world to go on ahead without them. The evening meal was *dinner*, always eaten at the table. This invariably made the twins appear feral. Though the grandparents declared how delighted they were to see their grandchildren, they soon tired of the twins, and waited for them to be taken to bed. It was the custom for adults to stay up long enough to watch a little of the evening news, and then for everyone to head to bed at the same time. External doors would be locked, lights turned off, glasses for water found and filled. With unnecessarily loud and jovial cries of *Goodnight, then!* the household members would retire to their bedrooms, where they would wait awkwardly to see who would go first to use the only bathroom in the house.

Helen and David found themselves sat upright in the narrow double bed that was provided for guests. They had propped up the pillows so that they could lean back against the mahogany headboard. They were both wearing pyjamas, as they always did when staying with family.

'Are you OK?' Helen asked, flatly. David wondered whether this was a preamble to complaints. Had he seemed insufficiently engaged in the conversation over dinner?

'I'm fine, I think.'

'Good.' She didn't seem pleased for him, but at least she was not going to take him to task.

'And you? Are you OK?' It was the required, and the kind, response.

'No, not really.'

'I'm sorry. What's the problem?'

David waited for her. 'It's work. When it comes at you on a daily basis you just get on with it. But when you're away from it—like now—you realise just how shit it's become.'

'I thought you liked the cut and thrust of office life.'

'Oh, I do, up to a point. Yeah, I like the pressure, the competition, the occasional adrenaline high. But I expect people to play fair. Now I'm reporting to one of the directors, and he plainly doesn't like me, doesn't like women, and doesn't think I've got the balls for the job.'

Helen described how she was being undermined. She would be given tasks at impossibly short notice. Rather than talking in private through any concerns about her work, he would wait to air his criticisms in meetings. When she made a recommendation that could not be entirely backed by evidence—and such decisions are unavoidable in publishing—he would disassociate himself from it. 'Well, OK,' he would say, looking around at his predominantly male staff, 'I suppose we'll all have to put our trust in women's intuition.'

'And I can't let him succeed,' Helen said. 'The rest of them are OK, but I'm really just an honorary member of the Boys' Club. They could so easily side with him, and then I'd be very vulnerable.'

They sat and stared down at the ancient quilted eiderdown.

'I'm sorry,' David said. 'I don't think there's much I can do to help.'

'No, there isn't. You've no experience of working in an organisation.'

There was the sound of somebody vacating the bathroom.

Helen went on. 'But there is something you could change. It's always at the back of my mind that if I lost my job we'd be in serious trouble. Your earnings couldn't even pay the mortgage. I don't think you really make an effort to increase your income—you assume you can rely on me. That isn't fair.'

'OK, point taken. But I just don't seem to get the work.'

'That's because you don't put yourself out there. You're a talented artist, David. You need to work harder at marketing yourself. Remind your old clients that you're still around. Call in a few favours. And if you've got free time, you could start adding to your portfolio—something fresh and distinctive—in place of that dreary commercial stuff.

'Anyway,' she added, 'I'm going to the bathroom.'

He knew she was right. He detested pitching for work—*talking himself up*, as the Americans would say. He was, by nature, an unassuming Englishman. And yet . . . if Helen were not there as the family breadwinner, he would have to go out and find work, for all that he hated it. It was wrong to lean on her as he did.

Chapter 5

Once the Easter holidays were over, the usual routine returned. David made a genuine effort to respond to Helen's request to increase his earnings. He doubted he would succeed enough for it to ease the burden on Helen. She probably wouldn't even notice, or be grateful, or have more respect for him; but he knew he had to make the effort. Although Kat's twice-weekly coffee breaks at the studio continued—he could not bear to lose those—there were no more outings with the twins. On Wednesday afternoons, when he knew Kat was in the house, he had to battle the impulse to go across the path, like a dieter resisting the temptations of the fridge.

At the same time, he set about developing the foundations for more work. He forced himself to put in phone calls to old industry contacts who probably did not even remember his name, and to make cold calls to publishers and other companies that outsourced their artwork. Before each call he would sit with his hand resting on the phone in the studio, and try to hear himself speaking his opening lines, imagining his voice upbeat and confident. Usually, when he then phoned, he would get no further than a switchboard operator or a secretary indifferent to the tone of his voice. Little by little, nevertheless, he developed a list of invitations to send in copies of his work, or to *come in for a discussion.*

This, in turn, highlighted the need to freshen up his portfolio with some colourful and interesting pieces to offset the dull commissioned work from recent years. Whereas the phone calls were a hated chore, creative work felt self-indulgent. He realised that he couldn't merely follow his own whims, but needed to produce work that would sit comfortably within the fashionable aesthetic. That meant he had to do some research. He found himself sitting in his studio, flicking through magazines.

In the same spirit, he went into town and browsed the bookstores and record shops, looking for a trend that he could use and augment with his own artistic skills. He was in a bookshop when he came by chance upon Kat. She was with another woman—a woman with short blonde hair and wearing dark blue jeans and a check shirt. It had to be Andi, and it was. When Kat introduced her, Andi looked David in the eye and gave him a firm handshake. There was no sign she was a man-hater. They all stood together for a minute or two, blocking the aisle while they made the requisite small talk. Andi was warm and straightforward.

'Great to have met you,' she said, as the conversation started to conclude. 'I know Kat loves spending time with the twins, and with you. Would be wonderful to meet them one day.'

It was an obvious request. 'Well, of course you're welcome to meet them,' David responded.

He realised he needed to say more than that, to be more specific, more welcoming. He wanted to look away from Andi to Kat, to find her guidance, but felt he shouldn't.

'Umm, tell you what,' he started, 'why don't you both come round for a meal one evening? Then Kat can introduce you to the twins.'

'That would be lovely,' Kat said, signalling the approval he had been wanting from her. Yet still he had not said enough.

'Look, if you're free,' he said to Andi, 'why don't you both come round on Saturday for dinner? Need to check with Helen, though I'm sure it will be fine. I can let Kat know when she's at ours, OK?'

It was OK. Everyone seemed content, and the two women went on their way.

It was also sufficiently OK with Helen, though she wasn't enthusiastic. 'Kat is lovely, and I'm sure Andi will be fine. It's just that after a hard week I could do without the hassle of entertaining.'

'Well, don't worry,' David responded. 'I'll do the cooking, and I'll get the shopping on Saturday. You won't need to do anything.'

From Saturday lunchtime onwards, Helen didn't do anything. David had bought her a newspaper while he was at the supermarket in the morning, and she sat reading it in the living room while he did the vacuuming. 'Don't know why you're bothering,' she said loudly over the noise, lifting her feet for him to vacuum the carpet below. 'Kat's seen the house enough times with its normal quota of filth.'

David had negotiated a deal with the twins. They could stay up until Kat arrived, so that she could put them to bed. But he required, in return, that they would settle to sleep without a fuss. He got them both bathed and into crispy-fresh pyjamas, and then left them to watch TV while he set about cooking the simple meal he had chosen.

The twins rushed to the front door when they heard Kat and Andi arrive, and abducted them to their bedroom. Soon and inevitably, however, Andi was sidelined, and she came down while Kat got the twins into bed and read a story that had them giggling. Andi wandered into the living room and began chatting with Helen. David could hear voices that sounded friendly.

Eulogy for Love

When Kat came down, she went straight to the kitchen. David glanced up. He had begun to learn how to read her mood from small clues. 'OK?' he asked.

'You mean the twins? Yes, of course. A complete delight. I may have to kidnap them.'

'So—is something else not OK?'

'We eating here, David? Shall I lay the table?' He nodded. She was silent while she rattled the cutlery in the drawer.

'Well, yes, since you ask. I hope it won't show this evening, but me and Andi are not doing so well.'

'I'm sorry, Kat.' The ragu was gently reducing in the pan, the spaghetti simmering. 'What's happened?'

'I've pretty much moved in with her, and it isn't working. I think it's that odd thing that happens with couples. When they first meet, they're attracted to something in the other that they can't accept in themselves. It's obvious, to me at least, that Andi was drawn to me because I express a femininity she won't acknowledge in herself. But when the two people become a unit, an everyday public couple, they find themselves associated with the very qualities they've denied in themselves. So now Andi is forever chiding me for all those things she used to like. Complaining that I'm conforming to patriarchal gender roles, all that stuff.'

David remembered the pasta, and prodded it with a fork. 'Oh shit.' He quickly drained the water. 'Think I've overcooked it.'

Kat also prodded it. 'It's alright. And hey, David, it's only us you're cooking for.' She stroked the back of his wrist with a single finger, lightly and momentarily.

They worked together to organise the food on the table. The pasta went into a large serving bowl. David was still feeling the sensation of her touch. 'So, Kat, I need to ask.' He poured the ragu into a mound over the pasta. 'I guess Andi knows that you and I are friends. Does that bother her? You know—*consorting with the enemy.*'

Kat moved the parmesan and green salad to the table. 'God no. She's absolutely fine about it. Knows I enjoy your company. And also knows that even if I wear skirts and lipstick, I'm still a lesbian. Don't worry—you've got nothing to do with our problems.'

The others needed to be called to the table. David was left to feel guilty because he had been conceited enough to think his trivial friendship with Kat might have affected her relationship with Andi. Moments later, he was feeling guilty for worrying about his own conceit when he should have been feeling sorry for Kat and Andi.

The four of them sat to eat, bunched up around the small kitchen table. Towards the end of the meal the conversation turned to films. Kat mentioned a new release she thought might be entertaining. A disaster movie, she explained, about a comet heading for earth.

'Oh god, not another of those.' Andi said. 'What is this Hollywood obsession with the end of the world?'

Helen nodded. 'Millennium angst. It's definitely a theme in fiction at the moment. But Andi, I agree with you. Does nothing for me.'

'There are more obvious explanations,' David countered, 'at least where Hollywood is concerned. They now have the technology to do amazing special effects, and that's what gets people to the cinema these days. And, I admit it, I enjoy that kind of film.'

'I agree,' Kat said. 'They're good fun. And actually, if we're really going to get into subtexts, these films aren't about the end of the world. They're about the end being narrowly avoided, or finding a new beginning through adversity. Good things being born from dust and ruins.'

Andi harrumphed. 'Ah yes, those brave men who'll save the rest of us. And a president—male, of course, and American—who will drag us from the ruins with a new sense of hope.'

'Oh, come on, Andi! Who would be more acceptable?' Kat was sounding impatient. 'The British Prime Minister? The UN? Of course, you can always find a subtext—propaganda, if you like—but sometimes it's nice just to get absorbed in a good story.'

'Why don't the two of you go to see it?' Helen asked. She seemed to be saying it as a straightforward, practical suggestion.

David and Kat both waited, without looking at Andi, for her response.

'Yes, good plan,' Andi said, apparently without concern. 'The obvious answer.'

***

Thus it happened that, a few evenings later, David and Kat went together to the cinema with the full permission of their respective partners. David collected Kat from home. They had allowed such extravagant margins for the journey and parking that they had time for an unauthorised drink in the pub first. There was, however, only time to head for the nearest pub—a dingy place that mainly served the locals. The stench of beer and smoke still lingered from the night before. They bought drinks at the bar, and found a booth to sit in. Across a narrow aisle, a group of four middle-aged men were having a ponderous debate about football, staring in silence at their beers between each shared thought. One of them like to announce his authoritative contributions by leaning back to draw heavily on his cigarette, then tapping a forefinger on the table as he expelled the smoke through his nose.

David and Kat started talking about films, and about the terminology of cinema itself. 'When I was young,' Kat said, 'we used to talk about *going to the pictures*. I don't hear anyone saying that anymore.'

'Give it a few more years,' David added, supportively, 'and we'll have stopped talking about *seeing a film*. We'll all be *going to a movie*. Bloody Americans imposing their words and customs on us!'

'That's right—like doing Halloween instead of Bonfire Night.'

'And *rookie*,' she continued. 'I'd rather have a virgin any day.' She winked at him.

David noticed, but pressed on. 'And this stuff about *stepping up to the plate*.'

'I know,' Kat answered, then continuing in a silly posh voice: 'It just isn't cricket, is it?'

David was often surprised by the things she knew. 'And,' he said, becoming bolder, 'there's changing the meaning of *fanny* from front-bottom to back-bottom.'

Kat said, 'And *pussy*.'

It brought David to a halt. She could only have meant it sexually. To cover his thoughts, he quickly tried to make a debate of it. 'Well, yes, but in that instance, I must say I prefer it to our Anglo-Saxon term.' Suddenly he realised he was at a boundary he could not cross. They were being frank, but he did not dare say the word in question. 'You know,' he said, 'the *c* word. It's such a harsh, hard word for something that's so soft.'

'Oh, but that depends how you say it.' Kat sat up and leaned towards him, willing him to look at her lipsticked mouth. 'You can make it sound very soft and womanly. I'll show you.' Her tongue moistened her lips, and she looked at him directly. She said the word slowly, sensuously, accentuating every letter:

'C . . . u . . . n . . . t.'

He saw her tongue flick down between her teeth on the last consonant, and how she left her mouth open to him when she had said the word. The effect was heightened by the louche look on her face. Then she said it again, and just as slowly:

'C . . . u . . . n . . . t.'

'Alright, I agree,' he said, quickly. 'Obviously, the clue is to say it the way you say your full forename.'

As a ploy to stop her saying it again, it was misjudged. 'I say,' she declaimed, and just as slowly as before, 'what a splendid cunt, Kateryna. In fact, I'd go as far as to say it's a completely cute cunt, Kateryna. Hey, everyone, come and have a look at Kateryna's cunt.'

She stopped and smiled naughtily at David. He swivelled his eyes to tell her to look discreetly across the aisle. He had noticed that the four men were longer talking, but instead looking at each other. The smoking man's fingers were about to get burned by the cigarette smouldering between them.

Kat turned gently back to David. Her cheeks were pink from the effort not to burst into laughter.

***

David's reluctant efforts to promote his work led to invitations from several contacts in London. He tried to herd them together into a single day, but the best he could manage was a list of meetings over a Thursday and Friday in late May. He would have to stay in town overnight.

On that Friday morning Kat took the twins to school as usual, returning to do an hour of housework. She knew that David was away, and saw it as an opportunity.

After completing chores in the house, she made her way to the studio, dragging a vacuum cleaner as it bumped across the paved garden path, and carrying a plastic bowl filled with cloths and cleaning fluids. She let herself into the studio with a key that David always hid outside under an old tile, and began her work.

She thought it would take an hour, but it took the morning. Nowhere was filthy, but there was a thin layer of grime and dust on everything. The greyness, previously barely noticeable, stood out against the areas she had cleaned. She washed and wiped the lower glass of the glazed end wall, and then realised she would have to go back to the house to get a chair so that she could clean the upper part as well.

Kat took care as she worked that everything was left where it had been found. In the far corner there was a muddle of boxes. She cleaned the top of most with the vacuum. One, however, was covered with a loose sheet which she decided to shake outside. When she pulled it away, she discovered it was not covering a box, but a rack of wide canvasses. Curious, she carefully took them out of the rack and propped each one around the walls.

The paintings shared a feature. They all conveyed a sense of transition from one side of the canvas to the other. Kat thought she could see the order of the canvasses from the way the theme developed. The first, she decided, must be the one that was almost abstract. It showed a tiled floor. On the left the tiles were plain and symmetrically laid out, their edges straight and sharp; but as one looked toward the right of the painting, the tiles melted and curved into irregular organic shapes.

Eulogy for Love

A second painting also featured tiles, but this time on one wall of a men's public lavatory, complete with a row of porcelain urinal bowls. On the left of the painting the room was orderly and sterile. But, as the painting developed towards the right of the canvas, green stems pushed their way between the tiles, the tiles cracked, and foliage gushed from the urinals. By the right edge of the canvas, the room was a jungle.

Another showed a long view of the inside of a railway station—perhaps one of the old London stations. At left it was an unflattering view from a high position of grey platforms and cast-iron columns supporting a glazed roof. A passenger train in smoke-smudged blue livery stood against one platform. Again, the dull order at the left gave way to nature. But this time the built environment was not overpowered, nor broken by organic growth. Instead, it was transformed. The blue train became more intensely blue and flowed itself into a river. The grey platforms became green riverbanks, the pillars trees, the roof a canopy of branches and leaves.

The last painting was the only one that included people. Three miners, dirt-faced and almost as dark as the tunnel in which they are working, attack a coalface at the left edge of the painting. A cart stands on rails behind them to carry the coal away. But, at the right side of the painting, the side of the tunnel has collapsed. The miners, apparently, are not underground. The collapse has revealed a scene of English countryside in sunshine that might have been painted by Constable. The miners, either oblivious or indifferent, work on.

Kat shook out the dustsheet, returned the paintings to the rack, and covered them again.

When Kat came to the studio with coffees the next Monday morning, David made a joke about having an infestation of cleaning elves. 'Either that,' he said, 'or I must blame you.' He smiled at her. She hunched her shoulders and smiled back at him in faux guilt. 'You shouldn't have done it, and I must pay you for the extra time.'

'No way, David! It needed to be done, and I did it as your friend.'

***

Kat's help with childcare, and her visits to the studio, had become an established and seemingly permanent part of life in the Barber household. She looked after the twins for a full day over half-term, and then went back to her usual routine until the term ended. The fickle English summer brought bright warm days in the last weeks. The twins, in their blue and white cotton check dresses and summer sandals, went skipping to school but returned irritable and thirsty from the heat. In the last few weeks of term, the school abandoned its focus on lessons. The normal timetable was disrupted by traditional end-of-year activities—the sports and daytrips, the concert rehearsals—and parents were made to fret even more about sending their children to school with the correct items for each day.

One of these end-of-year occasions was the school sports day. The absence of parents at such events was always conspicuous, and the twins were unimpressed when Helen told them she could not be there. So was Kat, when David told her over coffee the same morning.

'I know it won't be as good as having their mother there, but I'd love to come along.'

David wondered whether, as far as the twins were concerned, it might be far better.

'That would be lovely,' he answered, 'but it might look a bit odd for the two of us to be there.'

'Don't be silly. I'm seen at school three days a week. I talk to the parents in the playground. Most think I'm the nanny, and the rest are trying to work out how old I must have been when I had them. But nobody's going to be bothered. And if they are, so effing what?'

They agreed that Kat would come to the house after lunch, and they would walk to school together.

Kat visited the house so often on her own that it felt absurd to ring the bell, so she came around to the side door, and called out as she went into the kitchen. David had been upstairs changing his clothes, but came down when he heard her. They stood and looked at each other from the opposite ends of the room. David saw a pretty young woman in a loose blue dress that fell to her calves. It was V-necked, low enough to show she was not wearing a bra. Her shoes were heavy black platform heels. Kat looked elegant and fashionable. And sexy too, David caught himself thinking.

Kat saw him assessing her. 'Yes, I know. A bit different for me.' She looked down at herself, tugging at the sides of the dress as if about to curtsy. 'Hope you don't mind. Just seemed the day for something summery.'

'Of course I don't mind,' he said. 'Far from it.' He stopped and looked at her. 'You must know by now that I think you're utterly lovely.'

He regretted it immediately. 'I'm sorry, maybe I shouldn't have said that. I do realise that nothing is ever going to happen between us . . . nothing more than friendship, I mean. Please, just take it as a compliment.'

Kat was smiling at him. 'Thank you, David. It's lovely that you feel that way. Now, for goodness sake, get a bloody move on. You're worse than your own daughters at getting ready for school. Go and put your shoes on!'

He was grateful to her. 'Or what?' he asked, playfully.

'Or nothing. If you were thinking I might give you a spanking, you're out of luck.' She winked. 'That's not the way we do things in this family, Mr Barber.'

The school had adopted a fashionable dislike for competition in sports between young children. The programme for the afternoon involved putting the children into groups and then rotating the groups through a series of obscure physical tasks. This made scoring impossible. The twins were assigned to different groups, so David tracked Lauren through her events and Kat followed Hannah. After an hour of chaos, the process had been completed. Orange squash was distributed.

It turned out that there was one element of the traditional school sports day that still continued in highly competitive form. This was the parents' races. The twins wanted Kat to compete, and had to be reminded that she did not meet the eligibility criteria. When the dads' sack race was being readied, it became clear that there was a shortage of entrants. The head teacher used her megaphone to ask for volunteers.

Kat said, 'Go on, David—you do it!' The twins heard her and started lobbying. He had no choice.

An area of the playing field had been chalk-marked into lanes. David made his way to the end of one that was empty, and picked up the sack. Soon all the lanes were filled, the dads poised. It was then that David realised how much he wanted to win. It was a ridiculous event—unfit men bouncing awkwardly towards a length of tape—yet for the moments of the race it might, for David, have been a medieval joust, and one that was being watched by a princess.

Eulogy for Love

Three-quarters of the way to the finish, David was in third place but not far behind the lead. He put in even more effort. Then his feet lost their rhythm and became tangled inside the sack. He was still holding the sack as he fell, and landed on his face.

He was the only failed-to-finish contestant, but won applause as he hobbled back to Kat and the twins. Kat found a graze at his temple, and insisted that they all go back to the school building so that the cut could be cleaned. She made him wait on a bench outside while she scavenged, returning with moistened tissues that she used carefully to clean away the dirt and grass stains. The twins watched as she fussed over their daddy. David felt loved.

Chapter 6

S ometimes the ending of happiness begins like the losing of health: a small ache, a pain in an unfamiliar place. The hand unconsciously seeks to soothe, and to acknowledge; but the conscious mind does not engage. Only much later will it be remembered as the moment the misery began.

Kat came to the studio with coffee, as usual. She had already agreed she would look after the twins for two afternoons when they had finished the morning summer playscheme. This meant that David would have two days a week when he could work without interruption. However, as Kat now explained to him, she had needed to speak to Helen about a potential complication. She had found part-time work over the summer.

David tried to look pleased for her, but evidently managed only to show surprise.

'I'm sorry,' Kat said. 'It didn't seem worth telling you about it when I didn't think there was a real chance I'd get it. And it's only two days a week.'

She went on to explain that she would be working with something called a *community outreach team*. It was a new project set up to tackle the number of young people—mostly kids who had been in care—falling into crime and drug abuse.

'God,' David exclaimed, 'that sounds heavy! Are you comfortable doing that sort of stuff?'

Eulogy for Love

'No, don't worry—I won't be out in the community working with the kids myself. There's trained social workers to do that. I'll be based at the project office, doing admin, being a friendly face to any young people who drop in. But I hoping they'll let me go out with the social workers sometimes.

'The thing is,' she went on, 'the work over August is about getting my foot in the door. If they like me, there's a chance it will continue into the autumn. And I really need some income to get me through uni.'

David felt reassured. She would still be able to help with the twins. His work had picked up a little, so he'd be glad to have two full working days each week, but it didn't matter which they were. He'd still be seeing her. She would still be in his life. There was no good reason to feel anything other than happy for her.

Kat started the job in early August, once the police checks had been completed. On the face of it, there were no problems. She was able to agree, a week in advance, which days she would have the twins. The morning coffees in the studio were no longer possible, but David instead spent a while in the house with the three of them at lunchtime or at the end of the afternoon, and he would chat with Kat when the twins allowed.

The difference was that now she talked about the job. So far, she had mostly met the young people when they came into the office to see their social worker. She laughed with David about some of what she had seen: the silly swagger of some of the lads, their corny chat-up lines, the absurd excuses they offered for not turning up to appointments. Much more of it troubled her, especially the young women who came in, under-dressed, emaciated, and dirty. The social workers confirmed what Kat had guessed: these girls were selling sex on the street to support a drug habit. What David noticed most, however, was Kat's admiration for the social workers who seemed to take it all in their stride.

After a while he grew impatient with Kat's stories, and he knew that what he felt was jealousy. Not towards any individual, or the social workers as a group, but with the whole damned thing—this exotic, high-intensity world that she had entered. He, his work, and his children, had been outclassed. Ridiculous though he knew it was, he felt humiliated, as if he had been made a cuckold.

Towards the end of August, the four members of the Barber family went away for a holiday in Rhodes. They had decided to go to a large resort with all-inclusive food, multiple pools, and evening entertainment. It was not, as Helen and David had taken care to assure each other when they booked it, the kind of place they would have chosen for themselves. But the twins would enjoy it, they agreed, and would not need to be entertained the entire time.

Helen adapted easily to resort life. Once the buffet breakfast was done, the twins changed into their costumes, and all their remaining visible skin covered in sun cream, she would settle herself on a lounger by a nearby pool and read novels for as long as she was allowed. David, in contrast, was restless. He found himself pleased to be disturbed by the twins, and would escort them around the resort even when they were safe enough on the own. As he went, he would look at the people enjoying their holidays. The majority were British. To judge from their accents, there had been recent incoming flights from Newcastle, and he suspected they were from very different backgrounds to his own. But, whatever their lives might be back in England, these people seemed happy. The older couples, once they had chosen their seats and arranged their towels, settled themselves in companionable silence. Young couples pulled their loungers close together, touched each other, whispered. Teenage girls in sexy bikinis stood together in the water to gossip, their backs against the side of the pool.

David felt a need in himself that he couldn't satisfy. It was a need for Kat; for her smiles, and laughs, her little mannerisms. He contemplated phoning her, but Kat would have found that odd—as would Helen, of course, if she had discovered him. Then he thought he might send her a postcard, ostensibly from the family but perhaps worded in a way that would make it subtly from him to her. The next morning, on the way back from breakfast, the twins came across a rack of cards and decided they wanted to send their own to Kat. Cards were bought—two, to avoid arguments—with stamps for each, and once back at the apartment the twins filled them with pictures of life at the resort. When they had finished, David picked up the cards, and discreetly dropped a pen into the pocket of his shorts.

Helen was in the bedroom getting the twins ready for the pool. David called out, 'I might as well put the cards in the box before they get covered in jam or sun cream.'

'OK,' Helen called back. 'See you at the pool.'

Once safely away from the apartment he stopped and put the cards out on top of a low wall. He had to be quick. He wrote sideways, down the seam of one card, *See you soon, Kateryna x*. It was pretty lame, but he believed she would understand.

The usual domestic routine was restored the following week. When Kat brought the twins back from playscheme on the Monday lunchtime, she first took them into the house to get drinks, but then opened the side door for them. They leapt out into the sunshine. David saw her standing at the kitchen door, and she waved at him in that way of hers. Putting down his pen, he went over to see her, and they stood side by side watching the girls play on a swing that was now too small for them, and grown rusty.

David had some news he wanted to share. On return from holiday there had been a letter waiting from the old friend he had met that evening in London. The letter formally confirmed that David could have a space at an illustrators' fair in September. Even better, he was to be a featured artist.

'He told me about it when I met him in London,' David explained, 'but I didn't want to set myself up for a disappointment.'

'Wow, David! That is such good news. I'm so pleased for you. Wish I could be there to see it.'

'I wish you could. It's going to be two long days—setting up very early, and then trying to respond positively to people who come up. Inevitably there's long quiet gaps, and then three people will want to talk to you at the same time.'

He paused, and then looked at her. 'Would you be interested in coming along?'

'Love to, if I'm free. But would Helen mind?'

'Let's see.'

David realised he had been talking too much about himself. 'And you? Work OK?'

'Actually, I've not been having a great time, but nothing to do with work.' She looked over at the twins.

'I've split with Andi.'

'Oh no. You'd said things weren't easy, but I had no idea they were as bad as that.'

'I know. It was the constant sense of her disapproval that got me down. Got to the point where I'd simply had enough of it, and I told her.'

'So—how's she?'

'Hurt. And very angry.'

The twins, bored with the swing, and hungry, came over to them. Kat squatted against the wall of the house, lowering herself to their level. 'Hannah and Lauren have been telling me that they had a great holiday,' she said. 'And I've thanked them for their lovely postcards.' She looked up at David, and smiled at him.

***

David had already told Helen about the fair, but raised the subject again while they were eating dinner one evening. He let her know that he was working hard to have a good range of work to put on display. 'It isn't the preparation that's troubling me,' he added, as if an afterthought, 'it's the event itself. The assembling and dismantling, then minding shop for two days. It physically isn't possible to be there all the time, and Sod's Law dictates that the potentially most valuable contact of the whole event will pass by when I'm taking a loo break.'

'Why don't you ask Kat?' Helen suggested, casually and on cue.

'You wouldn't mind?'

'Not at all, provided you pay her something for her time, and of course pay for her to have a decent hotel room.'

'OK, and thanks. That's a really helpful idea. I'll ask her.'

***

By the start of the autumn school term it had become clear that Kat's help with childcare was no longer reliable. The outreach team wanted to keep her, but could only offer irregular hours. It was the Barber household that had to adapt to Kat's changing availability. She was also needing to prepare for the start of university, hunting for a place in shared student accommodation. Helen found an afterschool club, and helped the twins get used to going there.

David realised that he would soon lose the pleasure of Kat's morning visits to the studio. On the other hand, he would have Kat's company for two whole days at the illustrators' fair, and—emboldened by Helen's indifference—they also went twice on evening visits to the cinema. He began to believe they could have a friendship that would stand on its own, separate from domestic life, openly declared.

David had decided they would travel to the fair very early in the morning, giving them time to set up ready for the opening at ten. This made it necessary to load up the car—Helen had agreed he could take her estate—the evening before. Kat came to help. David had said there was no need, but she argued that if she was going to be useful, she needed to know what he was taking and where it was packed.

He had already collected up the materials to pack by the time Kat arrived. She found the middle of the studio cluttered with boxes, portfolio cases, and display boards. David was now starting to move them to the car. She joined in, carrying each load to the side of the car and watching how he packed them.

She stood and rested for a few moments in the studio, leaving David to collect up another load. It was then that she noticed the rack of paintings, still in the corner of the room, still covered by the dusty sheet. She went over to them, crouched down, and lifted away the sheet.

'David—you're surely taking these, aren't you?' But he was heading across the grass to the car, and did not hear.

Kat saw that were now five canvases, not four. She lifted out the one at the front, and knew instantly that it was the addition.

Eulogy for Love

It plainly belonged in the same series as the others. Here again there was a sense of transition from left to right across the wide canvas: From drab greys to iridescent colour; from manufactured to organic. But this time the scene was the studio where she was now standing.

She realised, as she looked more closely, that it was a changed version of the studio. Things had been moved, the layout altered. The filing cabinets, pots of pens, computer, and David's drawing board were at the left side of the painting. They, and the walls and floors, were all painted in dirty greys. At centre was the antique chaise longue, painted grey at left and then becoming progressively more blue—first the dusty blue it was in real life, and then deeper and brighter, until, by its raised end, it was a vibrant cobalt. The glass wall had been relocated to the centre and right of the painting. It no longer looked onto a tired lawn and an ordinary English terraced house. Instead it revealed an Italianate landscape painted in High Renaissance style, with heavy luminous clouds hanging over distant church buildings, thin cypress trees and rocky outcrops in the foreground. It glowed with colour.

The chaise longue was occupied. Venus was there, reclining. But this Venus was fully clothed. This Venus was wearing black leggings and a dark sweatshirt, holding a coffee mug, and gazing serenely at the artist. Kat recognised herself.

David returned from the car at that moment, and saw her. 'Oh,' was all he could say.

'Wow,' Kat replied. 'It's . . .' She was going to say *beautiful* but worried that might sound either twee or vain. 'It's very striking.'

'I think you've already seen the others. I had an idea that things had been moved when you did your cleaning here.'

'I did. I'm sorry.'

'Don't worry—it doesn't matter. The other ones are old. I painted them years ago.'

'When did you manage to paint the new one?'

David picked up a box for the car. 'It was easy to do some sketches—all those mornings having coffee together. You didn't know you were modelling for me. And then I did the painting over August, when you weren't around.'

'Please tell me, David, that you're going to put these all in the car.'

He put the box down again, and looked at her. 'They're kind-of private. Don't know whether they're any good. I showed the four of them to Helen once—back in the days when she took some interest—and she wasn't impressed. I still remember her words. She said they were *too calculated, too knowing, to count as serious art.*'

Kat looked at the new painting. 'Well, David, fuck that. In fact, if I may say so, just this once: Fuck Helen!' She turned to David, and he saw that her cheeks were flushed. 'Please David, put them in the car.'

He paused, bit on his lip, considered. 'OK. We'll put them at the end.'

***

It was agreed that in the morning Kat would come through the side gate and meet David at the car. It was still dark when she arrived, and every sound they made—even the click of the latch on the gate—felt loud in the stillness of the streets and houses around them. Kat had brought a small case and a thermos flask. The car was so full she had to tuck them by her feet.

It was too early for conversation. They travelled mostly in silence while the sun rose, orange then gold, to their left. Kat got out the thermos flask and passed capfuls of coffee to David as he drove.

The journey went easily, although they began to slow in the morning traffic as they made their way over the top of the capital to their East London destination. It was a converted church, squat and plain, probably Baptist or Wesleyan. There was a small yard at the back for unloading, but not large enough to leave the car, so they quickly transferred the contents of the car to their allocated space inside. It was a good space—larger than most, and close to stairs that led to the gallery, so unavoidably seen by anyone visiting the upper floor.

David went to park the car for the day, and left Kat with the heaped materials and with firm instructions not to make any attempt to set them up. When he returned, he saw how she had used her time. The leggings she had travelled in had been replaced by high-waisted denim jeans. She had also put on a crocheted, sleeveless top that barely fell to the waist of her jeans. It had a pattern in a deep, bluish red—rose madder, David thought—and she had put on lipstick of the same colour. He could not ignore the change.

'My, my, Kateryna, you're looking good.'

'Why thank you, Mr Barber!'

They had the display ready a little before the opening time at ten. Kat had to cajole David to do it, but in the end the five canvasses were put out at the centre. Though a little cramped, they summoned the gaze of all who walked by. Better still, the Venus piece was at the centre of the group, and just above Kat as she stood at the table. People were amused, and thought themselves clever for noticing, that the same attractive young woman was there both in flesh and acrylic. This first day of the fair was geared to *the trade* and had brought in the predictable quota of leering middle-aged men who would pause to talk to her because she was a pretty young woman. 'Ah, I see you're the model, and the lovely *assistante*,' they might say, glancing enviously at David. Others wanted to know whether there might be further pictures in the same series, pictures that would show Kat, as one enquirer put it, *with her kit off*. Kat held her smile.

As David had expected, she was useful in looking after the display, dealing with easily answered enquiries, and encouraging those with more complex or important questions to wait until he was free. But she did much more than that. The common logic—of men especially—is that a middle-aged man can only attract a beautiful young woman if he is successful; and if he is successful, he must be good at what he does; and if good at what he does he must, then, be taken seriously. Even David fell for this. With Kat close by, he felt successful, and acted as if he were successful; and so, in a sense, he became successful for that day.

By the end of it, David had been invited to display at two art exhibitions, and three publishers were expressing interest. It had truly been a success. They emerged from the building to discover it was a warm evening. David needed a drink, and they found a bar nearby with tables outside, facing the street. Kat took a seat at a table while he went to the bar. When he got back, he sat down and impulsively grasped her hand. 'Thank you so much, Kat. You were an enormous help today.'

'Pleased to do it. It was fun!'

They talked comfortably together. David told her about the promising contacts, she told him about the ridiculous leering men. They agreed to find a straightforward restaurant and eat early, so they could get to bed in good time, as they were both tired.

A car drew up in front of them. A *supercar*. Everything about it was designed to draw attention, from its crazily curved shape to its bright orange colour. For some moments the deep gurgling of the exhaust halted all conversations at the outside tables. Then the engine was cut. The doors rose up like guillotines. From the driver's side emerged a young man, casually dressed in denim jeans, a gaudy soft shirt, and white sneakers. In contrast the woman who struggled onto her feet from the passenger side was dressed for the evening in a short, halter-necked, black dress. She was slim, tanned, and wearing elaborate make-up. The doors descended, and the two of them walked into the bar.

'Blimey!' David said. 'What do you think? Would you like one of those?'

Kat shrugged. 'Well, I wouldn't mind taking her for a spin around the block a couple of times. You know, tickle her throttle and see if I can rev her up a bit. But I suspect she'd be awfully high maintenance.'

Kat leaned forward and tapped the table. 'Oh, sorry David.' She winked at him. 'I didn't realise you meant the car!'

David guffawed. 'Kateryna, you are outrageous! You'd be shocked if I talked like that.'

'Nah! You're a sexually alive man. I know you have those thoughts. I'm just saying them out loud. And a lot less vividly than I could have chosen to.'

David said, 'Yeah, I'm sure you could. And maybe I do.' And then he imagined them sitting together watching women walking past—discussing each one, awarding points, perhaps even whispering fantasies. He found the vision simultaneously impermissible and liberating.

'So, go on, then, David. Would you like one of those? And yes, I do mean the car.'

He stared at the car where it sat at the kerb, a few yards away.

'I suppose I'd take it if you offered it to me. You'd also have to give me the money to run it, and the fancy house with the high security garage to keep it in. But I don't hanker for it especially.

'The truth is that I'd be much more likely to fantasise about having a car that I might, just conceivably, be able to afford one day. A nice Volvo, maybe, or a Saab if I'm in a daring mood.' He lifted his beer glass and waved it at the supercar. 'Those things are so far from my reality that I can't even get serious about the idea of having one.'

'So you never want things you don't believe you could have?'

He looked up at her, and frowned. 'Wow, you are in the mood for big questions.' He paused, checking she wanted an honest answer, and then stared at the supercar.

'I don't suppose it's the same when you're young, like you. *You* could throw away everything you have and start again, and the cost would not be very great. But by the time you get to my age you've invested everything. I suppose some lucky people are happy with the life they've found, but I reckon most of us can't bear to dream, because it would confront us with the truth that our lives are far from what we wanted.

'Don't ask me to do this too often, Kat, but if for a moment I start to think about the life that I'd want, it has almost nothing in it that I have now. Yes, I'd keep the twins, but that's about it. And the awful truth is that they couldn't have a place in this alternative reality, because I wouldn't have travelled down the path that led to their existence.'

He halted and bit his lip. Kat noticed.

'I'm sorry, David.' She found his hand and squeezed it sympathetically. 'I should have realised we were heading into difficult territory.'

Eulogy for Love

'And you know,' David said, struggling to calm his voice, 'what makes it worse is that Helen would almost certainly say the same thing. In fact, I reckon most of the middle-aged people I know, with their kids and jobs and mortgages, would say much the same. None of us thinks about our dreams anymore, because we know we have fallen so far short of them.'

Kat said: 'I wonder if I'll be saying the same thing in twenty years. I'm going to try so hard to live with authenticity, to follow my true path.'

'I wish you well with that, Kat, I really do. But you may find that your true path is a lonely place. And I suspect you'll compromise, like the rest of us.'

They fell into silence until Kat grasped his hand again and gave it a little shake. 'C'mon,' she said, 'let's go find somewhere to eat.'

They found a little place where the tables had red gingham tablecloths, and thick white candles with wax that dripped down the sides. The restauranteur and the music were both Greek and too loud. Kat and David sat close as they talked. As ever, there was never an awkward pause. There was a point, though, when David stopped listening to her words. He only watched her mouth and heard the sound of her voice—the softly flowing water of a moorland stream, he decided—and thought how lovely she was.

It was no longer early when they collected their overnight bags from the car, then checked into the modern budget hotel. Kat scooped up the key cards while David paid the bill. Kat gave him one of them as they stepped into the lift. David didn't notice that Kat had pressed for two floors, and was taken by surprise when it stopped.

'It's OK,' Kat said, as the doors opened. 'For some reason they put us on different floors.'

85

She quickly stepped out, and then turned. 'Thank you for a great day, David. I've really enjoyed it.' Her smile had an intense warmth, but he could see there was also a knowingness in it. 'Goodnight. See you at breakfast.'

They were still looking at each other when the door closed between them. The lift started upwards. She had done that deliberately, he realised. She had known that he had wanted something that was beyond his reach. It crossed his mind that she too had wanted it, but he suppressed that dream. It was only later, before he went to sleep, that he allowed his mind to downgrade the unattainable romance into a sexual fantasy of what might have happened if they had gone to the same room.

***

The second day of the fair went well, and quickly. It was geared more to the public, less to trade, and there were fewer serious enquiries that David needed to deal with. Kat sent him the interested amateurs with their technical questions but kept the families and children for herself. David enjoyed watching how she responded to them. Sometimes she would come out from behind the desk to the front of the display, where she could kneel to talk to the little ones. And whereas, yesterday, the *Venus* picture had attracted leering men, today it provided magic for the small children who stood looking solemnly into her face while pointing their small round fingers at the canvas on the wall.

At the end of the day they reloaded the car hastily, and drove home as the light failed. It was fully dark by the time David manoeuvred the car through the big side gates and parked it by the kitchen door. It would be safe enough there for the night.

When Kat got out, and came round to David, they both knew that these two special days could not be ended with a little wave of farewell. They leaned into each other and hugged. It was a carefully innocent hug, with no accompanying kiss, and their bodies did not touch below the shoulders. As they embraced, Helen opened the back door.

They separated. 'See you Friday,' Kat said brightly, for the benefit of their new audience.

'Sure,' David answered. 'And don't let me forget to pay you. You've been a great help.'

Kat wished goodnight to Helen, and left. Helen said, 'Well, I don't need to know whether the two of you got on OK. Did you actually get any business out of it?'

'Not the sort of place I'm going to clinch deals,' David responded as he locked the car, 'but if a tenth of the contacts made and proposals discussed come to something, then it will have been very worthwhile.'

Chapter 7

K at had agreed to provide childcare on the Friday of the following week, both at the start and end of the school day. The day before, she phoned David at the studio to say she would have to cancel. The permanent admin worker with the team was sick, she explained, and it was likely she would be off for several weeks. For Kat it was very good news, as she was now being offered increased hours. It was a chance to show them that she was a reliable and capable person. And, that being so, she would have to give the team priority over the Barbers.

David reassured her. 'Sad for us, Kat, but don't worry. The twins would be far happier with you, but there's no good reason why they can't go to the afterschool club. And I think we all know that your days of helping us are coming to an end.

'To be honest,' he went on, 'I'm just hoping we don't lose touch entirely. I know the twins will want to see you. You're already well on the way to being Auntie Kat. And I can't see anything to stop you and me continuing to meet for a drink or film, if you can spare the time.'

As soon as he had said it, he felt vulnerable. He became unusually aware of the difference in their ages. She had so many opportunities ahead, while he was the trapped and lonely man. He didn't want her to agree out of pity.

'Well actually, David, that's the other thing I wanted to tell you.' There was a pause.

'I've met somebody new.'

Eulogy for Love

'Wow, that's great!' David responded, over-enthusiastically. 'Really pleased for you. You don't hang about, do you!'

'I know, it is a bit quick, but honestly, I didn't two-time Andi. Meeting someone new, someone fresh and interesting, makes you realise it's time to end a relationship that is no longer working.'

'Oh, I can see that.' More forced enthusiasm. 'So tell me, who is she, and how did you meet?'

'That's the thing, David. His name is Mark, and he's the outreach teamleader.'

David couldn't speak for a little while. He heard Kat's voice down the phone saying, 'I'm sorry, David.'

Another silence. Then she said, softy, 'I can understand why you'd be surprised. I suppose I'm learning that what people have between their legs isn't the most important thing for me. I let myself be labelled as a lesbian, and sort-of accepted that's what I was. Maybe I should be re-labelled as bisexual. But I don't really want to be labelled at all.'

David didn't find that helpful. He wasn't used to Kat sounding uncertain.

Eventually he recovered sufficiently. 'You don't have to explain or apologise, Kat. I'm a little surprised, that's all. We're simply friends, and I'm happy for you. There's no reason why we can't see meet up sometimes, is there?'

'I hope there isn't, but we need to let things settle a bit. It's all very new with Mark. I've told him I have a friend called David, and that we sometimes go to the cinema together. He didn't express any concerns.'

David said he should leave her to get on with her day. Kat said she'd try to sort out whether she could offer time with the twins the next week, and would phone. The call ended.

Kat did phone. It was early on Monday morning, when David had barely started at the studio. But not to offer childcare.

Over the weekend she had encountered Andi in town, and stopped to talk. Kat had stupidly followed her inclination to be honest, and had told Andi about Mark.

'Oh,' David said. 'And how did she take that?'

'She's absolutely furious. There's all the usual stuff about betraying the lesbian cause, surrendering to patriarchy. But this time it's far worse because it's personal. She's concocted a whole theory about how I was seeing Mark—sleeping with him—while I was still with her. The thought of it—my body being entered by a man when she thought it belonged to her— is driving her crazy.'

'But you weren't . . .' David began.

'No, but she's not going to be convinced otherwise. I've already tried.'

'Well, she'll just have to live with it. You've done nothing wrong.'

'Unfortunately, David, it's not that simple. She's on the warpath. She's already phoned Mark this morning. She talked to him while he was in his office, and me just feet away. She now suspects that you and I were up to things. I know because Mark came out and told me. He just said, very coldly, that he didn't want me to see you anymore, and that he and I would talk about it this evening. But Andi has obviously insinuated that there were things going on between us – between you and me, I mean.'

'I'm so sorry.'

'There's more. And I'm so sorry, David. It's all but certain that Andi will phone Helen and tell her the same story. She's probably already called her at work, so you need to be ready.'

90

'But we haven't done anything! And anyway, she doesn't seem to care what I get up to.'

'You don't understand. This is about ownership. It's one thing not to care about you. But if she's told directly that you're being unfaithful, she can't afford to ignore it. It's a matter of pride.'

'OK. Thank you for warning me.'

'David, I'd better get back to work.'

He was about to let her go until he realised the significance of the moment. 'Wait, Kat, not like this. I can't say goodbye like this. Can I meet you—today?'

There was a silence. 'It's difficult, but I agree this is not the way to end our friendship.' Kat paused again. 'I can escape at lunchtime, pretend I need to do some shopping. But only for half an hour. There's a place nearby—Walter's Bar—that's not the sort of place anyone here would go to. I could see you there at one. But only for a little while.'

***

Walter's Bar was all glass and leather, and quiet on a Monday lunchtime. David had not been sure he could find it, and arrived far too early. He thought it was the sort of place where one should drink gin rather than beer, and by mistake ordered a Happy Hour double. He found a pair of sofas at the far end of the room, where he sat and felt the alcohol passing unhindered through his empty stomach.

Kat arrived, bought herself some bottled water, and sat down on the sofa opposite David. She leaned back and let out her breath.

'What a mess,' she said, with a rueful smile. 'I think we both know that we have to stop seeing each other—that this is the end.'

'We could still stay in touch, couldn't we?' He heard himself sounding pleading and pathetic.

'That would be difficult with Mark, I'm afraid. And anyway, I'm not sure there's much point.'

David looked at her. He felt lightheaded from the gin. There were tears forming behind his eyes.

'In that case,' he said, 'I want to be honest with you before you go.'

He found the strength to look at her. 'I've been falling in love with you.'

When he'd said it, he felt there should be more to say. But that was it—the single truth he needed to share, the knowledge he wanted her to have and keep.

'I know you have, David. But you have Hannah and Lauren. They're the ones you need to think about. It would hurt you terribly if anything happened to them. And me too.'

There was a long silence. Kat poured and drank her water. David watched, trying to memorise the image of her.

'I need to go soon, David,' she said, softly.

He reached into a pocket of his jeans and brought out a small plastic bag. 'I wanted to give you something that would remind you of me, and us, and our funny friendship,' he said, and pulled open the bag. 'I'm sorry it's not all nicely presented in a box, but there wasn't time. And of course I don't know whether it will fit on you.'

He held out a ring for Kat to take. It was silver, simple in design, with black jet and small white crystals laid around the band in an alternating pattern. 'I'm sure it isn't valuable,' he said. 'It was my grandmother's, and she wasn't wealthy.'

Kat took the ring and tried it on. It was too tight for her ring and middle fingers, but she discovered it slid neatly onto her little finger. 'I can wear it like that, if that's OK.' She held her hand up to show him, and smiled. 'Thank you, David. It's lovely.'

Then she put the same hand on his, and said, 'Really, I am going to go now.

'Goodbye David. I hope you find happiness.'

He managed to say, 'Goodbye, my Kateryna,' but then the tears came, and he was forced to bite his lip to stay silent. Kat got up and walked out. She did not turn to wave. David lowered his head so that nobody would see him weeping, and fumbled in his pockets for a tissue.

Helen arrived home that evening as David was giving the twins their tea. She said little, and seemed grumpy, but that was not unusual. It was only much later he knew for sure. He was coming downstairs after putting the twins to bed, and she called out to him from the kitchen:

'David, we need to have a talk.'

He had decided to pretend he knew nothing about Andi's phone calls, which meant he needed to look surprised and curious as he sat down at the table.

'Andi phoned me today. I gather Kat is not so exclusively lesbian as we all thought.' Helen was watching his face for reactions. 'Andi thinks that the two of you may have been doing things you shouldn't. I need to know the truth, David.'

'There's nothing to tell, Helen. She told me she had a new boyfriend, but it's no business of mine to question her sexuality. That's it. End of story.'

'Did you fuck her?'

'No, I certainly did not!'

'Did you want to?'

'Oh, come on Helen,' David said, offering as much exasperation as he judged appropriate. 'That's not a fair question. You may have forgotten, but I am a man. And men, on a daily basis, want to fuck any attractive woman who passes them by. Doesn't mean they're going to.'

'OK. But did you make any attempt to seduce her?'

'No'

'Did you love her?'

'I was fond of her. She was nice company, and she was good with the twins.'

'I don't mean that. I mean, were you in love with her?'

She looked hard at David. He held her gaze. He needed to answer quickly, unequivocally, and there was no doubt what the answer should be. It was a choice between saying something to save his marriage, and indulging in a pointless romantic gesture. Yet he struggled to say it.

Finally: 'No,' he said.

He felt disgusted with himself. He had betrayed Kat, betrayed the love he felt for her, betrayed himself.

'I'm going ask you one more time, David. Are you in love with Kat?'

It seemed he needed to be more emphatic.

'Absolutely not. I am not in love with Kat. Not in the slightest.' He made himself look straight at Helen's eyes. Inside, he felt his soul wither.

'OK, I believe you,' she said. 'And that's the end of it.' She released his gaze. 'We won't discuss it, or her, again. And, needless to say, I expect you to have no further contact with her. I do mean *no contact*. Never, ever, again. Understood?'

'Understood.'

PART 2

He feeds upon her face by day and night,
And she with true kind eyes looks back on him,
Fair as the moon and joyful as the light:
Not wan with waiting, not with sorrow dim;
Not as she is, but was when hope shone bright;
Not as she is, but as she fills his dream.

Christina Rossetti
"In an artist's studio"

Chapter 8

David had always promised himself he would stay with Helen until the twins left home. He kept the promise, but, less than a month after Lauren and Hannah had started university, Helen announced that she wanted a divorce.

They had learned, by that point in their marriage, how to live without ever having heartfelt conversations, so Helen had first to announce that she wished to talk to him. When they met, she delivered a speech that felt to David as if it had taken a decade to prepare. She said she hoped they could part amicably and wait the two years that the law required for them to divorce by mutual consent, without blame. She said that it would probably be best if David found somewhere else to live, and she hoped David would understand that she would want to stay in the house so that the twins could continue to come and stay in their own bedrooms.

David was delighted to agree to find somewhere else to live, but pointed out that the house remained as much his as hers, and that he considered he should have access when he needed. Helen, suddenly less conciliatory, said he should appreciate her need for privacy in what was, for all practical purposes, her own home; and that she couldn't have him coming and going on a whim. She reluctantly agreed, however, that he could continue to access the studio via the side gate.

Eulogy for Love

He managed to find a place to live a couple of miles away. A dull redbrick box on a newbuild housing estate, it was not the sort of place he would want to stay long, but it got him out of the marital home. He committed only to a six-month letting. Though pleased to be free of Helen, he felt the loss of his everyday identity as a father. In the heavy silence of his new home, he would yearn to hear the thudding of teenage feet on stairs, the dull thump of the music they liked to play in their bedrooms, their voices as they laughed together with the friends who came to *hang out*. He missed the teasing that was their way of saying they loved him. Their passing touches to his shoulder, and their less frequent hugs, had been—ritual business handshakes aside—the only human touch he had known for many years. Now even that had been lost. He did not mourn the end of the marriage, yet he had many reasons to grieve.

He also needed time to create an image of the future he wanted to build for himself. He had, over the last decade with Helen, become much more successful in his work. He was in no doubt the change of fortune could be traced back to the illustrators' fair in London and, more specifically, to those five canvases. People had liked them, wanted to buy them. A hotel chain paid well for permission to make reproductions of the picture of the railway station, eventually hung in thousands of their rooms. He was now in demand as an illustrator for book covers and upmarket magazines. If there were time to spare, and that was not often, he would experiment with new ideas and themes, always confident his work would sell.

As a consequence, his income had risen to the point where it outstripped Helen's. They had become an affluent family. They could have bought a second home, or gone on luxury holidays. But Helen and David invested nothing in their marriage, and wanted nothing that would cause them to spend more time together. Instead, the money was put into investment funds where it silently accumulated.

Now fifty-three, David was in good health. His hair had receded a little, and sometimes he used reading glasses, but he looked good for his age. After he had moved to the rented house, it started to bother him that he had acquired a small paunch. It was slight, but looked unappealing on a body that was otherwise lean. He decided he would take up jogging.

He disliked the need to go back to the house to work in his studio. It had become a museum of his own past. He would catch himself looking wistfully out of the studio window at remembered scenes of the twins playing on the lawn. In his mind he saw them as toddlers, as lithe little girls playing ball, or as slouching teenagers in secretive conversations. Inside the studio, there was still the chaise longue, unused and dusty. He would think of Kat lying on it like a reclining Venus, and of those few happy months. Often these thoughts pervaded his mind so much that, by the time he locked the studio door and went home, he would be soaked in melancholy. On the other hand, it didn't seem the time to be finding a new studio, and Helen was at work when he went over, so there were no awkward encounters. He considered it a situation he could survive for a year or two.

One day, about a month after this arrangement had started, he left his phone at the studio. He didn't notice until he had started cooking an evening meal, so thought he would drive over to get it afterwards. But then he decided he would jog over after his meal had settled.

It was late when he finally set off, and dark, but his route was on streets with good lighting. He let himself through the side gate and walked across the grass. It was then he realised that, of course, Helen would probably be at home. The light in the kitchen suggested he was right, and, when he came nearer, he saw Helen inside. He also saw she had a man with her, a man he did not recognise.

They were both standing, Helen at the sink, the man passing things to her—crockery from the table, probably. He was middle-aged, with not much hair, a little overweight, and heavy jowled; the sort of man who needs to shave twice a day. The view was limited by the windowsill, but David thought the man was wearing a plain white shirt, undone at the collar. He looked like a businessman home after a day at the office.

David let himself into the studio without turning on the light. He stood at the window and looked across at the house. Helen had moved away from the sink, leaving no one visible. Then the kitchen light went off. A few moments later, the windows above lit up. These, David knew, were the windows to the main bedroom. It crossed his mind that the man might have gone, leaving Helen to retire to bed on her own, but he saw the man pass the window. David was watching his estranged wife going to bed with another man. And yet they weren't playing it like new lovers—embracing, removing each other's clothes, falling onto the bed. These two took their own clothes off, and talked as they did so. The man removed his shirt and gesticulated while it was still hanging on him by an arm in the sleeve. Helen walked casually past the window in her bra. They were going to bed like an old couple at the end of an ordinary day.

David found his phone in the darkness, and left the studio. As he exited onto the street, he saw a white Mercedes parked outside the house.

Within the week, David had instructed a solicitor to inform Helen that she was being sued for divorce on grounds of infidelity. It wasn't about vengeance. Months later, when he had learned to be angry with Helen, he would fume and curse her for the parsimonious way she had rationed sex to him while she, he imagined, was fornicating eagerly with another man. At this stage, however, he felt sorry for her. The two of them had each wasted almost twenty years of their lives in the belief that their children needed them to make the sacrifice. They had both lacked courage, both surrendered their integrity, both lost. At this point David had simply had enough of all the deceits. He wanted out, and as fast as possible.

Not much more than six months later, he was out. Helen, as she had wanted, kept the house, but had to pay off David with a large proportion of their financial assets. He had enough money to set himself up well. He bought an old farmhouse a half-hour drive from his old home. It was on the edge of a pretty village where most of the residents commuted to well-paid jobs. The farmhouse was a square, two-storied building with the symmetry of a doll's house. The central front door lay under a wood-framed porch, with four windows set square around it. It was so neat and pretty one might have looked for giant hinges under the ivy at the corners. There were three bedrooms, so the twins could always feel welcome. It came with gardens at the back and on one side, but faced onto a farmyard, now gravelled over, where David could park his Volvo estate. And, at the side of the yard, there was a cowshed, which David paid to be converted into a bright and spacious studio. He had the chaise longue reupholstered in its original vivid blue, and put it in the studio.

He had sold all but one of the five canvases that they had taken to London that day in 1998. He could not part with the Venus. When he first moved into the farmhouse, he installed it over the head of the bed in the master bedroom. He discovered, however, that guests who made it as far as his bed would ask questions about the girl on the couch. For all he tried to give a brief and breezy account, they always seemed to hear something in his voice that left them feeling intimidated by her. So he moved the canvas to his studio, where she was his quiet companion as he worked.

There were a few guests in his bed over those years. With the exception of the barmaid from the village pub, who was incautiously invited one New Year's Eve, they were all people he met through his work. He lacked other interests that might have broadened his social contacts. He wasn't interested in football, ballroom dancing, or motorsport. He moved almost entirely in the overlapping worlds of art, illustration, and publishing. People met the public persona of David Barber, *the artist and illustrator*, and only afterwards got to know David. It meant that he tended to attract women who saw a quality in the artistic works—passion or elegance, perhaps—but then failed to find it in the man, and so ended up being disappointed by him. As a result, most made their excuses after three or four dates.

There were two who saw the real David, and still liked him. Each earned temporary promotion to resident status at the Barber farmhouse, but neither stayed for more than a few months. Before they left, each gave a similar speech. They said that although he was a lovely guy, and treated them very nicely, they got a feeling that he wasn't one hundred percent committed to the relationship. David felt this a little unfair. He genuinely cared for each of these women. He could look them in the eye and say, honestly, that he loved them. He enjoyed their company, and, now recovering from the years of Helen's humiliation, enthusiastically participated in sex with them as often as they were willing.

The problem, and he knew it, was that he hankered for something more. It was like drinking blended after tasting single malt, or travelling Economy after flying First Class.

This standard-issue love was real, honest, and heartfelt. It was the kind of love that made the world go around. It was the version of love that David had once felt for Helen, and for one or two others before her. But David now knew there was another kind of love. It was not something he had fully experienced. He had seen but not visited, as one might glimpse a sunlit clearing through the trees of a shadowy forest. Yet he had a certainty about what he would have found, had he been able to take those last few steps into sunlight. It would been a love that existed without qualification, and without limits: Perfect devotion.

He told himself that he was yearning for this kind of love as an abstraction, as something that might one day become manifest through, and with, someone who lay in his future. To assign it exclusively to one individual, a young woman whom he had already met and lost, was too unbearable to contemplate. He knew, nevertheless, that he could have loved Kateryna with this perfect devotion. He would have loved all of her: the shape of her toes, the set of her teeth; her bones, her blood. He would have been devoted to her in this way, not for a few months of early romance, but for as long as they had lived. He would have counted it a privilege to watch her grow old, as one savours the signs of summer fading into autumn, knowing full well that winter follows. He would have kissed each new crease at the side of her eyes, cupped his hand lovingly, year upon year, into her softening belly as they spooned in sleep. He would not have loved her *in spite of* this or that failing. No exceptions, no limitations. All of her would have been included within this love's paradigm. All; everything; always.

That woman had gone. Though he tried to believe that he could find someone else who merited such love, all the candidates proved disappointing. They knew they had disappointed him, and he knew that they had been hurt by this knowing. So he stopped looking, and journeyed through middle age on his own. The twins did visit, but not often, and they rarely stayed. They preferred to be based at their mother's house, in their own bedrooms, and in the neighbourhood where they still felt rooted.

In his membership of the village community, as in his professional life, his position was secure. He was often to be seen running a circuit around the village outskirts. Though he would not stop to talk to people, he unfailingly acknowledged them with a wave. Most weekends, he would walk to the village pub and drink a pint while seated on a stool at the bar, ready to make conversation with anyone who came within chatting distance. He always helped with the annual fête and other village events. There was only one occasion when he refused a request for help with village life, and that was when someone thought he might do some small black-and-white illustrations for the parish magazine. He explained, a little too abruptly, that he didn't do that kind of work.

In this way, the years passed. Freed from the cage of marriage, financially secure and professionally recognised, he considered himself no longer oppressed by other people's expectations. The illusion of happiness depended, however, on his ability to contain the expectations of life that he allowed himself to have. He managed, most of the time, to be content by only wanting those things that he knew were within his reach. Occasionally, the curtains would draw back. He might be paused in thought, or talking on the phone. His eyes, unneeded in those moments, would randomly gaze around the studio. And then he would become aware that they had rested on his reclining Venus, his Kateryna. She would be looking out at him, and once more the images of Kat in his old studio, smiling at him as she lay on the chaise longue, would have an immediacy that stung his eyes. In those moments he felt a terrible yearning. His mind would rush to shut the memories away, but not before he had been reminded that the only important thing he wanted in life was something he would never have.

Chapter 9

'So, what's the answer?' Mark asked, as he took the cardboard folder. 'Still looking good?'

He was in his office, separated by a glazed wall from the rest of the project team. From here he looked across the open plan area to the public entrance. He was a general who led his troops from the rear. As always, he was sharply dressed. It was another way in which he kept himself separate from the team. Whereas the social workers dressed informally, he wore designer casual when he was at the office all day, a suit when he had meetings elsewhere.

The admin desk was close to Mark's office door. In her first weeks of casual work, Kat found him remote and haughty, and stayed away from him. Slowly he thawed, and they began to have little chats or quips when she took him reports that she had prepared. This time, she had brought him a printout of actual and budgeted expenditure, a spreadsheet she had soon learned to update.

'Yes, we're maintaining the excess from delayed implementation. Not cutting into it at all.'

'Great.'

She turned to leave. 'Hold on, Kat. In that case there's something I want to ask you.' She turned back to him. 'I'd be interested to know whether you'd like your position put on a proper contract. I thought we might agree on twenty-two hours. Three days a week, give or take.'

'Wow, that's very kind. But I don't yet know which days I'll need to be at uni, so I wouldn't be able to commit to working here on specific days.'

'Doesn't matter. You can work flexible hours.'

'Does this mean Jane isn't coming back from sick leave? You can't really need two admin workers.'

'I wouldn't worry about it. As you've just told me, we're running a surplus. If we haven't spent it by April, it will simply return to government coffers.'

Kat wondered what to say. The guaranteed income would be lovely, but she wasn't quite sure it was all above board.

'Come along, Kat,' he said, laughing at her, 'I'm offering you a job, and a wage that that will be a big help through university. It could even carry you into another job after the project has ended. And yet you're stood there, apparently trying to talk yourself out of it. Why don't you just say yes, and then I can ask you whether you'd like to come out to dinner this evening.'

She could have been outraged. It was tantamount to buying her company. Yet she found something reassuringly plain about it. For almost three years, destiny had called on her repeatedly to do the right thing, to act selflessly. Each time she had obeyed duty and principle, but nothing had been given in return. She had sacrificed a life in the States, and set aside her plans for university, to care for her dying mother. She had tried to be the woman that Andi wanted her to be, yet had been rewarded only with criticism and spite. Just a few days previously, she had been given the chance to spend the night in a London hotel with a man she liked very much; but—out of some moral sensibility she didn't even understand—she had turned the chance down. In that light, the bargain Mark was offering made a refreshingly straightforward exchange.

In any case, he was a good-looking, well-spoken guy. It would be no hardship to go on a date with him.

Kat agreed to both Mark's invitations, and asked if it would be OK to go in the clothes she was wearing, as it would be a rush to go home and change. Her glanced at her leggings and jumper, and suggested she leave a little early. He would collect her from home.

She found a softly feminine dress that she had bought in Italy, but had never been able to wear with Andi. Mark arrived in the coupé he drove in those days, and took her to a hotel restaurant where they still put white linen on the table and brought the food in silver dishes. He obviously felt at home. Kat coped well enough. Afterwards she made him take her home, and only allowed him a kiss. She wouldn't be bought so easily. But he took her out again on the next Friday. This time they went back to his smart town apartment, and to his bed.

As the dates coalesced into a relationship, Kat would realise that Mark was not as straightforward as he had seemed at first. The air of confidence proved to be only the subtle arrogance, the presumption of superiority, that is the gift of a public school education. Though Kat never saw it directly, and Mark would never admit to it, she came to understand that self-doubt churned like magma below his surface. He also had odd habits. He always locked the bathroom door. He had an obsessive need to brush his shoes each evening. He never cuddled in bed. If she reached out to him in the darkness, he would turn away from her, shifting closer to the edge of the bed. These oddities, she guessed, were also consequences of a boarding school upbringing.

Kat learned, though only in outline, that other childhood experiences might have added to his psychological injuries. Mark was of mixed heritage. It was clear to see, once he had told her, that he had Chinese blood. His father's English genes dominated in most respects, leaving him with only a hint of Asia in the moulding of his features. However, his skin was slightly olive, as if he enjoyed a permanent holiday tan, and his hair was thick, naturally glistening, and a profound black. In those days he wore it long with a centre parting, the hair swept back symmetrically over the top of his ears.

His father, Charles Smallwood, had been with the diplomatic service, and had been posted early in his career to Hong Kong. Charles had soon fallen for a pretty Chinese girl, Jing, and married her. Kat got the impression, as Mark told the story, that the marriage had met with disapproval amongst colleagues. Within a year the pretty new wife gave birth to a boy, Mark. The posting ended some months later, and the family returned to England in 1971.

Kat understood that Mark could have little memory of his first years in England. Still, he was oddly vague about the chapter that followed. He would only say that his mother had died two years later. His father soon remarried, and this time he chose carefully. Mark's stepmother was very English, and privately educated. Peggy, as Mark had put it, was a woman who had floated through the 1960s, advantaged by a rich daddy and her long, openable legs. Charles provided Peggy with a soft landing in the '70s, and she soon gave him a second son, the favoured Thomas.

***

In those early days, the complexities of Mark's past and personality seemed insignificant to Kat. In so many ways he was a very good catch. She realised, once she saw the nice car and the town centre apartment, that Mark was already comparatively wealthy for his age. She did not know it then, but he was being assisted financially by his father. Charles was not motivated by love, for which he had limited capacity, but by a vague sense of guilt for neglecting Mark in his early childhood. In any case, Charles had been advised by his accountant to start offloading his wealth. Kat only knew that Mark had enough money to give them both a very good life, though constrained by her university commitments. Their evenings and weekends were filled with restaurant meals, visits to the cinema and theatre, and late nights on the clubbing scene. Mark liked to show her off, liked it all the better when she looked sexy. Kat obliged by losing the t-shirts and leggings, replacing them with crop tops and short dresses.

They had fun in private too. On the days when Kat worked with the team, she would stay at the office until Mark was ready to drive them both home. This often meant they were the only ones left. The opportunity for role play was irresistible. One day, bored with reading reports, Mark complained loudly that he was feeling stressed. Kat, working in the open area just outside Mark's office, heard him.

'Would Sir like a little something to help him relax?'

Mark knew what she was offering. She crawled under his desk, unzipped his trousers, and brought him to climax. She did not see his face, and he saw nothing at all of her until he had finished. Kat crawled back out of his office and returned to her desk. She glanced round at him, expecting an exchange of naughty smiles, but he had already returned to his papers.

She had not foreseen that this would become a common practice on days they were alone in the office. She didn't mind—she liked the feel of him in her mouth, and she liked to hear him groaning above the desktop. Nevertheless, she thought it would be nice if he sometimes reciprocated. She imagined sitting on his desk in front of him, her legs apart so that she was fully visible and available to him. She even tried wearing a short skirt to work, and letting him see during the day that she was naked underneath. He never took the bait. It was only at night, in bed, that he would go down on her. Even then it was plain that he regarded it only as an obligation, an item on the checklist of modern mating protocol. He had neither the skill nor the patience to satisfy her by that means. It was better when he fucked her—from behind, usually. Often, though, she helped herself by fantasising she was having sex with a woman. If need be, she could rest on her shoulder, leaving a hand free to attend to the needs that Mark ignored. He seemed not to notice. All in all, the sex was good enough at a physical level. She found it impersonal and unloving, but assumed that sex with men was always like that.

It wasn't until close to Christmas that Mark drove Kat to her father's house so that they could collect her belongings. Symbolically, that was when she moved into his flat, though for all practical purposes she had been there since October. She needed to set her father at a distance, and the flat was convenient for the university campus.

Mark's apartment was a chic and pleasant place to be. It was on the fifth floor of a renovated Victorian factory building. On the outside the building retained its original redbrick facades. The communal corridors had also been left with their cold brick walls. Whether it was due to a lingering odour, or something more paranormal, there was always an unappealing sense in those hard, echoing corridors of the building's grimy industrial past, and of the oppressed people who had once worked there. Once through the heavy apartment door, however, it was fresh and fashionable. Each apartment occupied one of the old factory rooms, now subdivided by modern plastered walls. Only a large living and dining area retained the high ceilings, with one small area of redbrick wall still exposed for decorative purposes. Mark had formed a living area by grouping a sofa, armchair and TV below the tall windows, while the dining area was defined by a glass table. A galley kitchen lay to one side, accessed through a doorless opening. Further round, a short passageway led to two bedrooms and a bathroom.

By November, the easy first weeks at university were over, and Kat was starting to worry about approaching deadlines for assignments. One evening she was busy on an essay, books spread across the glass dining table, when Mark arrived back from the gym.

'God, you're not at it again, are you? I was hoping we'd go out this evening.'

She didn't look up. 'Got to do it. Deadline is Monday.'

He sat down at the table, still in his gym kit, still sweaty. He pulled up the jogging top he was wearing and used the hem to wipe his forehead. 'I don't know why you're doing it. It's just getting in the way of us having a good time, and you don't need it. Once we're married I can earn enough for the both of us.'

Kat wasn't sure how to react. He had just announced he wanted to marry her, which was lovely. Then again, it was a rotten way to make a marriage proposal. He had no right to assume.

'Mark, it's lovely that you're willing to support me,' she answered, sitting back from the papers on the table, 'and thanks for the proposal of marriage, if that's what it was. But I still want to be educated to a level where I can support myself financially.'

'So what're you saying? Sounds like you're thanking me for wanting you as my wife, but also planning for a life after we've divorced.'

'That's not what I meant.'

'Isn't it? Well, your choice. But I think you're being silly. I was thinking we could go to the Caribbean in January. Best time to be there. But not if you're going to spend the whole time doing coursework.'

He got up and went to take a shower.

Kat met the essay deadline that time, but Mark continued to sabotage her commitment with both complaints and distractions. When university paused in December, she knew she would have to make a very serious effort to catch up before it recommenced in the New Year. Then, on Christmas Eve, Mark gave her an envelope containing tickets for a holiday in Jamaica at the start of January.

***

Of course, in many ways Kat had been delighted by the prospect of a holiday in the Caribbean. She had travelled in Europe and the USA, but as soon as they landed in Jamaica she discovered it had a vibrancy that she had not known before. This realisation came to her vividly in those few moments when the two of them wheeled their suitcases between the airport terminal and the air-conditioned transfer coach, and when she was flooded with the ripe aromas of sub-tropical flora and sweaty human bodies. Soon they were at their upmarket resort, positioned on a peninsula of land where the sea and the security guards kept them distanced from any realities that might have tainted the tourist fantasy.

Whether strolling the beach or, more fully dressed in the evening and hanging out in the bars and restaurants within the resort compound, Kat and Mark made an attractive couple. A large proportion of the resort's guests were American, and the rules of acceptability proved to be American as well: if you had money, you were OK. The good looks of this young Brit couple, and the air of confidence that Mark exuded, helped to suggest wealth. Thousands of miles from the usual wealth indicators of houses and cars, they only needed to tip generously, and avoid gawping at the yachts in the bay, for the Americans to assume they were the kind of people worth knowing. Over the first three days, they became absorbed into a loose social circle, to the point where they could not walk into any of the restaurants without finding one of their new friends beckoning them loudly to their table.

Then, suddenly, the social circle acquired connections with wealth beyond the boundaries of the resort. On the fourth evening their companions at dinner insisted on taking them out to a bar along the coast to meet up with other friends. Then the other friends insisted they come on their boat the next day. The following morning, the day beginning to heat up, Kat found herself alone on the curved white foredeck of a luxury catamaran. She was half sitting, half stretched out so that she could hold onto the hand grabs in the deck. There was a good breeze and a slight swell, and sometimes the falling bows would catch a wave with a bump. Behind her was the cockpit, concealed from her by tinted glass. She knew that someone would be at the wheel, looking over her. Most probably a man—a man who would also be taking the opportunity to survey her body, barely concealed by her pink bikini. Mark was there as well, no doubt, toadying to the Americans, enjoying the fantasy of serious wealth.

Kat knew it was a fantasy, yet it remained seductive. As the catamaran moved through the glistening water, she felt she was riding into a brighter, more exciting life. That morning she had noticed the date, and realised that back in England it was the start of the new university semester. She lay on the deck in the sunshine, listening to the cascades of spray as the twin bows dropped into the water, the edge of the taut mainsail humming in the wind. She imagined the students making their way to the campus, their breath making mist in the January air as they waited for grimy buses and overcrowded trains. That was a life she had wanted so much, but now she was moving away from it. Did it matter? It was hard to believe that it did.

Chapter 10

K at wanted, for the sake of self-respect, to finish with university before it finished with her. She waited a week before going to see her tutor, allowing time for the pink tinge from her Caribbean tan to fade, but the story she told of financial pressures and long working hours could not have been convincing. Nevertheless, it was done. For the third time in her life, her plan to get a degree had been cancelled.

Now she was free to work for the project, and for Mark, fulltime. When, in April, the project started its second year, Mark arranged for her to have a small salary increase. It was still low-paid work, but, as Mark paid for all the major household costs, it was all money that could be used for leisure and luxuries. As he explained to her, personal relationships between staff were generally frowned upon, especially if one were the manager of the other. However, as the project was distanced from the rest of the charity, it seemed the only people likely to worry about it would be the other members of the project. So, Mark said, it would be best for them not to behave in front of colleagues in ways that would highlight their relationship. During the working day, Mark stopped being more friendly to her than to other members of the team, and she was required to do likewise. She did think he applied the policy too excessively, and often seemed cold. It was only when other staff had gone in the evening that he allowed her to show affection, and in the way that he preferred.

Kat did not deny that Mark had his odd ways. He was possessive of her, but she learned to avoid situations that would upset him. He liked to be in charge, but Kat discovered that, despite her feminist beliefs, she appreciated a man who was decisive. What's more, his decisions were usually sound. In return for tolerating his peculiarities, he gave her a wonderful life. In their first six months together, they used weekends to explore European cities, were pampered at a spa hotel, and caught shows in London. In early summer they rented a villa on a Greek island. There, as they sat on the veranda under the stars, Mark pushed the wine bottle and glasses from the centre of the table, and put a small box in front of Kat.

He flicked the box open. 'Do you need me to get down on my knees?' he said. As Kat had expected, it contained a diamond ring as beautiful—and no doubt as expensive—as she had foreseen.

She looked at him. 'Do you need me to say yes?'

***

Mark insisted that they should get married the following spring, almost a year ahead. Kat knew, even before they went to bed that night, that Mark had very definite ideas about the wedding. The idea of it excited him. On the flight home, as Kat was quietly reading a magazine, he started talking about where they might stay on the night after the wedding, before they went abroad for the honeymoon.

Kat waited for him to pause. 'Mark,' she said, 'it's lovely that you're so excited about the wedding. But you realise, don't you, that my father couldn't possibly pay for that kind of wedding?'

'Of course we do. Don't worry about it. It may be tradition for the bride's family to pay, but never mind that. We've got it sorted.'

Mark wanted to talk about the timing of the wedding, to make sure they could catch a flight for their honeymoon the same evening. Kat was thinking more about the way he had said *we*, and wondering what it meant.

She soon found out. On the evening of the same day, Mark got on the phone to tell his father the good news, and she heard Mark agree that they would visit the following weekend. It was obviously to be a planning meeting.

Charles and Peggy lived in a converted barn—a long thin building, stylishly appointed but ergonomically disastrous, with the kitchen at one end and the dining room at the other. Charles had aged into a thin man, bald but for a horseshoe of grey hair at the sides. He always seemed to be suppressing his own agitation, as if making the effort to stay though he really ought to be doing something important elsewhere. Peggy, perhaps in compensation, was forever wafting about, doing things that didn't need to be done, and finding ways to do them that took far longer than was needed.

Kat and Mark arrived in time for lunch. Mark's younger brother, the favoured Thomas, was already there with his family: Tina, who was trying hard not to move her head too much for fear she would mess up the platinum blonde hair she had worked so hard to straighten that morning; and the two boys—a four-year-old, and a toddler with a snotty nose.

They assembled around the mahogany dining table, though within ten minutes the two boys had been transferred to the floor with toys. Peggy brought in a meal of roast chicken, slowly. Family meals in the Smallwood household,

Kat would now discover, were little more than business meetings with refreshments. Charles, as chair, thanked everyone for coming, and then received reports from the two sons. Thomas's report, on the state of commodities trading, was well received. Mark's account of his work with troubled teenagers was duly accepted, though without questions.

As Peggy gradually removed the remnants of the first course, and replaced it with dessert, the discussion turned to the main item on the agenda, and quickly focused on the best venue for the wedding.

'I think you should go for St. Margaret's,' Thomas suggested. 'Vicar was very helpful.'

'Yes, I agree,' Charles added, 'and the vicar did you a nice chat—nothing too religious.'

Peggy departed for the kitchen in search of dessert plates.

'But All Saints is so much prettier,' Mark pitched in. 'And much more space in the churchyard for photos.'

Tina, head carefully upright, chipped in her thought: 'Couldn't you get the vicars, y'know, to swap? Pick and mix sort-of thing?'

Thomas, sitting next to her, patted her thigh. 'I don't think it works like that, really. Not unless you're royalty.' The toddler, at the opposite end of the table next to Kat, had stood up in search of an adult to wipe his nose on, and was whimpering. Thomas looked at Tina again. 'Darling, could you do something about Benjamin?'

'Don't worry,' Kat interjected quickly. 'I can help him.' She took her napkin from the table to wipe Benji's nose, and then got down on the floor with both boys. There were some wooden bricks nearby, so she built them into a tower. Benji watched blankly, but pushed the bricks down with a listless backhander. Kat built the tower again, and Benji knocked it down again, this time with a little more pleasure and energy.

His brother joined in. All Kat could see of the adults were their legs under the table, but she heard them continuing to discuss her wedding. *Her* wedding, she thought.

Both boys were soon giggling with delight as they smashed the wooden towers. The adults were having their conversation disrupted. They stopped talking and looked down at Kat.

'Sorry,' she said, peering up at them. 'I'll take them into the living room.'

'Come on, you two. Help me pick up the bricks.'

The three of them carried the bricks to the other room, where they settled. Kat closed the door to the dining room so that the boys could make a noise without disturbing the meeting. Peggy wandered through from time to time, carrying things, but otherwise Kat was on her own with the children. She remembered the twins, and the happy times she had spent with the Barbers. For a moment, she found her mouth twisted in melancholy.

Later, on the drive home, Mark gave her a report from the meeting, summarising the lavish arrangements for the wedding. Kat felt obliged to register her objections.

'That all sounds lovely,' she said, 'and of course I'm really grateful to your dad for being willing to foot the bill for it all.' She paused to pluck up courage. 'But I've got to say that I wasn't very happy about being left out of the discussion. Do you really think it was OK for the rest of you to plan the wedding without me being involved?'

Mark, driving, looked ahead in silence for some seconds to imply he thought it was a point that deserved to be considered.

'I don't think it was like that,' he said. 'You were there at the start, and free to offer your thoughts. You chose to go to the other room with the boys. No one made you go.'

'Not exactly,' Kat persisted, 'but someone had to do something about the boys, and I wasn't being involved anyway. It was just you three men, with Tina occasionally saying something stupid.'

'Oh, for goodness' sake, Kat, you're not really going to make this into an issue about feminism and the patriarchy, are you?' His tone of voice was a warning. 'It was simply the three men of the family doing their best to plan a great wedding for us. For *you*! You just said you liked the plan. So please, Kat, stop complaining—it only makes you seem ungrateful.'

They drove on, in silence.

***

They were to marry in 2001. This was also the year that the project would close, as funding ceased at the end of March. One cold afternoon in January, the office windows steamed up, and darkness already falling outside, Kat was at her desk when she noticed a conversation Mark was having in his room. He was with Samuel, the oldest social worker in the team. Samuel had a social sciences background, and had been taken off other duties to start work on the evaluation that had to be delivered as a condition of the government funding.

'Don't blame me, Mark,' Samuel was saying. 'It was you that promised an evaluation based on outcomes.'

'So what's the problem with that?'

'Well, Mark, what outcomes did you have in mind?' Samuel sounded impatient. 'Yes, we can get some hard figures for offending, but interpreting them is very difficult. Some data are available for rates of homelessness at the end of our involvement, but there's lots of gaps and we've no idea where the kids were living six months later. And as for prostitution, how would we know? What would you like me to do—walk around the relevant streets and see how many offers I get from girls I recognise?'

'Well at least we can say something about offending rates.'

'We can say something,' Samuel answered, tartly, 'but not what you're hoping for, I suspect.'

'Why not?'

'Because the figures for our lot don't have anything useful to say unless we can set them against a comparable group of young people. If you make the comparison with young people as a whole—all those nice wholesome, law-abiding kids— then it's going to look like we've driven our lot into a life of crime. Our kids are a mix of troubled teenagers, with only some of them having been in care. Finding data for a comparable group is probably impossible. And that means, of course, that we can't show any real evidence that the project did any good.'

Kat heard Mark say *shit*, heard the clatter of his pen as he threw it onto the desk, and then the scrape of a chair being pushed back. She looked round and saw him gazing out of the window at the urban twilight, hands in his pockets. Samuel, still seated, was fretfully stroking his beard.

Kat looked down at her work as Mark turned back to Samuel. 'So, Sam,' Mark said. 'Please start giving me some answers.'

'We'll have to rely on the subjective stuff instead,' Samuel replied. 'The stuff from the user satisfaction questionnaire. The only snag, and it's a big one, is that the forms haven't been completed for an awful lot of the kids. I know the team felt that, after all their efforts to gain some credibility with the kids, it went against the grain to start shoving forms in front of them.'

'So come on, give me some good news. What do the questionnaires tell us?'

'They tell us that twenty-five percent of the respondents thought that the project had helped them *a lot*. Samuel held out his fingers to serve as inverted commas. 'And another thirty-five said it had helped *a bit*.'

'That's more like it! Sixty percent of the kids felt they'd been helped. Makes the project a resounding success!'

'Except it also suggests that forty percent either felt it had not made any difference, or had made things worse. The finding will be even less impressive to any reader with the intelligence to check the number of respondents. We've got twenty completed forms. So what we're really saying is that, at the end of three years' work, costing hundreds of thousands of pounds, the only real achievement we can show is that twelve kids think we helped them in some unspecified way.'

'Shit,' Mark repeated. 'Do we really have to show the number of respondents?'

Samuel made a hollow laugh. 'Yes, we do. Be hung out to dry if we didn't.'

Kat heard the sound of chair legs on wooden flooring, and guessed that Mark had sat down again.

'Sam, let me ask you a few questions. Do you think this project has been a real help to the kids we've worked with?'

'Yeah, I do.'

'Do you think other kids could be helped if there were more projects like this one?'

There was a pause before Samuel answered. 'I think that there are some things to be learned, things that could be done better. But in principle, yes. It would be good if more kids got the same kind of help.'

'OK,' Mark went on, lowering the volume of his voice, 'then why don't we focus on that bigger picture, Samuel? We know the project was a success, we just lack the data to prove it. For the sake of all those kids who need help, let's adjust the data a bit. The questionnaires are anonymous, so why not add another twenty, maybe thirty, with some really positive answers. They could be done on behalf of the kids who didn't fill them in, putting down the answers we think they would have given.'

Kat decided to go and look for something important in a filing cabinet. Stood in front of it, she could glance sideways and see the two men. They were staring at each other across the small table.

'I'm hoping to retire fairly soon,' Samuel answered, 'but not that soon. I'm not going to falsify the data, Mark. I'll give you the actual data, and the tables, and as much of the draft as I've written. You do what you like, but I don't want my name anywhere near it.'

'I'm sorry you can't see what's important here,' Mark said. 'You're putting your concerns with accuracy and some fanciful notion of professional integrity ahead of kids who desperately need help. If you won't do it for them, do it for yourself. You said you're not wanting to retire yet. It will help you to move on to a well-paid job if you can say you've worked in a highly successful project. Will also help if you've got a good reference from me.'

Samuel looked down at his papers on the desk, then started to gather them up. 'You do what you like, Mark, as long as you don't involve me. But I know I've done good work in this project, and that I deserve a good reference.'

He looked up again and fixed his gaze on Mark. 'If I get anything other than a good reference from you, I'll start telling people about the conversation we've just had.'

Samuel stood up and headed out of the office. He brushed past Kat as if she had not been there, and she saw fury on his face.

***

Over the weeks that followed, Mark often asked Kat to go home from the office without him. He said it was because he needed to work into the evening on the project evaluation report. But she saw the accumulating heap of professional journals on his desk and knew what he was doing. He was planning to jump ship before his career could be tainted.

Mark only admitted he was looking for a new job when he had been offered an interview. It was the last week of March when he told her, the week when the project was being wound up. Two social workers had been on fixed contracts with the project, and were leaving the organisation, but the rest of the team would be returning to the main offices to be redeployed. There had been no enthusiasm for a final party, so the team gathered briefly at the end of one afternoon for a drink. The office had already been partially cleared, leaving patches of dust where furniture had stood. The team members perched on the remaining desks with their glasses of wine and listened to an unconvincing speech from Mark. Kat noticed that afterwards the whole team, except for Mark and herself, left together. It was obvious they had made a plan for their own evening event to mark the end of the project. Mark went back to his desk. Kat, alone in the main office, gathered up the wine glasses and washed them.

Mark told her about the job interview on the way home. It was for the regional office of an organisation providing care and education for children with special needs. A larger company than the charity they now worked for, he explained.

'Company?' queried Kat. 'Not a charity?'

'Technically, no, not a charity, but really it makes no odds. Doing exactly the same kind of work.'

'But doing it for profit,' Kat challenged. 'Doing it to make money for the shareholders.'

'Kat, you're being prissy! What difference does it really make? Charities try to maximise their income, and their managers want salaries that match the private sector. There really isn't any difference these days, except that the private companies do it in a more business-like way.'

Kat sighed. 'I suppose, Mark, the difference is that I wanted to think that you came into this work to help people, not to make a profit.'

'Of course I did. But I don't see why I shouldn't be paid well for what I do.

'Anyway, let's not argue about it. I haven't got the job yet.'

***

The interview was in mid-April, just four days before the wedding. Kat was now glad that the Smallwood family had taken charge of the plans so efficiently. She had little more to do in the week before the wedding than to collect the wedding dress, and pack for the wedding and honeymoon. A room had been reserved for her for two nights in a hotel conveniently located for the church. That allowed her a whole day to settle and rest, and to receive every available beauty treatment. Tina had been appointed to supervise.

Mark had taken a day's leave for the interview, but was in any case working at home all week to finish the evaluation report. Kat came home the evening before his interview to discover that Mark had been to the barbers'. The long hair that had swept stylishly from a centred parting was gone. What little remained was parted at the side, and flipped into a small and unconvincing quiff. The back and sides were razored. As Kat looked at him, he appeared to have entered middle age.

'God, Mark, you might have warned me.'

'Just decided it was time to grow up and look business-like,' he explained. 'Want to give the right impression tomorrow.'

Tina came up the following evening to collect Kat, her wedding dress, and her extensive luggage. They were about to leave when Mark phoned. He'd got the job.

Chapter 11

To an uninvolved observer it would have appeared the perfect English wedding: A bright spring day, a pretty country church, and a bride whose dark curls and crimson lips brought to mind a Disney Snow White about to be united, at long last, with her Prince Charming. As is so often the case on these occasions, the truth was less happy, and far more complicated.

When her father, Eric, arrived at the hotel, ready for the journey to the church, Kat had endured Tina for more than a day, and was already irritable. Tina's comprehension of the world was as thin as her voice, and a mishmash of the obvious, the trite, and the superficial. Tina, Kat decided, was plain stupid, and couldn't help it. The blame lay with Thomas for taking her away from the community of simple folk where she belonged. The only mystery was why he had done it. As Tina had knelt in front of her to check the fall of the wedding dress, Kat had looked down at her little mouth and her manicured hands and wondered what sexual tricks they could perform to have caught—and kept, what's more—a man like Thomas.

Tina supervised Kat into the hired Rolls, lifting the hem of the dress inside. Once the car was moving, Eric squeezed her hand. 'You alright, my love?'

'Yes, I'm fine. And you?'

Eric could not lie so well. He pursed his lips, nodded his head, and squeezed her hand again.

Steve Dowson

They were the appropriate five minutes late to the church. Tina arrived at the same time, and again adjusted the dress at the church door. The appointed pair of bridesmaids, two unappealing second cousins of Mark's, swung into formation behind her like fighter jets escorting a hijacked Boeing. They passed from sunlight into the gloom of the church. The warmth of the day had not penetrated the old stone. The air was cold and musky. The pews seemed full of men wearing long heavy overcoats, as if they were attending a funeral at Westminster, interspersed with shivering women in absurd hats.

Kat walked arm in arm with her father down the aisle, and she could feel him shaking. She knew he must be terrified. They arrived at Mark and his haircut, flanked by Thomas. So far, Kat had remembered to smile. The ceremony began.

They reached the point where the vicar asks if anyone knows of any reason the couple should not be married. Kat found herself hoping someone would speak up. Why, she then asked herself, was she going through with it, if that was how she felt? Even as the vicar recited his words, she silently recited a familiar mantra: *Because he's from a good solid family. Because I have a good life with him. Because he's going to be successful in life and will provide a stable and secure home for the children I'll have by him. Because, as men go, he's not a bad man, even if he does have his flaws.*

The vicar was waiting for her to speak. She took a chance, and said, 'I will'. He continued. There was a hymn, and then they made vows to each other, and then she was holding out her hand for Mark to put the ring on. It already had a ring on it—a simple ring decorated with alternating black jet and small crystals, as always on the little finger of her left hand.

Eulogy for Love

When Kat had been getting ready, Tina had seen it and said, 'Shall we take that other ring off? Don't want to take attention away from your lovely new wedding ring, do we.'

'It stays where it is,' Kat had answered sharply. 'It was my mother's, and I always wear it. Mark knows that. It's my way of keeping her with me, and she's coming with me today.'

Dull though she was, Tina knew better than to argue.

The vicar beamed a well-practised wedding beam, and Mark slid the ring onto the bride's finger where it claimed a place next to the ring that David had given her.

The service continued through the vicar's address, the signing of the register, and then they were out into the churchyard for the photos. Soon she was back in the Rolls with Mark next to her, heading for the reception at the country hotel. The Smallwood wedding production, planned in every detail, appeared destined to be a triumph. Kat felt distanced from it all—not outside the scene, but as if buried deep within her own body while it followed its pre-programmed instructions to walk, wave, smile, speak.

The wedding plan included a reception line to greet guests on arrival at the hotel. Charles, in an act of selfless generosity that would be much admired, allowed Kat's father to head the line. Eric, left to face the onslaught of strangers, abandoned any attempt at speech, and only grinned while channelling the tremor from his nerves into a thundering handshake.

Kat had nothing to say to the men in suits or their wives with their stiff painted faces, or they to her. That did not matter as long as the line kept moving—an exchange of platitudes about the dress or ceremony was enough to fill the few seconds before the guests shuffled on. But, for Charles, at the far end of the line, the occasion was a meeting of the clan. He was lingering with his guests, often guffawing loudly.

Upstream, the flow halted. Strangers were stuck together for a length of time that was at first awkward, and then unsustainable. The line fractured. Mark merged into a cluster of young men. Eric left for the hotel bar. The guests that had still been waiting at the doorway assumed they were excused from the process and swirled in, more interested in finding a drink than meeting the bride or groom. Kat stood alone.

There was one guest still making her way into the ballroom: an elderly woman who walked slowly and painfully while a young woman discreetly pushed a wheelchair behind her. The older woman walked with such determination that Kat stood still and left her to make slow passage across the carpet sea between them. When she finally arrived, she grasped Kat's arm like a mooring post in a choppy harbour.

'There you are, I made it! You don't know me. I'm Norma Bellwood.' The woman had to pause for breath between each sentence. 'Actually . . . I'm surprised Charles thought to invite me . . . my husband was a colleague of his decades ago, when Mark was a little boy. But I'm very glad to be here!'

Kat smiled and studied Norma. In her eighties, Kat reckoned. It was obvious she had gone to great trouble to look good for the wedding. Her silver hair was newly permed and topped with a little hat of feathers. The pleats on her floral print skirt were crisp, the creases on her face softened with powder.

Norma shifted painfully to face Kat, then grasped both her wrists. 'I already know that you're a lovely young woman. Years since I've seen Mark, so I've no idea whether he deserves you. But doing well, I hear.' Another pause for breath. 'I heard somewhere that he's in charity work. Is that right?'

Kat imagined the kind of thing that Norma had probably assumed. Mark devoted to the poor of London's East End,

130

perhaps; or driving vital medicines across the endless sands of Africa. There was nothing to be gained by correcting her.

'Yes, that's right, he is.'

'Well, well, how lovely. Such a surprise—never would have imagined any son of Charles in that line of work. . . I suppose it must be the effect of his difficult early years. These things have a way of working themselves to the surface. Especially his mother's suicide.'

Norma must have seen the surprise on Kat's face. 'Surely you knew?'

'I knew his mother died when he was little. But nothing about suicide.'

'Oh, I'm so very sorry. I've spoken out of turn. I should have guessed—Charles always wanted to pretend it never happened. For goodness' sake, though, you're family!'

Kat was too interested to let the chance pass. 'I'd liked to know more, please.'

Norma straightened herself to look closely at Kat. 'Then I think I'd better tell you, if you have a moment. There really isn't much to it anyway. But only on condition it stays between you and me. And only if I can sit down first!'

The assistant saw Norma signal, brought up the wheelchair, and helped Norma settle into it. Kat pulled in the hem of her white dress, and crouched down at the side, her hand on Norma's arm.

'Hard to imagine, but Charles was once an impressionable young man. And inevitably he found Hong Kong—especially back then, in the 1960s—completely irresistible. Everything about it seemed exotic and exciting. That, of course, particularly included the young Chinese women. I don't know how he met Jing—in some bar, probably—but he thought he'd fallen in love with her. I did once see a photo of Jing in a qipao—y'know, the traditional Chinese dress—and I must say that she was exquisite. Anyway, he married her.

'Of course, she was just a toy to him, a doll in silk dress that was easily removed. She was poorly educated and spoke little English; and, to be frank, she was not very bright. After the baby, she didn't even have the figure. She loved Charles, no doubt, but simpered over him in a way that became tiresome.

'As soon as they returned to England, Charles saw Jing for what she really was, and was only embarrassed by her. His solution was to exclude her from his life beyond the home. After a while, people didn't even think to ask where she was. Can you imagine? She must have been horribly lonely, shut away in a house in a foreign country, abandoned by the man she loved. Hardly surprising that after a couple of years she took an overdose. Charles found her dead one day when he got back from work.'

Kat said, 'My God.'

Norma patted her hand. 'But enough! That's all I have to tell. And this is your special day—so go and make the most of it! I'm going to find a drink, and I shall accost that scoundrel Charles before the day is over!'

Kat knew she had to revert to role. 'Thank you, Norma. What a terrible story. I'm so very grateful you've told it to me.'

She squeezed Norma's hand, kissed her cheek, and walked away.

Norma called after her. 'Don't forget. Between us two.'

***

Kat headed with some urgency to the nearest toilets. In the confines of the cubicle, it was a struggle to heave the underskirts safely out of the way, and once she had managed to sit she decided to reward herself with a few minutes of solitude. She needed to pull herself together, take more control of herself. She couldn't even start to think about the information from Norma.

Over the months of planning, she had accepted that the day would run the way that the Smallwoods wanted. There had been a few points she had queried, but in almost every instance she had conceded. In the end there was only one wish that she had held against sustained objections. It was small, but symbolically it made up for all the times she had let the men overrule her. She was going make a speech of her own at the reception. It was going to be a simple speech, and she might not deliver it very well; but she would show them all that she had a voice and views of her own. She was a grown-up, competent woman, not a man's chattel. These days, it wasn't even a radical thing to do.

That morning she had given Tina an envelope, explaining she would need it back when they assembled at the high table for lunch. It contained Kat's notes for the speech. She planned to start by saying, in a caricature of militancy, that in the new millennium the wedding should reflect the equality that exists between woman and husband. She would go on to offer her own thanks for the generosity that had made the day possible, while not identifying its source, to spare her father's feelings. She would thank the guests for attending, and for their gifts. Briefly changing to a more sombre tone, she would share her sadness that her mother was not present on this special day. To end on a lighter note, she would make an affectionate quip about Mark's new haircut, and say she felt sure that Thomas, in his role as Best Man, would be sharing more entertaining stories about her new husband.

Kat felt better. The solitude had done her good, and she was reassured to find she knew her speech without needing the notes. She exited the toilet cubicle in a decent but dishevelled state. Another guest was checking her make-up at the toilet mirrors, and helped Kat smooth her dress. Then she rushed to find Mark.

'For God's sake, where have you been?' he said angrily, as soon she reached him. 'The photographer's been waiting to start taking the formal pictures, and he can't get far without the bride.'

'I went to the toilet, Mark. No easy thing in this getup.'

He pulled her into line next to him and turned his head down to hers. '*Getup*? Do you know how ungrateful you sound?'

The photographer had set up his camera pointing towards a corner of the hall, and had been passing the time taking pictures of guests who happened by. When Kat and Mark arrived, he got started with the traditional group photos. He made a quip each time to provoke a smile at the moment the camera flashed.

As the minutes passed, it began to seem that the photographer was intent on recording every combination that was mathematically possible.

'Jeez,' Kat eventually said to Mark, between shots, 'do we really need this many photos?'

'No, I don't think we do,' Mark said, still looking towards the camera, 'and actually, we have a problem. We've been getting further and further behind schedule. The meal should have been served forty minutes ago.'

The photographer made another weak joke. The group smiled; the camera flashed.

'Oh, that's not good,' Kat said. 'But there's not a lot to be done about it, is there?'

'A few things. I'll ask Tom to talk to the hotel staff, get them to keep the meal moving along as much as possible.' Another combination of guests moved into position around them.

'And I think,' Mark went on, 'that we need to cut out all the non-essentials.'

'Like what?'

'Well, I'm sorry, but I think we'll have to do without your speech.'

'Right ladies and gentlemen, let's get you all smiling by thinking about something nice you did last evening.' The camera flashed. 'Oh dear, that much fun, eh? Glad I didn't come round to your house.' There was mild laughter, and the camera flashed again. But, as the photographer would see later when he reviewed the shots, Kat was not smiling.

'Oh, come on, Mark! It's always been obvious you didn't want me to speak. You're just looking for excuses. I don't suppose I'll speak for more than about five minutes, so it makes no odds whatsoever.'

'Each little saving adds up, Kat. We've got to cut wherever we can.'

'OK, ladies and gentlemen, please could we just have one more shot with the bridesmaids and bride and groom?'

'So cut your speech, Mark, or Thomas's. They'll both be far longer than mine.' Kat was barely aware of the bridesmaids stepping into line.

'Now you're being stupid,' Mark said softly, leaning into her. 'As you well know, it's the tradition for the groom and best man to speak. No one expects the bride to speak, and no one will care if you don't.'

'Ladies and Gentlemen, Bridesmaids, I know you've been stood there a long time, but I'd be grateful if you could look at the camera and give me one more big smile. Ready?'

Kat stared indifferently at the camera until it flashed.

'I'm sorry, Mark, but in all the months of planning, this is the one thing—the one and only thing—that I've asked you to agree to. I'm not giving up on it for the sake of five minutes.'

'Thank you very much for your patience, everyone,' the photographer announced. 'You'll be pleased to know that we're all done with the photographs.'

As the group and the onlookers dispersed, Mark caught Kat by the wrist and pulled her over to an alcove. He pressed her against the wall, grabbed her other wrist, and moved close to her. To anyone passing they would have looked as if they were sharing loving words, perhaps kissing. But Kat could see his face, and there was no love in it.

'I was going to leave this for another day, Kat, but maybe today is the right day. Let's establish something right from the beginning.

'Every ship needs one captain, every government needs one prime minister, every company needs one chief executive. It's the only sensible way to get things done. And that's how it works in marriage too. So let's get it straight, now. In this marriage, I'm the one in charge.'

Kat had no choice but to keep looking at his face. It scared her. She had seen this Mark before, but only flickering through him for a second when he lost his temper. Now it seemed to have arrived in him in a different form—a still coldness, a quality that could endure.

'If we don't catch up time, we'll leave late; and if we leave late we may not get to the airport on time. And if that happens we'll miss our flight. So, I have decided that you will not give a speech today.'

He stared hard into her eyes, as if to press the message into her brain. 'I've decided, Kat. That's all there is to it, and I'm not going to discuss it further.'

136

Eulogy for Love

He broke away from her, retaining his grip on one wrist, and pulling her. 'Come on,' he said, 'they'll be waiting for us.'

***

Kat left most of her food. When the speeches were being given, she stared at the linen tablecloth in front of her. Tina had dutifully passed the envelope of notes to Kat, and when the formalities were over, Kat tore it up and threw it on the floor.

'I'm going upstairs to change,' she told Mark. 'I'll take longer than you, and I wouldn't want to cause any delays.'

Tina had checked all the luggage into a hotel room, so Kat went to get the room key from her. Tina wanted to come up to the room and help her change. Kat didn't want her company, but found she no longer felt impatient with her. Tina was doing her best.

'Thank you, Tina, you've been really helpful today. But I'd rather be on my own for a while if you don't mind. Tell you what—come to the lift, and unzip the back of my dress when it arrives.'

Kat, unzipped, made her way to the room unnoticed, and stood in front of a full-length wall mirror. She reached behind herself, pulled the zipper the rest of the way down, and let the dress fall around her feet. In the mirror she could see herself dressed in the lingerie she had worn all afternoon. She was wearing an exquisite white, strapless, basque. It was matched by white stockings with embroidered tops, and an embroidered thong. The only item that did not match was a frilly blue garter on her thigh, the 'something blue' that Tina had brought for her to wear—or, technically, had lent her.

It was the most expensive and beautiful underwear she had ever owned, and she had paid for it herself. Tina had been impressed. It was also an absurd extravagance, as it had been entirely covered by the wedding dress.

She had wanted to wear it mainly so that it would keep telling her, through the difficult hours of that day, that she was a beautiful, sensuous, desirable woman. She looked in the mirror, and saw it was true, even if no one else would see it. She had foolishly imagined that, in a lull during the wedding day, she might have brought Mark to this room. She would have let the dress fall away and put herself on display for him; let him see the delicious woman who had vowed always to be his. Against all her experience, she had believed that he would respond—not only out of lust, but to love and adore her.

She knew now that it wasn't going to happen. She wanted the underwear off her body before he could find her. She had worn it for little more than five hours, and she vowed never to wear it again.

She watched herself in the mirror as she took it off. First, she kicked off the white stilettos, and pulled off the garter. She released the stockings and let them fall to her ankles, then pushed each one off her feet. She rotated the basque around her torso so that the laces were at the front where she could undo them. Loosened, the basque also fell to her feet and she kicked it away. Lastly, she pushed down the thong and stepped out of it.

Kat, now naked except for the two rings on her left hand, reassessed herself in the mirror. She was no longer the bride, nor the seductress. The artifice had gone, and she was plain, whole, female. And within that moment, time itself fell away, and she saw herself in all the forms her body would ever be. She could see the breastless child; the full and fecund woman;

the stooped crone. This was the ever-shifting physicality that would contain the single person, Kateryna, through all her life.

Then she saw defenceless flesh, and utter vulnerability. What, Kat wondered, would become of her?

***

In the short term, she became a newlywed on her honeymoon. They arrived in good time at the airport, and by mid-evening were at thirty-five thousand feet in the night sky. It was a little late in the year for skiing, too early for the Mediterranean, so they were on the overnight flight to Mexico. For all her misgivings, Kat found Mark much the same as he had always been: superficially impressive in public, insecure in social situations, aloof and condescending in private; and, as ever, unloving in bed. The resort was splendid, the skies cloudless, the sea warm. Mark had favoured Mexico because he wanted to see the Mayan ruins. He did, however, allow Kat generous time on the beach.

That, perhaps, was the one difference Kat noticed. Mark no longer negotiated with her. She got her way sometimes, but only because he allowed it. She no longer had rights or entitlements, but depended on his largesse. On this ship, he was now the master and commander.

Chapter 12

The speech that Mark had made in her face, as he had pressed her against the wall of the reception hall, stayed in Kat's mind throughout the honeymoon. It scared her, and it outraged her. If she didn't call herself a feminist, it was only because the feminist cause was embedded in her identity, not a label added to it. As a matter of principle, and for her own self-respect, she had to challenge Mark's outdated assumptions.

On the other hand, what worthwhile response could she make? Mark wasn't going to change. If she tried to discuss it with him, it would only lead to a row with no useful outcome. If he could not be changed, and she did not accept his rules for their marriage, the only thing she could do would be to leave him. Yet, here again, her sense of principle held her back. She believed in keeping promises, and only a short time ago she had stood at the front of a church and vowed to be with him until they were parted by death. What's more, if she left him it would look foolish. Pop stars might end their marriages weeks after starting them, but that was not what real people did. People would see what she had done—let his family pay for a fabulous wedding, taken the luxury honeymoon holiday, and then left him. 'Little hussy,' they would say. 'Feckless, money-grabbing minx!'

The truth of the matter, she told herself, was that Mark's private speech had done nothing more than articulate views she had long sensed he held. What's more, they were probably not that different from the view that most men held, deep down. Other husbands might play the game more gently, smile more, pretend to concede more, but ultimately they also liked things their own way; and, Kat suspected, most wives let them have it.

And what would be achieved by leaving him? Her job was poorly paid. She had no qualifications to get anything better. She could not afford to rent a place on her own, and would have to return to her father's house. Leaving Mark would mean crashing out of the comforts she had become used to, and sliding back into being a nobody, a single girl still living in her childhood home—a high price to pay for an act of principle.

It was a calculation that Kat would make many times over the years to come. And Mark seemed to know, each time, how to ensure that the result of the calculation would never quite convince her that she should leave. While he slowly subjugated her, he increased her habituation to material comforts, as a pimp might jack up the dose in the syringe, so that the prospect of losing her supply became ever more unsettling. Though there was always a part of her that rebelled against him, he ate away at her belief that she would be able to take control of her life. She still rebelled, but only through secret small acts of defiance. Although these acts demonstrated she could still disobey him, they had a quality of naughtiness that reduced her to playing the child to Mark's autocratic father.

Only two weeks after they had returned from honeymoon, he moved to end her financial independence.

Mark had to honour his two months' notice of resignation with the charity. With the end of the project, they had both been moved to the main regional office, located on an industrial estate outside the town. It made for a lengthy bus journey for Kat, so she continued to commute with Mark as much as possible. They were based in different parts of the building, so often only met at the end of the day when Mark called or texted her. On this particular day they arrived home together, and Mark indicated it was a day for gin and tonic. While Kat went to the kitchen to make the drinks, Mark put his briefcase on the glass-topped dining table and popped it open.

'I picked up a form today from Toby', he said, lifting out a single sheet of paper as Kat returned with the drinks.

'Toby?' she said, puzzled. 'Oh—you mean Toby who does all the payroll stuff?'

'Yes, that's the one.'

Kat stared down at the form he pushed in front of her.

'It's just a bank authorisation form,' he said, 'to switch over the arrangements for your monthly salary payments.' He lifted up the drink she had put in front of him. 'Cheers, Kat. *A ta santé*.' He sounded uncharacteristically jovial.

'All you need to do is sign at the bottom,' he continued, pointing at the form. 'I'll fill in the rest.'

'But why do I need to change my payment arrangements?' she asked, staring at the form.

'We did talk about this.' Kat had no memory of any such conversation. 'We agreed that as husband and wife it makes sense for all our earnings to come to one place. So the form is to authorise the payments to come into my account.'

'Why the fuck should *my* salary go into *your* bank account?'

'For goodness sake,' he said, no longer jovial. 'This is not a *mine* and *yours* issue. Now we're married we need to think in terms of *ours*.'

She was feeling angry. 'But it will still be *your* bank account that the money comes in to!'

Eulogy for Love

'Kat, I don't like the way you're sounding so untrusting. It's nothing more than a convenience, so that we can see how much money we have coming in. I'm also arranging for a new joint account, and I'll put money in that for our outgoings. One route in for the money, and one route out for our household expenses. Everything tidy and easy to monitor.'

'What about my personal expenses? How will I pay for them?'

'You're being silly again. I'll put plenty enough into the joint account for you to have some spending money for yourself.'

Mark found a pen and pushed it across the table towards Kat. She was looking down at the form. She felt sure this was not right. She knew she would be signing away another slice of her independence. She hesitated. There was silence.

'I'm getting impatient, Kat. Maybe I need to point out that without me, and without my family, you couldn't possibly afford the kind of life you have now. I suggest you start being grateful, and start trusting me on things like this.'

Kat stared at the form a little more, and reviewed her choices. Then she picked up the pen and signed.

Mark did put enough in the joint account to meet Kat's ordinary personal expenses, and even enough for small luxuries. However, he liked her to give him all the receipts, and the thought of him seeing what she spent on herself made her feel embarrassed and guilty. Sometimes he would glance through the receipts when she handed them over, and he might frown over the price of her lunchtime sandwich, or quiz her about the need to buy such expensive moisturiser. Fortunately, he slowly grew tired of checking the receipts and, as time went on, Kat learned how to bend the system that Mark had imposed on her. She could claim, as long as she didn't do it too often, that she had lost a receipt. Then she could buy something from the supermarket but tell him she'd bought it for cash, no receipt. It pleased her that she was able to fool him. *Silly bugger*, she would think, as she added another banknote to the envelope that she kept in an old handbag at the back of her wardrobe.

***

One late evening, a few weeks later, they were both in the bedroom, undressing for bed. By this time Mark had decreed that they should wear pyjamas in bed, but inevitably there was always a moment when they would each be naked. That evening Kat was a little late coming to the bedroom. Mark was already in bed, so he watched her as she took her clothes off.

'You know,' he said, as she released her bra, 'I think you're getting fatter.'

Kat would have liked to escape to the bathroom, but felt obliged to stand in her knickers and let him inspect her.

'Yes,' he said, 'you definitely are. I looked the other day at our honeymoon photos, and I'm sure you've got a tummy now that you didn't have then. And your tits are bigger too.'

'I don't think they are,' Kat said, looking down at herself. 'But anyway, wouldn't you like me with larger breasts? I thought that's what men liked.'

'God no. I see men walking down the street with their fat wives, and feel sorry for them. I bet their women weren't like that when they got married. All that wobbling flesh. And big sweaty thighs. Disgusting. Don't let yourself get like that.'

'I promise I won't.'

'Please don't.'

Some weeks later they were both getting ready to go out on a Saturday evening. He was in the bedroom when she walked through from the bathroom after a shower, and unthinkingly let the towel drop from around her.

'I still think you're getting fatter,' he said. He was already fully dressed.

'Oh Mark, please, not that again,' she said, suddenly feeling naked, her hands moving to cover her breasts. 'It really isn't true. I often check my weight, and it's no different from when we were married.'

'It isn't only a matter of weight. It's also to do with muscle tone, and the balance of fat and muscle tissue.' He leaned against the wall, assessing her. 'Go and stand in front of the mirror.'

There was a full-length mirror on the bedroom wall. She went in front of it and looked at herself.

'No, not like that,' he said. 'Turn sideways.' She turned and looked at her image in profile.

'See!' he said. 'Your stomach sticks out. And your nipples are beginning to point downwards.'

Kat remembered herself in the mirror on the wedding day. She had been certain, then, of her young beauty. Now, under his onslaught, she was having doubts. She put her hand on the slight curve.

'Yes—there!' Mark said.

'Oh, Mark,' she sighed. 'that's hardly a bulge. It's the way we women are made. We weren't supposed to have six-packs.'

'Well I don't like it. Make sure it doesn't get any worse.'

***

Mark started the new job. He had to visit establishments that the company ran, and, on those days, he took to wearing sharp suits. It was unnecessary for someone at his pay grade to wear suits—particularly suits that were so obviously expensive. It seemed to Kat that he did it to let people know he was too good for his current position, and would soon be rising higher.

His visits meant that he was often much later home than Kat. Mark presumed that Kat would use the hours after she left work, and before his return, to do the shopping and housework, and prepare his dinner. At first he feigned surprise when she put the evening meal in front of him, and thanked her for it. In another six months, he would complain if it were not ready when he got home.

With Kat on her own at the charity offices, she had to commute to work on the bus. Years before, she had learned to drive, though now she was out of practice. She asked Mark about whether she could get a car.

He looked disapproving. 'Jesus, Kat. Running another car would use up most of what you earn. You might as well stay at home. How about a bike? Much cheaper, and the exercise would help get you back into shape.'

'You've always said it was a matter of principle that I should go to work,' she countered, 'even if the income wasn't important. You can't have it both ways. And if you want me to be the one who does the food shopping, and arrives back here to cook your dinner each night, I need a car.'

She got the car, though it was a battered old thing with no style or comfort.

***

Always, when Kat bled each month, she had welcomed it, and though she hated the pain that came before it, she still perversely savoured that also. She had a modern woman's attitude to menstruation, and quietly enjoyed the affirmation of her fecundity.

The change in her feelings, after a year of marriage, caught her by surprise. She started to see the blood as a symbol of the fertility flowing out of her. Her eggs had become finite, and she found herself mourning the loss of each one. She could see her thirtieth birthday not far ahead. Suddenly, she wanted babies.

There had always been an assumption, barely discussed, that they would have children one day. Now Kat wanted a more specific plan, and she tried to get one agreed while on a weekend break in Madrid.

It was a brief conversation. She told Mark that she had discovered that powerful yearning that people call being _broody_, and was hoping very much they could try for a baby soon. Mark told her that they would need to move house first, and he wanted to reach a higher income, ready to meet the increased living costs. He would not discuss it further.

They returned from Madrid on the Sunday evening. There had not been an opportunity for a meal on the way, and by the time they reached home it was too late for dinner. Mark was hungry, so Kat made him an omelette with toast. Although she chose only to have a mug of tea for herself, she felt obliged to sit across the dining table and watch him eat.

'I've been thinking,' he said, before putting the last piece of toast in his mouth, 'about you wanting to start a baby.' Kat felt hopeful.

Mark pushed the empty plate away, and sat back. 'The decision to have children should be made jointly, of course,' he continued. 'So, by the same token, the decision _not_ to have children should also be one that is shared.' Kat was now feeling puzzled, and less hopeful. 'I realise that some couples share the contraceptive decision together all the time—like when they pause to put on a condom before sex, or simply agree not to have sex. But you make the decision every day by yourself when you take your pill.

'I don't think it's fair for you to be burdened with that responsibility on your own,' he went on. 'So from now on, we're going to do it together, a small daily ritual to show that we are jointly deciding the time is not yet right.'

Kat took a moment to understand what he meant. 'You mean you want to be there when I take it?'

'Yes, that's it,' he confirmed crisply. 'Of course, it will be you that actually swallows it, but I'd like to share the moment with you.'

'Really, Mark, I don't mind. You can trust me to take it. I always have since we got together.'

'I know you have, darling, and I'm grateful for that. But I'd like to be part of it, too, from now on.'

From then on, he was. He would bring the pack of tablets to her each morning, and put one pill in her hand. He also brought her a glass of water, even though she said she didn't need it. He liked to see that the pill was washed down. Sometimes he had to go off early on one of his work visits, and on those mornings she would feel him shaking her awake, and open her eyes to see him stood over her with the pill and the glass.

He didn't want to be more involved than that. She had always shielded him from the reality of her periods because it obviously offended him. He used the daily ritual to turn menstruation into nothing more than the popping of each pill from the pack until they had all been used. For the rest of the cycle, he only wanted confirmation they had worked. Kat and Mark achieved this with a one-word code.

'Started?' he would ask, without feeling, on the day it was due.

Eulogy for Love

There might be another day to wait, but each month she was always able to reply, 'Yes, started,' and hide her feelings as she spoke.

***

As they had been to Mexico in April, they holidayed late that summer, and less extravagantly, with a stay in Cyprus. Again, it was chosen by Mark because it had ancient ruins for him to visit. He went off to see them on his own, leaving Kat at the resort. She didn't mind, as it gave her a chance to sunbathe in her bikini, which she no longer dared to wear when he was around.

Chapter 13

By the time they returned from Cyprus and settled themselves to another English autumn, they had been together for three years. Kat was now in a time of waiting for the only thing that really mattered to her: motherhood.

It would be another year before Kat confronted the truth that she no longer loved Mark, and doubted that she ever had. At this point it was more an indifference to him, an absence of pleasure in his company. She also no longer felt excited by the lifestyle—the upmarket flat, the long-haul holidays, the weekends away. She had become accustomed to it; and, in any case, she considered it no more than she deserved for the services she provided to her husband.

She categorised sex as one of those services. Mark had abandoned any honest attempt to satisfy Kat sexually. He still went down on her, but it was purely symbolic, like saying grace before a meal, and over almost as quickly. Kat would respond after the shortest feasible time with a symbolic orgasmic groan; and, having met his need to pretend that he cared, Mark would set about the main course. Kat was saddened to notice that now, almost always, he wanted sex that did not involve looking at her. He still wanted oral sex, sometimes when he came home from work, when it served only as a release of his stress—an act devoid of desire, let alone love. If she looked up at him she would find him red-faced and staring somewhere else. His preference in bed, always, was to fuck her from behind, wordlessly.

Sexually unsatisfied by her husband, she had to make up on her own. She had long used her fingers, aided by a little pot of Vaseline she kept in the bedside drawer. For her dry lips, if anyone asked. Eventually, however, she took some of the notes from her secret stash in the wardrobe and went, nervously, to the new, *women-friendly* sex shop that had opened in town, where she bought a vibrator. It was two-pronged, noisy, and alarming, but worked magnificently. Sometimes she would get home from work and go straight to bed to use it. As she lay with it humming inside her, her mind would deliver a comforting, unfocused montage of soft flesh, and tongues that knew how to please her, and the taste of female juices. She would imagine putting her hand down towards the focus of her pleasure, and finding a woman's soft hair to stroke and pull, and beneath it a head that she could press down as she climaxed.

Kat also started paying attention to her intellectual needs. At work she signed up for every in-service training course. The following spring, she was promoted to a job that included support to local playgroups and family support groups. This sometimes required her to visit them in order to assist with their own administrative and financial systems, and sometimes the visits had to be outside office hours. It meant she had been released from the clock-watching regime of the office. It annoyed Mark when she had to go to meetings in the evening, but it meant she got time off during the day.

She also renewed her interest in English literature. Mark had allowed her to have her own account on his home computer, though he insisted that she told him her password, *just in case*. Kat signed up to an academic email discussion group on modern English literature, and accessed it through the Web, clearing the browser history each time. When the email discussion topics focused on a particular literary work, she would aim to find a second-hand copy. She sensed that Mark would not approve of her attempts to better herself, so kept her accumulating library under the fitted units in the kitchen. She hid the vibrator with her secret cash in the wardrobe, so that he would not be confronted by the tube of pink plastic that had bettered him in the bedroom.

In this way she lived through the months while she waited for Mark to decide that the time had come for them to have children. Her work and her discreet leisure interests kept her mostly cheerful, but there was another need that remained unsatisfied. She was lonely. Her work colleagues were pleasant, but not the sort she felt would make good friends beyond the office. One or two of the men had come on to her, but she wasn't looking for an affair. And anyway, she couldn't imagine a friendship, however innocent, or with either man or woman, that Mark would tolerate.

On a Thursday afternoon in March, Kat had come home early but then decided to go to the supermarket. She headed along the corridor from the flat to the lift and stood waiting for it to come. She could hear voices rising up the shaft, and the slight sound of the lift cables vibrating, yet the lift did not arrive. She was about to take the stairs when she heard the familiar sound of the motors. Half a minute later the doors opened. Kat saw a woman accompanied by a sofa. The sofa was stood on its end, and not only taller than the woman, but also taller than the lift doors.

'I'm so sorry to keep you waiting!' the woman said, breathlessly. Kat thought there was a slight Australian accent. 'Helluva of a job getting this thing in. In the end I dragged some kind man off the street to lend a hand, but now I've got to get the damned thing out again.'

Eulogy for Love

She was slim. Late forties or early fifties, Kat guessed, but she looked fit. Her tanned, creased skin and bleached hair, held by a band in a ponytail, suggested an outdoor life. She was wearing a full-length cotton dress, too insubstantial for March in England, but with a cardigan to cover her shoulders. A bag with a long strap was slung diagonally across to her hip.

The woman bent down and started heaving the base of the sofa towards the lift doors.

Kat's first instinct was to stop the doors closing while the woman pulled, but then it became apparent that the sofa was not going to move. Kat put down her purse and shopping bags, and got into the lift. They both heaved. The sofa reached the critical angle where the lower end had enough horizontal force, and shot out of the lift. The other end slid down the back of the lift and banged onto the floor, causing the whole compartment to bounce and vibrate. The lift doors started attempting to close, only to encounter the sofa and withdraw.

Kat managed to squeeze between the back wall of the lift and the sofa, and found a way to lift it. The woman lifted the other end.

'Where to?' Kat said.

'Fifty-seven, please.'

The two women shuffled along the corridor to Number 57—fortunately, not too far from the lift. They had to put the sofa down while the woman found a door key and opened the door. Together they shoved it over the threshold.

'Hey, thank you so much!' the woman said, still struggling to calm her breath. 'Do you live here?'

Kat pointed back down the corridor to a door they had already passed. 'Number fifty-three.'

'Wow, that's great!' the woman said, and held out her hand. 'I'm Barbara.' She smiled in an intense way that gathered the creases around her blue eyes.

Kat already liked her. 'I'm Kat,' she said, and shook Barbara's hand.

'We've just moved back to the UK,' Barbara explained. 'As usual the tenants didn't look after the place, and the sofa was just too vile to sit on. Been out today and bought this one in a hurry, but the damned van driver wouldn't bring it up for me.'

Kat sighed in sympathy.

'Why don't you stay and have a cuppa?' Barbara asked abruptly, as if it had been an inspiration.

'That's really kind of you, but actually I was just on my way to the supermarket.'

Barbara put her hand on Kat's arm. 'Are you really? Could I ask another really big favour of you?'

'Of course.'

'Could I come along with you? I've no car, and not so much as a snag in the fridge.'

Kat said yes, of course. She went back to the lift to retrieve her purse while Barbara scribbled a note to tell her husband where she had gone.

They talked all the way to the supermarket, and went on talking as they walked the aisles. Kat learned about Barbara's life, and liked her all the more.

The hints of Australian in Barbara's accent were misleading, it turned out. She was, she said, *a Pom, and proud of it*. But she and her husband, Tony, had spent the winter in Southeast Asia, often in the company of Australians, and were still imbued with Aussie speech patterns. They had for many years lived a life of migration, following the sun with the seasons. They would base themselves in the Med. from May through to September, and then head south of the Equator for the rest of the year, often stopping off in the Caribbean on the way back north.

154

Eulogy for Love

Australian immigration rules were a problem. Sometimes they could get in for a few weeks on tourist visas, and quietly pick up enough work to cover their living costs, but it was always awkward. Southeast Asia was far easier, and the money better. Tony was a trained diving instructor—the serious deep stuff, with air tanks, Barbara explained—and that usually brought in the best money. She also taught scuba, and had acquired a handful of other certificates and skills. She could offer herself as a professional masseuse and personal trainer. Sometimes, when the pay was good enough, she would even do impromptu childcare for rich people who wanted to dump their brats for the day.

In warm climates they lived inexpensively. They got to know the places away from the tourist spots, where the food was good but cheap. It meant they only needed to put away enough money to pay for the flights out at the end of the season.

'Sounds wonderful!' Kat had said, at several points.

'It's been great,' Barbara agreed. 'But we've been doing it for twenty years, and we've finally admitted to each other that we've gotten weary of it. Made good friends all over the world, and every time it's great to meet up with them again. But now we're thinking we'd like to be in our own place, surrounded by our own stuff, and be able to close the door on the world. And we're also starting to see the time coming when we can't go travelling any more. No kids, no pension. Looks a little bleak. The one good thing is that we have this flat—bought with money Tony inherited from his father three years ago.'

'You never had kids, Barbara?' They were facing the canned beans and pulses, though not seeing them.

'No. Wasn't a gift that nature was willing to bestow upon us, maybe because we left it too late. Eventually we thought of adoption, but I guess we didn't look the kind of upstanding, reliable folk the adoption people have in mind. To be honest, they were right. We were too used to doing as we pleased, enjoying our freedom. We'd become selfish, you might say.'

As they drove back, Barbara made Kat talk about her own life. Kat gave her the bare facts, and apologised that it was so dull by comparison. 'Hey, don't apologise,' Barbara said. 'Tony and I have lived twice as many years as you. Plenty more time for you to have adventures. What matters, as they say, is whether you're happy.'

Kat focused on her driving, and said nothing. She knew Barbara had slipped a question in front of her, and would be noticing the absence of an answer.

As they travelled up in the lift, Barbara again invited Kat to come in for tea. This time Kat agreed, calculating that Mark would not be home for at least another hour. Barbara waited inside the doorway of Kat's flat while Kat transferred items to the fridge, taking the opportunity to glance round.

'Wow, very nice,' she said. 'Somehow I don't suppose our place will ever look like this.'

They continued round to Number 57, and Barbara held open the door for Kat. It was plain to see why Barbara thought her flat compared poorly. It felt small. The carpet was thin and dirty, and mostly covered by cardboard boxes and their partially unloaded contents. The new sofa, now vertical again, was stood in a corner. An old beige sofa, stained and sagging, had a man sitting on it. He got up as soon as he saw Kat.

'Babs, I don't remember putting one of these on the shopping list.' He winked at Kat.

'Nope,' Barbara answered, still holding bags of shopping, and obliged to push the door closed with her shoulder, 'but they were on special offer this week.'

'Looks very nice. Reckon you should have got a couple more while they're cheap.'

'Now stop being rude, Tony,' Barbara said, 'and say hello to Kat, our neighbour and new friend. And our Good Samaritan too. Helped me bring in the sofa and then took me to the supermarket.'

He held out his hand to Kat, and shook hers, warmly. He was wearing a t-shirt and shorts, and she could see he was as tanned and as weathered as his wife. He was thin, but in a lean, healthy way. His salt-and-pepper hair was thinning on top, to a degree that would have led many British men, hoping to look more masculine and *hard*, to shave themselves bald. But Tony seemed content to let the remaining hair on top sprout up and then fall back in sparse curls.

'G'day, friend,' he said, winking again, and waved her into the room. 'If I were you, I'd sit at the table. We can't work out where this sofa's been, but it wasn't anywhere nice.'

'Jesus, Tony, you've got it hot in here,' Barbara said. Kat silently agreed. The humid air had struck her face as she had walked in. She sat down at the table.

'Sorry, love. Haven't acclimatised to Pommie weather yet, I guess. I'll turn it down a bit.'

Barbara went to the kitchen to assemble tea. Tony picked up some spectacles and went over to a thermostat on the wall and fiddled with it, leaning back awkwardly so that he could see the dial through the glasses on the end of his nose. He returned to the sofa and smiled across the room at Kat. This time he had to peer over the rims of the glasses to get a proper look at her. 'So,' he said, 'are you feline and cool, or a companion for Kit?'

Kat, uncomprehending, frowned.

'*Cat*?' he said. 'Your name.'

She understood, and smiled. 'Neither, really. I'm Kat with a *k*. Short for Kateryna.'

'Well, Kateryna,' he said, 'I reckon that makes you exotic and exciting.'

'Hardly. Just my hippie parents being fanciful.'

'Well, they gave you a person that you could choose to become, but the freedom to be someone else. Or maybe a Kat for now, a Kateryna later. Are they still alive, your parents?'

'Dad is, Mum died five years ago.' That sounded rather stark, Kat felt. Tony was looking at her in a kindly way but saying nothing. She thought she had better say more, so she added, 'I went back home to look after her when she was ill for the last time.'

Tony nodded. 'How was that for you?'

'In a strange way, good. I think I did right by her.' Kat paused to reflect, and again Tony waited for her in silence. 'Not just a clear conscience thing,' she started again, 'more something to do with achieving a balance. She'd brought me into this life, and then I cared for her until her death. Not doing right by her, really. More like doing what was right and proper. Sounds a bit twee, but like completing the circle of life.'

She paused, staring at the floor, suddenly full of the memories of those last months with her mother.

'It was tough, though,' she added, looking up at Tony again, 'to see her in discomfort for many months.'

'I don't think that's twee, Kat. And that's good you feel you completed your shared journey. But I guess you paid a high price for it, putting your own life on hold.'

'Yes, I did. In fact, I never really got my life back into a normal pattern afterwards—never made it into university, where I'd always wanted to go.'

Eulogy for Love

Barbara brought in mugs of tea on a tray, and a packet of biscuits on a plate. Kat and Tony watched her as she pushed aside the clutter on table and slid the tray gently into the space. Kat welcomed the moment's pause. She was feeling unsettled by the conversation she'd found herself having. It was as if the surface of her had been cracked like thin ice, leaving her depths exposed. And it had been cracked by a stranger—a man, even—she had met only minutes before. Whether by chance or by skill, he had touched it exactly where it was easy to shatter. Yet she didn't mind.

Barbara opened the packet of biscuits and shook them onto the plate. 'Is it still the done thing in England to have digestives with tea,' she asked, holding the plate out to Kat, 'or does everything have to have chocolate in it these days?'

'Kat's been telling me about looking after her mum until she died,' Tony said.

Barbara sat down on another dining chair, close to Kat. 'Ah yes,' Barbara said. She looked into Kat's eyes and touched her arm, as if examining her thoughts. 'That's such a difficult experience, but so important.'

She kept her hand on Kat's arm, but released her gaze. 'Tony had the opposite experience with his father, didn't you, love? He was taken ill very suddenly, and went straight into hospital. Tony got word from his brother and came charging back from Thailand, but his dad had already gone. So you could say it was a wasted journey—especially as his father had been unconscious the whole time he was in hospital. There was the funeral, of course, and some other things to be sorted out, but . . .'

'But the flight,' Tony interrupted, 'was what I needed to do to say goodbye to my dad. Those hours sat on a plane with my head full of memories of him. Sitting alone on a plane was the final journey I had with my father.'

Kat was learning that Barbara and Tony had difficulties with small talk. For them, small talk was swimming on the surface. They preferred to dive, to go deep into inner worlds, and they had the ability to swim into hers whenever they wished. When she started talking, she found that what she wanted to offer was the Kat she used to be, in the life before Mark. It was a past that had laid inert inside her, a place she had stopped visiting. Here, however, as she sat on a dining chair in this humid, cluttered apartment, she wanted to talk as if the talking would give it life again. These strangers had opened her. Her brittle surface had broken and fallen away.

She talked openly to Tony and Barbara. She summarised her travels as an au pair abroad, how she had come back to care for her mother. She mentioned her life as a lesbian. She also found herself needing to tell them about David, to make him real again also. Yet what was there to say? A man she'd only known six months. A married man with whom she had not had an affair. She had shared coffee with him twice a week. They had once gone together overnight to London and slept in different rooms. Anyone would dismiss it as a girlish infatuation. Maybe it was.

In the end she only said, in that first conversation, that David was an older man, and someone who was very special to her, but unavailable. She did not tell them he was married. That would have made it seem sleazy, and it never had been.

'So now you're married to Mark,' Barbara said, leading Kat to the next stage of her story. 'How are you getting along?'

Kat gave a little sideways shake of her head. 'To be honest, marriage is not what I expected it to be.'

She looked at her wristwatch. 'Talking of which, I really ought to get back and start making dinner.'

'No problem,' Barbara said. 'It's been lovely to meet you. We'll hope to see lots more of you. And we need you to be our guide to an England that seems very changed.'

'I hope so too. It's been great to talk,' Kat replied. She turned away momentarily to put her mug back on the table. 'Please,' she said, 'I think I need to ask you a favour.'

'Of course.' Barbara again touched her hand.

'Could we keep this between ourselves? Our friendship, I mean. Mark can be a bit possessive, a bit choosy about who we're friends with. I think the two of you are absolutely lovely, but . . .'

Tony had seemed preoccupied with the digestive biscuit he was eating, but stopped nibbling it and looked at Kat over his glasses.

'Of course, Kat,' Barbara said. 'That's not a problem at all. If we see the two of you together, we'll walk straight past. But we want *you* to come around whenever you like, OK? Like today—if you're home a bit earlier than Mark, come and knock on our door. Will you do that?'

Kat nodded and got up. 'I will,' she said. Barbara stood up and hugged her. As Kat moved toward the door, Tony came across to her. He put his hands on the sides of her shoulders, and then leaned in and kissed her slowly, melodramatically, on both cheeks. Still holding her shoulders, he looked into her eyes. 'You take care of yourself, Kateryna, OK?'

Kat nodded. Barbara opened the door for her, and Kat walked into the corridor. She turned, saw them in the doorway, and gave them a little wave: her hand, palm to the front, moving briefly left and right in front of her. Then she turned and walked down the corridor with a girlish spring in her step.

Her home felt cool and quiet. Her heels clicked sharply on the solid wood floors. Hurrying to put away the rest of the shopping, she picked up a box of eggs without seeing it was half open. An egg fell onto the top of the dining table, breaking open and oozing out across the glass.

With the tabletop cleaned, and the shopping cleared away, Kat started scrubbing some potatoes. She had nearly finished them when she heard Mark turn the key in the lock. He came in, threw his briefcase on the sofa, and then looked into the kitchen area where Kat was standing at the side of the sink.

'Christ, is that all you've done?' he said. 'You've been home ages, haven't you?'

He left her in the kitchen, and went to change out of his suit. Kat put her head down as she finished the last potato. A teardrop fell in the saucepan.

Chapter 14

O ver the following weeks, the centre of Kat's life shifted two doors sideways. Number 57 became her true home, her refuge. Tony and Barbara's apartment was the place she discovered love and acceptance in a form as undeniable as the humid air that enveloped her whenever she visited.

She didn't visit every day. Sometimes the gap between the end of her working day and Mark's arrival home was too small, or she had chores she could not postpone. But it soon became the understanding that she would text or call them if she was not going to be visiting that day.

It also became less certain, as time went on, that she would find them at home. Barbara got work on the staff team at a fitness centre. It was only part time, but she was allowed to develop her own business as a personal trainer. Tony struggled more, and was obliged to take sessional work as a quarry-diving instructor. 'Great way to learn,' he said, 'but sitting a hundred foot down in total darkness on shit and supermarket trolleys is not my idea of fun.'

A while further on, after they had given Kat a key, she didn't even need them to be at home. They made space for her to keep her secret library in their spare bedroom. And after she had told them that she suspected that Mark checked the height of the gin in the bottle, they put a bottle of vodka in their fridge with a supply of orange juice, and told her to help herself whenever she liked.

It was mainly for their company that she went round, however. Barbara gave her love in quiet ways: fussing to make her tea; touching her hand or arm; hugging her on arrival or departure, usually both. Tony, in contrast, always greeted her loudly. 'Well, well,' he might say, 'it's the lovely Kateryna!' Or, 'G'day to you, Kat, light of our lives.' Or simply, 'Hello, beautiful!' It was cheesy—that was the fun of it—but the affection was wholly honest, she knew, and Tony the most genuine, open man she had ever met.

While Kat was getting to know Barbara and Tony, she was puzzled by the way they talked about deep emotions as easily as other people discuss the weather, and yet sometimes became wildly, even childishly, frivolous. If a conversation reminded Tony of a quote from Shakespeare, he would pluck *The Complete Works* from the bookshelf and read it out loud—not sat with the book, but stood up and acting out the scene from the play. Once he stood on the dining table and recited *The Jabberwocky* from memory, slashing the air with a broom as the vorpal blade went snicker-snack. The two of them would sing old musical-hall songs so loudly that Kat worried for the neighbours. And they had an act—they admitted it was a party turn—when Barbara would blacken her eyebrows and put circles of lipstick on her cheeks, and sit on Tony's lap as a ventriloquist's dummy. Though Tony was a rotten ventriloquist, it was a well-practised performance. Kat had to take her turn as dummy, and did it so badly that they all fell helplessly into giggles, and had to stop.

It was after they had calmed, and Barbara had gone to clean her face, that Tony explained, in his own way, why they were like this.

'It's so lovely that you get into the spirit of things,' he said. 'It's such a great quality. You know something, Kat?'

Eulogy for Love

Kat recognised these last words as a cue for one of the pearls of wisdom that Tony liked to offer. Even though they were often genuinely insightful, Barbara sweetly teased him for it, and had taught Kat to do the same.

Kat said, 'Tell me, O Wise One.'

'It's often thought,' Tony said, too familiar with the mockery to take any notice, 'that people who are shy, and hold back from joining in, are being humble. It's really quite the opposite. It's a kind of conceit. People who are shy are more concerned with preserving their appearance than getting involved. We have to set aside such vanities if we want to be fully in this world.'

***

One Saturday morning, Kat went to find Barbara and Tony. She had never visited before on a Saturday, and thought she had better knock. Tony opened the door. 'Buenos días, Señorita!' he said. He was wearing a striped apron, and had a polishing cloth in his hand.

'Sorry, Tony. Is this a bad time?'

'For you, never. Come and see.' He took her hand, led her to the door of the kitchen, and stood behind her as she looked into the room. Usually it was untidy, and a little grubby. Now it was clean as new. 'Wow,' Kat said. 'You've been working hard.'

'Taken me all morning, but doesn't it look smashing!'

'It does.'

'You know something, Kat?'

She heard the cue. 'Tell me, O Wise One.'

'Y'know, we expect to find beauty in what is perfect, and hence rare. And yet, through patience and effort, we can find beauty also in the ordinary and imperfect. Today, this kitchen is beautiful in my eyes.

'It's the same with love. We expect love to grow through what we are given, but it only truly grows through the effort we give to it. Choose carefully, though. Some things, and some people, will never grow.

'And if you do it very, very tidily, you can make us both a coffee.'

Kat started to make the drinks, while Tony sat down.

'Babs is doing sessions this weekend at the centre', Tony said, loud enough for Kat to hear over the boiling kettle.

When Kat carried out the coffee, Tony had settled on the sofa. By this time, they were using the new sofa. The old one stood upright in the spare room. Kat sat down next to him. Tony looked up from his paper to take the coffee, and then peered over the top of his reading glasses at her.

'So,' he said, 'what brings the delightful Kateryna to us on a Saturday morning? I've a feeling it isn't something joyful.'

'No, it isn't.'

Tony took off his glasses and shifted into the corner of the sofa so that he could look at her fully.

'You know he always likes to go visiting places on a Saturday?' Kat said. Tony nodded. 'Well,' Kat went on, 'today I told him I didn't want to. I crazily took it into my head to say No. OK, I can be interested in castles and Roman villas, but just not today.'

'And?'

'He was angry, of course. Big lecture about how he works hard all week to support me, and how it's surely reasonable to hope he could have the company of his wife at the weekend. And then a lot of stuff about how lazy and stupid I am. And

166

then he stormed off out—presumably to whatever ruin he had planned for today.'

'How's that left you feeling?'

'Right now, mostly angry. But I'm already starting to feel guilty because I've disappointed him, not done my duty as a loving wife.'

Tony looked at her, reflecting. 'You may be married,' he said, 'but you're surely still not obliged to do whatever he wants to do. Arguably, the sensible grown-up solution has been found. He wanted to go look at ruins, so he went. You didn't so, so you stayed. If he's not happy with that, it's his problem.'

'Yes, but he'll make it my problem when he comes back. He'll spend the rest of the weekend seething.'

'Aha, so he's still managed to make sure your day is in ruins.' Kat smiled to acknowledge the small joke.

Tony looked hard at her over the top of his glasses. 'He doesn't hit you, does he?'

Tony had never asked that question directly.

'No. But he often looks like he wants to. Sometimes he shouts at me. Mostly it's just the cold seething anger. Hour after hour of it gets you down.'

Kat smiled at Tony, her eyes full of tears.

'Do you think I'm stupid to put up with him, Tony?'

'Never think you're stupid, Kat. You're a bright and lovely woman. You must decide whether he's worth it.'

'You know why I'm staying with him, Tony? I want babies. That's the only really important thing to me right now. I want children, and I want them to grow up in comfort and security. He can provide that.'

Tony nodded. 'I understand that—as well as any man could understand. For years I watched Babs suffering through all our failures to have a child.'

Kat nodded. 'Well yes, absolutely. I can hardly bear to think what that must be like. And of course, it could be like that for me. Another reason not to jump ship in search of a nicer man. And aren't all men much the same?'

'What're you saying, Kat?' Tony was pointing to himself, and wide-eyed in fake shock.'

'No, not you! But you're such an exception! Can you tell me honestly that most men aren't like Mark?'

'Jesus, there's a depressing thought! Of course, I haven't met the fella, but from what you tell me I'd say he's got some special problems of his own. You're right, though, much as I hate to say it. Most men I come across don't know how to be with women—even their own women. You often get the impression they don't really like them or understand them.'

'Well, there you are,' Kat agreed. 'My point exactly.'

'I've gotta tell you, Kat. One thing I got right in my life was finding Babs. We are so good together. I don't think many couples are really friends. It's the sex that first glues them together, and then when that's gone they find some way to rub along in a vaguely friendly way. That's if they're lucky. But with me and Babs we're best mates, and still great lovers, still got that deep man-woman thing.'

'I've seen that. It's lovely, and you're both very lucky.'

'Well, I want you to know, Kat, that we aren't judging you. You have to choose your path in life. But in these last weeks we've become very fond of you, and we feel sad when we see you in pain.'

'Thank you, Tony.' She put her mug down, leaned across the sofa, and hugged him. 'Life would be really tough without the two of you.'

***

Eulogy for Love

Not long after, life—or life on weekdays, at least—became a little easier.

That evening, Mark arrived home at six-thirty. The pasta bake Kat had made for dinner was already in the oven, but she was still in the kitchen making a salad. Mark went straight to the bedroom, pulling off his tie.

'We're going out for dinner,' he shouted as he changed. 'Put something nice on. I want you looking good this evening.'

Kat was puzzled, and went to the bedroom doorway.

'Table's booked,' he added, glancing up as he changed. 'We need to leave in twenty minutes.'

'Why?'

'Tell you when we get there.'

Kat had to wait until they were seated at the table, their dishes ordered, champagne in their glasses.

'I've got a promotion,' Mark announced, smugly. 'Acting Regional Manager.'

'Great! Well done!' Kat began calculating when she might become a mother, then realised there was a problem. 'But what does *acting* mean? Is it only temporary?'

Mark told her it would probably be for three or four months, running over the summer, until they found someone to fill the post permanently.

'Why don't they just give it to you as a permanent job?' Kat asked.

'They probably want to see first whether I'm up to it. It is a big jump up. But I don't think I'd want it anyway. I don't want to be up there for long. They're all heathens, and anyway I think people who get posted to the sticks can find themselves forgotten when the promotions are being handed out.'

Kat sensed she'd been duped. 'OK, so which region are we talking about?' she asked, stiffly.

He shrugged and waved his hand, as if fending off her rising anger. 'Northwest Region. Manchester office. But look—we don't have to move. I'll go up each week, Monday to Friday. There's some spare staff accommodation in one of the residential schools we have up there. And I'm going to get a better company car, plus all the mileage.'

The thought of weeks without Mark was wonderful, but Kat was still furious. This plan had obviously been in the making for days, if not weeks, yet he had not even told her, let alone consulted her. She plucked up the courage to register her objection, if only to preserve some respect for herself.

'I have to say, Mark, that I'm really disappointed and upset that you haven't shared any of this with me earlier, so I could have a chance to offer my thoughts. But,' she continued, trying to lighten the mood, and even add a hint of affection, 'please tell me there's some good news. Does this mean we can try for a baby now?'

The waiter came with the first course, so they fell silent. When he had gone, Mark drank from his champagne glass, very slowly. He put down his glass and looked at her.

'No, sorry. I think there's going to be some changes at work in the autumn, and I plan to be one of the winners. But at the end of the day we can't make decisions on the basis of a temporary promotion. We can look at it again in September.'

He took a mouthful of the savoury mousse. 'Incidentally,' he said, using a finger to recover a fragment from his lip, 'I'm expecting you to honour that policy even though I'm not going to be around to do it with you.'

She frowned, puzzled. He leaned forward and dropped his voice. 'I mean,' he said, 'that I won't put up with any accidental pregnancies. I'm trusting you to avoid the need for an abortion.'

Eulogy for Love

***

Tony and Barbara helped her to see things in a positive light. She had at least got a promise from Mark that he would review the position in the autumn, and if he did get a permanent promotion, he would surely have to agree that they could start a family. Moreover, in the meantime, she would have four evenings a week to do as she liked. Tony and Barbara were already planning what the three of them might do together.

Once June had arrived, and Mark had started the new job, it became apparent that he intended to phone her every evening, even if there was nothing to be said. He always called the phone in the flat, not Kat's mobile. 'Perhaps I'd be more understanding if I met him,' Tony had said, when he heard about Mark's evening calls, 'but I do find myself appalled by his need to control you.'

'I don't want to defend him,' Kat had answered, 'but it isn't just about control. I'm sure you know that. During the day he'll be strutting around playing Mr Big, but he has to spend evenings on his own in his room. He'll be lonely and insecure. It's like his ego wilts if it isn't constantly watered. Yes, he's checking up on me, but he's checking that he still has someone he controls, someone who depends on him.'

'And the irony,' Tony had commented, 'is that he needs you far more than you need him.'

As Barbara and Tony pointed out, Mark's evening calls still allowed her to go out during the day. Their first suggestion for an outing was to go to the cinema together. It was, they explained, something they hadn't done for years, because they had rarely stayed in the kind of place that had a cinema, let alone one that showed films in English. They appointed Kat to be their guide to cinema-going in Twenty-First Century Britain.

Kat contrived to do some evening work, which allowed her to finish early the following Wednesday. She called round to Barbara and Tony's flat to pick them up in time for a late afternoon screening.

'Kat's here, Tone,' Barbara called, when she saw Kat in the doorway. 'Are you ready?'

Tony appeared from the bedroom. 'Well 'ello, my darlink,' he said to Kat, in a cod French accent, 'you are looking *très belle* today.' Kat smiled and purred inwardly. It was such foolishness.

'Are you sure you want to wear your shorts today, Tony?' Barbara queried. 'If the cinema is a fleapit you might get bitten in some strange places.'

'Barbara, my dearest, I'd love you to bite me in strange places, but you might embarrass Kat.'

Kat giggled. 'Fleapit, Barbara?' she answered, laughing. 'Where do you think you are? We're about to be the customers of a twenty-first century palace of entertainment. I'm sure they don't have fleas!'

Barbara and Kat were awkward and out of place in a modern multiplex cinema, and bemused by the lines of people queuing for refreshments. They bought a bucket of popcorn. 'When in Rome,' Tony said cheerfully, before discovering the price. Kat carried it in. 'You go between us,' he said, when they had found their way through the gloom to the correct row, 'so we can all reach the popcorn. Kat settled into her seat, Tony and Barbara protectively on either side of her, the popcorn on her knee. She felt like a loved child.

On their return, parking the car outside the block of flats, they scanned carefully for Mark's new BMW. There was no sign of it, so they walked in together and shared the lift. Kat needed to go to her flat to be ready for Mark's call, and they parted at her door.

'Well,' Barbara said, as she hugged Kat, 'I judge that to have been a great success. Agreed?'

'Agreed,' Tony said, before solemnly kissing Kat in his customary extravagant way. 'We should do more of it, and very soon.'

'Agreed,' Kat said to the two of them, and watched as they turned towards their own apartment. 'And thank you both so much.'

Kat's evening routine on weekdays soon became fluid. She might call on Barbara and Tony when she got home from work, perhaps lingering with them until she needed to go back for Mark's evening call. Barbara liked to cook dinner for the three of them, though Kat made sure to contribute ingredients or a dessert. They would sit at the table and good-naturedly debate politics, most often with Tony leading the discussion, absentmindedly waving forkfuls of food as he talked; or they would explore facets of the human psyche, drawing on their own inner lives. Kat shared with unhesitating honesty. She never felt vulnerable, never judged.

Sometimes she would go back to Number 57 after Mark had phoned. On other evenings she would stay at home and find pleasure in watching her choice of TV without Mark scowling beside her. She often went to bed early to read. As the weeks passed, the bedroom came to feel like her exclusive territory, invaded by Mark for three nights a week. Her current book, and her vibrator, were no longer hidden away, but left in the bedside drawer for easy access. Her new weekly chore took place on Thursdays, when she had to clean and tidy until the flat was restored to the standard that Mark expected.

Chapter 15

'We've got a proposal for you,' Tony announced one evening after they had shared dinner. It was late June, and the windows were opened to catch the slight breeze. 'You must decide whether you want to do it. It does involve a degree of risk, but we think it would be wonderful.'

'Wow!' Kat said. 'I'm intrigued. So, what is it?'

'We'd like to take you surfing. Or, to be more exact, we'd like you to take us surfing.'

Barbara and Tony laughed at the expression on Kat's face.

'But I can't surf. And anyway, there's no sea around here to surf on.'

'Perhaps we didn't tell you.' Tony winked at her. 'We're both surfing instructors. So that puts paid to the first objection. And we have a way to get you to the ocean.'

Tony set out the plan. She would need to take a day off work—annual leave, maybe, or sick leave. The evening before she would phone Mark, as early as she dared, to get his phone call out of the way. And then they would all pile into Kat's car and head to the North Devon coast. 'Provided we do it soon, before the start of school holidays, we can do the journey in four hours, five tops,' Tony told her, 'so we should be there well before midnight.'

He had remembered that an old friend used to have a little wooden bungalow close to the sea in Devon. 'Primitive shack of a place. The authorities have been trying to get it bulldozed for years. But it's still there! And he's happy for us to use it. Need to take bedding, but that's it. He even has a couple of boards stashed away.

'So, surf as much of the morning as we want, have lunch and chill, and then head back around three. Should be home by seven, in good time to receive his lordship's call. And even if we're a bit late you can surely make up some story. You were asleep, or out shopping, whatever.'

'God,' Kat said, 'it would be amazing to do it. But it's a bit risky, to say the least. What if Mark phoned a second time?'

'Why would he? If he did, you could always find excuses. And he'd probably try your mobile, so you'd be able to say you were out at the supermarket.'

Kat stared at the floor. Barbara said, 'You don't have to decide now. And you don't have to say yes. Don't let us pressurise you.'

Kat continued looking at the floor. The others waited for her.

'Oh fuck,' she said. 'It feels a really dangerous, disobedient thing to do. But it would be wonderful, and I think I'd regret it forever if I said no. Hey, let's do it!'

Tony punched the air. Barbara hugged her.

'We'd be free to travel down on Wednesday, back Thursday,' Tony said. 'How about you?'

'Works for me!'

***

Kat made up a tale about needing to know plans for the weekend, and called Mark at seven. Half an hour later they were in the car, heading for the motorway. Tony went in the back, the bedding and a coolbag of food piled in the seat next to him. Barbara pulled out Kat's stash of CDs, and they all debated which one to play. They ended up with Queen and R.E.M. When those ran out, and Tony was snoozing, Barbara put on George Michael, but saw that Kat was driving through tear-filled eyes. She hurriedly took it off again. Kat noticed and glanced across at her, wiping a tear from her cheek. '*Heal the pain*,' Kat said. 'Funny how some songs pin the butterflies of your life. And sometimes they're so beautiful you can't bear to look at them.'

Barbara found a tissue for her. 'Your David?'

Kat nodded. 'Yes,' she said, when she felt sure of her voice. 'But everything, really.'

They stopped briefly south of Bristol to give Kat a rest. Barbara switched to the back seat and handed round sandwiches as they travelled onwards. By the time they had left the motorway and were heading north to the coast, the sun had set in a cloudless sky. It was only when they neared the end of the journey that they sensed an absence of land to their left beyond the trees at the edge of the road. A minute later they were driving on the side of a treeless headland with the sea clear to the left and ahead, painted the palest lemon by a low moon. Tony wound down the window. At a distance the water looked motionless. Then the car came around the headland and drifted downhill towards the bay, and they could hear the slow beat of waves dropping heavily onto the beach.

Tony directed Kat to turn briefly inland before swinging behind high dunes, the sea no longer visible. A cluster of small buildings appeared in the headlights. He asked Barbara to pass him a torch and went to investigate. Two minutes later his head appeared at the car window. 'Yes, this is it. Found the keys, unlocked the door. We're in business.'

Once they had arrived, they did no more than organise their beds and make hot drinks. Then they slept.

Eulogy for Love

When she woke, Kat's first sensation was the sweet-and-salt aroma of timber that has aged in damp sea air. The entire property was built of pine. It appeared to be mounted on a raft of wood in place of foundations, with part of the raft extending to form a veranda accessed through French windows. The whole construction looked as if it could be dragged somewhere else if the need arose. This was perhaps the intention, because the bungalow, and its four similar neighbours, were all positioned behind a bank of high dunes, with the beach on the other side. Although mostly tethered by vegetation, the dunes evidently leaked sand, grain by grain. Even on this summer's day, thin trails of sand would be pushed off the edge. Where they had fallen around the bungalow, and onto the veranda, the sand grains had been caught and heaped by eddies of wind. One day, unless moved, the property would be submerged.

Barbara was starting to make a breakfast of eggs and bacon on the little bottled-gas hob. Tony was outside, rooting around under the back of the wooden raft, and he eventually pulled out two surfboards. He hauled them onto the veranda, then came inside.

'Good morning, Gorgeous. Ready to surf?'

Tony explained the plan as they ate breakfast. 'We reckon you'll fit into Babs' wetsuit.'

'But what will Barbara wear?' Kat interrupted.

'I'll be fine,' Barbara said. 'I don't need to surf. We're going to play catch with you. Tony will go with you into the deep water, and send you on your way. I'll be waiting for you in the shallows. On a day like today, I'll be happy to paddle.'

Kat managed to put on the wetsuit by herself, though Barbara pulled the zip at the back so that it was closed snugly around Kat's neck, and then they were off to the beach—Kat walking behind Tony, the two boards held between them at their hips, while Barbara followed with a bag of refreshments. It was only when they came around the side of the dunes that Kat had proper sight of the bay, and felt the warm, salty wind coming off the sea, strong enough to sing in her ears. There were thin, fast-moving clouds, and the bright light seemed to put everything in sharp focus. Rounded headlands on either side formed a deep bay, pure sand meeting the sea halfway. The waves, seen first from a distance, looked gentle and regular. For Kat, marching behind Tony, the world in that moment looked new and clean.

'The serious surfers won't be happy,' Tony shouted over the wind, 'but these conditions will be fine for you.'

They stopped walking towards the sea before the sand became too wet, and Tony gave Kat a lesson in surfing theory. As Tony talked, Barbara demonstrated the correct position to stand, and, later, how to move into the standing position, hitching up the hem of her long dress so that Kat could see her feet on the board. And then Tony led Kat into the sea, the board rearing up gently against her hand with each oncoming wave, the water rising up her body until the waves slapped against her tummy.

After an hour, Kat was confidently catching the wave, and had managed to get to her knees by the time the board was in the shallows, but felt unable to progress further. Barbara, indifferent to her wet skirt, waded out to Kat as she again reached the shallows. 'You're tired, my love. Tell Tony to let you have a break, and then try again when you've got a bit more energy. You're nearly there.'

They sat on the surfboards and drank coffee, eating biscuits from the packet. Kat had been cold from the sea, but the day's warmth was increasing as the sun climbed, the clouds almost gone.

Half an hour into her second session, Kat managed to stand on the board. She was so surprised by the achievement that she immediately lost her balance and tipped into the sea. But now she knew she could do it. Another half hour on, she managed to stand and ride the wave in; wobbling, unable to steer, but standing. Tony came in on the next wave, and they all met at the edge of the beach.

'Brilliant, Kat! Don't you think, Babs?'

'I do', Barbara said. She had already hugged Kat twice. 'But enough for one day, I think.' Kat nodded, brushing water and sand from her face.

Back at the bungalow, Kat wrapped a towel around her waist and sat down in one of the chairs on the veranda. 'You two crack open a couple of tinnies and take a rest,' Tony said. 'Give me ten to change, and I'll put some lunch together.' He pulled some beers from a cooler box, and then went inside.

Kat smiled across the table at Barbara. Barbara gazed back warmly.

'It's lovely to see you looking so happy, Kat.'

'It's wonderful to feel so happy,' Kat answered. 'I don't know when I last felt so full of it. Mark and I have been on trips to all sorts of exciting places, and fancy resorts, but they've never made me feel like this.'

'As they say, simple pleasures . . .'

'And the right company,' Kat said, and gave out an empty laugh.

They fell silent.

'You know,' Kat said after a while, 'I think that sums up why I admire the two of you so much. You figured it out early—it's the simple pleasures that count. And you've lived your lives accordingly.'

'Ah, you mean the years of hedonism, easy living in sun-kissed lands, all that?'

'Yes, all that.'

'But, Love, we've paid the price, just as much as you're paying the price for taking the path you've chosen.'

'You mean about not having children?'

'That, for sure. But so much more. I left home and went travelling as soon as I was out of my teenage years, and I didn't bother to contact my parents more than twice a year.' Barbara stared at the beer can she was holding in her lap. 'It was only years later I realised how agonising that must have been for them. They didn't deserve it. We wish now we'd put away money for our old age. And because our friends have been spread around the globe we often haven't been there for them when they were in crisis. Some of them have died, and we weren't with them, never said goodbye. We just carried on with our lives.

'And that's the big regrets. Add the countless little ones. Scuba customers who had a bad experience and will never do it again. Meeting people who were plainly in distress and needing help, but pretending I hadn't noticed. Y'know— walking past on the other side.'

'For goodness sake,' Kat said, 'you can't take all that kind of thing on your shoulders, surely?'

'How else can we measure the value of our lives? Me and Tony, I mean. We can't point to the children we've brought up to be good people, or to the business empire we created. We can't flaunt the wealth we've accumulated. All we've got is one apartment, and that was bought with inherited money. So how else can we judge the worth of our lives, except by the way we've touched the lives of other people?'

Tony, now in his shorts, started to bring out an assortment of cold foods for lunch.

'Kat and I have been talking about regrets,' Barbara said, looking up at him.

180

'Oh, those,' Tony said. He laid the food out on the table. 'I notice we're talking more and more about those.'

He brought out some cutlery, and then joined them. 'I have my own way of thinking about regrets.'

'O Wise One, please tell us,' Kat said, and laughed affectionately.

'No, I'm being serious, Kat. Maybe it's obvious, but it is something important.'

Tony slid onto a chair and leaned in towards Kat. He took one of her hands and cupped it between his, looking at her intently as he spoke.

'I've been having such a special day today, and I'm guessing you have too. I think of memories like this as helium balloons attached to our shoulders. We get them in the moments of joy, on those times when we know that others have been helped by our kindness, and when we have been true to ourselves without hurting others. We're lifted up by such memories.

'But, on the other hand, there are all the regrets, and guilts, the moments of stupidity and selfishness. Those are the lead weights on our feet, pulling us down.

'When we're children, unless we're very unlucky, we quickly gather balloons, and float up. Later, as we become adults, we start to accumulate the lead weights. If we're lucky we still have enough balloons to stay afloat.

'But the balloons leak. Our memories of joy, of the special moments, start to fade. We look back and find it harder to recall the good times, the things we have done that make us worthy of love. The lead weights, on the other hand, stay as heavy as ever. So, as we get older, we start to sink. I suspect that, in a way, that's how we become old. And I think that the moment we die inside is when, finally, the memories of joy have gone, and we hit the ground.'

They were home in good time. Barbara insisted that Kat should shower in their flat, and leave her clothes for them to wash, so that Kat didn't take any sand into the apartment. And Barbara oversaw Kat making a dash along the corridor back to her own flat wearing only a borrowed towel, and giggling. Kat got back in time for Mark's call, and his mood was, reassuringly, no different from usual. Afterwards, she went down to the car and cleaned it thoroughly. It seemed they had got away with it.

When Mark arrived home on the following evening, he asked Kat to make him a gin and tonic, and watched her do it.

'You look like you've been out in the sun,' he said.

'Oh, yes,' Kat replied, looking down to check the tonic flowing into the glass. 'It was such a lovely day yesterday that I went to the park after work, and sat in the sun for a while.'

Mark said no more about it until they were having dinner. Kat was eating when she became aware that Mark had stopped, and was watching her.

'What did you wear yesterday?' Mark asked her.

'What a strange question, Mark. I don't know,' she answered, at first picturing the blue t-shirt, still at Barbara's, that she had worn for the journey home. Then she remembered she had spent the morning in a wetsuit.

'For goodness sake, you must know what you wore yesterday.'

'Well, OK, it was just one of my work blouses, I think.'

'Collarless?'

'Yes, collarless.'

'Odd then, isn't it, that you have a tan line around the middle of your neck. And all you did was sit in the park for an hour. Maybe you sat very still, with the shadow of a tree falling in the right place. Oh, and moving very, very slowly to compensate for the changing position of the sun.'

'I've really no idea,' Kat said.

After breakfast the following morning, Mark told Kat that he was going down to fill up the screenwash in his car, and would put some in hers as well. He had never been helpful in that way. As she would tell Barbara later, Kat's first panicky thought was that he was going to look for sand in the car. But, she realised, he had no reason to think he might find any. However, as he went, he picked up a piece of paper and a pen, and stuffed them in his pocket. She sensed that he wanted her to see it.

'I'm sure,' she explained to them, 'that he went to make a note of the car mileage reading. Something there's no way I can disguise. He was letting me know that if I go on any more unauthorised outings, he'll be able to tell.'

Chapter 16

Although Kat could no longer risk driving long distances, Mark's absence during the week meant there was nothing to stop her spending time with Barbara and Tony in their home. On warm summer evenings they went out together, finding the sunshine in local parks or on nearby countryside walks, and usually winding up at a local pub where they could sit and talk as the heat went out of the day.

This pleasant routine continued until the last Thursday in August. The weather had been growing humid and oppressive all day, and it started to rain heavily when Kat left the office, falling in crystal rods that shattered when they hit the ground. Kat protected herself with an umbrella as she hurried from the car into the apartment building, but her feet still got soaked. It had been such a sticky day that she'd worn a short dress to work with neither socks nor tights. She called briefly at her own flat, kicking off her shoes and throwing the umbrella, still opened, into the bath, and then went straight on to see Barbara and Tony.

They were both at home. Barbara was ironing. Tony was in the kitchen making a salad. They had pushed open the living room windows as far as possible, and the flat was full of the sound of rain falling onto the car park below, water gurgling as it fell through a downpipe outside.

Tony insisted that the salad was intended for the three of them, so she stayed and ate. The sky was so dark that they

184

turned on lights and closed the windows to lessen the noise of the rain.

Kat decided, at about seven, that she should go home to carry out her Thursday evening duties—to restore the apartment in readiness for Mark's return the next day. She walked along the corridor in her bare feet, and opened the door; and saw Mark stood by the window, his arms folded.

'Where the fuck have you been?'

It was the voice of a parent shaking with anger, a stern father already considering the punishment due. As Kat faced him, her mind was imagining the apartment as she had left it, with unwashed dishes, the bed unmade. She thought she might have left an academic book lying on the duvet. And the vibrator? Still in the bed?

'I'm sorry, Mark. You hadn't told me you'd be back today.'

'I bet you're sorry. Obviously, I've been far too predictable. And I'm still waiting to hear where you've been.'

Kat looked beyond her husband to the still-falling rain, and realised her choice of lies was very limited.

'Take care,' he said, as she looked at him, uncertain of what to say. 'I've been here more than an hour. And your car has been parked outside the whole time. And anyway, I can see you haven't been outside in this weather. What the hell have been doing, wandering around half dressed like that?'

Before she could react, Mark had stepped across the room to her and pulled up the hem of her dress. 'Surprised you even bothered to put your knickers back on.'

He let go of her dress, but stayed where he was, close in front of her. He was so furious that she could feel him breathing fast, snorting the air into her face. 'So who are you fucking when my back is turned? Or is it some lesbian bitch?'

Kat twisted her head away. 'For goodness sake, Mark, it's nothing like that.'

She needed this to end, even if it meant sacrifices. 'I've been round at some of our neighbours. A couple. Completely harmless, lovely people. I've been on my own a lot, and it's been good to have some friendly people to talk to sometimes.'

'So where are these lovely, harmless people? Which apartment? And what are their names?'

She told him. He picked up his shoes and put them on. 'OK, I'm going to see whether this lovely couple exists. Wait.'

Mark left. Kat sat uneasily on a dining chair, her heart pumping.

Tony, calling out from the sofa as Barbara opened the door, greeted Mark as 'fair Aphrodite'. It is not certain whether Mark heard him. Fortunately, they immediately guessed who their visitor was, and were welcoming. Mark, though plainly surprised that Kat had been telling the truth, also recovered quickly.

Ten minutes later, he was back home. Kat, by then, was busy tidying.

'I've invited them for dinner,' Mark said. 'Saturday night, seven-thirty. Now please get me a G&T.'

Kat brought the drink to him as he sat on the sofa. She had made one for herself, but didn't want to sit down with him, so again perched on a seat at the dining table.

'I'm sorry,' he said after a long silence. 'I was just worried and confused when your car was here, but you weren't. It's been a long, hard week.'

'Problems?' Kat asked, in her best loving-and-supportive-wife voice.

'Not problems, exactly. Just a lot of politics. We're being taken over. Some streamlining going on, people being asked to clear their desks, that sort of thing.'

'God', Kat said, 'sounds dreadful. But what about you?'

'You don't need to worry about me,' Mark replied, sitting back, 'there's always opportunities for people who know how to grasp them. And I'm one of those people. They're making me Director of Development. Got a meeting in the morning to thrash out the details. That's why I came home tonight.'

***

Barbara and Tony took care to arrive on time on the Saturday evening. Kat had popped round the previous morning, while Mark had been at his meeting, but only Barbara was at home. She had assured Kat that they were both relaxed about the dinner invitation. Now, as Kat opened the door to them, Tony looked ill at ease.

Mark was standing behind her. 'Hello again!' he said, with improbable bonhomie, and shook them both by the hand. 'I was going to offer to take your coats, but you haven't travelled far, have you!'

He called to Kat. 'How's the food coming on, darling? Ready to eat yet?'

'Whenever we're ready.'

'Then why don't we go to the table now?' Returning from the kitchen, Mark opened his arms as if to sweep Barbara and Tony to their seats.

Kat had wanted to serve good food for her friends, but without fussing, so she settled on coq au vin, and a salmon terrine starter that she could serve in a way that would bring a little pizazz. Now she needed to hurry to the kitchen to plate it up. Conversation at the table was proceeding pleasantly, though it seemed only Mark and Tony were talking. Kat realised, when she came out of the kitchen with the first course, that Mark had placed Tony opposite himself. Barbara, next to Tony, was already being sidelined. Kat handed one of the starters to Barbara, who mouthed back, 'Thank you, Kat. Looks lovely!' It was an affirmation of solidarity.

An opening exchange about the weather had been completed. Now Mark invited Tony and Barbara to talk about their lives, showing an interest in other people that Kat had never seen before. He was apparently trying put his guests at ease. It was working, too. First, Tony outlined the itinerant lives they had led. Then, when he saw Mark looking fascinated, he started sharing stories about their lives abroad. Dining table anecdotes were not Tony's forte, but—with Barbara's prompting—he fell into telling tales about foolish scuba customers and awkward conversations with immigration agents. Mark guffawed over each story. Thus encouraged, Tony moved on to racier tales of misplaced bikinis and beach parties that got out of control.

Then Mexico was mentioned, and Mark grasped it, with an ostentatiously loving glance at Kat, to describe their honeymoon. He had redirected the conversation, leaving Tony adrift and exposed. Barbara, out of kindness, completed the transfer with a question about Mark's work.

Kat noticed, during the lengthy account that followed, that Mark identified entirely with his organisation. *We*, he explained, *help children who have special needs*, and *we work with them both in the community and in our residential schools and home*s. As far as Kat knew, he might never see a child with special needs from one month to the next, and never worked with any of them.

He went on to tell the guests that he had a new role as Director of Development. The day before, he had told Kat—

reciting the job description verbatim—that his new role was to *ensure the rapid growth of the organisation by seeking out new business, whether in new markets or by taking business from competitor organisations*. Now, as he explained it to his guests at the dinner table, his job was to *find ways we can help more troubled and needy children*.

By then the starter was finished. As soon as Kat began to collect up the plates, Barbara was on her feet and helping.

'Going OK, isn't it?' Barbara whispered, once they were in the kitchen.

'Yes, so far,' Kat whispered back, 'but I think he's up to something. Not acting normal at all. Tony needs to be careful.'

As the women carried in the main course, Tony was congratulating Mark. 'All credit to you,' he said. 'It's obviously important work. And you've done really well to achieve a directorship at your age.'

'It's only a matter of putting in the effort,' Mark responded.

Conversation at the table became fractured as the main course was served and eaten. Afterwards, Mark glanced up at Tony.

'So, Tony, you and Barbara have had lots of good times, but did you never think of making more of your lives?'

Kat and Barbara frowned at each other. Tony, however, seemed to be taking the question at face value, thinking on his reply as he chewed a mouthful of food.

'Well,' he said, pausing again to wipe his lips with a napkin, 'I think it's all bound up with my father. Born into a poor working-class family, he discovered he had a flair for numbers. There wasn't any university or college option for him, but by sheer hard graft he managed to become an accountant, and eventually had his own business.'

'That's what I was saying earlier,' Mark interjected. 'It's only a question of putting in the effort.'

'I'm not sure it's quite as simple as that. But anyway, I've always respected him for achieving what he did. The thing is, though, that he was an incredibly dull man, and he lived a terribly dull life. A short, dumpy man with a moustache that was always carefully trimmed. Everything done to a strict routine. Meal on the table for six o'clock, fish on Fridays, church on Sundays. And so out of touch with his feelings that he didn't know what the word meant. He may have loved my mother, but you'd never have known it, and I suspect she was a very lonely woman. In the whole of my life, I never felt any real, honest affection from him.'

'He showed you love through the medium of money,' Barbara commented.

'So how does this connect with your own life choices?' Mark asked.

'Put simply, I wanted to be different from him. I don't only mean a different kind of life from his. I wanted to be a different kind of man.'

Kat listened to Tony developing his theme. He had taken a dive into his inner world. She had heard him talk on this subject before. This sort of conversation was ordinary at Number 57, but here, with Mark present, it seemed exciting and risky—as if allowing an outsider into a secret club. But where was the harm, when Mark was outnumbered three to one? He might even learn from it.

Tony continued with his monologue, indifferent to all the conventions of dinner party conversations. Moving away from his own psychology, he set out his view that real gender equality calls for changes in male identity and consciousness at the most fundamental levels. He told Mark how he had been working to achieve this change in himself for over three decades, but still needed to be guided and corrected by Barbara. 'Possibly,' he said, 'the young people who grow up in the new millennium won't have this baggage, but older men—you and me, Mark—we'll always be struggling to exorcise it from our hearts and minds.

'The other thing,' Tony went on, 'is that it's such a tragic irony. We're the oppressors, and yet we're missing out on something really precious. In terms of basic equality, where the currency is power, then of course we men have benefited enormously from patriarchy, and women have had to fight to take the power away from us. But at this other, deeper level, men have been the losers.

'I mean, take these two wonderful women sat next to us while I prattle on.' He waved a hand towards Barbara and Kat. 'I know they have ways of communicating, of cherishing each other, of standing in solidarity with each other, that are completely unknown to most men. And it's something that most women do without even thinking about it. It's like the old biblical story of the Egyptians and the Jews. The Egyptians were the oppressors, but it was the Jews, oppressed though they were, who carried a special knowledge that sustained them and bound them together. Instead of learning from them, the Egyptians feared them and killed them. I believe it's the same with men and women.

'OK, sorry everyone. I'll stop. But Mark, you're a bright and educated guy. You must have that same sense that, notwithstanding the need for women's equality, men could gain so much by learning from women.'

Mark looked at him coldly. 'Actually, Tony, I don't.' He sat back in his chair. 'What I do see is that you're the only one of us who hasn't finishing eating.'

191

Tony looked down at his plate. He still had a fork in his hand, but dropped it next to the unfinished food on the plate. He looked across at Kat and muttered 'Sorry.'

Barbara and Kat cleared the table in silence, and returned from the kitchen with a supermarket cheesecake. Kat was now glad she hadn't bothered to make a dessert. She was hoping Tony would let the subject drop. He didn't.

'Come on, Mark. Are you telling me that nothing in what I said has any resonance with you at all?'

Kat cut the cheesecake into wedges and silently pushed it to the middle of the table.

'Well,' Mark said, extracting a wedge onto his plate, 'if you insist on pursuing this, Tony, the answer is no. It doesn't resonate at all. Or make much sense. My organisation has a strong equal opportunities policy, which of course I support. But you seem to be arguing that I should turn myself into a woman, and I don't want to. I love my wife. She's a woman. I'm a man. I wouldn't have it any other way. And I've not the slightest idea what the Egyptians have to do with it.'

Kat wanted to intervene, but hesitated for fear she would been seen to be taking sides. Barbara started to ask Mark about his leisure interests, but Tony would not be deflected.

'Sorry Babs, my love,' he said, waving his spoon, 'but I want to take Mark up on what he just said.' The spoon swung to point at Mark. 'You see, Mark, you just said it yourself. You're a man, Kat is a woman. You acknowledge that you're different in a fundamental way. Don't you sense that Kat, as a woman, is able to express herself—to be *in the world*—in a way that remains hidden and unexpressed in yourself? The feminine that rests inside your masculine, one might say.'

Mark laughed in contempt. 'No offence, Tony, but I think you're spouting a load of hippie nonsense. Yes, of course there's differences between men and women. After all those depraved beachside parties, you should know that better than me. It's also obvious that Kat and I are different people— different skills, different personality traits. But the whole point of equal opportunities—as we go to so much trouble to teach it to our staff—is to stop making generalisations. Yet here you are, posing as Mister Politically Correct while making the most ridiculous sweeping statements.'

Tony was about to speak again.

Barbara got there first. 'Tell us more about the new job, Mark. Will you be based here, or will the two of you be needing to move?'

Mark turned to Barbara, but Kat could see he still had that coldness, the suppressed temper, that she knew so well. He wasn't done yet.

'I'll be travelling quite a lot,' Mark said, 'as I'll have national responsibilities. But no more weeks away. I've obviously been doing that far too much.' He paused, leaving time for his point to be understood.

'But I'm thinking we might move house soon. I expect that one day we'll have children, and we'll need somewhere bigger and better than this place.'

Kat took care not to show any reaction. This prediction, without a timescale, was nothing new. He was playing to his new audience, not her.

'So, you and Tony have never had children, I gather?'

Barbara mistook this for a straightforward question, and started on the explanation Kat had heard from Tony about her difficulties in conceiving, about the possibility they should have tried earlier. 'Of course,' she said, if I'd become pregnant, we would have come back to England, or settled somewhere, at least for a few years.'

'Really?' Mark asked. 'I'd have thought you'd have carried the thing on your back until it was old enough to go scuba diving on its own.' He snorted at his own joke.

Barbara pressed on with the standard account. 'We made some enquiries about adoption, but it was soon obvious we didn't meet the requirements.'

'Christ no!' Mark guffawed. 'I'm sure you didn't. Adoption is not my area, but I'd say the agencies would have run a mile when they saw you two coming. More than that,' he went on, 'I'd say nature did us all a favour by preventing you from having children, not least the sprog that was saved from having you for parents.'

Barbara stopped talking.

Unchallenged, Mark continued. 'In fact, I'd say that you're two of the most feckless, idle, selfish people I've ever met. Well, OK, I've come across worse in the lower classes, but they're too thick to know any better. You two, though, purport to be educated middle-class people. You had it all going for you, yet you've frittered your lives away in total self-indulgence, trying to justify yourselves with hippy mumbo-jumbo nonsense. Bet you didn't even pay taxes when you could avoid it. And now you've come home and expect British taxpayers to look after you in your old age. Worst of all, you fucking chose—with daddy's help—to move in next to us.'

Kat said, 'Shall I get some coffees?'

'No,' Mark responded. 'I don't think the meal extends to coffees.'

Barbara put her head down. Tony kept switching his glance between Mark and Kat, looking to Kat for guidance.

Barbara, a tissue held to her nose, reached with her other hand to Tony. 'Come on, Tone, leave it alone. Let's go.'

Eulogy for Love

'Before you go,' Mark said, 'I want there to be a clear understanding. I don't like people like you. I don't want to have any further contact with you. And I don't want you to have any contact of any sort with my wife. Please don't give me that crap about her right to choose. When people like you have a bad influence on her, it affects Kat, and that affects my relationship with Kat. So I have rights in this as well.'

Mark went to the door, held it open, and looked pointedly at Barbara and Tony. They got up, and walked through the door into the corridor beyond, Tony's hand round Barbara's waist, as if supporting her. Mark closed the door behind them.

'I'll have that coffee now, please.'

Kat was standing at the table, staring across the room away from him. 'I'm absolutely speechless about what you've just done,' she said, without turning around.

'That's good. Then don't say anything.'

'How could you be so cruel to them? Lovely, harmless people.'

'Alright, I'll make a cafetière myself. Then you can have some if you want it.'

Mark went into the kitchen. She left the dining table, uncleared, and sat on the sofa.

At that moment she was close to leaving him. She already knew he could be cruel and condescending, but not to the depths of nastiness on display that evening. If she could not do it for herself, she felt she might have to leave him simply to honour her friendship with Tony and Barbara.

Kat remained silent on the sofa. Mark cleared the table, drank his coffee, and then announced he was going to bed. Kat refused to speak to him.

'Y'know,' he said, pausing as he was about to head into the bedroom, 'you need to learn a lesson from this.' Kat refused to look at him. 'This happened,' he continued, 'because you started making friends without telling me. In future, we'll choose our friends together. I know you liked them, but they're really not our kind of people. So no more secret friends, OK?'

Kat remained on the sofa. She had no wish to share a bed with him. After a while she turned on the TV and flicked between channels. When she reckoned he must have gone to sleep, she found her phone and risked texting Barbara:

So desperately sorry about 2night. Had no idea he was going to do that. Xxx

A reply came immediately:

Course you didnt. Dont worry—we r OK. Take care of yourself, plse. Talk when things have settled. xxx

Half an hour later, Mark came out of the bedroom, and stood in front of her wearing only his underpants.

'I do wish you'd come to bed, Kat. You can't sit there all night. And I wanted to talk to you.'

'About what?'

'Come to bed and I'll tell you. Nice things.'

'Tell me first.'

'OK.' He paused, waiting until she looked up at him. 'Now that I have a job on a much better salary, I thought we could start looking for a house. And on the basis that we'll have moved into the house by the start of next year, I thought we might set about getting you pregnant. I don't mean tonight—but, y'know, when you've stopped the pill.'

***

On the Monday, Mark texted Kat at work to ask whether she could be sure to be home by five on the Thursday afternoon. He wanted, he said, to have an electrician round to do a small job. She had no reason to disagree.

The electrician standing at her door on Thursday afternoon was wearing blue overalls with *ST Security Services* embroidered on the chest. He introduced himself as Simon Taylor, and Kat figured he was not from a company with global reach.

Once inside, the man explained that he was there to install a security camera at the door. Mark had never suggested that there was a need for one of these, so Kat was surprised; but she left the man to get on with his work at the doorway while she started preparing dinner. After only a short time, and some brief noisy drilling, he came over to the kitchen to say he had finished. She went to see what he had installed. He pointed to a small camera outside in the corridor, attached to the wall near one corner of the door; and a cable running inside to a video recorder on a bookshelf close by. This system, he said, would continuously record the view from the camera, and the recording could be viewed either on the small integrated screen, or via the VHS recorder connected to the TV.

Kat went out to look at the camera, and saw that its position to one side of the door meant that it looked at an angle, not only covering the door but the view along the corridor.

'Wouldn't it have been better,' Kat said, staring up at it, 'to put it the other side, so that it showed the view towards the lift?'

'Ah,' the man said, 'your husband said you might ask about that. But he was very clear he wanted it this side, where it is.'

To make sure she was right, Kat went back inside, and looked at the image being displayed on the screen of the recorder. As she suspected, it showed a view that extended along the corridor, and included the door to Tony and Barbara's apartment. Mark had put them all under surveillance.

***

Kat found satisfaction by defying her husband, and contrived to see Barbara and Tony again; but the pleasure was not the same. They had to meet in pubs or cafés, or walk together in a park when the autumn days were dry. Even though they chose the meetings in places where they were unlikely to be seen by people they knew, it always felt furtive, and Kat would worry about getting home before Mark returned.

Kat also knew, though they talked very little about Mark, that Barbara and Tony were saddened that she remained with him. Indeed, it was the absence of discussion on this topic that spoke so loudly about their disappointment and concern. It was also apparent that Tony and Barbara had been disappointed by England. As they sat together in a little café, the windows misting up against the chill October air, Tony and Barbara told her they had decided to head to Thailand for the winter. They would put most of their possessions back into storage, and rent the flat.

They left on a bright, frosty morning in November. Kat, after deciding that, for once, she didn't give a damn about being late for work, drove them to the railway station where they would catch a train for the airport. She pulled up the car in a waiting area, and offloaded their bags.

'God,' Tony said, 'I won't miss this cold.'

'But we'll miss *you* terribly, Kat,' Barbara said, as she stepped forward to hug her.

'As I will miss you,' Kat answered. 'You've become so important to me over these last months.'

Barbara released her, and Kat turned to Tony. He reached out and took her hands.

'Do you know something, Kat?' he said.

'Tell me, O Wise One,' Kat answered with a smile that made the tears run down to her cheeks.

'Nothing wise this time, my love. Just a simple truth.' He gripped her hands tightly, pulling her closer. 'In case you haven't realised, you've become the daughter we never had. And now we're doing what all parents have to do, sooner or later—letting their child go free. But we're having to let you go when we've barely got to know you. It's terribly, terribly hard.'

Kat could see he was about to cry. But he leaned into her, held her for a moment, and then kissed her slowly, softly, on her cheek. 'Look after yourself, Kat,' he whispered into her ear, 'and find the happiness you deserve.'

Then, quickly, Barbara and Tony collected up their bags and walked away, turning just once to wave as they walked through the station entrance. Kat, forlorn, waved back, but too late for them to see.

Chapter 17

Kat had once imagined that she would be impregnated in romantic circumstances, perhaps lying on silk sheets in a bedroom suffused with rich perfumes and the warm light of candles. It would never happen that way with Mark. As a gesture, on the evening when she calculated she had ovulated, she put on a short dress and some make-up. She made a meal she knew he would like, and found a battered candle at the back of a cupboard to put on the table.

'What's this about?' he said, when he got home.

'I'm hoping we might make a baby tonight.'

He dropped his briefcase, and went to shower and change, as he always did.

When they went to bed he took advantage of her offer, but followed his usual routine. Kat tried to focus on the biology—that, after all, was what mattered—and not store any images that she would forever associate with her future child. When he had finished and fallen, panting, to his side of the bed, she quickly turned onto her back and lifted her hips to encourage conception.

It was all in vain, that month. The next month she didn't bother with the dinner or the dress, instead using more direct methods, once they were in bed, to get him in the mood. This time it worked. By Christmas she knew that, all being well, they would have a summer baby.

It was clear, as soon as the housing market became active in the New Year, that they would be able to sell the apartment without difficulty. Mark took it on himself to start searching for their next home, using criteria he did not explain to Kat. She was only allowed to view the properties he had shortlisted. It was obvious that they were going to take a large step upmarket, which she imagined would require more family money as well as a large mortgage.

They moved in March to their new home, a double-fronted Georgian house on a street where all the properties sat behind long gardens and well-tended shrubbery. It was in good condition, but Kat had not foreseen how much more work would be required simply to maintain a property of this size. Mark was immersed in his work, and expected her to act as estate manager, strictly following his instructions. If she used her initiative, he would almost always find fault. Sometimes he found fault, and shouted at her, even when she had done exactly what he had told her to do.

Mark's organisation was constantly in crisis after being taken over by a holding company. Sometimes when he came home, he was so stressed that he could barely speak. He would sit down to dinner and stare at the food, the muscles in his face pulsing slowly as he clenched and unclenched his jaw. It made Kat frightened to see him like that, a bomb that might explode unless touched with extreme care. She tried, where she could, to help him relax, by encouraging him to go for a run or at least making him a drink. If necessary, she would fellate him, which seemed to work, but she hated doing it. There was violence in the way he used her, often holding her head as he came. It was as if he were offloading the poison he had brought back from work, venting it into her mouth.

When he did talk about work, he told tales of conspiracies between board members, of managers being fired and made to leave immediately. As Director of Development, he fretted about meeting his targets. Capacity, he said, was growing at a satisfactory pace across all the regions, but units were lagging behind. She had to ask him, one evening as they sat eating, to explain what *units* were.

'Units are kids,' he said. 'Or, strictly speaking, they're child-nights. The number of places that are occupied by a child on a particular night. The number that are generating income.'

'God, that sounds so cold-blooded. What happened to the idea of helping children in difficulty?'

'Oh, the helping bit. That's done by people further down the organisation. They're the ones who worry about outcomes and regulations, all that stuff.'

'So the children are not your concern, except as bodies in beds?' Kat asked.

Mark caught her frowning. 'Don't go all sanctimonious on me,' he said. 'It's just a fact of life. We're owned by a holding company. They don't give a damn what we do, just as long as we bring in the money. Most of their companies are in the hotel and tourist sectors, so that's how they think. Bums on beds. Doesn't matter whose bum it is.'

'But you can care, surely?'

'Caring is a luxury I can't afford. We're a private company, and it's our job to make money for the holding company. To maximise profit. And what do you think they do if they reckon we're not doing our job well enough? Eh? Do you think they come and help us do things better? Like hell they do. They just fire the manager they reckon is to blame. Tomorrow that could be me.'

'Poor dear,' Kat said, wanting to calm him. 'It sounds awful. I don't understand why it has to be like that.'

'You mean why it isn't all cosy, like it is at your place. I'd like to point out that we've expanded fifteen percent, year on year, for the last three years, while you lot haven't grown at all. And every March you reach the end of the year struggling to balance the books. And the staff get paid fucking peanuts.'

Kat could see where he was heading, and decided to get there first.

'Yes, darling, I know. It's thanks to you that we live as well as we do.'

'Good,' he said, picking up his fork and stabbing his steak. 'Make sure you remember that.'

***

Although Kat, now pregnant, had got what she had so much wanted, the morning sickness in the first months was so unpleasant that she rarely managed to enjoy the journey she had just begun. Then, as winter ended and the days grew longer, she entered the quiet second semester, and felt a deep contentment. Not yet fulfilment, but a confidence that she was travelling towards the realisation of herself as a woman. She liked to look at herself each day, naked in the mirror, lifting her enlarging breasts with gentle amusement, turning sideways to assess the growth of her bump. She only did it when Mark was not around. She could tell he found her newly emphatic womanhood distasteful, but she did not care. Sometimes he still needed stress relief after work, but at bedtime he ceased to make any requests, which she found liberating. And whereas Mark was not interested in the development of his own child, the women in Kat's office fussed over her, and were excited to feel her bump when Baby started to move.

They took an early holiday. Kat did not want to fly, so in May they drove to South Wales and stayed in a cottage on the coast. Large windows at the cottage provided views across farmland to the sea. Mark went off for much of the time, hiking and visiting castles, leaving Kat to look out of the windows and learn, clumsily, to knit baby clothes. She found a lonely contentment.

Then Kat was into the last semester: the weeks of waddling in the daytime and playing the beached whale at night; of breasts that were anticipating their new role; and the sense each morning that a different life might begin before bedtime. Fortunately, the weather was cool for August. She passed her due date but then, one morning after Mark had left for a meeting seventy miles away, she could feel the baby was on its way. She texted Mark to come home, but he presumed he could safely finish his meeting, and before he returned she had been forced to call an ambulance.

He arrived at the hospital half an hour before the birth. As far as Kat was concerned, he might as well not have bothered. He had only attended one antenatal class, and had forgotten what little he had learned, and now behaved like an am-dram actor forced to ham it up on first night because he had never come to rehearsals. Kat could tell, afterwards, that he was furious because he had looked inept in front of the hospital staff. That evening, she did not care. She lay, sore, exhausted, and fulfilled, with baby Jonathan asleep in the Perspex cot next to her bed.

Once the initial euphoria had passed, and she was settling into the new life at home, Kat discovered that her feelings were more complex. She adored the baby. When he was at her breast, or sleeping, she would gaze down at him and be amazed that her own body had produced this perfect being. At the same time, she felt a sadness. It was as if something had been taken from her; as if the bright flame of her own vital energy had been passed to the baby, a dark cave left within herself.

204

Eulogy for Love

***

Kat was now on maternity leave, and Mark took this to mean that she had total responsibility for all domestic duties, and for all the baby's needs; or, more to the point, that he was now at liberty to disengage entirely from life at home. For the first three nights he scowled and puffed when she put the bedside light on to tend to Jonathan. On the fourth night, when Jonathan cried out, he gruffly announced that he had an important meeting in the morning, and went to the guest room. Within two weeks of the baby's arrival, Mark had simplified the arrangement and went straight to the guest room at bedtime. It would be four months before he next slept in her bed.

It seemed that he had taken his sexual urges with him, because he stopped making any demands on Kat. It was no surprise. She noticed that he avoided going in the bathroom or bedroom when she was also there, undressed. She could tell he tried not to look closely when she was feeding Jonathan, and sensed it was not merely awkwardness, but distaste.

Kat would have been glad of some reassurance that she was still an attractive woman, but it was a long time since she had hoped for that from Mark. On the whole, Mark's disengagement suited her well. It left her in peace in the night in the companionship of her baby, singing and cooing over him as she changed him, and sleepily watching him as he suckled, his cheek caught by the warm light and long shadows of the bedside lamp. She would get up late, after Mark had left for work, and not see him until evening. Her days, especially as autumn drew in, were mostly spent alone in the house with Jonathan, doing household chores in the times that he was settled. It was a quiet, introspective way of life, but she avoided loneliness by meeting up with mums she had met at the antenatal classes, dropping into the charity offices where her women colleagues would reliably fuss over the baby, and—occasionally—driving over to see her father.

This gentle routine was interrupted when Christmas arrived. Mark was off work for a week, with the consequence that the two of them spent more time together than felt comfortable. Christmas Day was an empty ritual. He gave her extravagant gifts—a Cartier watch, a necklace with diamonds. They felt to Kat like payments, and she accepted them in that spirit. The two of them spent much of the afternoon and evening watching television. Kat let Mark choose what to watch, so the day was mostly good tempered, though he was annoyed when she read a magazine during the Queen's Speech. At bedtime he went, as usual, to the guestroom.

The following day, Boxing Day, Charles and Peggy came to stay. They had identified a village close to their route with a hunt that still followed the tradition of running with the hounds on Boxing Day. This was the last Christmas before fox hunting would be made illegal in England, so these events were now gatherings of the gentry to lament the loss of rural tradition. Charles and Peggy, though not members of the gentry and entirely ignorant of rural traditions, attended as an act of bourgeois solidarity.

As a consequence, Charles and Peggy did not arrive until two in the afternoon. In the spaces that the baby allowed, Kat prepared a roast chicken lunch, set a fire in the living room, and made up a bed for the guests. Mark was persuaded to peel potatoes. In the new house there was a decent dining area in the kitchen, and they had filled it with a solid pine table. Kat decided that, for simplicity, they would eat lunch there.

Jonathan, upstairs, obligingly slept while they ate lunch. It was only as Kat served the Christmas pudding that she heard Jonathan gurgling over the monitor. She left the other three at the table and went to see him. He had now learned to smile when he saw her. Kat took him out of his cot and changed his nappy, making faces and silly noises at him to win smiles in return. Once he was dry and tidy, she sat down on the bed, intending to feed him.

She changed her mind. Although Kat had no wish to sit with them in the kitchen—and in any case the men would behave awkwardly if she fed the baby in front of them—she felt disinclined to be banished from the ground floor. So, baby in her arms, she padded down the stairs in her slippers, went past the half open kitchen door, and entered the dining room. The room had a deep bay window, and in it a high-backed armchair that faced over the front lawn to the street. Kat liked to sit there sometimes, watching the birds. By now it was late afternoon, and darkness was falling rapidly. In the street beyond the garden, the cars passing noiselessly were already using their headlights.

Kat had no need of lighting. She settled in the armchair, pushed aside her blouse, opened her bra, and sat contentedly in the gloom as Jonathan fed.

Kat realised she could hear fragments of the conversation in the kitchen. The only voices were male. She could also hear plates and cutlery being moved. She guessed that Peggy was washing up but had chosen, in her customary style, to eschew the dishwasher and instead wash each item by hand.

Kat could hear enough of the conversation to recognise that they were talking about a party to celebrate Charles' retirement in March. Charles had decided that the occasion called for more than the customary bash laid on by his employers, and attended by the staff team at the London office. He wanted something larger—an occasion that would reunite him with colleagues past and present, as well as family and personal friends. The date and venue had been decided, and it was now only a matter of finalising the programme for the evening, and the invitation list. These were the matters being discussed in the kitchen.

The conversation stopped for a moment. There was the sounding of scraping chair legs as someone stood up, then the bang of a cupboard door. 'Damn,' she heard Mark say. Then, 'Not to worry—there'll be another bottle in the dining sideboard.'

A slight increase in the glow of light from the kitchen indicated that Mark had pushed open the door. Charles called after him. 'Hold on, Mark.' He also got up from his chair, catching up with Mark in the dining room doorway. Mark had his hand on the light switch, but did not press it.

'Son,' Charles said in a low voice, 'I just wanted to have an extra word with you, away from Peggy. Kat's upstairs with the baby, I take it?'

'Yes, she must be.'

'Good. I just wanted to say quietly to you that I'd much prefer not to have any mewling and puking babies at the dinner.'

'Jonathan, you mean?' Charles must have nodded. 'I'm sure that could be arranged,' Mark said. 'But you realise that means Kat won't be there either?'

'To be candid, Son, I don't think that would be a great loss. I'm not saying I don't like her—we've talked about this before. It's just that I see this as an occasion for family.'

'Technically, Dad, she is family.' Mark sounded as if he were correcting Charles simply on a point of fact.

'Yes, of course she is, technically. But you know what I mean. She's not real family. She's not kin, not our lot.'

'Will you say the same to Thomas about Tina and his kids?'

Eulogy for Love

'I fear it may be more difficult to argue the case, given that the boys are older, but I'm planning to give it a try. It's the same principle. It's strange how you both chose to marry down. Not that I'm judging you. They're pretty girls, or at least they were, and they've turned out to be good breeding stock. But—well, you know what I mean, don't you? On this sort of occasion, they don't belong.'

'Understood. I'll talk to Kat about it. Sure it won't be a problem.'

'Thanks, Son,' Charles said. 'I was certain you'd understand.' He turned and went back to the kitchen. Mark flicked the light switch and headed towards the sideboard. Jonathan, deeply asleep in Kat's arms, was startled awake by the bright light, and drew in breath sharply, causing a little sound like a snore. It was enough to make Mark look up. He saw Kat in the armchair. She did not turn around to look back at him, but she could tell he had seen her. Mark reacted by ignoring her entirely. He grabbed a bottle of single malt from the cupboard, and left. He even turned off the light as he went.

After a while Kat went back to the kitchen, and sat at the table, cuddling Jonathan. Peggy was still washing and drying the dishes one at a time. The men talked on, ignoring Kat. After a few more minutes she left and went to watch television.

Mark and Kat never spoke directly about the conversation she had overhead in the dining room. From then on, however, there was an understanding that she would not be attending Charles' retirement dinner.

***

Charles and Peggy left the following morning. Mark and Kat faced another seven days before he would return to work.

It was not going to be easy for either of them to be so much in each other's company, but it was Mark who grew increasingly restless and irritable as the days passed. They tried going out together, for walks and a pub lunch, with Jonathan in a baby carrier, all of which seemed pleasant enough to Kat. She also encouraged Mark to go to the gym, and didn't complain when he shut himself away in his study. Yet nothing seemed to lighten his mood.

On the Friday, New Year's Eve, they agreed not to stay up until midnight, and went early to their separate rooms. Kat had already put Jonathan down to sleep in his cot by the bed, so she read for a few minutes and then turned the light off. She was very nearly asleep when she felt Mark get into bed at her back. He spooned into her, close enough for her to know what he wanted. Then he put an arm over her waist and reached between her legs.

'I need you,' he said. The tone made it clear that the need was purely physical.

She lifted her leg to let him in. 'Alright,' she said, 'but please be gentle. It's been a very long time.'

It was now almost three months since the baby. Kat was beginning to sense her physical sexuality returning. It had come gently, sometimes, when she was feeding Jonathan, but she had no idea how her body would respond to Mark's intrusion. She felt apprehensive. She imagined she must also be very dry, but Mark had learned, long ago, how to shortcut that problem. He spat on his hand, and then applied it as a lubricant.

There was no pain, she was relieved to discover, but there was no pleasure either. She was entirely passive, unresisting, waiting for him to finish his business inside her. He got into his rhythm, and she felt hopeful that, after so long without sex, he would climax quickly.

Eulogy for Love

It did not happen. After several minutes of thrusting, he started to grow tired. 'I need you on your knees,' he said, panting into her ear. Kat knew this routine well, and obliged. He knelt behind her and entered her again. He was now able to go much deeper, and she waited once more for it to hurt. It did not. She thought that, perhaps, her body was responding, even though she was emotionally distant.

Mark was in the position he liked best, and thrusting with persistence. Kat, her eyes closed and her head pressed into a pillow, waited for that familiar and welcome moment when the thrusts would be replaced by spasms and grunts. Instead he slowed, and withdrew from her. She felt his finger against her anus, and then suddenly, shockingly, she felt the finger pushing its way in. This had never been part of their sex life. Occasionally he would touch it, as if intrigued; but he had never asked for more, and she had certainly never invited it.

She lifted her head from the pillow. 'What are you doing?' He said nothing, but moved the finger back and forth a few times before removing it. She briefly thought that was the end of it, until she heard him spit. He was motionless as he attended to himself. Then Kat felt him pushing again. This time it was not a finger. For a moment she thought he wouldn't get in; but then he forced her open, holding her hips so that she could not twist away. A deep aching pain emanated in waves as the muscles were violently forced apart, and it was followed immediately by sharp stinging pains as the delicate skin was torn.

Kat cried out uncontrollably. The baby woke, and cried out as well. Somewhere within Kat, below the layer of pain, there was a frightened yet still rational woman who recorded what was happening to her. Mark was indifferent to the cries of his wife and baby son, apparently only concerned to complete his invasion. He seemed to be succeeding, though she didn't know whether the lubricant was spit, or blood, or shit. She only wanted it over, so that she could comfort her baby. She leaned forward and screamed into the pillow.

He only managed short, slow movements inside her, but evidently it did what he needed it to do. She felt him jerk to completion. Then he pulled himself out, causing her a last soprano chorus of pain. He got off the bed and left the room.

Kat, still kneeling, crawled across the bed to the cot and scooped up Jonathan. Holding on to him, she cautiously turned over, then lowered herself onto the bed so that she could sit against the headboard. She gave her breast to Jonathan. She watched him suckle, and wept tears of anger and humiliation. She had no real sense of the physical state she had been left in, but, in her imagination, Mark had speared a raw, dirty hole into her that would never close.

After a while, Jonathan let her nipple fall from his mouth as he slept, and Kat nodded off where she lay. An hour later she stirred and lowered Jonathan into his cot. She went to the bathroom, cleaned herself as much as she could without taking a shower. She took some painkillers, put on some pants. Then she attempted to sleep again, though for some hours without success.

Kat stayed upstairs for a long time in the morning. She bathed Jonathan, and made him sweet-smelling, and showered herself when he gave her the opportunity. Eventually, once fed, he fell asleep in the cot, and she came downstairs in a tightly wrapped dressing gown.

Mark was at the kitchen table with a mug of coffee, reading an out-of-date newspaper. 'Happy New Year,' he said, before looking up. Kat walked slowly, gingerly, towards the kettle. It didn't make any difference to her soreness, but she wanted him to know she was hurting.

Eulogy for Love

He watched her over the rim of the newspaper. 'You alright?' he asked, lightly.

'What do you fucking think?'

'I don't know. What should I think?'

'You hurt me, Mark. Right now, I don't feel I'll ever be the same again.'

'Oh that,' he said, closing the newspaper. 'I'm sorry, but it wasn't working for me, you know . . . the other way.'

How telling, Kat thought as she filled the kettle, that after all this time together they still had no intimate language of their own.

'I think you're. . .'—he was searching for words again— '. . . a bit looser since the baby.'

She turned round to him. 'That's as maybe. But it doesn't entitle you to fuck me in the arse.'

He winced disapprovingly at the language. 'Plenty of couples do it, I understand—and enjoy it, too.'

'Maybe they do. But they do it with care and kindness. And, for God's sake, with consent!'

'Well, I'm sorry. And sorry that Jonathan woke up. It was just a spur-of-the-moment thing. I didn't realise I needed to get my own wife to sign a consent form first.'

'That spur-of-the-moment thing is called anal rape.'

'Oh, for goodness sake, Kat, stop being so melodramatic.' He turned the page of his newspaper.

Kat made a cafetière of coffee. She waited in silence while it brewed, and then poured it into a mug. 'You really have no idea of how you made me feel. And I don't mean the physical pain.'

She picked up her coffee. 'I'm going back to bed,' she said, and left the room. She emerged again at lunchtime, but they barely spoke for the rest of the day.

***

Superstitious people might say that Kat should have expected something else bad to happen.

The following week she had a call from her father's neighbour. The front room curtains of her father's house had been closed for two days, and he had not put out his rubbish bin for collection. The neighbour had tried ringing the doorbell, but got no response. *Not like him*, the neighbour had said. Kat went round immediately, with Jonathan in his travel cot at the back of the car. The neighbour saw her, and came out, and stood by Kat as she opened the front door. Eric's body lay in a heap at the foot of the stairs. He had obviously been dead for some time. It would be determined, in due course, that he had had a heart attack, probably while going upstairs.

As she stood there at the front door she was filled not only with grief, but also with regret and guilt. Lead weights were binding to her feet, and they would forever draw her earthwards.

Kat did not know the correct procedure on such occasions, so she phoned for an ambulance.

Then she phoned me.

Chapter 18

I became a part of this story in the moment Kat phoned me. That being so, it's time I introduced myself.

I am Kat's elder sister, Annie. Anichka for legal purposes, or for affectionate teasing by a privileged few. I was at Kat's wedding, and I saw how unhappy she was on that day; and I felt no sympathy. It seemed to me, then, that she had made a bargain with the devil, and she had only herself to blame if she didn't like the price.

There were six years between us, and we had never been close. The problem was not the years but the contrast in our early life experiences. I was born in the back of a horse-drawn Romani wagon, a year after our parents had embarked on their itinerant hippie lifestyle. When I was a toddler, my toys were mud and sticks, my second-hand clothes acquired by charity. If, by some chance, I got to know another child, we were only friends until my father hitched up the nag and returned us to the road. I spent most days alone inside the wagon, accompanied by the grind of the wheels on tarmac, and the aroma of cannabis as my parents sat sharing a spliff while the countryside flowed slowly past.

Then Mum fell pregnant again, and they decided it was time to give up travelling. Kat was born in a rented house on a council estate. I was sent to school—a year later than the normal kids—as soon as we had moved in. And when I went off to school, I left behind baby sister Kat, snug in a warm house, growing up to be a girl who could wear pink clothes and play with dolls that had been bought new and clean. By the time she started school she been imbued with little girl culture, and easily made friends.

Life on the road had made me untrusting, and desperate for certainty and control. I did well enough, but kept away from the popular kids, instead creating my own little circle of playmates where I could set the rules. No child could be my friend until they had successfully passed a lengthy process of testing. Later, I would set the same condition for adult friendships. In schoolwork I was drawn to the unambiguous world of mathematics. I grew up to be a cautious and contained young woman. Most of the time I would have appeared confident and capable, but this was an illusion achieved by ensuring that I had control of the conditions in which I operated.

I had fashioned a persona for myself that was reliable. I can admit now that it was not who I wanted to be. I wanted to be Kateryna: girly, flirty, confident. And because I denied those qualities in myself, I both admired and disliked them in her. When she came out as a lesbian, I pretended to myself that I disapproved, whereas in truth I was envious—not because I wanted to have sex with women, but because I wished I had Kat's confidence to seek out what I wanted, and to enjoy it when I found it.

As I reached adolescence, my academic leanings towards mathematics shifted into computing. Fortunately for me, this was in the 1980s. Personal computers were new and exciting. It is the accepted wisdom, endorsed by the millions who have sat cussing at a screen, that computers behave in unfathomably inconsistent ways. This is a misunderstanding. They are the most consistent pieces of machinery ever invented. Even when they go wrong, they go wrong for good reason. If we find them unpredictable, it is entirely our fault for not comprehending the patterns that underlie their behaviour.

For a young woman who wanted to live in a controllable world, a career in computing was the perfect, if unusual, choice. I studied computer science at university, and then honed my skills in a couple of unexciting jobs—one of them in council social services, where I first encountered the generation of public school boys like Mark who had come to conquer it. I lived on my own. Few men wanted to meet my conditions for friendship, and I had never learned how to present a needy feminine self that would make them ask for more.

In that decade, computing technologies and software languages changed so fast they were a succession of waves that lifted up formidably and charged forward, but were soon spent at the shoreline. We, the programmers, rode them like surfers, heroes for a little while. A few of us had the energy to swim out for another ride, but most were left in the shallows, stuck in some backwater office maintaining out-of-date technology for a company that lacked the vision or the money to pay for an upgrade.

I only caught a wave once, but it was a good one. I found employment with a company developing traffic management systems, and got so good at it that I was able to go freelance, and even to be subcontracted by my old employer. Advanced traffic management systems had become something that every modern city wanted. Though I kept putting my prices up, I still got more offers of work than I could accept. For ten years I was leading on the implementation of new systems around the world, and for another ten I found steady though less glamourous work, doing maintenance, extensions, and minor upgrades. But then I was on the beach. The new waves were being caught by a newer generation.

I wasn't worried. I had put away enough money to keep me secure for the rest of my life. I had also spent too long working crazy hours, living in hotels, or in ex-pat compounds in oppressive foreign countries. I barely had social networks, let alone friends. I had also neglected my father, and I stepped away when my mother was taken by dementia, leaving Kat to carry the burden. The voice of my conscience didn't keep me awake in the night, but it muttered at the back of my mind.

All in all, I was glad to settle back in England. For want of reason to go elsewhere, I returned to my old home area, bought a nice terraced house and gave it a stylish makeover. I realised that the cold, exacting world of computing was a refuge that had become a prison. I yearned for great adventures and passionate love, but believed it was too late for me to have them. In compensation, I took them, second-hand, through art and literature.

I still needed some shape to my life, so I drew on my old skills. I set up a small computer maintenance company that served small businesses and private customers. It's nothing special, but customers like that I am a woman, not the male computer nerd they had been expecting. I soon had an adequate customer base, and as much work as I wanted. If there's a day when no work comes in, I'm happy to call it a day off.

***

Now, with our father's death, Kat and I were forced together, first to organise the funeral and then to deal with his estate. The funeral was a small affair at the crematorium. Kat, Mark, and I sat in the front pew, Jonathan in a carrycot beside Kat. Nine mourners sat behind us: some obscure relatives on our mother's side, and a few of Dad's neighbours and drinking companions. The brief and clichéd ceremony insulted him. He was an unremarkable man, with no achievements the world would remember, but he had known the delights of love, the joys and fears of parenthood. He had fought to live by his principles, done his best to raise his daughters. He might, for all anyone could judge, have experienced his life with as much intensity as any king or poet. Yet we sent him to the furnace in half an hour. As we stood to watch the coffin move behind the curtain, I felt Kat curl her hand round mine, and I was grateful. I was suddenly glad to have a sister.

After the inhumanity of the crematorium ceremony, we honoured our father as we disposed of his estate. In legal terms it was straightforward. There was only the house and its contents, and he had left everything to be divided equally between the two of us. It was a small but solid property, a former council house that our parents had been sensible enough to buy when, in the 1980s, they were given the chance. It was still furnished and decorated much as it had been when we were children, though there were signs that Dad had used his carpentry skills here and there: some tongue-and-groove panelling, and the old kitchen units refitted, unfashionably, with plywood fronts and doors. Then, when we started to explore, we found cupboards, and a loft full of boxes, that contained children's clothes, toys, and photo albums. For the first time we saw how much our parents had savoured those brief family years, and had clung to these material residues. It made me recall the way I had turned my back on my parents, not out of any wish to abandon or hurt them, but simply because I was selfishly preoccupied with my own young life. Those murmurs of guilt and regret grew a little louder. I said as much to Kat, and I recall it was the first time she warned me about lead weights.

We could have thrown everything in a skip in a couple of days, and that is where much of it ultimately went. First, however, we honoured the family we had been, and made it a task that stretched over weeks.

We met for half-day sessions. Slowly, indulgently, we mined our way down through the stratigraphical record of a family's life over three decades. At first it felt like grieving, the tears sudden and often. Kat struggled to exorcise the memories of our mother's last months. Gradually, though, it turned into a celebration. When Jonathan was asleep, we would leave him in his carrycot on the kitchen table with its red gingham oilcloth. Then Kat and I would be together, going through the boxes, giggling and reminiscing as we went. When he was awake we would take it in turns to hold him while the other rooted out the memories. Jonathan could, by now, keep his head upright and look around, and he was happy to sit on my lap. Initially, out of habit, Kat would feed Jonathan discreetly, but I gradually persuaded her to be more open. At thirty-seven, I knew that I was unlikely to have a baby, and so these times on our own, with my sister and her baby, were as close as I would ever come to suckling a child. Sometimes we sat close beside each other on kitchen stools, my shoulder against the back of hers, one arm around her waist to pull her into me. The kitchen had west-facing windows, and the afternoon sun would throw a beam across the room, catching motes of dust. I could look down over Kat's shoulder at baby Jonathan, and Kat would let me lift her breast to him until his mouth grasped her nipple. These were days when we felt so peaceful, so content, that the three of us would remain like this until the sound of Jonathan's breathing changed and his mouth opened in sleep. When I think back to those moments, I still recall the rich, sweet odour of breastmilk, the touch and perfume of Kat's hair against my cheek.

It was as if we had returned to the nest for a second chance to learn, joyfully, to be sisters. We practised being little girls, giggling and teasing. Sometimes we were teenage sisters, reminiscing about boys and favourite popstars, teasing each other about the clothes we wore those years ago. We could be crude and contrary with each other; and loud and cackling too, as Jonathan permitted. And we were women together, united in kinship and womanhood. I also came to love Jonathan, and not merely as my sister's child. By then he had learned how to laugh, and how to make me pull the silliest faces to win his smile. I soon discovered that, even as I was doing it, he had taken my heart.

I had discovered my sister, and found her a warm and generous woman. She was, in only the best sense, straight-forward: reliable, honest, and unpretentious. She was not, however, plain or simple. She was smart, and knowledgeable, and funny too, in a quirky, quick-witted way. For most of my life I had known enough of these qualities, and her pretty looks, to resent her. Now they made me admire and love her.

There was, though, a shadow. When we were not busy with the house, or with the memories it stirred, we talked about our lives since the end of childhood. I doubt there was a detail of her life that Kat withheld from me. She told me about her years abroad, her return home to care for our mother, and the relationship with Andi. One day she gave me the full story of her friendship with David, her face quivering as she smiled and wept at the same time. Even at the end of the story, by which point she had a tissue pressed to her nose, she was still looking at me. I saw the fresh tears sparkle in her eyes. It was only when she had finished that she looked down at her feet, paused in silence, and then laughed as if she had been foolish.

When she talked about Mark, it was different. A mention of him—sometimes even the mere thought of him—was all it took to call up his oppressive spirit. When she spoke of him, she always looked away from me, and her voice became flat, her face expressionless. It was upsetting to see the way her energy and wit drained out of her, but I felt far more disturbed by the absence of anger. Mark disgusted me. I told her I would help her in every way possible to leave him. She could come with Jonathan and live at my house. I offered to sell my house, and then combine the proceeds with our new inheritances to buy a house for us all. When we talked about such possibilities she would brighten with enthusiasm, yet she was never able to commit to a plan that would make it happen.

In any case, Mark had started laying claim to the inheritance even before the funeral. Kat unwisely shared some ideas about how she thought she might invest it, and Mark was angry. After all the money that had come from his family to her benefit, he said, it was only right that Kat's legacy should be added to the assets of the whole family. Moreover, he said, he was in a better position to judge where to invest it. The money was duly passed straight to Mark, and Kat knew nothing more of it. Her best chance to break free of him was gone.

Still, if I could not rescue Kat from her marriage, I would at least do as much as I could to protect her and Jonathan from its effects.

Kat's employers were more honourable in their treatment of staff than they could afford to be. It was their policy to continue paying full salary to staff on maternity leave for five months. If the new parent continued to take leave beyond that point, payments fell to the minimum amount required by law.

Eulogy for Love

As Mark said to her, Kat's weekly income from six months onwards would be *less than she could spend at the corner shop getting something for dinner*. Mark's organisation never paid more than the legal minimum for maternity care. In any case, it managed quite successfully to avoid employing women who looked inclined to *germinate*, as Mark and his senior management team enjoyed calling it in their private conversations. Mark wanted Kat back to work at the end of five months. It wasn't so much the money, he insisted, it was simply the need to continue to invest in one's career. Plenty of other women didn't have the choice, he pointed out. And anyway, he added, she surely wouldn't want to squander the right to equal opportunity in the workplace that generations of feminists had fought to secure on her behalf.

As far as Kat was concerned, those arguments did nothing to offset the nightmarish prospect of handing over Jonathan, five mornings every week, to a childminder or nursery. He was far too young, she believed. She imagined him being left unattended in a cot for hours, at first crying but then gradually withdrawing into a thumb-sucking, foetus-shaped bundle. She wanted to remain enveloped in the love affair she had been having with her baby. Kat had learned, more and more, to defer to Mark, rather than provoke an argument that would almost certainly yield no response except shouting and long silences; but this time she put up a fight. She won a three-month extension, in return for a promise that she would make sure that alternative care arrangements were ready from month nine.

When I saw that Kat would win no better deal, I made a counteroffer. I would have Jonathan on two days each week. None of my customers ever needed a service from me that could not wait twenty-four hours. Kat was delighted. Mark was not, except on financial grounds. He had never liked me, and thought it gave me too large a role in the family.

I had eased Kat's pain, and as my reward I ceased to be an aunt. I became Jonathan's second adoring mother. Kat nevertheless faced the end of the honeymoon with her baby, the cessation of those few months of complete mutual absorption. Before Jonathan started at the nursery, she had begun to put him on a supplementary bottle and baby foods. Her own body was no longer enough for him. Not long after, she realised his cot would have to be moved to a different room. When he woke in the night, and he saw her in the bed next to him, he would start trying to get her attention. He would first try charm, then complain by banging the cot. If that didn't work, he would try crying, which invariably succeeded. He did all these more effectively once he had learned how to stand in his cot. Kat was, of course, easy prey to his charm, immediately hooked by his cries. She recognised that their relationship had changed. For close to a year he had unhesitatingly asked her to meet his every need. On the other hand, when those needs had been met, he asked for nothing more. Now, like most others in Kat's life, he wanted more of her than he needed, and had developed strategies to take it from her. Her baby son had acquired artifice.

Kat grieved for this lost time of innocence, but knew she could find it again with another child. For that to happen, however, she needed to be inseminated by a husband who slept in another room and showed no signs of desire for her. She had come to prefer sleeping alone. Any small residue of desire she might have had for Mark had died that night he had forced himself into her. He might do it to her again, wherever in the house he crawled to sleep, but she felt a little safer without him next to her in bed. She also did not have to tolerate the light on because he wanted to read, or find herself sitting in darkness, the book still on her lap and the sentence unfinished, because he had decided he wanted to sleep. There was no tut-tutting when she got up to Jonathan in the night. Her sex drive, like so much else that had made her a joyful, sensual woman, had fallen into a dark pool of memory that lay beyond her consciousness. Sometimes, though, her dreams would bring it in fragments to the surface. When that happened, there was no one next to her in bed to stop her drawing them out, her fingers teasing open the forgotten pleasures until, with a small shudder, she let them fall back again.

And what price did she pay for the loss of her husband as bed companion? He had never cuddled into her, or held her in his arms, or asked in a whisper how her day had been. He had been only a man-shape lying across the bed from her; silent, his thoughts concealed.

She needed him, nevertheless, for one specific purpose. One evening, while he watched one of the few television programmes that he considered worth his time and intellect, she announced she was going to bed, but then added a question:

'Are you ever going to come back to sleep with me, do you think?'

He looked at her as if she had suggested something ridiculous; frowned, and then said, 'Why?'

'I suppose because that's what husbands and wives usually do.'

'Do we have to be bound by convention? Nobody's even going to see, nobody who matters.'

'Jonathan will see. It's not offering him a very good example for him to follow when he grows up.'

'Come on, Kat. Let's not start playing make-believe for the benefit of a one-year-old.'

'I don't see why it has to be make-believe. In fact, I think it's really sad that you think it would be.'

He looked at the television, letting her know she was disturbing his leisure time. It was absurd of her, but she felt upset. He had said nothing that was not already obvious. She knew their marriage was a make-believe. She preferred her own bedroom, and he was surely entitled to feel the same. She watched him sitting on the sofa, his head resting on his arm so that his hand hid his face from her. Of all the hurts he inflicted, she thought to herself, the worst was that he considered the predicament so obvious, so established, and hence, presumably, so far beyond any possible change. This, he was signalling, was how it would be, always. And he was prepared to put up with it.

The credits rolled up the TV screen. Now he had less excuse not to talk.

'Can you see nothing nice about sharing a bed with me?' she asked. Then, as if wanting to hurt herself, 'Do you really not find me attractive at all?'

He switched off the TV, and slowly turned to her. He stared in her direction, considering his response.

'I'm sorry you're making me say it again, Kat. I did say before. You're not how you were when we married. Physically, I mean.'

'Jesus, Mark. I've had a baby. Your baby!'

'I know. But it seems there are plenty of women who have babies and then get themselves back in shape.'

'Yeah, the sort of women who have personal trainers and cosmetic surgeons.'

She could think of nothing more to say. She went upstairs to Jonathan's bedroom, where she sat in the pale glow of the nightlight, looking down at him as he lay sleeping in his cot, big-bottomed in his nappy, and adorable in his sleepsuit.

Eulogy for Love

***

Mark was more concerned about convention than he admitted. When Charles and Peggy came to stay that autumn, he moved back to the main bedroom. It was so long since he had been there that he looked awkward as he undressed for bed and put on his pyjamas.

Kat was near enough to the middle of her month to make it worth an attempt. Mark turned off the light and lay with his back to her. She reached over the top of him, found the gap in his pyjama trousers. He turned on his back and let her continue. She kneeled up, undid the top of his pyjamas, and sucked him. He said nothing, but allowed her to continue. When she thought he was close enough to climax she straddled him and rode him, adding two fingers between her legs to give him the extra tightness he seemed to crave. He groaned. She had taken what she needed from him, and lay back on her side of the bed.

Nothing more was said that night. The following morning, Sunday, they said goodbye to Charles and Peggy. Kat stood a moment at the front door, Jonathan on her hip, watching Mark carry the luggage to the car. She then returned to the kitchen, dropped the baby into his playpen, and cleared away the breakfast.

Mark found her before she had finished tidying. 'I know what you were up to last night,' he said. 'Do you think once will be enough?'

'Enough for what?' Kat said as she loaded the dishwasher.

'You know what I mean. Enough to get yourself pregnant.'

She gave him the smallest glance. 'Probably not.'

'Well, I might be willing again,' he said, 'but I think we need to have a little more give and take in this relationship.'

'I don't understand.'

'Yes, you do. I give you what you want, then I have a little of what I need.' He smiled at her without warmth. 'My turn tonight, I reckon.'

***

Jonathan had been put to bed, the kitchen was tidy, and she had checked she had clothes for the morning. She thought she might be able to slip away to bed unnoticed, but he guessed.

'Off up?' he said. Reluctantly, she nodded. 'Excellent,' he said. 'I'll be up in ten minutes.'

Kat had engaged in anal play with her lesbian lovers, and enjoyably so. She had discovered how the muscles can be relaxed, and had felt it done to her. But that had been with loving, careful partners. Now the bedroom was a cell where she waited for the sound of her torturer's footsteps. She lay back, legs bent, trying to prepare herself, but her body rebelled.

He came into the room, naked and already hard. She sat up. He got onto the bed, grabbed her head, and held it while he used her mouth, pushing himself in so deep she choked. When he had had enough of her that way, he told her to kneel on the bed and face away from him. He made no attempt to prepare her. She felt him trying to enter her, and instinctively moved herself away. He shouted at her: 'Fucking stay where you are!' and she moved herself closer to him. This time he got himself into position, and then grabbed her hips and pulled until he was inside her.

She had at least managed to apply lubricant, and his entry was not such searing agony as that time before. There was still physical pain, but the emotional hurt went far deeper—the humiliation of being told, wordlessly, that this was the only way he wanted her. While he grunted behind her, she wept into the pillow. He withdrew from her as soon as he had climaxed, and left to sleep in his own room.

Kat took her payment the next night. She had to go to his room to get it, and was glad to find he had already switched off the light. He did not see her shaking with fury and disgust as she pulled back the duvet and touched him. She even, when she found she was not pregnant, made the same bargain in the following two months. Finally, she made a better match with her ovulation, and got the result she wanted.

Unfortunately, as far as Mark was concerned, Kat had now given her consent to anal intercourse as a continuing part of their sex life. It was, in fact, the entirety of their conjugal relationship. Through the years that followed he would signal in the evening that he intended to visit her, and that she should prepare herself. For a few years this might happen once a month, though it became less frequent as the children got older. It helped, in a way, that it was never discussed. It enabled Kat to separate his nocturnal visits from ordinary domestic life. Were it not for the lingering soreness, she could almost regard them as nightmares to be dismissed when daylight came.

***

For all that, Kat had what she wanted. She was pregnant again. This time she planned to give birth at home; and, this time, I was going to be there. One morning in May 2006, Kat knew that labour had begun. She phoned the midwife and me, and we came immediately. She texted Mark, and he came when he had finished his meeting. By lunchtime, Kat had become feline, a cat searching for a place in the house to safely have her kitten. The midwife and I followed her with polythene sheeting. Mark lost interest and went to his desk in the study. Kat finally settled in her bedroom, the place in the house that was as close as she could find to sanctuary. When the baby started to arrive, Kat kneeling and groaning at the side of the bed, I went to find Mark, and he came up. He stopped as the bedroom doorway, where he stood and watched. He was ill at ease, sensing this was woman's business. The midwife hurriedly arranged towels on top of the sheeting as Kat pushed. I caught little Rachel in my hands as she fell into the world.

Chapter 19

Kat could find no way to persuade Mark to review his policy on maternity leave. From the spring of 2007 she had the double misery of handing two children over to the nursery for three days each week. I, on the other hand, came close to having the family that I thought destiny had denied me. Until Jonathan started school, they both came to me for two days each week. I established a bond with the children that would never be lost, and, the older they got, the more rewarding it became. Kat was the one who first tired of referring to me as Auntie Annie, and started using the initials instead. The children made me Ayay, the second most important adult in their lives.

Part-time motherhood was a privilege that suited me well. I didn't have to juggle work and kids. I had the rest of the week to attend to business and household chores, leaving me free to enjoy the children when they came to me. It was Kat who endured the morning routine–that frantic process of supervising children through dressing, breakfast, toothbrushing, while also putting on makeup with one hand and the dishwasher with the other. I could rise serenely, eat a little breakfast, and wait until the children arrived with Kat, usually late and always stressed.

The regular childcare also guaranteed that Kat and I spent time together. For better or worse, it helped her survive her marriage through those years. She often paused for a cup of tea with me in the afternoons before she rushed on to her duties at home. My house was a sanctuary to her almost as much as it was to Jonathan and Rachel. Even when I no longer served as childminder, they often came over to see me, Kat always happy to linger over mugs of tea in the kitchen. In time, the children began to stay over for weekends, each with their own bedroom.

That made me useful to Mark, but he openly disliked me. He was the domestic dictator, I the guerrilla force encamped in a place where he could not attack. He disliked the possibility that I might enter his house, and if he saw an extra used mug at the kitchen sink he would want to know whether I had visited. On the few occasions when he found me there, he would speak to Kat as if I were not present.

Mark's shadow lay heavily on the family home. As the children grew older, Kat had to teach them how to endure him, and the three of them conspired to become a secret single-parent family. Kat treasured Jonathan and Rachel, and when the three of them were on their own she was a lively, indulgent, slightly disreputable mother. They had fun together.

They learned to be a different kind of family when Mark was present. If they were eating when they heard the sound of the front door as he arrived home from work, they would look knowingly at each other, fall silent, and improve their table manners. On weekday evenings he was not interested in the children and did not want to talk to them, but silence made him suspicious. Conversely, talk that did not include him made him resentful and suspicious. Kat had to fuss over him so that he would not notice. It was only at weekends that he would pay attention to the children, and this was only because he wanted to act out his image of a cultured middle-class family. He would announce that they were all going out to a museum or to visit a ruin, and then wait impatiently while Kat cajoled the children into getting ready. On their return, and having concluded the performance, he would retire to his desk in the study.

Even before the children were at school, Mark had begun to fret that he could rise no further in the company, and should find a job elsewhere. Fortunately, this risk was made less likely by the financial crisis in 2008. The company, always lean and ruthlessly competitive, seemed as good a place as any to shelter until that storm had passed. As it turned out, the parent company was less robust, and ran into difficulties. After weeks of negotiation, Mark's company achieved a management buyout, and he became one of the owners. He had now invested far more in the company, and so had far more to lose. Mark declared that the family would have to cut back on expenditure, and for two years their summer holidays were confined to Europe. By then, though the climate in public services was difficult, the company was expanding once more.

The Smallwoods settled down, and came to look the epitome of a well-off English professional family. By 2010, both children were at primary school. Kat, still with the charity, had become overall manager of the finance, admin, and human resources teams. Mark liked to remind her that, compared to him, her job was still lowly and miserably paid. Nevertheless, Kat was a respected senior member of staff, and enjoyed the responsibility. That year, the family acquired the first of a series of au pairs, giving Kat more time for herself. Mark opened a family membership at the local health club. The children liked to play in the pool at weekends, while he would sometimes go to the pool early in the mornings to thrash his way up and down the swimming lanes. Kat made use of the gym.

It may well have been a typical English middle-class family in one other important respect. It was built on a marriage without love or respect. Mark and Kat had honed the division of roles to the point where they barely needed to speak. This division was straightforward: Kat carried the family, Mark paid for it. She performed a role for him, and delivered it efficiently, though he would find fault if he could. There seemed to be nothing that he wanted from her as a person, or as a woman. Even the late night visits to her bedroom had become very infrequent. In any case, those had nothing to do with love, or desire for her as a woman. She had an orifice that happened to be the right size. Nothing more.

There was only one service she provided to him as a woman, and that was to escort him on social occasions. He wanted other men to know that he could bag a beautiful woman. He had no use for what he possessed, but he wanted to parade it in front of other men to let them know they were denied it. In addition, as Kat had realised over the years, his public school arrogance still concealed awful insecurities. He had a dread fear of being left standing awkwardly on his own at a party. With Kat by his side, he would never look alone.

Kat's libido had fallen into line with the level of sex she had in her life. At a purely physical level, she did not often get aroused any more. However, that didn't stop her missing the idea of being aroused. She was only in her mid-thirties, but middle age was starting to seem close. She wondered if her body was permanently shutting down its sexual appetites. Would she never again know what it was like to shudder in orgasm as she was filled by a man—or, for that matter, tongued by a woman?

Kat had her own way of checking to see whether she still rated as attractive. She tended to wear a dress or skirt to work, unlike most of her colleagues, and she often wore heels as well. She would walk out to get a sandwich at lunchtime, her stilettoes clicking on the pavement, and watch to see if men still looked twice at her. Invariably, they did. That was reassuring, but it still was not enough. She craved adult affection. She wanted a man to tell her she was beautiful. She wanted to be touched. There was no one who gave her that.

Almost no one. In 2011, Kat started having regular sessions at the gym with a personal trainer. He urged her through the demanding circuits he set for her, praising her when she completed them. He also touched her when she was doing floor exercises. It was always legitimate, never anywhere more intimate than the back of her thighs, and always with consent; but, after so long without being touched by a man, it still had its effect on Kat. He would also send a text if she didn't book for a week or two, and say he was missing her. It was simple good business practice, of course, but she still felt flattered.

Nat was a young man—barely in his twenties, she reckoned. He wore his dark hair in a top knot, which Kat thought a little silly, and he had a fashionably bushy dark beard which she didn't like. On the other hand, he had lovely light blue eyes, and a delicious body. It wasn't muscly, simply well defined. Sometimes she noticed him doing his own workout, and felt her own body responding.

A lot of the banter was legitimate, friendly encouragement, but he became more and more flirty. She enjoyed it. He could see that she did, and so he did it more. He would stand at the side of the treadmill and tell her how great she looked—more gorgeous, he would say, than the women half her age who came to the gym. She'd be looking ahead as she pounded, but smiling, and hoping her pink cheeks could be put down to the exertions. He started suggesting, jokily, that they could meet up later for a coffee. She would laugh, and point out she was a married woman twice his age. Some weeks after that, he suggested they could meet up somewhere more private, if that would suit her better. This time, he wasn't so obviously joking.

He was a decent young man, and no fool. If she had turned serious, told him to stop, he would have stopped. She didn't. Instead she giggled, said she didn't fancy men with beards, and gave his a little tug.

He was away the following week, and unavailable for his usual session with her. She texted to check that he would be back the week after. He replied to confirm, and said he had something to show her.

She almost missed Nat when she walked into the gym. He had lost the beard. His blue eyes shone twice as bright, and Kat fancied him twice as much. 'See,' he said, stroking his naked chin, 'did it all for you. Well, and for the job interview I had last week.' He winked.

Kat laughed. 'I'm not sure whether to consider myself flattered, but I have to say you look a lot better without it.'

'That's good,' he said. 'As it happens, I got the job, and I'll be leaving in a couple of weeks. So I'm now a strictly time-limited offer. Really hoping you'll snap me up before it's too late.' He looked at her very hard. 'Please. Kat.'

Kat said, 'Never mind all that now. I'm waiting for my personal training session to start.'

She knew he wouldn't let her go without asking again. At the end he waited while she wiped the sweat off her face with a towel. 'And?' he said.

Kat glanced around to check no one was watching. She reached up and stroked his newly smooth cheek, just quickly with the back of her finger. 'OK,' she said. 'let me see what I can sort out. One evening next week?'

He grinned. 'Any evening you like!'

236

Eulogy for Love

***

Kat had been giggling to me about Nat for weeks. Now she phoned, confessing that she was going to let him have what he wanted. She asked me to be her alibi, and planned to tell Mark that we were going out for a meal together. Mostly, I was pleased for her. Her horrible husband had lost any right to expect her fidelity. She deserved a little fun, and a boost to her ego. My only concern was that she was going to his flat on the first date, but she insisted that he hardly counted as a stranger.

'OK,' I agreed, 'but I'm going to insist we follow safe dating rules. Give me the address before you go. Text me when you arrive. And if you haven't phoned by ten, I'll be calling the police. Oh—and don't assume he'll be ready with a condom.'

'Annie, you worry too much. He's a decent guy, I'm sure of it. But I'll stick to the rules, I promise.'

She sent the address when Nat gave it to her. When the evening came, I got a text at seven to say she was parked up outside his place. It was only an hour later when my phone pinged again:

See you in fifteen. Yeah, don't ask. xxx

Kat stood on the doorstep, dishevelled and smiling ruefully. 'Are you OK?' I asked.

She shook her head slowly. 'Absolutely. But I told Mark I'd be home around ten, and I can't possibly go back yet.' When we got into the kitchen she sat down heavily at the table. 'I hope you've got something to drink,' she said. 'Alcohol, I mean.'

I fished a bottle of gin out of the cupboard and waved at it at her.

'So, what on earth happened?'

Kat waited until the drink was in her hands. 'It was a very plain little flat. I suppose he can't be blamed for that, at his age, and on his PT income. Though it would have been nice if he'd put fresh sheets on the bed.

'Anyway, he lets me inside but only as far as the hallway. Then he stops and looks me up and down. 'Jesus Christ,' he says, 'been wanting you for months. You are one hell of a MILF!'

'Oh dear,' I said.

'Of course, I knew what he meant,' Kat continued, 'and I suppose I'd figured that was how he saw me. But I was so surprised at him saying it out loud that I said *sorry*, as if I hadn't heard him right.

Mother I'd Like to Fuck, he says. Then he starts kissing me. Which was fine, I suppose—that was what I'd come to do—but we were still in the hall. And the next thing he's got his hand between my legs. Not going through the bases and working his way down. Just straight to business.

'I wanted him to slow down a bit, so I pulled away and suggested we should go to the bedroom. *Yeah, can do*, he says, as if it's a surprising idea, and points behind me to a door further along the hall. So I head towards his bedroom. He follows, stripping off his t-shirt as he goes. By the time I turn around in the bedroom he's well on the way to having his jeans off too. And, as that really was all he was wearing, the next thing he's stood in front of me, naked.'

'Nice view?'

'Oh yes, a very nice young male body, as I knew it would be. There was only one bit of him I hadn't been able to check out in the gym, and that turned out to be OK as well. Nothing exceptional but, you know, fit for purpose. The problem is that he knows he looks good, and he stood there waiting to be admired. Or, more exactly, waiting for me to get down on my knees and worship.'

'And did you?'

'Well, yes. Would have seemed rude not to. And at that point I wanted to. Something I used to enjoy doing, and—to start with—I enjoyed doing it to him. But then he grabs my head and starts pushing himself in far too deep. I was starting to choke, and all I could do was wave my arms about and hope he'd notice. He did, fortunately, and stopped. Took me a minute to recover, and he was terribly embarrassed and apologetic. Said he'd assumed that, as an older woman, I'd be OK with it.

'Just to make sure he didn't do it anymore, I stood up and kissed him. Keep in mind that at this point he's stark naked, and I've still got all my clothes on. So we kiss a bit, and then he pushes me down on the bed, pulls my knickers off, and lifts my legs up until they're practically next to my ears. He gets down on his knees and starts licking me—which might have been nice, except that he's doing it with his tongue flat, like a tiger.'

'I'm beginning to get a feeling about this guy.'

Kat laughed. 'My problem was that I wasn't getting any feeling at all. He'd completely left me behind. At that point my main concern was that my dress would get creased if I didn't take it off. Fortunately, he stopped after a couple of minutes, and that was my chance to get the dress off. He'd stopped, I realised, because he was putting on a condom.

'And then he starts fucking me. He wasn't nasty about it. It wasn't like I was being raped. More like we're back in the gym and he's demonstrating a new set of floor exercises. Except, of course, that he's inside me. One minute he's pumping away on top of me, then he's got me on the side. It wasn't exactly unpleasant, just meaningless. He never spoke a word through the whole thing. And I expect you can guess what's coming next.'

'I'm fairly sure he's coming next, all over your face.'

'Nearly right. I managed to turn away, and got it on my neck instead. And that was it. He'd finished, and so he got up. Very thoughtfully passed me a box of tissues, then pulled on a pair of shorts and asked me whether I'd like a drink, which sounded like the best offer I'd had since I got there. I found my knickers, pulled on my dress, and followed him to the kitchen, only to discover that the drink he was offering was a quinoa smoothie. I mean, really! At that point I gave him a little kiss on the cheek, thanked him for the hospitality, and got the hell out.'

I grasped Kat's hand. 'Don't be hard on him, Kat, or on yourself. You know what he was doing, don't you?'

'What?'

'He was offering you sex the only way he knows. You've just described an online porn scene. I've seen enough of it to know that the ordinary stuff—the kind I mostly find on my customers' PCs—follows this standard sequence. It satisfies the varying predilections of the viewers. Nat was simply doing what he'd watched. He didn't talk to you because he doesn't see people talking in porn movies. And that's because most porn these days is made for an international market. A man in Saudi or Japan doesn't want to hear people talking in some obscure East European language, so the films avoid conversation entirely.

'Did he at any point talk to you, check you were enjoying what he was doing to you?'

'Only when he realised he'd made me choke.'

'That must have been a shocking discovery for him. He obvious assumed that all women do deep throat. Including MILFs.'

240

Kat nodded. 'Just to be clear,' I asked, 'Did you signal that you were enjoying what he was doing to you?'

Kat laughed. 'What, *Give it to me, Big Boy*, that kind of thing? No, I didn't. But there'd never been any doubt about what I was there for. And if I'd clearly told him to stop, I'm sure he would have. It would be wrong of me to claim he didn't have consent.'

'I don't mean that. Did he actively think about making it pleasurable for you. I suspect he was surprised you didn't sound like you were enjoying it. It wasn't enough to stop him, though, because he's never been programmed to consider that possibility. He lives in the land of porn where men do what they want, and women always enjoy it.'

'But not old MILFS like me,' Kat said. 'God, you're managing to make me feel simultaneously naive and ancient.'

'Don't be silly. None of it was your fault. You should be feeling sorry for the young women in Nat's generation. When we were young, the boys had no idea what they were doing, but at least they knew they had no idea. Nat's generation reckon they've got it figured. They think they know what women want, when it's quite the opposite.'

'Well, I've learned my lesson,' Kat said, staring into her glass, now empty. 'It's terribly sad, though, to face the fact that you may never experience joyful lovemaking again.'

'Yes,' I said with feeling, and suddenly thinking of myself, 'it certainly is.'

PART 3

Look in my face; my name is Might-have-been;
I am also called No-more, Too-late, Farewell;
Unto thine ear I hold the dead-sea shell
Cast up thy Life's foam-fretted feet between;

Dante Gabriel Rossetti
"The House of Life"

Chapter 20

D avid had spent Christmas Day on his own, like many before. That year, 2012, only Hannah had come back to her mother's house to spend Christmas.

More tender hearted than her sister, Hannah had promised to visit her father before she headed down south again. They agreed she would come to the farmhouse early on the Friday evening after Christmas, and go for a meal at the village pub.

David showered and changed in readiness, but then realised he had time to spare—even supposing that Hannah, uncharacteristically, arrived on time. A publisher was expecting sight of some artwork. He doubted they would look at it until the New Year, but it would be good to get it off his conscience. He headed over to his studio in the darkness, feeling the strong but unseasonably mild wind swirling around the courtyard.

These days he often sent his artwork using a flatbed scanner and a high-speed broadband connection. In principle a simple process, but in practice it involved powering up the equipment, fiddling with the scan settings, and then dispatching the file with a note. He was still at it when he heard Hannah's little car on the courtyard gravel. She could see him through the large studio windows, lit brightly as he sat at the computer desk.

'Hi!' he said, as she walked inside; then, after staring at the computer screen for some moments, 'Sorry—just thought I could get this job done quickly. Nearly there.'

She came over, put her arm over his shoulders, and gave him a symbolic sideways hug. 'Don't worry,' she said, and started to wander the studio, glancing over the equipment and drawings. Through all life's changes, she had always had a father who worked in a home studio. It was a point of constancy. She found it comforting to be there.

David focused silently for a minute or two. 'There, done,' he said, as he shut down the computer. He sat back, and saw Hannah stood looking across the room.

'What do you think happened to her, Dad?'

He followed her gaze to the painting of Kat on the chaise longue.

'Kat? Oh, I expect she's had an enormous brood of children. She obviously loved kids. And middle-aged by now. Must be hitting forty. Fat and frumpy, I should guess.'

David did not believe it, and could not imagine it. He had sometimes attempted to age her in his mind, as if it would lessen his sense of loss, in the way an insurer might mark down the value of a piece of furniture due to wear and tear. It didn't work, and he was glad it didn't. When he called up a mental picture of her, he still saw the slim and pretty girl he had known fifteen years before. He could still hear the sound of her voice as it was then, the way she moved, her little mannerisms. That was his Kateryna, and that was the way he was going to keep her.

He picked up the keys at the side of the computer. 'Shall we go then?'

***

David had been invited to attend a private viewing in March of an exhibition that included some of his work. It was at a small gallery in Manchester. Though he was grateful that his work was still well regarded, he no longer needed to mingle with people who would flatter him, and generally sought excuses not to attend such events.

This was an exception. He was going to be shown alongside other artists he respected. He liked the idea of seeing his canvasses next to theirs, liked even more the prospect of meeting up with them for an hour or two over some drinks and canapés. He began to think he might make it a little outing to mark the start of spring, and researched what else he might pleasurably do while in Manchester. It turned out that the Lowry Theatre was, for once, putting on a show with a bit of substance. He could go to a matinée on the Saturday, the following day. There was, he remembered, a decent hotel near the Lowry on the new MediaCity development. A room and a seat were booked, and the plan was made.

The private viewing was as pleasant as he had hoped, and he slept well that night. However, he had to vacate the room before lunch, so drifted over to the Lowry complex and spent awhile at the permanent Lowry exhibition. With the time for the theatre performance approaching, he went upstairs to get a drink from the bar outside the auditorium. People were arriving for the performance, but not yet finding their seats. He noticed, beyond the bar area, some glass doors that gave access to a balcony. It provided a view of little more than acres of concrete, but he found it good to get some fresh air. He stood at the balustrade with his drink, looking down at people arriving for the performance.

He became aware of some other people coming out onto the balcony. They walked across to share the view from the balustrade, standing not far from him. He continued to look down at the concrete, but the hand of the person next to him was resting on the chrome railing, and inside his field of view.

A woman's hand. It took him some moments to pay attention to the hand, and then to realise the significance of what he was seeing. The hand had a ring on its little finger, a silver ring of small crystals interspersed with jet.

David looked up at its owner. She had lost some weight, and it showed in her face. Her cheekbones had become more prominent, resulting in an unfamiliar elegance. Her hair, more coiffured, was straighter, with blonde highlights, and a little shorter. Much later he would discover that she had also acquired some small creases at the side of her eyes, but at that moment he was oblivious to detail. He only knew it was Kateryna. His Kateryna.

Kat knew immediately that it was David. She saw the look of recognition turning into delight. She began to smile back until she realised what the consequences would be. In milliseconds she had played out what would happen: the impossibility of civilised introductions; Mark full of suspicions because she had spoken to any man, furious if he realised who this man was; the silence and sulking through the play and on the journey back; interrogations once home.

David saw the smile begin to grow but disappear. She shook her head like a tremor, formed her mouth into a silent 'No!' Then she turned her back to him and spoke to her companion: 'Mark, do you think we should go and find our seats?'

David understood the message enough not to watch them leave the balcony, but a few minutes later he was in his seat, well up in the auditorium, and scanning the rows below. He found their heads, eventually. Quickly, before the lights went down, he pulled a biro from his pocket, and an old receipt from his wallet, and scribbled down his phone number.

Mark never bothered to ask his wife's views on art or culture. They added nothing to his own opinions. On this evening that was fortunate, because Kat was unaware of the first half of the show. Kat recognised the absurdity of her reaction to seeing David. She could have found a way, at any point in the last fifteen years, to get in touch with him. She had done nothing. Now, after setting sight on him for a matter of seconds, and not even speaking to him, she knew he was back in her life and would stay there—unless, she reminded herself, he did not want it. He had been a memory. Now he was a present reality. More than that, she already saw him as a portal in the dull fabric of her life that could lead to something wonderful. She only needed the courage to walk through it.

When the lights came on for the interval, David stayed in his seat and watched. As he had hoped, Kat got up, leaving Mark seated, and walked towards the exit. She passed the end of David's row. He tried by telepathy to attract her attention, unsuccessfully as far as he could tell, and then manoeuvred to the end of his row and followed her out. Kat had moved clear of the exit door, and was watching from a distance.

'I'm so sorry I had to do that to you,' she said softly, when he got to her, 'but he would have been horrible.' They were stood close. She touched the back of his hand, and gave him the smile he had believed he would never see again. 'I dare not stay and talk,' she said. 'I told him I was going to the ladies, but he might come out.'

David held out the fragment of paper with his phone number. 'Please get in touch. Please.' She looked at it and laughed. 'I was going to use your email address, but thank you!' He frowned, puzzled. 'From your website,' she explained. 'I love your work, and I'm so pleased it's been recognised.'

There was a moment when they only looked at each other. Then she whispered, 'Gotta go!' David stood and watched her hurrying towards the toilets. She was about to be lost amongst the gathering of people when she stopped and turned. She glanced around quickly, to make sure it was safe, then smiled, and waved—that little wave of hers, from side to side, hand at chest level, her palm towards him.

***

It might be said that their first few exchanges by text were wholly innocent. There were some facts to be established, some corrections to be made. They were both pleased, and quietly relieved, that neither of them had moved to Manchester. Kat explained that Mark had been required to attend a work event later on the Saturday and, much like David, had decided to leaven the chore with a theatre visit. Kat had been brought along to be the candy on his arm and the cover for his social inadequacies.

Kat had been visiting David's website ever since he had paid to have it developed, but it told her nothing about his personal life. He now recounted by text how his marriage had ended, and delighted Kat with recent photos of the twins. He explained that he lived alone. Kat reciprocated with photos of Jonathan and Rachel. David had already seen some hints of the state of Kat's marriage, and at first she only added, opaquely, that she had learned to be more realistic in her expectations.

In truth, Kat and David were merely getting into position to begin a slow dance, one that would be conducted through the medium of texts. It was a dance that could only have one ending. They performed it intuitively yet also impeccably, their steps closely coordinated. For several weeks they did not acknowledge even to themselves what they were doing, and they only admitted it to each other, laughing at themselves for being so silly, long after the dance was ended.

Those texts reveal it to have been a dance of four parts. The aim of the first part was to create possibilities. David took the first step by sending Kat vivid and improbably detailed memories of the things they had done together fifteen years earlier. He still remembered the clothes she had worn when they first went to the cinema together, and he knew the date they went to London, as if it were an anniversary he still honoured. Kat read these texts and knew then that he still loved her. David had already seen the ring on her finger, and so knew she had feelings for him. He did not, however, know exactly what her feelings were, or whether they were strong enough for her to allow him back into her life. He took a second step, expressing mild concern that she might be regretting that by chance he, old guy that he now was, had re-entered her life. Kat understood what he was asking, and began sharing the little miseries of life with Mark. He stopped worrying, as she had intended. By this means she had told him there was a space for him in her life, perhaps a large one. Finally, and completing the turn, she made disparaging remarks about the size of her house, and the cost of the family holidays, and reassured him that she usually bought her clothes from ordinary high street shops. She was, she was telling him, still the same Kat she had always been. She might take her husband's money, but her mind was still her own.

In the second part of the dance, they made a space for intimacy, though not directly with regard to each other. David offered the tale of his misjudged night with the barmaid from the village pub, including a few risqué details. In response, Kat indicated vaguely that her marital sex life was unremarkable. That was as much as she could let him know. If he had thought it was good, he might have felt she was making it a competition he could lose. Then again, she was afraid that, if he knew the horrible truth, he might think her frigid or tainted. She also decided against telling him about the unfortunate hour with the personal trainer, in case it made her sound slutty.

Instead, and with deft footwork, Kat turned David's attention to the succession of au pairs at the Smallwood residence, intriguing him with thoughts of lesbian liaisons. In reality there never had been the slightest possibility. The girls were far too young to be sexually interesting, and none pretty enough to appeal. In any case, it would have been an outrageous breach of trust to have seduced them. None of that mattered, though, for Kat's purposes. Her frisky, mildly fictionalised account of life with young women in the house let David know that she was still sexually alive and exciting. She could tell that he loved it.

In Part Three, they used this intimate space, and the revitalised and extended intimate language they had now established, to acknowledge their feelings towards each other. However, this potentially explosive discussion was made safe by being placed in the concrete-clad context of *what was*, or *what might have been*—never *what still could be*. They laughingly discussed all the opportunities for naughtiness they ignored during those months when Kat was coming to the house, though they agreed that the dusty chaise longue would not have been good for making love—and, in front of the big window, far too public! Most potently, they conducted a detailed review of the last moments of that evening at the London hotel, when Kat had abruptly exited the lift. David read, with turbulent feelings, the text in which Kat admitted how sad she had felt, and how hard it had been not to invite him to her room. David agreed that it had been awful, and admitted he had lain in bed a long time thinking about her.

Eulogy for Love

Kat texted back:

Just thinking? Is that all? I could feel insulted! xxx

David texted back and queried, in an exaggeratedly prim manner, what she could possibly be meaning.
She replied immediately:

If you're the man I think you are, I'm sure you eased yourself to sleep with a little hand relief. I remember my fingers were busy! Xxx

From then on, all their texts carried an erotic charge, even when they were ostensibly sharing titbits of news about their days. They travelled through their separate and mundane lives in a constant state of mild arousal. Kat's body had fully reawakened, and David's once illicit fantasies played freely in his mind as visions of the pleasures he might yet experience.

They had not, however, explicitly acknowledged these feelings—these present and overwhelming urges—to each other. Some unwritten convention, a protocol of the English middle classes, perhaps, prevented them from doing so. As a result, they had to complete the fourth and final part of the dance, in which they took steps backwards. *Yes, it would be nice to meet up again, but let's not make assumptions. Let's just see how it goes. After all, we were only together for seconds in Manchester. We don't know how we'll get on together after all these years.* They debated where it would be appropriate to meet, and nearly decided on a café. They were only saved from this by Kat, who said it really might be easiest if she came to David's home.

***

The dance had taken almost two months. They met in May. Kat took a half day in lieu, went home at lunchtime to prepare herself, and then drove to the farmhouse. David, though innately disinclined to dress up in his own home, found a soft green linen shirt to wear over his usual white t-shirt and blue jeans. When he saw Kat on the doorstep, he came out and held her, but was still tentative. Here, in her vivid presence, he wondered whether he had misread all the implied promises in her texts. He had a bottle of champagne already open, and said he could put out some lunch if she hadn't had any. Kat said she might have something to eat later, but took a glass of champagne and sipped it as she walked around the kitchen.

David watched her. She was wearing a cream dress in light cotton, with buttons at the front, and heels, and she had left the dress unbuttoned enough for him to catch glimpses of a white lace bra. He had always found her beautiful and desirable, but never more than at this moment. Even as he had put fresh linen on the bed that morning, he had told himself that he would let the afternoon unfold naturally, with no expectations. Now, as he watched her, his body said otherwise.

Kat was pretending to look around the kitchen, but she was parading for him, loving that he was watching. She knew him well enough to know that his awkwardness was a sign of desire. She knew men desired her, but it meant little, and was no compensation for a husband who only used her as a masturbatory aid. Now a man she loved—in truth, the only man she had ever loved—was watching her and wanting her. Her body was alive and ready for him.

She had had enough of the procrastination. 'What a lovely house, David. And you've made it so nice.'

'Thank you. Would you like to look around the rest of it?'

'Maybe later. Right now, I'd like you to show me the bedroom.' She removed her stilettos. 'Come on, bring the bottle. Show me the way.'

When they arrived in the bedroom, David drew her to him. He kissed her more freely this time, yet still hesitated to go further. After so many years of waiting, and so afraid to be presumptuous, he could not entirely grasp that there were no longer any impediments. She inwardly smiled and loved him for it.

She pulled back a little. 'Maybe we should get undressed,' she said gently. Without waiting for an answer, and without any affectation, she undid a few of the buttons of her dress and let it fall to the floor. She took off her bra and thong, then laid all three items on a nearby chair. When she turned back, David was making no attempt to remove his own clothes.

He was looking at her, mesmerised. He had always thought of her as completely wonderful, but now that he saw her naked, he had the final proof that she was perfect. He found it astonishing, unbelievable, that she was waiting to give herself to him.

'Aren't you going to take your clothes off, David?'

'Sorry,' he said, and hurriedly removed them, throwing them into a heap on the chair. He seemed embarrassed to stand naked in front of her. Kat reached out and touched him for a moment. He gasped, but her aim was not pleasure. It was an act of unconditional welcome, a symbolic breaking of the barrier that had stood so long between them. He understood.

She kissed him quickly on the lips. 'Come on, let's get onto the bed.' He followed her as she lay on her back, and moved above her. They kissed again, no longer holding back. David moved down a little to her breasts, and then started lower. Kat realised where he was heading. She caught him and pulled him back up to her face.

'I'd love you to do that. But not now. All I want now,' she whispered, 'is to have you inside me.'

They were both so ready that David needed only to shift position a little. The pleasure was exquisite for them both, yet it meant so much more. It was as if all the interlinking wheels of the universe had, for that one moment, moved into their proper position. As they lay on the bed at the farmhouse that afternoon in May, the world seemed at last to have come right.

Chapter 21

Kat had to be ingenious to make times to be with David. She twice, in those spring months, risked taking a whole day off as annual leave, but otherwise had to find excuses to be away from the office in working hours, or used the gap between the work and the time she needed to be home for domestic duties. It meant that they were rarely together more than once a week. Still, when they were together, it was perfect. They only had to avoid Tuesday mornings, when David had someone come into do the cleaning, and they were assured of solitude. The farmhouse had no overlooked windows, and even Kat's car was hidden from the lane when it was parked in the courtyard.

In the first weeks, David would be ready for her arrival with a cold bottle of Prosecco to take upstairs. By June they had agreed they preferred to stay clear-headed, and he would put the kettle on when Kat texted to say she was on the way. They always went straight up to the bedroom, except on those times when, charged full with lust from many days apart, the first kiss of greeting became the start of urgent lovemaking. Kat encouraged it on these early days of summer by wearing only thin cotton dresses and leaving David to find her nakedness underneath. It did not delay them long from the bedroom. The floor would prove too hard, the kitchen table too insubstantial. They would part breathlessly and go hastily up the narrow staircase, giggling at their own foolishness.

These times were their private, temporary heaven. The hours were spent in a meandering of conversations and caresses, of indulging each other in the giving of pleasure, and of moments when the talking would give way, briefly, to cries and groans. They never slept afterwards, though sometimes they would have to rest for a few minutes. More often, though, they would laugh with delight and carry on.

In these times together, they hid nothing, denied nothing, found nothing unpleasurable in each other. When they had become lovers, they had both brought old wounds with them: the violence and degradation of Kat's treatment by Mark; the emptiness and humiliation that David had experienced with Helen; and the more generalised judgement and rejection they had both suffered in the long years of their marriages. Now, in the peace of the farmhouse bedroom, warmed by the heightening summer, they healed.

***

Kat had got away from work mid-afternoon. The au pair had been briefed to make tea for the kids and start them on homework. Kat had mentally run through a familiar and reliable choice of excuses for her absence in the unlikely event that Mark got home before her. And, as a result of all this, she was now, at around four o'clock, lying on David's bed at the farmhouse. The sun had fallen far enough to send its light, shaped by the arched window, across her naked body.

She was lying on her back, though with her upper body tilted a little so that she could look at his face as he lay close next to her. He was on his side behind her, her legs hooked over the top of his hip. In this position he was able to be inside her, and he had been there for the best part of half an hour. He moved gently, enough to sustain their arousal, but without any particular plan to head for orgasm.

David stroked her cheek. 'Do you miss having a woman?

'Only as a gift for you.' She winked at him, wickedly. 'Maybe on your birthdays. I'd like to watch another woman giving you pleasure.'

David laughed gently. 'I've an idea you wouldn't just watch.'

She giggled. 'OK, it's true. If she were busy with you in her mouth, I might slide between her legs. You know, just as a way of thanking her for her efforts.'

'Or the other way around, I'm guessing.'

They looked at each other, smiling. The images pleased them both. It made him grow a little harder inside her, and she felt it pleasurably.

'If you're asking seriously,' she said. 'Not really. You make love like a girl anyway.'

'Oh,' he said, and made a face as if he'd been terribly hurt.

'Hey!' she said. 'That's actually an enormous compliment. The point is, when women make love together, they want to please each other.'

She moved her head a little, as a shrug. 'Alright, I'm generalising. There are some who like to be rough, and of course plenty who are plain selfish. But in my experience women take care of each other. A lot of the time we take turns, preferring to please and then to be pleased. You know how it is doing sixty-nine. Seems like a good idea, but usually turns out to be far too much at once. What I mean is, lovemaking between women is more likely to be loving. Which makes it a lot more pleasurable.'

'A bit late in life,' David said, 'but I'm realising that. Watching and hearing you climax gives me almost as much

257

pleasure as coming myself. Not that I've become saintly—I simply get enormous pleasure from pleasing you.'

Kat laughed. 'Right now, lying here, I'm not likely to accuse you of being saintly.'

'You know what I mean. It's such a shame. Men missing all the pleasures of the journey for the sake of arriving at their five seconds. I've heard it said that as men grow older, and their bodies slow down, they have to be less focused on their own orgasms. But I suspect young men simply haven't figured out the secret.

'Then again,' he continued, 'I have to plead guilty for some past occasions—not with you, I hope—when I've been lazy and selfish. Especially when they weren't telling me what they wanted. There'd come a point where I would give up trying, and please myself.'

Kat widened her eyes and opened her mouth. David had moved at an angle and depth that was exactly right for her. He understood, and smiled.

'Don't get me wrong,' she said, when she had recovered a little. 'I don't want you to be all kind and gentle the whole time. I absolutely love it when you get really aroused—most of all when you're about to come.'

'That's good to know,' he said. 'I sometimes feel embarrassed about it. Think I must look very strange.'

'No! You look powerful and masculine, and somehow also vulnerable. Please don't stop doing that. The important thing is that you aren't locked into your own private pleasure. I can see you looking at me when you're getting close, and I know that you're still loving me. It's me—all of me—that's driving you crazy with pleasure, not just my cunt or my mouth.'

The memories of David above her, his face contorted as he climaxed, moved Kat to a new level of arousal. The two of

258

them had been meandering in erotic foothills, but now Kat realised she had reached her base camp, ready for the ascent.

'Do you mind if I use the vibrator?' she asked.

'Of course not.'

Kat stretched out an arm behind her and walked her fingers, spider-like, across the bedside table until she found it—a pink pebble that David had bought as soon as she admitted she used a vibrator at home.

'But there's one condition,' he said. 'You must keep your eyes open, and look at me all the way to the end.'

'Ah,' she said. 'I know what you mean, and I'm sorry. For so long, having sex meant wanting to be somewhere else.'

The vibrator started to buzz, and David watched as she progressed. He saw her cheeks flush and her mouth open. When she knew she was not far off, she smiled at him out of love and delight. And then Kat suddenly drew in air, and her eyes widened. She released the air in a gasp, groaned, shuddered, and climaxed; and, through all this, she looked at David. He was so overcome by her beauty that he also came— softly flowing out, as if he were melting into her.

***

Perversely, these trysts were so perfect that both David and Kat felt a worry. It was so much on the margins of consciousness that they barely articulated it to themselves, and never plainly voiced it to each other. It was there, nonetheless. Individually, privately, Kat and David both worried that the world would judge them harshly. A vacuous relationship, it would say, based on nothing more than lust between a woman compensating for an unhappy marriage and a man old enough to know better. A relationship, moreover, that could never withstand the pressures of the real world, and which in any case would fade once the carnal desires were satiated. It was a child's birthday candle: an inconsequential thing that would soon be blown out or burnt out.

They believed it wasn't true. As evidence, there had been the friendship those fifteen years ago, the immediate warmth and rapport that had arisen between them. Admittedly, the desire had been there then, a flammable vapour that rolled heavily around them during those months, though it never ignited. The friendship had survived. And now, though they spent their time in bed, the friendship was still present. It wasn't cold, animal, impersonal sex. They laughed, reviewed the pleasures they had just experienced, shared intimate fantasies, made hypothetical plans, exchanged views. Talking in this way was not only something they did as they made love. It was a part of their lovemaking.

It was still not enough to silence the imaginary charge, the world's unspoken accusation, that they were engaging in nothing more than a dirty little affair. As if in rebuttal, they tried meeting for a walk or a drink. But, as soon as they met, they wished they were alone at the farmhouse. Sitting in the back of a pub or a coffee house, constantly wondering if they would know the next person who came through the door, was nothing like real life. The real world was cuddling up together in front of the TV, meeting friends, getting the kids to finish their homework on a Sunday evening. They could share none of those things. So, after a while, they gave up on the real world and its judgements, and met at the farmhouse in the magical, technicolour world that their love had put around them.

They did once venture out together in the middle of a day. They had come downstairs to find some lunch. David opened the French windows that faced the garden at the rear of the house, and the fields beyond. It was an old-fashioned English summer's day, with cloudless skies. A slight breeze sent the warm air through the doorway and to softy stroke their skin.

'We should be outside on a day like this,' David said. Kat, dressed only in one of his shirts, came over and linked her arm through his. They both gazed outside.

'Do you remember that day out with the twins on those little hills?' he asked.

'Course I do. I sometimes think you don't believe those times were as special for me as they were for you.'

'We could be there in twenty minutes,' he said.

They were there forty minutes later, by the time they had dressed and scavenged enough food to make a little picnic.

The car park, as ever, was on a flat area surrounded by hillocks, like the crater of a small green volcano. Kat made unhesitatingly towards the hillock where they had sat those years ago. 'You really do remember,' he said, putting his arm around her. She leaned into him as they walked, and kissed him on his neck.

They made camp at the top of the hill with a rug, and sat side by side. David said, 'Do you remember doing the rude thing with the ice cream?'

She laughed. 'I had so much fun teasing you!'

David nodded. 'We had some lovely times that summer.'

'And nobody gave a damn about it, because they didn't think we'd have sex.'

'And they were right. We didn't.'

'But they never understood. Sex alone is flesh. Friendship is where the joy happens, and where the trouble starts.'

They sat in silence. 'God,' Kat said, 'How different it was. You were in your prison cell, and I played the little bird that sang to you at the window. I somehow imagined you'd find it comforting.'

'But you *were* comforting. You made me look through the bars and see there was a life beyond the prison. I don't mean a life with you, not then. Just the hope of something better. I suppose I'm now officially the free one, but I don't feel much of a bird. I only fly with you.'

They were becoming melancholic. Kat pushed David's chest back until he was lying on the rug, and then stretched herself over him. 'Well,' she said, after she had kissed him, 'at least these days I don't have to pretend with an ice cream. I can do it for real.' Her hand moved to his groin, and she winked at him. 'Like right now, maybe.'

David laughed, but put his hand over hers, making her stop.

'Spoilsport!' she said with a giggle. 'I can feel you want me to.'

'Of course I'd like you to. It's just that there are people around.'

Kat made a pretend pout. 'Oh, alright. Just as long as we do it again later.'

He looked up at her face. 'Do you realise how wonderful it is that you like sex as much as I do? Not having to beg for it, or earn it?'

'You mean like it was with Helen?'

'Helen? God, no. With Helen it was more like begging her not to do it. No, I mean with women generally. Men always have to pay for sex, one way or another.'

Kat sat up and reached for the plastic bag with their picnic. 'Always? Do you really mean *always*?'

'Well, alright, maybe not always. Maybe it isn't true when people are on new dates. Or at least it will be cheaper—the price of the meal the man is expected to pay. But after that, yes. Listen to the way that couples talk about sex, the way a woman tells her husband she'll *let him have it*, but *only if he's good.* It's entirely one-sided. Men want. Women ration. Why isn't it a matter of both wanting the pleasure of it, just as we do?'

Kat rolled away from him and reached for a packet of tortilla chips. 'Perhaps that's because there's little pleasure for women. I speak from limited experience, of course. But I suspect most men are crap at sex.'

'Yes, I can believe that's true. In which case sex has no value for women except as something to trade. A sellers' market.'

'Absolutely. Hence any woman who offers it for free is a threat to the market, and considered a slut.'

'God, can you imagine it?' David said. 'Sex freed from the marketplace, and simply for the pleasure of all participants.'

Kat laughed. 'Lovely thought. But I'm not sure you'd like it. Well, let's leave *you* out of it. I suspect men in general like having a market for sex. It's the same for men as owning cars. They always have to compete over things. They feel superior if they own a more expensive car than the next guy. Same with owning women. Mark doesn't really want me. He never has. I'm the trophy wife, the proof that he's a successful man. All that would fall apart if men didn't have to purchase in the marketplace, whether it's cars or women.'

'Leaving a lot of other men at the bottom of the pecking order.'

'Wasn't that always the way?'

She leaned over and brushed back David's hair. 'Come on you,' she said, 'let's go home, where you can have me, no charge.'

'Hey, man,' he said, in his best American accent, 'free love. Right on!'

Steve Dowson

***

'I must get moving,' she said, though she remained by his side. 'I do hate this bit, you know,' she continued, 'this rushing away. It may seem odd, but I'm getting to the point where I would trade making love for the pleasure of simply getting up and doing ordinary things together. It would be unimaginably wonderful to wake up in the morning and see you next to me.'

'Easily solved,' he said. 'Let's get married.'

'Ha-ha.' She kissed him on the tip of his nose. 'There's one small impediment to that plan.'

'Oh, you mean the little problem that you're married already?' he said, as Kat got out of bed.

He understood very well what she meant. He, too, hated her rushing away, the impression of her body left where she had been next to him, her warmth dissipating in the forlorn entropy of happiness.

It was compensation to watch her getting dressed. She was, in his view, the perfect expression of womanhood. He saw it in her physical self, and in the way she moved. How she would put on her bra back to front, and then swivel it around. The way she would tuck a thumb at each side of the scarce material of her thong, stretching it to ensure it was placed symmetrically. Intellectually, he supported the idea of sexual diversity, the notion that people should not be pinned down as male or female. But he was also a romantic. Kat was, he believed, the manifestation of the magical otherness of authentic, deep-rooted womanhood. Her body, in its ability to receive, nurture, and bleed, shaped her being. Her womanhood, in turn, helped him towards a stronger sense of his own male self—not a masculinity expressed by control and violence, but through creation. It seemed foolishness in a

264

modern, urban man—a man in his late fifties, what's more—but she awoke in him the primeval urge to plant seed and crop babies.

He watched her pull up her dress and button the front. 'OK,' he said, 'so let's be less ambitious for the moment. Do you think there's any chance you could get away for longer? I've been wondering whether you could pretend to be going on a trip with Annie, so we could at least have a night and a day together. You could come here, or we could go away somewhere.'

Kat sat on the edge of the bed as she brushed her hair. 'Like where?'

'Anywhere you like. I was thinking of a nice hotel, far enough away that we can stop worrying about meeting someone we know.'

He looked at her closely, waiting.

'Or?' she said. 'I can tell you've something else in mind.'

He had to work up the courage to say it.

'Yes. I know it's a cliché, but it would be so utterly wonderful to go to Paris with you.'

Kat looked at him. 'Christ,' she said.

'We could fly over late one afternoon,' David persevered, 'have the whole of the next day together, and then come back in the evening.'

'What about passports? And what if the return flight was delayed?'

'You mean you can't get hold of your passport?'

'No—I know where he keeps it, and he wouldn't notice if it went missing for a day or two. But supposing they stamped it?'

'They never stamp passports in France. Or coming back from France. And if you tell him you've gone to London, you could tell him the train had been delayed, or that you were a silly little girl and missed it.'

'Supposing he phoned to check up on me?'

'Don't answer. Wait until we're somewhere quiet with wi-fi. At the hotel, say. Then call him back over wi-fi. No strange codes or extra charges on the monthly statement. Oh, and make sure Annie has my phone number as well as yours, to let us know if he calls. She can make up some excuse about you not being there.'

Kat made a sideways shape with her mouth. 'Gotta go,' she said, and kissed him. 'Let me think about it.'

She thought about it for all the time it took to drive home. It was a lovely, crazy idea. She remembered when Tony and Barbara, a decade before, had talked her into another lovely, crazy idea. She thought, too, about helium balloons.

'Sod it,' she said to herself, but out loud. She felt rebellious, girly.

'Let's fucking do it.'

Chapter 22

Whereas Kat helped David to ground himself in the foundations of his own elementary masculinity, she loved him for the way he allowed her to rediscover her full self.

David's love was a harbour where she sheltered for repair and renewal. She had started to understand how much she had been damaged by Mark, and she now rejected the pessimistic assumption that she could expect nothing better from men and marriage. It really didn't have to be like that. This unavoidably led her to the conclusion that she needed to get out of her marriage. In truth, the mission was not to run away with David, much as she loved him and wanted to share her life with him; it was to become the woman she was remembering that she could be.

Thus, in principle, Kat now had a goal for herself. Getting there was a different matter. Although she was beginning to feel her strength, she could not yet countenance going to Mark and cold-bloodedly telling him she wanted a divorce. On the other hand, she could imagine having a furious row with him that led to the point where she would feel able to say she had had enough, and that she was leaving. It would feel safer in the heat of the moment. This meant that, whereas she had always tiptoed around Mark to avoid arguments, she was beginning to like the prospect of a row so seismic that life could not continue unchanged.

Though she might not have entirely recognised the calculation she was making, this was why she was willing to risk Paris with David. The trip was a lovely idea, but even more risky than the dash to the ocean with Tony and Barbara. But so what? If it led to a row, she would make it a showdown.

***

Paris had been a place of pilgrimage for David in his art college days. He enjoyed his memories of staying in a little hotel where the lift had clanking scissor gates, and where, for lack of a restaurant, the only breakfast option was a croissant and a large cup of black coffee brought up to the room.

Kat had also visited Paris. Two years earlier, Mark had deemed it an appropriate educational experience for the children, though Rachel was not yet seven years old. They had stayed in a soulless international hotel outside Paris, then made forays into the city to push their way through the crowds at the Notre Dame and wait in the queues at the Pompidou Centre. He judged the Eifel Tower too vapid to be worth the time and money but, much to Kat's relief, he abandoned plans to cajole the kids around the Louvre. Kat had come home only with memories of long journeys, fretful children, and a sulking husband who walked ahead of his family.

David and Kat waited until summer was over to make their own Paris visit. The airports would be quieter, and with Rachel and Jonathan back at school it would be less obvious that Kat had slipped free of her usual Friday duties. She had also needed time to persuade Mark to agree to an overnight trip to London. After the long summer school holidays, when he had done nothing to take a share of the extra childcare, he was in a weak position to deny Kat a break of less than two days. He nevertheless pouted and protested, and tried not to give her a decision. In the end she threatened him with humiliation.

'For goodness sake, Mark. Lise will get them back from school on Friday and give them dinner. You've only got to get them to bed. She'd look after them on Saturday too, but that isn't fair on her. Are you really saying you can't entertain your own children for one afternoon?'

He could hardly admit it, so the argument was over, though, as the weekend approached, he behaved as if he were making an heroic sacrifice.

Kat had originally planned that she would simply slip out of work a little early on the Friday, but in the end decided she might as well take a half day's leave. It allowed David to arrange a mid-afternoon flight. She left the office at lunchtime. The team wished her a good weekend in London.

The flight departed on time, and, to the rest of the world, it was unremarkable. It appeared to be full of business people going home for the weekend, all of them tired and subdued. David sat by the window, and Kat leaned into him. They were silent, both pretending to be looking out at the pale blue sky. In truth they were each, separately, sipping these precious moments.

David, who could safely make the arrangements and willingly paid for them, had invited Kat to choose between the international hotel or something more characterful in the city centre. She chose the city centre, as he knew she would, and he found a place in the Fifth Arrondissement. It might once have been a primitive *pension de famille*, like the one of his memories, but now it was restyled as a boutique hotel. He had gladly paid extra for a room on the roof of the hotel. It was a small room, made smaller still by the bathroom that had been added, but it came with tall, shuttered windows on two sides. It felt remote from the street below.

It was after six by the time they reached the room. They kissed, at first only to celebrate their temporary status as Parisians, but it quickly became sexual. Kat withdrew her lips and looked at him. 'Do you want to go out, or stay here a while?'

'We should go out, don't you think?'

She put her hand between his legs and rubbed him through his jeans. 'Are you sure?' she asked again.

He grinned. 'Yes, sure! But not for too long. I think we need an early night.'

It was not difficult, once they had found their bearings, to navigate towards the Seine. It felt as if they had caught Paris returning to life after the August break. Students at the universities were arriving for the start of the autumn semester, and there was a pleasantly excitable mood in the streets. They emerged onto the river's edge where it faces the Notre Dame. Here the tourists dominated, drawn by the vistas and the stalls of art and print sellers lining the wall above the river. The sun was low but still warm. Kat and David strolled, arms around each other's waists, savouring the ambience, too happy to speak.

By the Pont Saint-Michel, and only a little way past the Notre Dame, they returned south and away from the river. A few hundred yards along the broad boulevard, they turned again into a side street where they could see a promising choice of restaurants.

On closer examination, they all seemed to be Italian. 'Do we mind?' David asked.

Kat shook her head. 'No, not this evening. I'd rather have something fairly light and straightforward. Maybe something more authentically French for lunch tomorrow.'

Eulogy for Love

The restaurant was quiet, but they preferred a table outside. While they waited for their pizzas, they held hands and smiled at each other.

'This is a wonderful dream,' David said, 'and I thank you so much for it.' He looked down at Kat's hand, and at the ring of jet and crystal on her little finger. 'I only want to believe it could be more than a dream. You and me in the real world.'

Kat laughed, but kindly. 'In the real world it would be me and you and a couple of kids. Probably playing with their phones and moaning because they're fed up waiting for their pizzas.'

'I can do that, Kat. I'd love to do that. You can put me to the test as soon as you like. But in any case, they'll be gone in less than ten years. Imagine what a great time we could have then.'

'My darling,' Kat said, and squeezed his hand, 'by then you'll be hitting seventy.'

'What the hell, Kat! If I have you in my life, I'll make damned sure I'm not just alive, but healthy enough to have all the adventures you could possibly want.'

'I believe you would. And anyway, who knows how life will turn out? You might outlive me.'

They sat and looked at each other again, smiling. The world around them—the people passing by, buzzing mopeds, a few cars—went unnoticed.

Kat said, 'You know I'll look after you when you get old? I promise I will. I love you, David. Always have, always will.'

David was looking back at her, puzzled. 'What are you saying? It sounds like you believe we're going to be together.'

'Give me time. Up until March I had this clear idea about my future. It wasn't a happy future, but it was familiar and predictable. Now, all that has gone. I love the idea of a future that is you and me—or, rather, you and me and two kids—but

271

getting there seems an awfully big jump. I'll get there, David, really I will. You just need to be patient.'

***

When they arrived back at the hotel room, Kat encouraged David to be the first one to use the shower. While he was in the bathroom, she removed a bag from her suitcase, and placed it discreetly near the bathroom door. Then, when it was her turn to use the bathroom, she managed to smuggle the package in with her.

As Kat was showering, she looked down and saw something familiar yet unexpected—and, that evening, desperately unwelcome. The water running down the inside of her thigh was pink. It was nowhere near her usual time of the month. As always, however, she had some tampons in her washbag for emergencies, and quickly returned to the plan she had made.

It took her ten minutes to get ready, and then she opened the bathroom door enough to look beyond. She saw David lying naked on the bed, looking up at the ceiling.

'What are you up to, David?'

'I'm being Parisian. All I need is a Gauloise.'

'OK. I've got something to show you. Are you ready?'

'Sure.' He turned his head towards the bathroom door. She opened it wide, and stepped into the room so that she was in front of him, fully presented. When he saw her, he immediately sat up, swinging his legs over the side of the bed to face her. 'Christ,' he said.

'Don't you mean *Mon Dieu*?'

Though Kat was laughing, she felt nervous. She stood in front of him wearing the lingerie that she had worn only once before, on the day of her wedding. She had put on the whole set: the white lace and embroidered basque, the matching thong, the stockings, even the white stilettoes. She had worn this outfit beneath her wedding dress in the hope that it would entice her new husband to adore her. He had not done so on that day, nor on any day since. She thought David would be different—she would not have taken the risk if she had not believed it—but all the hurt that Mark had done to her could not be dismissed. As she stood in the bathroom doorway, inviting David's inspection, she felt vulnerable, fearful he would laugh. When she had tried it all on at home, she thought it still fitted her almost perfectly. Now she started to fret. Perhaps, these days, she needed a smaller cup size. Perhaps, these days, the flesh bulged unpleasantly below the basque. But David's desire was very clear on his face. His body, in its crude and honest way, was telling her the same.

David broke away from savouring the sight of her, and looked into her eyes. 'Kateryna—my beautiful Kateryna. I want to explain something to you.'

She felt a little on edge. 'Never mind explaining, my darling. Holding me in your arms might be the thing to do now.'

'I will hold you, darling. I can barely wait. But I want you to understand something.' He reached out. In the small room, he was already close enough to take her hands as she stood in front of him.

'There are many things about you that make me desire you, and many reasons I love you. In this instant, I desire you because you look ravishing. But the reason I love you in this instant is that you chose to make yourself a gift to me. You're a wonderfully beautiful gift, in the prettiest of wrappings, but it's you, giving yourself freely and without condition, that makes you so special. I hope you understand.'

'Thank you. I understand. Now hold me.'

David stood up, and they embraced. He was hesitant to caress her, in case she might sense his desire more than his love, and so they kissed gently until she put her hand down between their bodies. He breathed in sharply as she grasped him.

'I'm sorry, but there is a snag,' she said, and paused her hand. 'It seems I've started my period. Completely unexpected, and such bad timing.' She looked at his face for a reaction.

'It hasn't stopped us before,' he said.

She shook her head. 'No, we can't this time—it's too heavy.' That wasn't the truth. It hadn't seemed all that heavy. It had seemed somehow different, and wrongly timed. That was what troubled her.

'Well, my darling, in that case I'll be happy just looking at you the way you look now.'

'Oh,' she said, moving her hand again, 'I'm sure we can do better than that.'

***

The daylight had gone by the time they returned to the room that evening. They had closed all the curtains but only some of the window shutters, judging as best they could how much light would enter in the morning. They should have closed more, because the light woke Kat early, soon after dawn. Yet she was joyful when she opened her eyes and saw David asleep next to her. This, more than making love, more than Paris, was what she had wanted to experience that weekend. She watched him a long time as he lay on his side. As she looked at him she grieved, on behalf of them both, that he would not be inside her that morning. After a little while, she realised there could be a compensation. Usually, he was

274

already hard when they began their lovemaking. There had only been one previous occasion—one of their precious long days together, when they had already made love twice—that she had needed to coax him back to life with her mouth. She had loved the sensation of it.

She stroked his cheek, watched as his eyes opened and focused on hers, and held still until he smiled. 'Good morning, my darling,' she said, and smiled back. Without waiting for him to answer, she slid below the duvet.

As soon as he had climaxed, she wriggled back up to the top of the bed, her mouth still loaded with his liquid, and kissed him open-mouthed. It had become a ritual for them to do this, as well as a strange pleasure for them both—a symbolic act of mutual acceptance, an erotic ritual of bonding. It was also a ritual for him to thank her when she had pleasured him like this; and for her to lick her lips and tell him that the pleasure had been all hers. When they had done all this, they laughed together.

'But I'm so sorry you can't be inside me,' Kat said, suddenly serious.

'Hey, don't worry about it. As we've often said, fucking is overrated when there are so many other ways to enjoy each other. And, on that note, it's my turn.'

'No, my darling, I'm OK. Truly. I only mean that thing we've agreed before—that sometimes there is no substitute.'

David nodded. 'Yeah, I know—leaving myself inside you, symbolically making babies. And, I admit, it would have been good to have done it here, on this special weekend.'

'I wish,' she said, stroking the side of his head, 'that we'd made real babies together.'

'What? That I'd left Helen all those years ago, and we'd run off into the sunset?'

'Yes, maybe.'

'But you can't want that, because you'd be wishing away Jonathan and Rachel.'

'I know. And I know that we both had to experience the lives we've had, before we could meet as the people we are now. But I still wish it. I still grieve what might have been.'

David sensed her distress, and pulled her to him. 'Silly, isn't it,' she said, 'the way we keep wishing to go to that damned place—that world called *Might Have Been*—the place we know we could never visit, even if we were willing to trample over the lives we have now.'

***

They ate breakfast in the cramped dining room on the ground floor, then packed and left the hotel, depositing their luggage at reception. This time they found their way more confidently to the river, crossing it at the Pont Neuf. For the rest of the morning they took scrupulous care not to have a plan. They did not want to be tourists cramming in the sights, taking selfies to prove they had been there. Kat wanted to undo the memory of being frogmarched by Mark through his approved educational experiences. They wanted only to be there, and with each other.

They wandered north, away from the river. On a whim they strolled, unimpressed, around the shopping centre of the Forum des Halles. Then they went west, bypassing the Louvre, and sat idly for a while amongst the regimented trees of the Tuileries gardens. After a while they headed north, and here chanced upon a shop selling luxury lingerie. Suppressing giggles, they went inside. Kat allowed an elegant young assistant to talk her into trying on some garments. It meant David was left sitting while she changed. He did his best to don the mantle of a wealthy Parisian gentleman indulging his young mistress, but felt he lacked the ebony cane and moustache to do justice to the role. The assistant came and invited him into the changing room to see Madame in the scarlet *brassière*, *culotte*, and *porte-jarretelle*. After David's approval the evening before, Kat was now more confidently coquettish. When the assistant was gone, the curtain closed behind them, she rolled her hips and caressed her breasts where the bra held them exposed, for David's amusement and arousal.

'Mon dieu!' he whispered.

'Ooh la la,' she whispered back.

He left her while she changed back into her street clothes. When she came out, he took the garments from her. 'I want to buy them for you,' he said, quietly.

She gave him an exaggerated frown. 'They're terribly expensive. And when will I have a chance to wear them?'

'I'll keep them for you,' he said, at the same time signalling to the assistant that he was ready to pay. 'You can wear them for me sometimes when you visit, and keep them once we're together.'

The lingerie had been packed in a pretty bag with a handle of ribbon, which Kat was pleased to carry. They left the shop, both excited and amused. But before the next street corner, Kat had slowed, drooped, and then stopped. David asked her whether she was OK.

'Just a little weary,' she said. 'Maybe I'm dehydrated—it's been a while since breakfast.'

'You're right. I could do with a coffee as well. Bound to be a place somewhere near here.'

The area north of the Tuileries is a place of grand buildings and designer brands, not cafés. David put an arm around Kat, and eventually they found a little restaurant with a few seats outside. Kat slumped into one of them and puffed.

'That's better.' She held out a hand to him. 'Sorry for being so pathetic.'

While they were waiting for drinks, Kat went inside to the toilet. She found she was still bleeding. When she returned to the sunshine, David was staring at his phone.

He glanced up at her, smiled reassuringly, and then looked back at the phone. 'I've just been checking,' he said. 'We can walk a short distance to Madeleine station, and get a metro direct to Pigalle. Then we can walk through Montmartre and up to the Sacré Coeur church. Amazing view. And Montmartre is mecca to any artist for its association with so many great French painters.'

Kat could see how enthusiastic he was. 'Is it a long walk up to the church?'

'No, no distance at all.'

After their rest, the short walk to the Madeleine Metro station felt easy, and then there was another rest for them on the metro train. Progress became more difficult when they emerged from the station at Pigalle. David's memory was less reliable than he thought, and they took an awkward zigzag route towards Sacré Coeur. He had also not mentioned that, by Parisian standards, the walk is a steep climb.

Kat flagged as soon as they began the ascent, and twice had to stop in the street. David was concerned. When she stopped the second time, he told her there was no need to continue.

'Don't fuss me! I'll be alright.'

After another slow walk they reached the entrance to the gardens, marked by a gateway and a few steps from the road. Kat looked up at the long flights of steps above her to the church. 'I'm sorry, David, but I'm not going to make it up there. I need to sit down.' Having announced it, she sat down on the dusty step where they had been standing. David thought he had better sit down next to her. There was no view except for the shops and cafés across the road, and much of the time that was blocked by the tourists who flowed to and from the gardens, intimidatingly close to where they were sat.

Kat looked pale. David said, 'I'm sorry, I should have realised you weren't up to doing this walk.'

'Of course I was!' Her sharp tone made him cautious. 'It's ridiculous,' she continued. 'I'm trying to work out what the problem could be. Wondering whether I might be anaemic. Or maybe it's nothing more than the excitement of the trip.'

David wanted to stay positive. 'I think there is a little funicular railway—you know, a diagonal lift—that goes up the side of this last bit.'

'No, thank you. I just want to sit and rest.'

He put his hand on her thigh, and she covered it with hers. The crowds continued to flow past.

'Why don't you go up on your own?' she suggested. 'I'll be OK here.'

'I'm not doing that. I've seen the view before. Rather be here with you.

'What about something to eat?' he asked. 'Maybe that would help you feel better. We did promise ourselves a good lunch before the journey home.'

'Maybe,' she said, without enthusiasm. David took her hand and stood up.

'Come on then. Let's get out of this and find a nice restaurant where we can sit in peace.'

Kat rose stiffly, and they made their way back onto the street. There were some cafés straight ahead of them. 'A bit basic for our needs?' David queried.

'I don't mind. I'm really not very hungry. Just want to sit down, to be honest.'

They found a table away from the worst of the noise. David had a beer, and Kat was brought hot water and a tea bag. The food arrived soon after. Kat found she was uninterested in hers, and instead watched David as he ate. She touched his hand, and he lifted his head from his croque monsieur to look at her.

'You said you wanted something authentically French today,' she said. 'I'd bet that isn't what you had in mind.' She smiled wanly, and her mouth formed a silent word for him to see. *Sorry*, it said.

***

When Kat said she was ready, they walked slowly down the hill to the Metro station. The line took them directly back across the Seine and to a station not far from the hotel. Kat insisted that she could manage the walk back to the hotel, but it wore her out. There was no doubt that they would need a taxi to the airport.

They were far too early at the airport. After they had checked in, they found seats where David could monitor the departure board. Kat lay across him and slept with her head on his arm. When, finally, the flight departed, she again leaned into him as if they were looking out of the window, as she had done on the outward journey. This time they saw the approach of the moment they would be separated, and feared it. When that moment came, as they stood in the airport car park, she apologised again.

'Kat, please don't keep apologising. These things happen, and it was still lovely. We'll be able to go back again—with kids, and without them. We'll have lots of perfect times together.'

Eulogy for Love

Her response was to lean into him and put her cheek against his. In her mind she heard some Latin words she had learned all those years ago in Florence or Wellesley. It was only a phrase: *Dis aliter visum*.

She knew the meaning very well: *the gods deemed otherwise*. She still wanted to be with David, and her faith in his love had only grown stronger. She even felt more certain that she had the courage to leave Mark. Yet the images of a future with David had dimmed.

She kissed him quickly on the lips, and walked away down the line of cars to find her own. As he watched her go, David reached up to touch his face, and discovered the tears she had left on his cheek.

It was twilight as Kat walked down the drive towards the house. Mark had turned on a light in his office, but not yet drawn the curtains. As soon as she entered the house she saw him through the office doorway, sat at his desk against the opposite wall, his back towards her.

He briefly turned his head towards his shoulder. It was an acknowledgement of her presence, but he had not turned enough to see her, let alone to welcome her home. 'OK?' he said.

'Yes, fine.' Then she noticed the silence in the rest of the house. 'Where are the kids?'

'I sent them to bed. They'd been playing up.'

'But it's only eight, and it's Saturday.' He didn't move or speak. 'And Lise?' Kat asked.

'Went out.'

Kat went upstairs with her suitcase. She stopped in her bedroom long enough to tuck her passport under the mattress of the bed—it could stay there until she had a chance to put it back in the office drawer—and transferred her wedding lingerie to the depths of the wardrobe. Then she went quickly to see the children.

Rachel was lying in bed in the dim light, wide awake. She sat up as soon as Kat walked into the room and held both arms out towards her mother. The arms wrapped around Kat as soon as she sat on the bed. Rachel was sobbing.

'Daddy was nasty to us. We were only playing.'

Kat had the kind of conversation with Rachel that she had had too many times before. Daddy doesn't understand *playing*, she had to remind her. Daddy doesn't know how to have fun and laugh.

When Rachel had finally calmed, Kat settled her into bed, kissed her goodnight, and went to see Jonathan.

Jonathan was also wide awake. Whereas Rachel had been tearful, Jonathan was angry. He had obviously been lying in bed composing a statement to present to his mother. 'I hate Daddy!' he announced. 'I never want you to go away without us again.'

'Where was Lise when this was happening?'

'Daddy shouted at her too, so she went out.'

The conversation that followed this time was more adult, but here too the child had to be asked to forgive the parent. Kat tried to convince Jonathan that his father loved him in his own way, though she struggled to find the evidence. She even had to ask him to forgive her for going away overnight.

To help him settle, Kat said he could look at his phone for a little while. Jonathan said Daddy had taken it away. Kat said he could read, just as long as he didn't let Daddy find out.

Kat went downstairs and looked through the study door. Mark was still at his desk.

'I'm going to bed,' she said.

'OK.' He didn't look round. Kat started to walk towards the stairs, but then stopped.

Eulogy for Love

She was out of his line of sight at his desk. He would hear her voice, nevertheless.

'Apparently it's true,' she called back at him. 'You really are incompetent to look after your own children for half a day.'

She heard no reply from him, and continued upstairs to bed.

Chapter 23

K at continued, over the following weeks, to feel tired and unwell. On the other hand, the bleeding was variable, and sometimes stopped, and this gave her the excuse she wanted to postpone seeing a doctor. She was worn out by life, she told herself as she swallowed an ever-enlarging range of dietary supplements. But, for the first time, she stopped looking for opportunities to see David, and started to find reasons she could not visit. He noticed but misunderstood, and concluded she was angry with him about the visit to Paris. He began to regret he had suggested it.

She could tell, even from the tone of his texts, that he was upset. It distressed her. She waited for a day when the bleeding seemed to have stopped, and then texted to say that she had at last found a short space to come and see him after work the same day. She contrived, once they were in bed, to make sure they made love briefly, and with a primitive urgency that had never been their style. Afterwards she wiped him before he could look at himself, then hastened to the bathroom, claiming she was desperate to pee.

The subterfuge worked, and David felt a little reassured that she still loved him, but he could tell she was unwell. She gave him the same excuses she had given to herself: that she was tired, and perhaps a little anaemic, or needing to increase her vitamin intake. He only let her change the subject when she had promised she would see a doctor within two weeks if there had been no improvement.

Eulogy for Love

She kept her promise, but by then it was October. She went to her health centre, where she was seen by a young male locum who declined to examine her but frowned when she admitted she was overdue for her cervical scan.

Kat sat by his desk while he said that he was going to refer her to the hospital. He did his best to ensure, in an insufficiently practised explanation, that the significant word, *cancer*, was not too prominent. But it was what Kat had been listening for, and she did not miss it. He judged it better, he said, that she should go to the hospital for examination, as that would mean she would already be *in the system* if any further actions were required. He would refer her to the hospital immediately, he said, tapping at a keyboard. And then he turned to her and said—as if giving a child a sweetie for behaving well—that he had put her through as a priority.

***

In the NHS of the twenty-first century, even priority cases have to be patient. It was more weeks before Kat attended the hospital outpatients' clinic. The appointment was in the afternoon. I had agreed I would pick up the children from school, and keep them at home until whatever time Kat was finished and felt ready to collect them.

The initial examination was done by a nurse; but she paused halfway through and said, in the reassuring tones that Kat was beginning to expect from all NHS staff—and never to believe—that she would like a doctor to repeat the examination. Kat pulled up the thick woolly tights that she had thoughtlessly chosen against the November weather and went to sit in the corridor. After a very long time a woman appeared wearing blue scrubs and a harassed expression, and went into the room where Kat had been examined earlier.

285

Kat was called back in soon after, and once more took her expected position at the side of the doctor's desk. Doctor Isabella Duran introduced herself and described the process and purpose of colposcopy. Kat was returned to the stirrups. She watched Dr Duran position her head between her legs and remembered happier times when a woman had taken that position. *How life had changed*, she thought. The instrument was brought to bear, the sample taken, and Kat heaved up her tights once more.

Doctor Isabella Duran checked the screen and then looked across at Kat and smiled at her. 'Kateryna, is that right?'

'Kat.'

'OK, thank you. Well, Kat, I've taken the sample, and it will be sent off now to be examined. 'But I think I should tell you that there is something very obviously not right with your cervix—a growth that shouldn't be there. There's a distinct possibility that this is a cancerous growth, and I suspect from what I can see that it's a kind that can develop very rapidly. And that means we need to get a better picture of what it's doing, and try to stop it before it goes any further.'

It was a carefully judged explanation, but Kat could read between the lines. She understood that she had an aggressive cancer that might even now be spreading beyond her cervix. At that time, on that evening, she didn't want it spelt out more bluntly. She was told only to expect appointments for further checks, which would be followed by a meeting with the oncology team.

It was almost five when she drove out of the hospital. Emotionally numb and very tired, she unthinkingly steered towards home. She needed a space to be on her own. She also needed a drink, and momentarily wondered whether the doctors would disapprove. She decided she didn't give a damn. Then she realised she should let me know what was happening. When she looked at her phone, it was almost out of charge.

Kat went upstairs with the second half of a large gin and tonic, got onto her bed without turning on a light, and plugged her phone into the charger she kept beside it. Then she texted:

> Sorry - only just left the hospital. Have come home for a bit of a rest before collecting the kids, if that's OK. Xx

I replied:

> Of course. We're fine - take your time. xx

And then, inevitably, Kat fell asleep. She had, however, made a mistake—a terrible mistake, and one she had never made before. She went to sleep so abruptly that she did not close the screen on her phone; and, because it was charging, it did not automatically lock. It remained on her lap, glowing in the dark.

When Kat woke, she saw Mark sitting at the end of the bed. He was studying the screen of a phone. She realised, horrified, that it was hers.

'Ah, hello,' he said, seeming calm. Kat pulled herself into a sitting position. 'Long days of passion in another man's bed, a weekend in Paris. No wonder you're too tired to cook dinner for your husband when he comes back from a hard day at work. I haven't yet determined how long this has been going on, but I shall. I've emailed the entire chat with your devoted David to my own phone, to read at my leisure.'

He looked round at her. The room lights were off, but there was a pale amber wash across the room from the streetlights. He would have seen the expression on her face.

'Of course,' he said, 'Maybe delightful David is only one of a long string of lovers. Who knows, maybe you run three or four of them at once.'

Kat managed a reply. 'There's only been one.'

Mark was looking at the phone again. The light varied on his face as he flicked from screen to screen.

'You'd say that, of course you would. But we now know, don't we, that you're a skilled liar, and nothing you say can ever be taken as the truth. You may say tomorrow that you're going to work, but for all I know you'll be heading off for an orgy.'

His finger stopped moving. 'Ah yes, here it is. I particularly liked this one. Shall I read it to you?'

He didn't wait for an answer. She remembered writing the words, but now Mark made them a parody.

My darling, I can't wait to be with you again. I love the way you want me, and I love to please you. I want to surrender to you, to be the object of all your desires. Know that I am here for you, to be used by you in every way you want.

Mark stopped reading, and shook his head. 'What a slut you are.'

He reached out to the bedside lamp and turned it on, so that he could see Kat's face more plainly. She turned her eyes away from him. 'It's so unfair, don't you agree?' he said. 'I work damned hard to give you and your children a comfortable life. Big house, plenty of money to spend, nice holidays abroad. And yet it's some other man, not me, that gets to *use you in any way he wants*.'

She could hear the rising fury in his voice, and thought he might be winding himself up to hit her. Then he reverted to the horrible calm voice.

288

Eulogy for Love

'I'm willing to forgive you for your ingratitude, Kat, and to let this marriage continue. But I'm not going to let you make a fool of me. So, for starters, I've prepared a little text for you to send.'

He put the phone in front of her face, but pulled it away when she tried to reach for it.

'No-no,' he said, 'no touching. Just read out what I've written.' She peered at the screen. 'Read it out loud!' he insisted. She looked up at him, sensed the anger trapped inside him. She returned her eyes to the words on the phone, and spoke them:

David

We've had some fun times together, but I've realised it has to stop. I should never have been unfaithful to Mark, and now I have to put things right before it's too late, for the sake of my marriage and children.

If you love me as much as you say you do, you will respect the decision I have made. We have to break off contact completely, and do it immediately. Please don't phone or text me, or try to see me. Just accept, please, that it's over between us.

Kat faltered, and looked away from the screen. The thought of David reading the message was unbearable. 'Keep going,' Mark said. 'There's only a bit more.'

Kat managed to focus again on the screen, and continued to read out loud.

I believe that you want me to be happy. In that case, leave me in peace to find happiness in my marriage. I need to block your calls and messages, and I won't read anything you send. I don't even want you to answer this message.

289

Thanks

Kat

'Excellent,' Mark said. 'Now press the Send button.'

Kat retreated from the phone, as if it might send the message on its own. It was all too much, too awful, for her to take in. 'I can't do that. It's a horrible message. I need to think about things.'

'You mean you need time to decide whether you're going to leave me? You don't. Because you won't.'

'Why won't I? Actually, I've been thinking about it very seriously. Don't you think I could live without your money?'

'Doubt you could, Kat—you've got very used to it. But that's not what I'm saying. I'm saying I wouldn't let you leave. If we're not going to be a complete family, all four of us together, then we're not going to be any kind of family. I've seen what happens when people get divorced. Husbands stripped of their money. Endless dreary arguments about access. I'd rather wipe the slate clean.'

'What do you mean, *wipe the slate clean*? Get rid of us? How could you do that?'

He watched her face looking back at him, letting her struggle to find an answer. 'There are ways,' he said. 'Freak accidents, house fires, unsolved murders while on holiday in dodgy countries.'

'God, Mark, you can be a cruel man, but you wouldn't do anything as awful as that.'

'Think of the benefits. I could find a new, young wife— one who would be appreciative and accommodating. Maybe have some new, nicer children.'

He held out the phone again. 'Press the button, Kat.'

'You wouldn't hurt your own children.'

'Try me.'

290

He kept the phone in front of her.

'Press the button.'

Kat looked at the screen. Then she realised that it didn't make much difference. She had cancer. At best she would be subjected to a series of hospital treatments when she would be no fun for David. She might be very unwell, lose her hair. The relationship with David, at least as something passionate and joyful, was over. At worst, she might be dead in months. In that case, choosing between Mark and David was an irrelevance. The only thing that mattered right now was to get through the next few months in a way that would keep the children safe.

She put her hand up to the screen. She paused. She pressed *Send*.

'Good girl,' Mark said as she put her head down and wept. 'I'm glad that's settled. Now let's have some dinner.'

She wiped away some of the tears with the back of her hand. 'You'll have to get your own dinner. I've got to get the kids back from Annie's.'

'Alright. But I should add, don't start thinking you can deceive me. From now on I will be monitoring you. I will want to see what's on your phone. I shall be checking for other phones you might have acquired and hidden, and looking through your computer account. I shall carry out unannounced calls and inspections to make sure you are where you say you are. And if you find that intrusive, you only have yourself to blame for being a lying, adulterous bitch.'

'OK,' she said, now beyond any argument, 'but please can I have my phone back?'

'Certainly not. I've still got more reading to do. And I'm curious to know whether he really loves you, or if he'll text back.'

Kat went to the bathroom and tried to tidy herself enough to go out. When she came out, Mark called to her: 'Oh, and I think I'd like to visit you tonight. You know, *to have you any way I want*. Please be ready for me.'

Kat went to each of the children's rooms and found fresh clothes for them, and put them in a carrier bag. She would have liked some fresh clothes for herself, but Mark was still in the bedroom. She could borrow some underwear from her sister. It only mattered that she didn't need to come back home that night.

***

David had noticed in recent weeks that Kat's texts were becoming less frequent, and he was especially pleased when he saw one arrive that evening. When he read it, the effect on him was so powerful that he started to hyperventilate, and became physically faint. He got himself a drink in the hope it would calm him, and started writing lengthy replies, only to delete each one. He did love her enough to let her go, if that was truly what she wanted. But he couldn't believe she would do it so abruptly. Eventually, and far from sober, he settled on a reply. A short message seemed less in contravention of her demand not to respond.

> My darling, I don't understand. Please don't cut me off like this. I will respect your choice if that's what you want. But please, please, can we talk first? I love you. xxxx

***

The children were both at the kitchen table doing their homework when Kat arrived. They leapt up to greet her. She hugged them but then manoeuvred them back to the table. A moment later the landline phone rang. It was Mark, wanting to know whether Kat was there. I told him she had just arrived, and asked whether he wanted to speak to her. He declined, but said he would like a quick word with the children. Rachel took the phone, thinking her daddy wanted a chat. Kat took the phone away from her.

'Mark, I'm going to stay at Annie's tonight. It's easier at this time in the evening to put the children to bed here than bring them home, and I need some space.'

'That's a shame. I was looking forward to having you later, if you know what I mean. Don't forget I'll be checking up on you. In fact, I may call again this evening.

'By the way,' he went on, 'your former lover sent a text, so he obviously doesn't love you.'

'Tell me what it said. Please.'

'Certainly not. It doesn't matter anymore. It's over. And I've deleted it from your phone, along with every other mention of him.'

I took Kat through to my living room, away from Jonathan and Rachel. I had to move between her and the children to supervise them as they finished their homework, watched a little television, and then prepared for bed. Bit by bit, I heard the entire story about the news from hospital, and about Mark's ultimatum. But the knife would be twisted in her heart once more that night.

After the children were in bed, the housephone rang again. I picked it up in front of Kat as she sat on the sofa. It was David, so distressed that he could only speak in staccato phrases. I mouthed his name to Kat. She shook her head forlornly, and heard the words that I spoke to him.

'I can't help you, David,' I said. 'She's not here, but she's made it clear to me that she doesn't want to speak to you.'

Kat was looking at me, her tears flowing so freely that they dripped from her chin.

'I'm sure it's very hard for you. She didn't want to hurt you, but it was bound to hurt whichever way she did it.'

Kat's mouth quivered as she tried to stay silent.

'Yes, she's absolutely clear about it. I'm afraid you just have to accept it, as she's asked you to.'

Kat had resorted to holding her hand against her mouth.

'I'm sorry, but that's all I can say. Please don't try to contact her again. Goodbye, David.'

As soon as I ended the call, Kat let out a howl—a terrible keening sound, so loud and full of despair that I thought it must have been heard by the whole street.

***

There was never going to be a showdown with Mark, never the cataclysmic end to her marriage. Kat had missed all her chances to walk that journey over rough ground to the life she had believed awaited her. Instead, she would grasp death's hand and slip away.

In the interim, she allowed her frail life to be taken over by her husband and the health service. She was put through a series of examinations at hospital. It was when she went for an x-ray, and they swung the machine over her chest, that she knew for certain to expect the worst. It was confirmed when she sat, with me by her side, and was told the results. Yes, it was an aggressive cancer that was already reaching out into her body. At this point it was no longer a question of cure, only a matter of slowing it down as much as possible, and trying to keep her comfortable. They recommended a radical hysterectomy. She had already been emptied of her capacity for joy and pleasure, she thought, and now they would scrape out her womanhood like the flesh from an avocado.

After fourteen years working for the charity, Kat deserved an extravagant farewell ceremony. She could not be given it, because they had to pretend that she would be coming back. Instead, she was handed a bunch of flowers and a *Get Well Soon* card.

Lise, the au pair, stayed on out of loyalty to Kat, despite a workload that was increasingly unfair. In the end it was the sense of gloom in the house that drove her away. She announced she wanted to go back home well before Christmas, and would not be returning. Mark hired a local woman to run the house and look after the children. In mid-December, Kat went for her operation, and afterwards began a course of chemotherapy. Within days she had to start picking clumps of hair from her pillow.

She was home for Christmas, but was beginning to disengage—not only from family life, but from life itself. Joan, the housekeeper, had gone into town to buy the few gifts for the children that Kat could not order online, and she had sat with Kat to help her wrap them. It was Joan who cooked the lunch on Christmas Day. Since coming back from hospital, Kat mostly wore loose clothes and nightwear, but she dressed for Christmas lunch, and chose a headscarf in festive colours to conceal her hairless head. Yet she was barely present. Joan, always efficient, set out the dining room table nicely, and served the meal on time. She was deferential to Mark, while subtly condescending to Kat. He was obviously pleased to have found a woman who provided most of the services he wanted from a wife. Mark found Joan had even put out a steel with the carving knife and fork at the end of the table where he was sitting. When Joan had put the turkey in front of him, Mark stood and made a ritual of sharpening the knife, whisking it back and forth on the metal bar, just as his father used to do.

When Kat began to help clearing away the table, Joan told her to go and sit down. Kat changed back into nightclothes and stretched out on the sofa in the living room that was now her customary place. From this position she was an observer of Smallwood family life as it was evolving under Mark's control. She looked on as the children were allowed to open the remainder of their gifts, as they watched Mark's choice of television, and as they ate the Christmas cake that Joan brought through to them. It was, superficially, a happy scene. But Kat knew that her children, uncharacteristically subdued, were feeling weighed down. They understood that their mother was very ill, and that saddened them. They knew they were no longer under her protection.

Kat smiled lovingly as she watched them. It was a mask she wore to reassure them. Inside, she felt a great emptiness. She knew this family life would be taken from her in a few months. For all she might watch, capturing the memories, they too would soon be taken. Life would vanish from her, and with it love, joy, fear, and sadness; and all knowledge of the world.

***

The worst of it, David found, was that there was so little left in his life to show that Kat had ever been a part of it. Yes, there were the texts on his phone, but nothing that had substance. No woman's coat on the hook by the front door, no half-read book on the table by the sofa, no clothes hung in the wardrobe. There was only the lingerie from Paris, unworn since that day. It lay in a bedroom drawer, kept inside the little bag with its ribbon handles, the delicate scarlet fabric interleaved with tissue. He knew that seeing it would be a torture he could not bear, and so he never opened the drawer. When he searched for evidence that his beautiful Kateryna had been a part of his life, the most irrefutable evidence he could find was his own searing grief. And so it was his grief that he clung to, ferociously.

The advent of Christmas added a terrible emptiness. For the first weeks after losing Kat, he became strangely hyperactive: tidying the studio, going out running more frequently and for longer. That, perhaps, was to divert himself from the only thing he really wanted to do: to go and find Kat. When that stage faded, he started to slide into despair and lethargy. The only good reason he could find for not taking his own life was that it would hurt the twins. The rest was merely cowardice. He was also exhausted from a lack of sleep, because he would lie awake at night replaying all his memories of their months together, seeking the clue that would explain why she had suddenly chosen to recommit to her barren marriage. Sometimes he wondered if she had been lying, and that there was some very different reason from the one she had given. He wondered if she had, in fact, found someone who could make her more happy. He tried very hard to be pleased for her.

For the first time ever, neither Lauren nor Hannah would be visiting at Christmas. They had busy lives and better places to be.

On Christmas Eve it occurred to him that, if he was not going to kill himself, he had better get some food to cover the holiday period. It was afternoon when he drove to the supermarket in town, and on arrival realised that anyone feeling depressed should avoid such places on Christmas Eve. Without the predisposition to good cheer, and with no prospect of festivities, the spell of Christmas is broken, the fraud exposed. David, looking around at the crush of shoppers with their overfilled trolleys, saw detestable people gripped by greed and gluttony, slaves to consumerism. He had thought to buy things he would like to eat, something to cheer himself through the solitary days. That plan was now abandoned. He limited his choices to food on shelves he could reach without shoving, closed his mind to the mockery of the piped Christmas songs, stoically endured the long checkout queue; and, at last, hurried home.

Until then, through his deepening depression, he had clung to the certainty that he must stay alive for his daughters. It was not that they needed him, only that they would be terribly hurt to think he had not loved them enough to stay alive for them, nor want to meet the grandchildren they would give him one day.

There is, however, a point in the long fall towards self-destruction when such obligations, even when held by the most loving parent, become invisible in the thickening darkness of despair. As David drove home, he fell past that point. It wasn't only Christmas that had become meaningless. Without Kat in his life there could be no joy; and without joy there was no value in home or work or family, or life itself. For the first time he started to think in serious practical terms how to end that life, mentally surveying his house for the tools he would need to complete his last task.

The light had gone from the day as he arrived home. The headlights swung around as he turned the car into the yard, and found reflections in two small eyes. David stopped the car quickly, the tyres crunching hard on the gravel, and looked more closely. It was a black and white cat. Not a kitten, he thought, but young and small. He had never seen it before, and there were no houses nearby where it might belong. He picked the bags of shopping from the car and took them inside the

298

house, for a moment leaving the door open. The small cat followed him into the kitchen and looked up at him.

David looked back down. *The gods are having a laugh*, he thought. *They've sent me a little cat. How very droll.*

The little cat waited inside while David locked the car and closed the front door, and then snaked around his ankles when he returned. He picked it up to inspect it. It had no collar. It seemed healthy but a little thin, and he thought he should give it some food. He could only find canned tuna, which it accepted.

David realised that if he was to have a guest for Christmas, he had better get some food that it would like. This time he drove the mile to the village shop, the only remaining commercial outlet in the village centre, the light from the window an oasis on a darkened street. Inside, he was the only customer. He put a bottle of wine alongside the cans of cat food in the basket, but still felt ashamed to have gone there for this emergency after taking most of his custom elsewhere. He felt worse still when the owner, a slim Polish woman, was not only friendly but emanated a quality of graciousness that had been entirely absent at the supermarket.

'You have cat now, Mr Barber?' she asked as she laid the cans gently into his bag.

'Apparently. It turned up on my doorstep this evening. I don't know who it could belong to.'

'We sometimes have people ask to put up notices in the window when they have a cat go missing, but we have none now. I will keep eye open for you.'

He paid by cash. As he took his change, she caught his eye and smiled at him with penetrating warmth. 'I hope you have very happy Christmas.'

'And you too,' David answered, embarrassed yet strangely affected.

The little cat had climbed onto an old armchair that David kept in the kitchen, and fallen asleep. They left each other alone for the evening, but when David went to bed it followed. As soon as he had settled, it leapt up and nestled into the bend between his stomach and his thighs, and stayed there all night.

David discovered the following day that he had flea bites on his shoulder. He didn't mind. Little Cat, as she soon became, had been a handhold for him to grasp as he fell into the abyss.

Chapter 24

Through November and early December, before her operation, Kat and I held to our long-established routines. Though she found it wearing, she still drove over at weekends with Jonathan and Rachel. She and I would sit at the kitchen table with drinks cupped between our hands, as we always had, and gossip while the children played, or bickered, or watched TV. But on those last visits she would soon seek a more comfortable chair, and watch while I made the lunch. These occasions, and we knew it, were no more than re-enactments of a life that was now ended.

Then Kat had her operation, returning home as a prisoner under house arrest, and with Joan as the ever-watchful warder. I continued to visit during the Christmas weeks, but it was more for the sake of the children. There was no pleasure in being in that house, nor privacy when he was so often there, scowling.

Once we rebelled and absconded. When the January weather proved mild, and the children were back at school, I bundled Kat into my car for a winter's afternoon, and we meandered through the grey lanes and little villages of Middle England. She looked out at the sunless landscape quietly, expressionless.

We stopped only once. At Kat's request, we pulled off the road near the top of an escarpment where we could look out across the fields and leafless trees towards Gloucestershire. I thought she was focused on the view, until I turned and saw that she was weeping.

'Oh, Annie, Annie, I am so angry at being cheated of all the good things I thought were still to come. But I can bear that for myself. What scares me, what terrifies me, is the thought of Rachel and Jonathan being left with him. God only knows what will happen if he gets his hands on them.'

She was still staring at the view ahead. I stretched awkwardly across the car and pulled her loose body into my arms. She shuddered and wailed as I held her.

'I can't stop it happening. But you can, Annie. I want them to be with you. Please promise you'll make sure they don't stay with him.'

'I will,' I said. 'I promise.'

***

I made the promise to Kat because she was my sister, and because I had no choice. But I also promised because she was right to be terrified. We didn't know whether Mark was so evil that he would carry out his threat to murder his own children, but the fact that we weren't sure was frightening enough. Even if he didn't, it was certain some woman of child-bearing age would be fool enough to believe he was a great catch, and he would be fool enough to think she could deliver him nicer children. Jonathan and Rachel would be pushed aside, exactly as Mark had been banished by his own father. And, whatever else might happen, we knew that Mark was a man incapable of warmth. The children were going to need a parent to help them through the loss of their mother. Someone who would hold them as they cried, be still with them as they raged, and play with them as they remembered how to be children. They would get none of those from Mark.

Eulogy for Love

The problem was that I had no idea how I could keep my promise. I researched online, took legal advice under a false name. There seemed nothing to be done. The world would regard Mark as a good man suffering under the tragic loss of his young wife. I would soon be the only one who knew otherwise, and cared enough to act.

And yet there was someone else who cared. I had made a promise to Kat that I would never contact him, but promises have hierarchies. Better to break one promise if it would help me keep another that was far more important. As March gave way to April, and feeling a growing sense of impotence and panic, I decided to phone him.

'David, this is Annie.'

I waited for him to assimilate.

'Hi Annie,' he replied, flatly. The two words were enough to confirm he was a man in pain. He waited for me to continue. I only said that I wanted to talk to him. He agreed, with no questions, and invited me to the farmhouse the next day.

The following afternoon I sat at the kitchen table in the farmhouse, and watched David make the mug of tea he had offered me. He was still a good-looking man, still slim, and with a good head of greying, unkempt hair; but his face was pale, his eyes surrounded by the darkness of someone who has not slept enough. He didn't make tea for himself, but brought over a glass of red wine, and the bottle too. Then he sat opposite me and waited until I chose to speak.

'How are you?' I said.

'How do you think I am, Annie?' He glared at me with his shadowed eyes. 'The last time we spoke was the day I stopped having a reason to live. Now I buy food, I eat. I sit in my studio and pretend to work. I go to bed. Sometimes I sleep. None of it matters.'

He turned his head from me. 'But I'm making progress,' he said. 'I no longer weep in the company of strangers.'

'I'm so sorry, David, I truly am. I've come today to explain some things. Not good things, but at least they may help you understand.'

My greatest fear was that he would rush out and do something crazy. Murder Mark, possibly, but more likely go to the hospital to see Kat. I made him promise he would not act unilaterally after he had heard me, though I was far from sure it would make any difference. Then I told him the whole story. He sat and listened, one hand on the wine glass and the other on the bottle. He said nothing, but I could see the emotions passing through his face. It was when I told him that our beautiful Kateryna was dying that he dropped his head. I wondered whether to go to him and hold him, but felt it might be an intrusion, so I gave him the last few dreadful facts as he covered his face with his hands, and cried almost silently, his body shuddering. I panicked when he got up, thinking that he might be about to rush to the hospital. He had only gone somewhere else in the house to hide from me.

I sat and waited for him. Eventually he returned, red-eyed, and sat down again. He poured more wine into his glass.

'I'm so terribly sorry, David. I never wanted to hurt you like this.' This time, I risked leaning forward and putting my hand on his. He let it stay. 'I hope you can understand that I hated keeping the truth from you, but my first concern was to keep a promise to my sister. Now that I've told you, I'm very worried that you'll contact Kat. It's vitally important you recognise that you mustn't do it, however much you want to be with her. The most important thing is the safety of Rachel and Jonathan. If you love her, and I know you do, then you must stay away from her.'

'So why are you telling me?'

'Because there's something desperately important that has to be done for Kat, and I need your help to do it.'

He looked exhausted. I wondered how much more I should say that day.

'David, there's nothing any of us can do to stop her dying. I believe she could at least go peacefully if she knew the kids would be OK. Right now, though, she's terrified by the thought they'll be left with Mark.'

'So what's the problem? Why can't there be a court order that gives someone else—you, I'm guessing—guardianship of the kids?'

He wasn't thinking very clearly. 'Because it isn't that sort of situation. It's not like divorce. Care of the children passes automatically to the surviving parent, no questions asked.'

'So what on earth can we do?'

'I don't know. But I do know that you and I are the only two people in this world who will do whatever it takes to let Kat die in peace.'

'That's true. Violent crime isn't really my thing, but I'll kill the bastard if that's what needs to be done.'

'Yes, I think you would. But please don't. Apart from anything else, you'd make me an accomplice to murder, and I wouldn't be able to look after the children if I were in prison.'

He made a thin laugh, then dropped his head and went silent, as if too weary to speak more.

'David,' I said, 'I don't like to leave you like this, but I think you need time to let all this sink in. Then we can talk again.'

He looked up at me, but only nodded. 'OK,' I said, standing up, 'maybe I can give you a call tomorrow.' He still said nothing, so I picked up the empty mug and took it over the kitchen area.

'Annie,' he said unexpectedly, while I was turned away from him, 'have you got plans for this evening?'

I said not, and it was the truth.

'Could you stay? This is the first time I've been able to talk to anyone about Kat.'

I stayed for the evening. As grieving people always do, we comforted ourselves with trivial things. We cooked together, talked about the weather and the news, and watched television. But, as also happens, the skin of normality kept rupturing, the painful memories breaking through. David found himself thinking of the foods that Kat liked, the TV programmes she enjoyed. He also said that I had mannerisms that reminded him of Kat.

'I'm sorry, David. Am I making things worse for you?'

'Not at all. It's so good to be with someone who understands, someone who's going through it too. I've had to deal with it entirely on my own these last three months. One of the many snags to having a secret affair. You can't tell people how wonderful it is, or about the agony of its ending. And anyway, people seem to think that an illicit affair can't be real love, so the ending of it can't be real grief. It's like adults dismissing teenage love. *Only a silly crush*, they say, as if a teenager's feelings aren't real. Falling in love with someone who's married is seen as foolishness, or naughtiness, or disgustingly immoral. Of course, it may be all those things, but that doesn't make the love less real, or the loss of it less agonising.'

Later, while we watched television, I looked at David and saw he was falling asleep. I teased him gently, said I was going home, and told him to go to bed. I stood to leave, but then leaned down and gave him a hug, awkwardly, where he was sitting. I realised, as I did so, that we had become friends.

Eulogy for Love

***

We exchanged texts the next morning and agreed to meet that lunchtime in a country pub halfway between us. It had an outdated style that featured wood panelling and high-backed seats with embroidered upholstery. The barman was polishing glasses for lack of customers.

David was already there, and looked calmer than the evening before. He admitted he had drunk too much wine, but said a morning run had dealt with the hangover. I was troubled to see he was now holding a pint of ale.

He had also been cooking up a plan to visit Kat without being seen by her. I had to squash it. 'Just think about it, David. If she saw you she'd be horrified, even if Mark didn't find out. You would certainly destroy my relationship with her. And if he did catch you—or hear that you'd visited—the consequences are unknown.'

'But really, would he hurt the children?'

'How could we know? He's a weird, screwed-up guy. Would you want to take the chance? Just to catch a glimpse of Kat asleep? And anyway, it was her genuine wish that you should remember her as she was before the illness.'

'You know, Annie, I feel hurt by that. It doesn't matter what she looks like now. I'll always love her. I thought she knew that.'

I wanted to move on.

'Well, David, the best way right now to show your love,' I said, 'is to make sure her children don't end up in the hands of their father.'

He nodded. 'OK.' He sighed. 'Let's talk about that.

'I've been thinking,' he said. 'Yesterday you said we couldn't challenge the kids staying with him after Kat has gone. But maybe we can find some evidence to mount a case against him after that.'

'What sort of case did you have in mind?' I asked, feeling disappointed.

'I don't know! Stuff the kids tell you, I suppose.'

'That's terribly vague, don't you think? Maybe if we wait a year or two, the kids might tell us things that amounted to enough to report to a social worker. Who'd probably do nothing about it. Hardly a comforting message for me to take to Kat on her last days.'

'Well, OK,' he responded defensively, 'then let's find some evidence now. I'm only thinking . . .'

He looked up at me, and I saw the tears forming in his eyes. He was fighting to hold himself together.

'. . . only thinking,' he eventually managed to say, 'that we haven't got very long.'

'I'm sorry, David, this is really hard for both of us. But I just can't see that working. Let's suppose for the moment he doesn't carry out the threat he made to *wipe the slate clean*, as he put it, if Kat left him. That will leave Rachel and Jonathan in the care of a man who is subtly but deeply abusive. At best it will take months to gather evidence from the children.'

'I wasn't thinking about that sort of evidence.'

'Then what?'

'I dunno. Involvement in financial crime, maybe. Paedophilia. Gambling addiction. Membership of a satanic sect.'

'Oh, I wish! God, wouldn't that be lovely. But he's not like that. You and I know that he's a controlling, emotionally abusive bastard with a personality disorder, but as far as the world is concerned he's an upstanding, hard-working citizen doing wonderful work with disadvantaged children. And it's standard policy to do police checks on people in his line of work. There's no chance we'll find that kind of evidence.'

There weren't many people in the pub, and it was hard to judge how far our voices were carrying. David leaned forward.

'That wasn't what I meant,' he said softly. 'We agreed yesterday that we'd do whatever it takes to keep them out of his clutches. I'm not talking about *finding* evidence. I'm talking about *manufacturing* it.'

David sat back and watched for my reaction. Then he leaned forward again.

'And if you're not willing to go that far, then let's not meet again. I'll just go and kill him. And you can honestly claim you had nothing to do with it.'

He'd played a move that had me cornered. If no other options were available, sheer logic pointed to fake evidence as the way forward. Better than David spending the rest of his life in prison for murder. That said, his proposal looked complicated and risky. And criminal.

We talked around the possibilities, but they all seemed very fanciful. David thought I could generate payments from Mark's bank accounts to dodgy organisations. Even if I could have done it, it seemed unlikely the police would be convinced that Mark was a jihadist or international drug smuggler. Briefly wandering into the territory of old films on daytime TV, we considered committing a burglary or a car theft and leaving Mark's fingerprints at the site of the crime. That strategy was also rejected.

Then we talked about paedophilia. 'We could get some child porn,' David said, 'and stick it on the hard drive of his computer.'

'Yes, we could,' I agreed. 'A few problems, though. Even if we could download some child porn—and, given time, I suspect we could—we'd have to gain access to his PC. And it wouldn't achieve anything unless the police found it.'

'We'd send them an anonymous message,' David said, as if it were obvious. 'Quickly, before he could find the files and delete them.'

'OK, we could do that. But there are still big problems. And I'll tell you what I like least. I'm sure there are special police teams monitoring the movement of kiddie porn across the internet. If they detect us downloading it, we'll be the ones in court, not Mark. If you're going to be locked up, David, I'd much rather it was for something comparatively honourable, like murder.'

We had run out of ideas, and fell silent. David had also finished his second pint of beer, and was turning the empty mug between his fingers, as if contemplating a third. I doubted he'd be safe to drive if he did. I was also keen to get over to the hospital to be with Kat, though I felt it would be unkind to tell David where I was going.

'Look, David, let's call it a day. We can think further.' He nodded. 'And, given the way this discussion is heading, I think we'd better meet in private.'

'Yes, good plan.'

We stood and put on our coats. 'Oh, and one other thing,' I said quietly. 'I suggest no ordinary texts from now on. Phone instead—or use text with encryption, if it's something incriminating. They've got no reason at all to be monitoring our calls, and the fact that we're phoning each other would be easy enough to explain.'

We hugged. 'Sounds terribly cloak and dagger,' he said in my ear.

'It is,' I whispered back. 'We're getting ourselves into some really serious stuff.'

Eulogy for Love

***

Those of us who make a living repairing personal computers see material that gives us a distinctive perspective on humanity. Our comrades who repair smart phones and notepads will encounter it too, but not in its full pungent richness. We are all maintenance workers in the sewage system that flows beneath the digital world, but they only deal with blocked U-bends. We're the ones who wade thigh-deep through the effluent.

All my private customers dislike giving me access to their PC, because they all have things to hide. When they come to claim their mended computer, they want to look in my eyes to see whether I have found them out, but they rarely dare. A few may have nothing worse to hide than embarrassing emails to former lovers, scurrilous gossip about their bosses, or membership of an online group that believes the Greek gods are a race of immortals who now live off-grid in the American backwoods. It's my professional judgement, however, that most people hide more than that. No—I mean most *men*. They are all at it. There are the predatory sexters, the dating site catfishers, and of course the social media trolls. And, if they aren't doing that, they'll be doing porn.

Most of it is only mainstream porn, the supposedly harmless stuff we all know that everyone watches but never confess to watching ourselves. I'll admit that I've seen plenty of it—mostly in the line of duty. This is the porn where low-level violence against women is so ubiquitous that it goes unnoticed. It is in this ordinary, everyday porn that you can see men thrusting remorselessly into women as if using a sex toy—a toy that offers the ultimate lifelike sensation of a real woman's flesh. Or watch the legally consenting but desperately vulnerable teenager, set upon by a group of big bellied, jism-spraying men, her mouth quivering in distress but her tears lost in the coating of semen on her face. Here you can see women, for men's pleasure, gagging as enormous penises are forced into their throats. These women, these paid victims, may be crying out in pain or in orgasm, but it can be difficult to tell the difference, and no one cares to ask which one it is.

So much for the mainstream. There is worse to be found, of course. I do my best not to find it, mainly because I might have to report it to the police. I haven't got time for that, and I suspect I would lose a substantial number of customers. I know the signs that it's there, however. These PCs belong to customers who plead with me to come and do the repairs on site, and then shuffle uneasily around me as I'm working. And there is always something about these customers that convinces me. The police can do their checks. I trust my intuition.

I thought about this as I drove home from the meeting with David, and started to develop a plan. I decided, however, not to tell him until I had some results. It took me most of two days to write and test some code, and then I made a list of the half dozen customers with the indefinable personal manner that, in my mind, made them hot favourites as peddlers of kiddie porn.

Dr Bowland was top of the list. If he was a medical doctor, I could only hope that he had been struck off many decades ago. He was certainly retired now, and that meant there was a good chance he'd be at home during the day. Sure enough, he answered when I rang.

'Hello, Dr Bowland,' I said in my brightest, most professional voice. 'This is Annie from PCP. How are you?'

Eulogy for Love

He managed to remember after a couple of seconds. 'Hello, Annie,' he replied, in the mucus-coated voice of a lifelong smoker.

He seemed to have no more to say, so I began my pitch.

'Dr Bowland, as you know, I've installed the latest and best virus protection software on your computer. Unfortunately, I've recently learned that there's a new virus, and your PC isn't protected against it. In fact, there's a very high chance it has already been infected. As a gesture of goodwill, I'm offering a home visit to all my Five Star customers to deal with the problem.'

I didn't know what a Five Star customer was, but hoped he liked being one.

'Oh, that's worrying,' he said. 'Can I download something that will fix it? Or maybe you could email over some instructions, so that I can get rid of it myself.'

'I know, Dr Bowland, that would be so much easier, wouldn't it? But I'm afraid it can't be done in this instance. With luck I can run an automated process to seek and destroy the virus, but I need to be there in case there are complications.'

There was a pause. He was weighing up the risks. 'Do I really need to do this? I mean, what would happen if it wasn't sorted out?'

'Well, it's a clever little virus, and its behaviour isn't always the same. Sometimes it will simply erase everything on the hard drive. But there are reports that sometimes it publishes a list of the contents of your computer on the internet, and lets everyone come and take what they like.'

He stopped protesting. He even suggested that I should visit the same day, which suited me well.

Bowland stood over me as I began to work on the PC, and it was an effort to conceal my disgust. He was a thin elderly man with a haggard face and a nicotine-stained beard that sprouted below his lip and waggled when he spoke. He was wearing a stained knitted cardigan over a check shirt, and baggy jeans that were barely lifted onto his hips, as if he were planning to drop them again very soon. I doubt he would have known what to do if he ever got his hands on an adult woman, but that did not stop him ogling me. Not that there was much to ogle, as I'd made a point of covering up.

I had put my high-capacity USB stick into a port, and initiated the programme it contained. 'There you are, Dr Bowland,' I announced reassuringly. 'The software is scanning your systems on a seek-and-destroy basis.'

As a general policy, I like to help customers understand what I am doing, though it can be painfully difficult. For once I was talking bullshit, and enjoying it.

A message on the screen appeared: *Scanning . . .* Below it, a message box announced the imaginary partitions that had been scanned, and—at intervals I had carefully randomised—reported that *virus instances* had been found. It was all nonsense. I was only interested in the full stops at the end of the onscreen text, which would increase if suspect image files were found. I had written the routine so that it would give low priority to images in places where images ought to be, and ignore the thousands of little gif and png files that are used to make a computer screen look pretty. Instead, it would be rooting around for image folders in unexpected places.

We were both getting too focused on the screen messages, so I tried to distract Bowland with conversation. He was very happy to describe his recent and current ailments. Fortunately, the screen message changed just as he began an account of his haemorrhoids. It announced that the scan had been completed, fifteen virus instances found. *Proceed and destroy? YES/NO,* it asked.

Disappointingly, the full stops had not extended. No likely porn found. I clicked the button for YES. The online message announced the *instances* were being deleted, with the number counting down. In fact, the software was saving a sample of images from the obvious folders, in case Bowland liked to keep his child porn mixed with photos of the family at Christmas.

'There you are,' I said. 'All partitions scanned, nasty virus removed. And new protection added to prevent the virus getting in again. Job done.'

He looked like a man who has just been told by the police that they won't be pressing charges.

I timed it carefully. 'Oh, Dr Bowland, I just need to check. If you've used any external disks in the last three weeks or so, the virus could have spread to them. We really ought to give them a scan. Do you have any?'

He looked crestfallen. On the other hand, he had seen how unobtrusive the procedure was.

He shuffled in his corduroy slippers over to some shelves, and brought out two disk drives from behind a row of books. 'I worry about being burgled,' he explained.

I took the drives and connected them both to the PC.

New drive(s) found, the screen message announced. *Extend scan YES/NO?*

I clicked *YES*, then turned to Bowland. 'Big drives,' I said. 'May take a while. So, you were telling me about your piles.'

By the time the scan had finished I knew too much about haemorrhoid surgery. But I had four new dots at the end of the onscreen text. I clicked *YES* to start deletion of the non-existent virus instances. The program would have already calculated how many files to take from each suspect folder, filling up all the available space on the memory stick.

I knew it could take some time to copy the files, and so resigned myself to more talk of ailments. Eventually the disks fell silent, and a message indicated that the virus had been removed.

'That really is all done now,' I said. 'I'm sorry it's taken a while.'

'What will the charge be for this?' he asked. For a moment I considered charging him something outrageous. Even if he were not a paedophile, he deserved to be punished for being such a vile human being. But I didn't want him to have a receipt that would record my visit.

'That's alright, Dr Bowland. All part of the premium service I offer my customers.'

I extracted the memory stick and escaped from the house as quickly as I could. I had cast my net in the murky waters of Bowland's PC, and was impatient to discover what little fish I had caught.

Chapter 25

It was already well into the afternoon when I left Bowland, and I was keen to visit Kat before Mark was likely to show up. I went home briefly, changed out of the clothes I'd been wearing, and put them straight in the washing machine. Then I went to my computer and browsed randomly through the images on the stick. Within thirty minutes I was on my way to the hospital.

A nurse was at the side at the bed, finishing a 'freshening up' routine. Kat turned her head to look past the nurse, and smiled at me. I waited until the nurse had gone, and then sat at my usual position between the bed and the window wall. I leaned forward over Kat, and we linked hands.

'Hello, sister dear,' I said softly. 'You're looking lovely and fresh.'

'Yes,' she said, 'but I could do with a clean bandana, if you wouldn't mind.'

'Of course. I'll bring in a couple tomorrow.'

'Looks like a nice day out there.'

'Yeah, for the end of March, not bad at all.'

We smiled at each other. Then her face changed, and even as the smile stayed on her face I saw her eyes become wet. I remained silent and stroked her hand. One can hardly ask a dying woman why she's crying.

'Don't ask me to be too much of a saint, Annie,' she said, holding my gaze. 'I'm doing my best, but I still miss life. Silly things, ordinary things. Sunshine, views of English hills,

317

being in a crowd. And having hair. And my kids. God how I miss them.

'It's true they tire me out,' she went on, 'but I still love to feel their energy, feel the life that will burn after I've gone. But he's sending them away because they're a nuisance to him in the school holidays.'

I nodded. 'Yes, completely typically bloody horrible of him. And he knows very well that I'd have been pleased to have them.'

'And they'd have loved being with you.'

Her expression changed again, her eyes searching my face for truth. 'Tell me you won't let him have them when I'm gone.'

'Good news, my lovely sister—I think I've got a plan.' It was more positive than I felt, but truth of a sort. 'Don't ask me for details, please. Just trust me. I'm making real progress.'

Trust from her deserved honesty from me. I knew, though, that in the end I would lie to let her die in peace.

***

I phoned David when I got home. It was gone five by then, but he was still in his studio.

'Is it OK to talk now?' I asked.

'Of course. I'm only sitting here pretending to work. It's such agony, Annie. The woman I love is dying a few miles away, and I'm not allowed to see her.'

'I understand, I really do. I respect you enormously for resisting. And grateful too.'

'How is she?'

'Actually, I've just got back from the hospital. She's not too bad. We had a nice chat.'

He stopped talking, and I wondered whether he was resentful that I had seen her. I moved on.

'David, I've got some good news. Are you ready?

'I've found some child porn.'

'Wow! Where? Lying around at the back of a drawer?'

'No. I managed to extract it from the computer of my most seedy male customer.'

'Hey, that's amazing! Well done! What's it like? Is it terrible to look at?'

'Actually no, or at least not the ones I've checked so far. They're photos of little girls with no clothes on. That's it. Probably taken in swimming pool changing rooms or on beaches. Personally, I'm relieved they're not more extreme.'

'But will they do the job? I've got photos like that from when the twins were little.'

'Yes, but I'm guessing you might have half a dozen photos like that, and they're your own children. This man has hundreds of these photos—maybe thousands—and they're of other people's daughters, taken in secret. I only managed to grab a few hundred, but I reckon they must be enough to condemn a man who's the father of a young girl.'

'You mean Rachel? Yes, and enough to finish his career.'

'Anyway,' I said. 'We've solved one problem, but now we have to make a plan, and the sooner the better. Can we meet this evening? If you feel like driving over, I'll cook us both a meal.'

***

I knew so much about David, from all that Kat had told me, and yet I didn't know if he was vegetarian. I made a vegetable lasagne. It was in the oven by the time he arrived.

I ushered him into the warm, bright kitchen, and we shared a hug.

'I do find that a strange sensation,' he said, as we separated.

'Gee thanks,' I laughed. 'It was a nice ordinary hug, I thought.'

'Oh sorry,' he said, 'I didn't mean it like that. It's simply that each time we hug I discover you're taller than I expect.'

'Taller than Kat, you mean? Yes, by about three inches. One of the reasons I used to envy her. She seemed petite and pretty, and made me feel all gangly and masculine.'

'For what it's worth, Annie, I don't see you as either of those. On the contrary, the reason the difference in height keeps surprising me is that you're alike in so many ways.'

'That's kind of you,' I said. 'And yes, I like to think there's a pretty and petite woman somewhere inside me, in spite of the inches.'

He held out the bottle of wine he had brought with him. 'You don't have to be petite to be pretty,' he said. 'You already are.'

'Thank you, David—for the wine, and for the compliment.' I focused for a few moments on opening the bottle. 'The problem was that my parents brought me into a world where I needed to be self-reliant and well defended.'

He watched me pour the wine. 'Yes, you did strike me when we met as more confident than Kat. But then I remembered that when I first knew Kat, she was confident too. If anything, she toned herself down so that she wouldn't threaten other people. But the new Kat was different. Still very competent, but she had lost the sparkle. The monster had ground her down.'

'I know. But I saw how your love was helping her become herself again.'

Eulogy for Love

We escaped into small talk. He pottered around my kitchen. He liked the way I had designed it, he said, and I was pleased he did. I'd invested a lot of money and creative energy in it. He laid the table for me, carried over the lasagne and salad, and the wine bottle; and then we sat and ate.

Neither of us could stay away any longer from the main matter for discussion. I suggested to him that this now divided into three problems: How to gain physical access to Mark's computer; how to insert the child pornography onto the computer's drive; and how to let the police know that it was there. The second question was easy to answer. I had retrieved a handbag from the hospital that contained things Kat no longer needed. These included a small notebook, and Kat had already pointed out a list of passwords inside the back cover. These, she had assured me, covered all her online accounts on the home computer she shared with Mark.

'But surely, you'll be putting it in Kat's account, so it will incriminate her, not Mark?'

'I can't get access to Mark's account without a password. They make this sort of thing look far easier in films than it really is. Maybe it can be done by governments with vast resources, and by teenagers with acne and autistic tendencies. But I can't, OK?

'However, if the two accounts are side by side on the computer, they're both relying on the same system software to run. This means I can insert the porn files deep down towards the root, amongst shared folders. Strictly, they could belong to either Kat or Mark, but it's inevitable the police will think it's Mark.'

I asked David to sort out a message for the police. Simply printing off a letter would be unsafe, I told him, because printers can have characteristics that make every document identifiable, and even have information deliberately encoded within the print. Much better, I suggested, to take the time-honoured, lo-tech option of cutting out letters from a newspaper and sticking them onto paper to make up a message.

'And for goodness' sake, don't lick the envelope. Oh—and please try not to give yourself away by getting too artistic.'

Gaining access to the house also appeared straightforward. I had Kat's set of house keys. It was now Friday evening, so we would wait over the weekend, and then go during the day on Monday. The children, at private school, had started their Easter holidays a week earlier than the state school kids, and were going on Sunday to Tina and Thomas. There was no reason for Joan, the housekeeper, to be at the house.

I could have done the whole thing on my own, but David gallantly insisted that he should come as well. If nothing else, he said, he could play lookout while I worked on the computer. He agreed to come to my house at ten on Monday, and we would drive together to Kat's. Cheered by a premature sense of success, we sat back and relaxed until I sent him home before he had any more wine.

***

Computer files, and even the folders that contain them, have a way of acquiring extra information about how and when they were created, and where they have been. This is *metadata*. Over the weekend I had contemplated trying to remove the metadata from Bowland's porn files; but, as I would have to do this on a computer, data might have been added that could incriminate me. In any case, image files normally only contain metadata about the camera used to take the photo, and where and when the picture was taken. If Bowland and his sources were stupid enough not to have removed it, that was their problem. Instead, I left the files where they were on the USB memory stick. The only change I made was to put them in a new set of folders, so that it would not look as if they had been lifted straight from Bowland's PC.

David arrived on time. I had put Kat's housekeys, the notebook with passwords, and the USB stick, all into a small bag. He showed me the anonymous message for the police. He had done it well. We seemed organised, and at first calm, as we drove away in my car.

When we were less than five minutes from our destination, David asked, 'Are you going to put the car on the drive?'

'No, I wasn't,' I said impatiently. 'That would make it obvious someone was at the house. I was going to park a little further down the road.'

'Which would look odd to anyone who knows you have a family connection.'

'Balance of risks,' I countered. 'But the other factor is that the car would get blocked in if anyone pulled in behind it on the drive.'

'OK. So we're going to walk together straight up to the front door. Supposing someone's in the house?'

We were running out of time. 'Alright, then, you can wait on the road,' I said, 'while I go in and ring the doorbell.'

'Leaving me to be seen loitering suspiciously, while my accomplice carries out the burglary.'

I pulled up on the road, fifty yards beyond the house, but we had to sit in the car until we'd agreed our plan. I gave the keys to David to lock the car, then walked back towards the house. David agreed to wait two minutes, exactly; then leave the car, lock it, and walk back along the road. As he went past the house he would look quickly to his right. If I was standing in the porch looking back at him, he would turn and come down the drive. If not, he would walk straight on, as if going elsewhere.

The house appeared empty, but I rang the bell and waited. Then I realised I had lost all sense of the seconds passing, and was torn between waiting to see if someone would answer the door, and my fear that David would march past. I didn't need him very much, but we were supposed to be sharing the risk. The house seemed quiet, so I unlocked the door while, at the same time, looking back towards the road in case David appeared. I had only just managed to get the key in the lock when he walked past, sauntering like a dog-walker, though short of a dog. I waved crazily at him. At the last moment he saw me and came down the drive.

Although double-fronted, the house was not symmetrical. The front door, with an elaborate brick and timber porch, was right of centre. The dining room, with its bay window, was to the left. The narrower front room, to the right, was designated as the study. The garden was also asymmetric: The tarmacked drive came off the road at the right-hand side of the property, in front of the study window, presumably to leave the best vistas of the lawn and flower beds to be enjoyed from the dining room. A small path led across from the top of the drive to the porch.

We entered the house, closed the front door, and went into the study that Mark considered to be his territory.

David stood at the side of the window to avoid being seen, edging forward to peer down the drive. I hurried to the desk and turned the computer on. While it booted up, I put Kat's little notebook to the side of the keyboard, and folded it out so that I could see the handwritten list of five passwords. I got to the account login screen, with the cursor in the password box, and started working down the list.

'Fuck,' I said after a short time, and then 'Sorry.' Swearing hadn't so far been part of our brief relationship.

'Problem?' David asked, briefly turning from the window.

'I've tried all five. None of them works.'

'Shit,' David said. 'What about trying zeros instead of the letter *O*? Or vice versa.'

'OK, I'm doing that now.'

'And changing between upper and lower case,' he added, unnecessarily.

'Doing that. But there is a problem.'

'Which is?' He had to wait for an answer while I carefully entered another password variation.

'At any moment I could hit the limit on the number of login attempts I'm allowed.'

'How many is that?'

'Don't know. It defaults to zero—which means unlimited attempts. But it could have been changed.' I pressed *Enter*, and watched as another attempt failed. 'And, if there is a limit, we could be locked out for two minutes, or maybe two hours. No way of knowing until it happens.'

I had gone past twenty attempts, and was slowing as I tried to think up more variations on the list of words, when David suddenly shouted.

'Oh fuck. Oh bugger! There's a big black car turning into the drive.'

'Oh Christ—that's Mark.'

I hit the power button on the computer, then dropped off the chair and crouched by the desk. I scooped the notebook off the desk and into my bag, and half walked, half crawled toward the office door. David was ahead of me. In his panic he somehow thought he could escape as he had entered, through the front door. When he realised that was impossible, he considered going further into the house, but feared it would leave him trapped. That left him stood, indecisively, in the hallway. A moment later, Mark's silhouette appeared in the frosted panes of the leaded glass in the front door. I waved at David as if trying to swat away a wasp, and he retreated into the dining room, his only other option.

I would like to be able to say that I had the wits, in that moment, to concoct an explanation for Mark. In truth I had prepared it, just in case. By the time he walked through the door I had moved to the foot of the stairs, and turned to face him.

'That's lucky!' I said, struggling to calm myself.

He stood in the hallway, expensively suited as usual, scowling at me.

'What on earth are you doing here, Annie? And how did you get in?'

'Don't worry, Mark, it's OK. Everything's in order. Kat asked me to take in some of her perfume. You know, to help her feel a bit nicer, get rid of those hospital smells. So thought I'd pop round.' My breathing was settling as I talked. 'The only thing is, I'm not sure which ones she likes the best. So now you're here, maybe you could show me.'

He looked unimpressed. 'Why couldn't you come in the evening when I'd be here? Or ask me to get it?'

'It's just that I'd promised Kat I'd take it in today.'

It wasn't a great story, but he couldn't be sure I was lying.

'Come,' he said, brushing past me to go upstairs. 'I'll get it for you.' I followed, not daring to look back. I could only hope David realised this was his chance to escape. Mark led the way into the master bedroom. Kat's make-up and perfume were still on the dressing table, untouched since she had sat that last time at the mirror.

As Mark was studying the perfume bottles, I glanced across to the window, and saw David dashing out of the drive. Mark held up a bottle. 'She likes this one,' he said.

I had guessed he would know nothing about perfume, or his wife's tastes, and he didn't. He was holding a cheap chain store brand.

'Great,' I said, and took it from his hand. Then, for no reason except cussedness, I reached past him and grabbed a bottle of Chanel. 'Maybe I could take this one as well,' I said, 'just to give her the choice.'

He turned to go downstairs, plainly requiring me to follow. In the hall, he said, 'I only called in to pick up some papers for a meeting. We can leave together.' He went into his study, and returned immediately with a folder in his hand. 'After you,' he said. He was seeing me off the premises.

I waited for him outside while he locked the door. 'Very good to see you, Annie,' he said, taking care to ensure the insincerity was obvious.

'And you too, Mark', I replied, doing my best to match him.

He came close to me, and held out his hand. I thought for a moment he planned to shake mine; symbolically letting me know, perhaps, that I had already ceased to be his sister-in-law.

'Maybe I could have Kat's housekeys,' he said.

He couldn't make me do it, and we both knew it. 'No, that's alright, Mark. I'll hang on to them. You never know when Kat might want me to run another errand.' And then I walked past him, pushing his hand out of the way. I had to walk on the damp lawn to get around his car, but I kept going until I reached the road.

As I walked along the road, I heard the low, expensive hum of Mark's car, and saw that he was backing it onto the road. I listened for the sound of it accelerating away, but it didn't happen. Glancing round again, I saw he had pulled up the car across the drive entrance, and was watching me. He wanted to see me gone, and he wanted me to know it

It was only as I approached my car that I realised he might be waiting some time. David, wherever he was, had my car keys. I could only hope Mark would give up waiting. I walked casually into the road, as if to get into my car. Mark still watched. I stood by the car door and gave him a farewell wave. He still didn't move. I reached for the door handle, as if about to get in. Mark sat and watched. Then, unexpectedly, the door clicked open. I got in, and as I did so I glanced into the back of the car. David was lying across the seat, hiding, and looking very undignified. He held out the car keys.

'You'd better stay where you are,' I said, as I closed the door. 'Mark is watching us.'

I started the car and gently pulled away. Then Mark's car overtook us, so fast and so close that it was menacing. When he was out of sight, I stopped the car again. David climbed out and got into the seat next to me.

'Jesus Christ,' he said as he sat back in the seat, and puffed. 'I'm really not cut out for this sort of thing.'

I smiled back at him, and gave the top of his thigh a reassuring rub. 'You poor old thing. I know you're not.'

'That's enough of the '*old*', thank you,' he said. And all at once, I suppose out of relief, we fell into giggling.

We continued to laugh as we talked through our experiences of the whole escapade. 'And you really didn't have to cower in the back of the car,' I said at the end. 'There's no reason why I couldn't have called round while I had a friend with me. I am allowed to have friends. He can't possibly remember what you look like.'

Sorry,' he answered. 'I wish I were a better partner in crime for you, Annie. You could have done with someone who stayed calm and decisive.'

'Yeah, of course, my action hero. A man who stays cool under fire, totally unemotional, always in control. Would have been just the man for a mission like this. Bloody useless for anything else, though. A complete fucking liability, in fact. So thanks, but I'll stick with you.'

I started the drive back to my place. We were silent for a little while.

'So, we got away with it this time,' David said, 'but now what? We can't risk getting caught again.'

'No, we can't. We'll have to think of something else. Damned if I know what it is, though.'

David went off as soon as I arrived at my house. We both needed to do some work, and I now had an extra reason to visit Kat that day. I belatedly realised that the perfume ruse had left me with a small problem. Mark would expect to see the bottles—would look for them, probably. Kat, on the other hand, would be puzzled by them, and might say so to Mark.

Towards the end of the afternoon, I made it to the hospital. A nurse was with Kat when I arrived, doing some routine checks, so I took the chance to put the perfume on the side where Kat might not notice it. The nurse did notice, however.

'Is that perfume?' she said. 'I'm sorry, but you can't leave that here. Hospital policy.'

I found a slip of paper to leave on the side where Kat could not see it, and wrote on it.

'Mark,' it read. 'In case you're wondering, perfume against hospital rules. Keeping it safe for her. Annie.'

Chapter 26

K at was sleeping more, perhaps because the painkillers were being increased. And even with the plastic tubes on her face delivering oxygen, she was working harder to breathe. I couldn't get a clear answer from the hospital staff, but it seemed to me that she was now moving into the last stages of her illness.

I phoned David. I don't know whether I was being kind or cowardly, but I made him discuss the weather first. Then I told him.

'David, I don't think we have very much longer. A matter of days.'

There was a long pause. I heard him sniffle.

'OK,' was all he managed to say, his voice thick. I waited for him to calm before I continued.

'If we want to be able to tell Kat the kids are going to be OK, we have to do something very soon.'

'I know,' he responded. 'I've thought about it endlessly. But I haven't found an answer.'

'OK. In that case,' I said, 'I want to ask you a question. We agreed we wouldn't risk going back to the house. But what if it was guaranteed Mark wouldn't catch us? Would you agree to do it then?'

He was unenthusiastic. 'Yes, I suppose I would, if it were totally guaranteed.'

'Good. In that case I'm going to buy some stuff that will help. It will take a couple of days to arrive, and then we can talk. I'll call.'

'You're being mysterious again, Annie, but OK. I'll wait to hear.'

He was about to end the call when I heard his voice. 'Annie,' I caught him saying, 'are you still there?'

'Yes, David.'

'I've been thinking,' he said. 'Let's suppose we can sort this out, and tell Kat that the kids will be coming to you. Problem solved. Wouldn't it be OK for me to see her then?'

'Yes, it would resolve one issue. But she was also absolutely, fiercely, insistent that she didn't want you to see her when she was very ill.'

'It wouldn't matter. I'd still love her just the same. If she doesn't know that, then she doesn't know how much I love her.'

'I don't think it's about love. She often talked about how wonderful it felt to be so loved by you. But she also said it was amazing that you found her so beautiful. That's the issue, I think. She wants you to remember her when she was beautiful.

'But look, David, this is something we can talk about when we've dealt with Mark. Maybe I could ask her for permission. Just let's focus on the main task for the moment.'

***

It took four days for the package to arrive. I called David immediately, and then drove to the farmhouse. We sat on opposite sides of the kitchen table with our coffees, and I put my purchase on the table. It was not much larger than a box of matches, and a similar shape. The box was made of brown plastic, but with a circle of metal on one side.

'It's a tracker,' I said. 'Been imported from the States, I think. Basically, it's like an automated phone combined with a satnav. The circular metal piece is a magnet. All you have to do is stick it to the underside of a vehicle. It does the same thing as a satnav to keep track of where it is, and then reports its location over the mobile network. Combine the messages it sends with a bit of software and an internet connection, and you can sit in the comfort of your home and watch on a map where the vehicle is travelling. Well, that's the theory.'

David picked it up and inspected it. 'Does it actually work?'

'Dunno. Only just got it. Once it's charged I'll put it on my car and see if I can track myself. But you can see the potential, can't you? We'll always know where he is, so if he heads home, we'll see him coming.'

'Hmm. . . yes, good theory. But even if it works there's the little problem of accessing the PC.'

'True, and I don't have a good answer to that one. The best we can do, I think, is to put the porn on a DVD and plant the disk in his study. I know it's less satisfactory, but it should still be damning.'

'Provided the police find it before he does.'

'Also true. We'd have to nudge them in the right direction. But it's all we've got.'

David was studying the tracker. 'Does it have batteries?'

'Yes, rechargeable batteries. You have to unscrew the lid, and that gives access to the charging point.'

'How long does the charge last?'

'Well, that is one of the snags. Depends on how much it's used—I mean how often it's asked to report its location—but unlikely to be much more than a week.'

David looked up from the tracker. 'Hold on a minute!' he said, frowning. 'So every few days someone has to go to Mark's car—presumably when it's in the drive at night—and collect the tracker to charge it. And then return sometime later to put it back on his car. Jeez, Annie. I thought you said this was the safer plan.'

'It is! It only means going down the driveway to the back of the car, either to take the tracker off or pop it back underneath. It'll be over in seconds. And, all being well, we can get the job done before it needs a recharge.'

David shook his head despairingly. 'Alright,' he said, 'but I think I heard you say *snags*, plural. So what are the other ones?'

'Only one, honest,' I said breezily, 'and I was going to leave this until later.

'The thing is, the computer with the map that shows where the car is located needs to have a solid Wi-Fi connection. In practical terms that means the person with the computer—me, I'm guessing—has to stay at home. . .'

'Oh, I get it.' David interrupted. 'That means I'll be playing burglar all on my own.'

'Yes, but constantly in touch by phone with me, so I can warn you if Mark comes anywhere near. And this time you've only got to tuck a disk in an office drawer, so you'll be in and out in seconds.'

David stared at me, his lips pursed. 'For Kat,' I said. 'We need to do it for Kat, and for Jonathan and Rachel.'

He sat back in his chair and nodded. 'OK. For Kat, and for the kids.'

***

I was impressed by the tracker. A brief test on my car suggested it identified the location very accurately, usually to within a few yards. The software on my laptop not only showed my car exactly where it was parked outside my house, but also drew a red line on the map of everywhere I had travelled, with times added to show when I had been there.

While out testing the tracker, I called in to my workshop and collected a PC gathering dust in a corner. It had come from a customer who left it behind when he bought a new one. There was a good chance he had bought it from someone else. This meant that it would not be easily traced to me, and fairly safe to use to burn Bowland's kiddie pics onto a DVD. For good measure I overlaid the UUID code that uniquely identified this particular machine, and set up a fake user account. I found a blank DVD that I'd had for some time, transferred the files and burned it, then finally wiped the surfaces with cleaning solution.

We went together to put the tracker on Mark's car. It was after dark on the Sunday evening, Palm Sunday, and after I had been to the hospital. I felt I owed it to David to be the one who put it on the car, and there was some advantage in using his car, as Mark would not recognise it. We first took a quick look at the house by driving straight past. Mark's car was in the drive. There were no lights visible from the front of the house, but both the kitchen and living room were at the back. Finally, we pulled up the car a few feet beyond the house, and I ran down the drive. I put the tracker under the car, far enough underneath for it to be invisible to anyone standing close by. It clicked firmly onto the metal. I ran back, and we left without incident.

'See,' I said, getting my breath back. 'Easy.'

***

Eulogy for Love

We decided to allow one day to satisfy ourselves that the tracker was operating correctly, and then David would plant the DVD on the Tuesday. Mark, inconsiderately, had a plain working day. He commuted to his office in the morning, stayed there all day, and then came straight home; or that, at any rate, was what the tracker said he did. I assumed he had come home for the night, and so never looked at the tracker display during the evening. It was only the following morning, when I opened my laptop, that I found a sequence of red lines across the map, suggesting that he had gone out again about eight. The trace showed an unlikely journey: First a brief stop in a supermarket car park, and then rushing onwards into the countryside before stopping again in a place that, as far as I could tell, was the middle of nowhere. According to the tracker, the car had started moving again at 9.32, and completed the same journey in reverse. It seemed such an unlikely journey that I was inclined to write it off as a technical glitch.

I called David to give him a report on the tracker's performance, including the little oddity in the evening.

'You're saying it was just a glitch, Annie, but a glitch is exactly what we don't want. OK, so this time it showed him driving around when he was actually tucked up at home watching TV. But today it might show him sat in his office when he's really steaming towards the house at the very moment I'm committing a burglary.'

'Let's be reasonable about this,' I told him. There's every indication that most of the time it works fine, and you'll only be in the house for about sixty seconds. The chances of another glitch during those few seconds are very remote.'

The was a moment's silence on the phone. 'Yes, I see that,' he said. 'Can we leave it for another twenty-four hours? Just to check out the tracker a bit more?'

I conceded. I told him I would monitor the tracker for the rest of the day, and report that evening.

As it turned out, Mark provided us with better data that second day. Shortly after I had spoken to David, I saw a red line starting to grow on the map as Mark left his office car park. He drove onto one of the main roads out of town, and kept moving steadily for nearly an hour. The tracker proved so accurate that I could tell Mark was disregarding speed limits as he passed through villages along the way. After forty minutes he turned off the main road and followed country lanes, then pulled into a carpark. The map only showed that he was outside an establishment of some sort, but when I checked a satellite view it was obviously a large country manor surrounded by smaller, more modern buildings. It was easy to get confirmation from a search online that this was a residential school operated by the firm. He was probably there for a meeting.

The ability to sit in comfort at a screen, watching someone's movements across the satellite image of a landscape, invites a sense of omniscience, as if one has become a Greek god looking down from Mount Olympus. I found myself tempted to sit and drink coffee, staring at the map. However, the software also included an alarm that would be triggered if the car moved. I set it, and did some housework. An hour later the alarm pinged, and the red line began to extend again. It retraced his earlier route. When he arrived on the outskirts of town it would have been a short detour to his house, but he didn't take it. He could have diverted a couple of miles to visit his dying wife in hospital; but, of course, he didn't do that either. He went straight back to his office, and stayed there until six, when he went home.

I waited until after nine, to make sure the tracker didn't show another mystery evening journey, and then called

David. He agreed we should go ahead in the morning, unless, of course, Mark was on the move.

***

David came to my house at eleven to collect the DVD.

He stepped inside the front door, and I gave him the disk inside a plastic bag.

'So tell me, where is he this morning?'

'In his office. Went in at eight thirty, hasn't moved since. Come and see for yourself.'

We went together and looked at the laptop on the kitchen table. 'See,' I said, pointing to the zigzag red line. 'It's so accurate you can not only see that he's put the car in the car park, but almost exactly which parking space he's left it in.'

I switched the display to show David the double red lines from the previous day, when Mark had gone visiting.

'That's impressive. And very spooky. Do you know if it's even legal?'

'No idea. Might be one of those cases where the law hasn't caught up with the technology. Do we care?'

'No, we don't.' David looked solemn, resigned. 'So let's get on and do it.'

'Good,' I said, holding up the disk in its bag, and Kat's housekeys. 'You'll need these. And don't forget to slide the disk out of the bag without touching it. No fingerprints, no DNA.'

'Understood. I'm in 007 mode, and ready to go.'

I smiled, then leaned forward and put my cheek against his. 'Then go!'

'Just one more thing, please, Annie. I know that strictly you only need to call me if Mark starts to move, but I'd feel so much happier if you were in touch the whole time. I've brought earphones.'

'No problem. We'll just hope the police never have reason to check your phone records. I'll call as soon as you're on your way.'

Then he left, disk and keys in one pocket, phone in the other. I poured myself another coffee, settled at the kitchen table with the laptop, and called him.

I sent the tracker a command instructing it to report its location every thirty seconds, and while David was en route I passed on the news to him almost as often. When he arrived at the house, the tracker showed Mark—or Mark's car, at any rate—still at the office five miles from his home.

David parked on the road in front of the house, but clear of the drive. After one more assurance that Mark was still at the office, he left the car and hurried down the drive. The door had a Yale lock, and I had shown David which key he needed to use.

'I've turned the key in the lock alright,' I heard him say, 'but the door won't open. There's a second lock, I think— looks like a normal deadlock.'

'OK, David, no problem. There's a key on the ring that probably opens that one. Just look through them. And relax! Mark is miles away.'

I could envision what David was doing. He would have had to take the Yale key out, and hunt for the other key on the ring. I was wondering whether it was significant that Mark had closed both locks.

'Alright, I've opened the other lock. Now going back to the Yale.' I could hear him breathing. 'Door opened. I'm going inside.'

Eulogy for Love

As he spoke, I heard a new sound—a two-tone sound, half beeping and half clicking, repeating in an insistent and ominous way.

'David, is that a burglar alarm?'

'Yeah, it must be.' He was trying to say the words calmly, but I could tell he was jittery. 'Guess it's waiting for me to enter the code. Do we know what it is?'

Even heard over the phone, the sound of the alarm system was aggravating, and I could feel my adrenaline rising. 'No, we don't. I can look in Kat's notebook, but I'm sure I'd remember seeing it. But never mind that. Concentrate on putting the disk in the desk. Somewhere not too obvious.'

'Annie, I am. But I think the door is locked.'

'Which door?'

'The study door. I'm just hunting around to see if the key is hidden somewhere close by.'

Then it became clear to me.

'David, forget it. Just leave.'

'Give me another few seconds. There's this dresser thing in the hallway. I'm checking the drawers.'

'David, go. Now! It doesn't matter anymore. Just get out.'

It was then that the alarm bell started sounding. I thought I heard David say 'Fuck,' but it was difficult to tell over the racket.

I shouted down the phone: 'Get out! And lock the door as you go. Lock the door!'

After that I had to wait to know what was happening. Then the volume of the alarm faded, and I could hear David breathing fast. I guessed he was heading down the drive.

I heard a door close. When David next spoke I could tell he was inside the car.

'Annie—give me a couple of minutes to get out of here.'

I waited as he drove away and then parked up again. He asked me to wait until he had calmed. I listened to his breathing as it gradually slowed.

'I'm sorry Annie,' he said, 'I was so focused on delivering that sodding disk that I wasn't thinking about anything else. But I've realised now. He was on to us.'

'Technically on to *me*; but yes. Or extremely suspicious, at least. That's why he locked up more thoroughly than usual, and put on the alarm. And I think that lock on the office door is new.

'Are you safe to drive?' I asked.

'Yes, now.'

'Then drive back here. I think we need to be together.'

***

It was barely lunchtime, but we both drank wine, sitting as usual at the kitchen table. The laptop was still on the table, but I closed it and shoved it to one side.

David said, 'I'm thinking we've reached the end of the road with the child porn.'

I nodded. 'Yes. Whatever we do now, he'll be ready for it, and he'll know it was us—or me, rather. He'll come home and see that the house alarm has been triggered. He'll search to see if anything has been taken, and he'll probably search again to see if anything has been left behind. I could imagine him giving my name to the police.'

'And we haven't got any other ideas.' It was hardly a question, more the concluding summary of a failed project.

'No,' I said. We looked at each other. I watched tears fill his eyes.

Eulogy for Love

David struggled to control his voice. 'Well, there it is. I had one last chance to help the woman I love, loved more than my own life. And I've failed her.'

He saw that I was also close to tears. 'I'm sorry,' he said, and reached out to hold my hand. 'I know you're suffering too. I wouldn't have got half as far as this without you. In fact, I'd still be at home believing Kat didn't love me.'

'Maybe that would have been better.'

'It wouldn't. Even though I haven't been able to be with her, I feel closer to her now.'

I went and found a box of tissues and put them on the table where we could both use them. As I sat down, we joined hands again, not even thinking about it.

David asked, 'Will you lie to her about the kids being safe from him?'

It was my turn to cry, but David cried again when he saw me weeping. Now beyond embarrassment, we wept and snivelled, and watched each other through the distortion of our own tears.

'I suppose I must lie,' I said, eventually, 'so that she can at least have peace in her last hours. But it will be such a betrayal of trust. And anyway, whatever I tell Kat, the reality will be that the kids will be left with their vile father.'

'And it will be Rachel and Jonathan who suffer.'

'Yes, it will. Every day. And there will be nothing we can do about it.'

We talked and sobbed until it was time for me to visit Kat. 'I've got an awful feeling,' I said, 'that she's going to want clear answers from me.'

'Would you like me to wait here until you get back?'

'Would you? Please do. And, if you like, you can root about in the fridge and see what we might eat later, if we have the appetite.'

That day, Kat did not ask about the children. She was sleepy, and talked little. I noticed her skin had yellowed. A nurse confirmed it meant the cancer had spread into her liver. When I persuaded the nurse to speak honestly, she agreed it meant that Kat had very few days to live.

I was glad to come home and find David there. He was making a curry. I told him about Kat's decline, and we cried again, and drank more wine. Then we ate, and found comfort in sharing tales about Kat. By then it was late evening. I made up the bed in Jonathan's room, and David slept there.

***

When I visited Kat the next day, the Thursday before Easter, I found she already had two visitors, sat side by side on the chairs at the foot of the bed. I recognised them to be Charles and Peggy Smallwood, Mark's father and stepmother. They did not recognise me, but made a skilful recovery when I introduced myself. We had met previously at family events, but Charles clearly considered me to be a member of the lower orders, and not the kind of person he needed to remember.

'I'm sorry,' I said. 'I'll come back later.'

'No, no. Join us, Annie,' Peggy said, beckoning me into the room.

'Well, there's supposed to be a rule about not more than two visitors at a time.'

'Not to worry,' Charles said. 'We gathered that Kat had taken a turn for the worst, so we thought we'd better pay our respects.' He had meant *last respects*, of course, but lacked the honesty to say it. 'She's been asleep since we arrived. You stay. I need to go and make a few phone calls anyway.'

When he had gone, I sat on the metal-framed chair next to Peggy. She had, uncharacteristically, come to a standstill. She was looking long and thin, and elegant in a faded way, in dark slacks and an expensive cream blouse. A coat was gathered

342

round her shoulders. We sat silently side by side and looked towards the end of Kat's hospital bed. It was as if we were in a waiting room, and in truth that was what the room had become. At the other end of the bed, a monitoring machine bleeped.

'You know what they say,' she remarked, breaking the silence, 'about cancer being caused by people suppressing their unhappiness, forcing it back into their bodies.'

She stopped talking, and continued to stare ahead. I had a feeling I should let her take her time.

'I'm sure it's nonsense,' she started again, 'but it does have a certain poetic truth to it, don't you think? Would totally explain why Kat has ended up here. Terribly sad. Poor Kat.'

Another pause, then she said, 'It must have been dreadful being married to Mark. I can't imagine what she's gone through. Of course, they're all pretty damaged, but Mark is in a class of his own.'

The remark made me glance sideways to check she was being serious. 'All?' I queried. 'All men? All husbands?'

She made a laugh with a little puff of air from her mouth, tilting her head upwards. 'Actually,' she said, 'I was referring to the male Smallwoods. But I wouldn't argue if you opted for the wider definitions.

'Larkin put it succinctly, don't you think?' she said. '*They fuck you up, your mum and dad. They may not mean to, but they do.*'

'You know it?' she said. 'Charles royally fucked up his firstborn.'

She was at last looking towards me, with a hint of a smile. I suspected she wanted to see if the language would surprise me. From her, it had.

'Are you talking about his mother's suicide?' I asked.

'Ah, you know about that. Do you know why she killed herself?'

'Not really. She was unhappy in England. I don't think Mark ever told Kat more than that.'

'No, he wouldn't. The Smallwoods keep these things to themselves. But here we are, on a night when Kat invites us to stare into infinity. It seems a good moment to tell you.'

Peggy put an arm over the back of her chair, and settled herself.

'My dear husband behaved appallingly towards Jing, Mark's mother. He picked her up on the streets of Hong Kong, where she had seemed beautiful and exotic, and eager to please. Once back in England, he discovered that his friends and colleagues were laughing at him for getting entangled with a stupid Chinese girl. Then he, too, despised her. His initial solution was to hide her away at home, and to continue his social life without her. But each time he came home, whether from work or from drinking with his friends, he saw her and despised her more. When she talked to him across the dining table, her language flawed and her thoughts uninteresting, he despised her yet more. She tried to please him in bed, but her eagerness made her boring.

'After a while, Charles moved her out of sight even within the house. He put an armchair and television in one of the bedrooms, and expected Jing to live in it with Mark. She had been demoted from wife to housekeeper, and Mark became nothing more than the housekeeper's child. She cooked Charles' meals, but he ate alone. Inevitably, it wasn't long before he went a stage further and brought women back to his home, and to his bed.

'So there she was, alone in a foreign country where she couldn't speak the language. Cruelly rejected by her husband, even obliged to serve breakfast to the women who had spent

344

the night with him. Jing may have been a simple soul, but she loved Charles, and must have been bereft. There can be no doubt about the reason she killed herself.'

'That's terrible,' I said.

'Yes, it is,' Peggy said, leaning closer to me. 'But there's more. Only Charles and I know this, and now you will too. Technically, Mark must know it, but I doubt he holds it as a conscious memory.

'Jing had managed to collect a vast supply of painkillers. She had nowhere to send little Mark while she ended herself, so that afternoon, after she had completed the housework, she put the child on the bedroom floor and surrounded him with toys and picture books. Then she lay on the bed and set about eating the tablets. Mark was a docile little boy, and when he tired of the toys he climbed up onto the bed and cuddled into his mother's back where she lay slowly, painfully, dying.

'She was still dying when Charles came home from work. According to the official record, he simply popped into the house and then, without seeing Jing or Mark, went out for a walk.

'But that's not the truth. When Charles got back from work, he went upstairs to tell her off for neglecting her duties. You can imagine the scene. He opens the door of the room where Jing lives, and sees her lying on the bed. There's all sorts of medicine bottles and tablets spread across the bedside table. She's alive, but her breathing is laboured, her lips are blue, and there's a pool of vomit at her mouth.

'It's obvious to Charles that she has taken a massive overdose. It is apparent that she wants to die. This is very convenient from Charles' point of view, because he too would like her to die. All he has to do is let the drugs take their course, and they'll both get the result they want.

'But there's a snag. And its name is Mark. He's three years old. He's on the bed with his mummy, calling to her, pushing her head, stroking her cheek, doing everything he can to wake her up. He's already terribly distressed. Then the door opens, and Mark sees his father looking in. Naturally, he climbs down from the bed and rushes towards his father for comfort, and for help to wake his mummy up. Charles has to make his decision quickly.

'The choice he makes is to shut the door, and lock it, even as Mark's little hands are clawing at the doorknob on the other side. Charles goes downstairs to the sound of his son screaming. Then he goes for a walk. An hour later he comes back, unlocks the door, checks his wife is dead, picks up his whimpering son, and calls the police.

'Only Mark had witnessed what had happened, but no one was interested in what he had to say. The details of the episode were buried.'

'My God,' I said. 'That's appalling.'

'Yes, it was.'

There was a silence. I thought about the damage it must have done to Mark. And then I realised there was a puzzle. 'But, Peggy, if you don't mind me asking—how do you know this?'

'Oh, because Charles told me. About a year after we were married. He's a fairly unpleasant man, but he's not totally evil. Ha!' she laughed, throwing up her head again. 'How's that for faint praise! It weighed on his conscience, and he confessed to me.'

'But you still stayed with him?'

'Yes, we were married. I was pregnant with Thomas.'

'You were still able to love him after what you'd heard?'

'Annie, let me explain my position.' She glanced sideways at me, as if checking that I was listening. 'Once

346

you've made that kind of decision, once you've agreed to stay in spite of the awfulness you've experienced or discovered, you will have handed over all control. For the last four decades, he's decided what we do, where we go on holiday, what he wants me to cook him for dinner, what newspaper we have delivered. Everything. But there's something he can't make me do.

'He can't make me forgive him. And I damned well don't intend to. One day I shall be where Kat is now, and I shall go on my way proudly unforgiving.

'And I'll tell you something else.' She turned at last on the seat to face me. 'I hope Kat doesn't forgive Mark before she goes. And I hope you won't either. After what I've told you, you might start to think Mark has excuses for being a such a despicable person. But they're all intelligent men with control over their actions. Mark was damaged by his childhood, but he has allowed it to determine who he is. They all choose to do what they do to us. They don't deserve forgiveness.'

'I entirely agree,' I said, 'that they don't deserve it, and you can be sure Mark won't be getting it from me. But don't you think that refusing to forgive hurts both sides? Isn't it a recipe for bitterness?'

'You're entirely right, Annie. It is. Look at me—I'm becoming a bitter old woman. The world is full of us. Do you ever look at the faces of elderly women as they walk down the street with their husbands? Or the timid, lonely widows pushing their trolleys round the supermarket? Mostly you'll see bitter faces. OK, so they may have all sorts of reasons— the dreams that never came true, the loss of those they loved— but I'm convinced they're bitter chiefly because they spent their adult years being hurt and disappointed by their menfolk. At first there was a sweet satisfaction in being unforgiving, a silent defiance, but in the end it soured, and the taste of it shows on their faces.'

The door opened. It was Charles. 'I've found the boy. He's just parking. Be along in a minute.'

'Well, I need to be going anyway,' I said. I went over to Kat, who was still sleeping. Her skin had become more yellowed. I kissed her on the space between her eyebrows and the hem of her bandana, and wondered how many more times I would say goodnight to her.

I turned to Charles and Peggy. 'Are you staying long?' I asked.

'No, we're going back this evening. Once the Easter getaway traffic has died down.'

'Safe journey, then.' I attempted to give Peggy a look that would acknowledge the new bond between us, but I didn't want Charles to see. I left.

As I walked down the corridor I met Mark. Neither of us slowed. 'Hello Annie,' he said, as we neared. 'How are you?'

'Fine, thank you, given the circumstances.' By the time I had said the words I was past him, and I kept walking.

When I got home, I phoned David and told him all that had happened at the hospital. I also asked him whether he wanted to come over.

'That's kind', he said, 'but there are things I really ought to get done.'

A few minutes later, he phoned back. 'About coming over this evening. Can I change my mind?'

'Of course. And you know you can use Jonathan's bedroom if you want to.'

I wondered, after the call, how I would feel if he signalled he would prefer to sleep in my bed. There was no overwhelming moral reason why we should not have slept together. The warmth of another body might have held off the

348

enveloping sadness, pushed back the taunting image of Kat alone in her hospital bed. An act of gentle sex—I could imagine moving together, wordlessly coupling, not even needing to mention it next morning—would have been a comfort. It would also have been a little act of affirmation that life, though it dimmed in my sister, would continue to burn elsewhere. For all that, there was something unavoidably creepy about the thought of Kat's sister and her former lover getting it on while she lay dying in a hospital bed.

David did stay over, but we went to separate beds. I noticed as I turned off the bedside light that I felt a mild, and oddly comforting, sense of disappointment.

Chapter 27

D avid stayed for breakfast. Afterwards, I thought it as good a time as any to remind him that we had some tidying up to do.

'I hate to mention it, but the tracker is still attached to Mark's car.'

'Yes, that had crossed my mind.'

'I'd feel much happier taking it off before someone finds it. And, while it has some charge left in it, we'll at least know where it is.'

'OK, but Lauren is up for Easter, and paying me a rare visit this evening. Can it wait until tomorrow? How much charge does it have left?'

'It's reporting over twenty-five percent, and I can change the settings to conserve the battery a little. So tomorrow's OK. Can we definitely agree on tomorrow evening?'

David nodded. 'I'll plan to go and get it once it's dark. I suppose that will mean around nine. But I'll be relying on you to confirm he's at home.'

He went on his way soon after. I decided I needed to get in some food for the Easter weekend. That done, I went to the workshop to tackle a backlog of repair work. I managed to do some of it but felt drawn to be with Kat. It was early afternoon when I arrived at the hospital. Kat was on her own.

I think it was my arrival that woke her. I sat in my usual position at the side of the bed, near the window, leaning close to her. I hoped she would be able to talk, but feared she would ask whether I had rescued the children. She seemed confused, however, even about where she was. She grew fretful about needing to be home, worried about unfinished work at the office. I tried to soothe her with words, and by caressing her brow.

She fell asleep after a while. For a long time, I continued to gaze at her, recalling memories and feeling grateful that, for nearly ten years, we had experienced true sisterhood. Then a doctor came in, escorted by a nurse. They had the sense to enter quietly, but I moved away from Kat so that they could carry out the customary checks of pulse, monitors, drips. When they had finished, the doctor made a sideways nod at me, indicating he wanted to talk outside.

He was a young man, I guessed a houseman, and still learning the assured manner that doctors are expected to have. 'You're a close relative?' he asked, once we were in the corridor.

'Yes, her sister.'

'I'm sure you've guessed,' he went on, 'that your sister is now very ill. To be frank, it's very likely that she won't be with us beyond the weekend. Then again, these things are always terribly difficult to predict, so it probably doesn't make sense for you to camp out here.'

'I appreciate that,' I said. He seemed to need comforting.

'The best I can say to you,' he continued, 'is that we can often tell when someone is finally slipping away, and we can phone to let you know.'

I nodded reassuringly.

'Are you the next of kin?'

'Yes, but she does have a husband.'

He looked confused. 'We should phone him?'

'If you wouldn't mind—it would be a great help—could you possibly call us both?'

'OK, I'll make a note for us to do that. But you need to be somewhere local, and be ready to come immediately.'

'Yes, we'll do that. Thank you, doctor,' I said, and added, 'You're very kind,' to cheer him up.

I went home, ate none of the food I had bought, and spent the evening alone. I envied David for having his daughter's company to distract him.

***

I woke the next morning exhausted, as if I had not slept, and wasted the morning on unnecessary chores. After eating a lunch I did not want, I decided to go and sit with Kat.

For me, this was now a vigil. I was glad to be left alone, yet angry that the world continued as usual, indifferent to the impending death of someone I loved. Kat slept quietly. Towards the end of the afternoon I came home again, aware that I needed to be ready to support David as he retrieved the tracker.

I had put the tracker into standby mode to conserve the battery, and had no record of Mark's movements for the past day. When I re-activated it at about eight, it showed Mark's car parked up at his house. I waited and watched for a while, to be completely sure, and then phoned David. He said he would call me once he was on his way.

He phoned as soon as he left, and chatted about his evening with Lauren. He seemed oddly calm about the errand he was now undertaking, considering the unpleasantness of the last two times he had visited the house. I said as much.

'You're right, I am. Not sure why. Perhaps I'm becoming adjusted to my role as petty criminal. Perhaps I'm past caring. I do know, though, that I'm more and more in touch with my anger towards Mark. I'm so furious that we're having to do this. If he'd been a decent husband, none of this would have happened.'

I couldn't resist saying it. 'And Kat, as a happily married woman, would never have agreed to have an affair with you.'

'Yes, I know that.'

'So, let's imagine this alternative reality. Kat's still in hospital dying, but she's had ten years of happiness with her loving husband Mark. Right now, he and the children are gathered at her bedside. Meanwhile you're at your farmhouse on your own, sadly remembering the girl who lay on your chaise longue and charmed you into loving her, oblivious to the fact that she is only a few miles from you, and about to die.

'Is that what you'd choose, David, if you could?'

'I'd have to choose it. I couldn't possibly prefer to deny her the years of happiness, merely so that I could have a parcel of memories from a few secretive assignations, wonderful though they were. And I'm still going to end up on my own for the rest of my life. Ultimately, from my point of view, it's only a question of which memories I get to carry with me into old age.'

'Well, yes,' I responded. 'Isn't that the ultimate question for us all?'

I had been staring at the laptop screen, but thinking about David's alternative realities. Suddenly refocusing, I saw that a red line had appeared

'David, he's on the move.' David cursed. 'Don't worry yet,' I told him. 'Maybe he's just popped out for a pint of milk. Keep going, and if need be, you can park up and see what he's up to.'

I sent a command to the tracker, telling it to increase the frequency of its updates, and the red line began to extend by the minute. Initially Mark headed towards town, but then the line made an angle, indicating that he had turned into a supermarket car park.

'OK,' David commented, when I told him, 'so he *is* getting a pint of milk.'

'He ain't getting milk at that supermarket,' I said. 'It closed an hour ago.'

The pause before Mark's car started moving again was so brief that the tracker barely registered it. It was then that I remembered the pattern on the map the previous Monday. I waited to see where the red line would go, and, sure enough, it started moving along the same route that the tracker had shown that other evening, the route we had dismissed as a glitch.

David turned his car and started to follow, guided by me as I watched Mark's progress. When Mark went by road junctions that could serve as waymarkers, I told David to report when he also passed them. In this way we could judge how far behind he was. It turned out there was only a minute's difference, and I told David to slow down.

I remembered where, on Monday, Mark had turned onto a minor road, and I watched as the red line cut left at the same point. It then switched directions at two junctions, going further into countryside. Then the line ended in a small spike, indicating that the car had turned off the road and stopped. I had to ask David to pull over while I found a satellite view, and briefed him on the final mile of his journey.

'You'll see the turning to Tettleton on the left. After that it's open country on both sides, but then there's a wood on the left that comes up to the road. Maybe a hundred yards further down there's a clearing in the wood with access from the road, and that's where Mark has parked up. But don't go down there—it's only a small area, and you'd bump straight into him. Keep going until the end of the trees. It looks like there's a farm track or gate where you can tuck in the car and walk back.'

I listened to the sound of the car moving, and David breathing, until he slowed. The engine noise stopped. 'OK,' he said softly, 'I'm here.'

I had assumed he would walk back along the road, but he instead headed into the wood.

'I'll have to stop talking to you,' he whispered shortly after. 'Got my earphones in, so you can go on speaking to me a bit longer.' From that point on I could only guess what was happening from the sound of his movements.

There was no moon that night, but a layer of low cloud was reflecting the light from nearby urban areas. Out in the open, visibility was adequate. Inside the wood, David found himself in almost complete darkness, except where gaps in the leaf canopy provided pools of thin light. The ground was uneven, and there were bushes and fallen logs. Even over the phone, I could hear he was making a lot of noise.

The risk of being heard as he blundered through the wood soon became greater than the risk of being seen. He had to give in and use his phone as a torch, cupping it so that the smallest amount of light fell on to the ground where he was walking. With the help of the light, he moved more quickly.

I was so invested in visualising David in the wood that I had become unaware of my surroundings at home. My concentration was broken when my phone started buzzing. The display showed that I had a call from the hospital.

Nothing could have distracted me from my commitment to support David. Nothing, that is, except a call from the hospital. I immediately feared they were phoning to say that Kat was minutes away from dying; or, possibly, that she had already gone. I needed to know.

'David, I've got to answer another call. I'll phone you back in two minutes.' I was about to cut him off when I realised I wasn't sure that his phone was on silent. 'No,' I added quickly. 'Give me a couple of minutes, and then call me back.' Then I ended his call and spoke to the hospital.

David was left on his own, in the middle of a very dark wood, not knowing what he was going to find at the other side. But he was now far enough through the wood to see the clearing beyond, and was trying to make sense of what he could see. Sheer curiosity drew him away from the safe shadows.

The first thing David recognised was Mark's car, its dark colour providing a feeble silhouette against the clearing behind it. The car was parked close to the wood, and sideways on, so that there was a private space between the car and the trees, hidden from anyone coming in from the road. The arrangement made no provision for somebody stumbling out of the wood on the other side. There were two people at the side of the car. One was obviously Mark. The other person was naked from the waist down, her pale flesh plain enough. She was leaning against the car, pushing her hips back towards Mark. Mark was dressed, but he must have been unzipped, because there was no doubt what he was doing: He was fucking her from behind.

All the anger that had been simmering inside David was approaching boiling point. After all the years of hurting and neglecting Kat, it now turned out that Mark preferred picking women up for anonymous sex under cover of darkness. Vile bastard!

And yet . . . had he read the scene correctly? There was something about the woman's physicality; and something odd about the way that Mark was angled into her.

Eulogy for Love

David moved even further forward until he was at the last tree, and then he realised his mistake. The semi-naked figure was male. The angle of the bodies was odd because the man was being buggered. The voice in David's head was shouting: *You vile bastard! No wonder you neglected Kat all these years.*

And then the final, the most appalling realisation: It wasn't a man. It was a boy, a child. The height, physique, and lack of body hair left no doubt. Probably a boy of eleven or twelve.

David's anger boiled over into uncontrolled fury. He came out into the open, almost tripping on a shallow drainage channel that marked the end of the woodland, and stumbled across the few yards to Mark. Those words he had been saying in his head—now absurdly inadequate—repeated themselves, but this time he found himself shouting them out loud as he rushed at Mark. 'You vile, disgusting bastard!' Mark, entirely surprised, turned towards David.

For a man who had never hit anyone, David launched an effective punch. It landed hard on Mark's cheek and made him stagger backwards. But it only unbalanced him for a moment. Mark said, 'Who the fuck are you?' and straightened himself up.

David, suddenly less brave, backed off. Mark advanced, and David was forced to walk backwards. As Mark moved forward, he gestured sideways to the boy, telling him to get into the car. It was a mistake, because as the boy opened the door an interior light came on, and when he had reached the car seat he looked out at David. It was only for a moment, but it was long enough for David to memorise the long, sallow face.

Mark seemed confident he could deal with the intruder, and was taking his time. He even paused to zip up his jeans.

357

David sensed that the space behind him was running out. He would soon be backing onto the uneven ground of the woodland, and wondered whether to turn and make a dash into the darkness. At this point Mark reached down and picked up a length of wood. It was large and plainly heavy, more log than stick. Mark was going to need both hands to wield it. It looked dangerous. David decided to run.

The call from the hospital had brought the news I had expected. Kat's pulse was weakening, her breathing very shallow. If I wanted to be with her at the end, I needed to go immediately. I used the bathroom, locked the house, and left. It was only as I hurried to the car that I realised David should have phoned me back.

I had no sense of David's circumstances at that moment, no idea of what might have happened when he reached Mark. It might have proved to be a fuss about nothing. And the chances were that David had put his phone on silent, in which case it would be safe to call him. He needed to know that I was going to the hospital. The news would be agonising for him, but he had a right to know Kat was living her last minutes. I had an obligation to tell him. I decided to get into the car and phone him before I started driving.

David turned to run from Mark, but had not realised he was at the drainage channel. He tripped on the edge of it, putting out a hand to stop himself falling all the way. It gave Mark enough time to catch up. David was barely standing when Mark brought the log down on him. Somehow David managed to hold up his arm to shield his head, and the log fell first on his arm, then crashed into the side of his ribcage. The pain was so intense that David put his arms across his chest and curled downwards. Now his head was undefended. Mark heaved the log back up and prepared to strike again.

Eulogy for Love

David had not put his phone on silent. It started to ring at the same moment that the log began its descent on his head. It's very possible that the sudden, incongruous sound put Mark off his stroke. It's also possible that David, in spite of his fear and pain, obeyed the ingrained compulsion to reach for his phone, shifting his position in order to find it in his pocket. Whatever the reason, the log failed to have the deadly impact it might have had. Instead of hitting David's head straight on, with a force that might have opened his skull, it caught the edge of his head and skittered down his temple. The force of it was still enough to knock him unconscious, and he fell face down into the mud at the bottom of the drainage channel.

Mark must have stood there and looked down at David, and made a judgement about what he should do next. Perhaps he believed that he had already killed David, or that he could be left to drown in the mud. Then again, perhaps he didn't need David to die. As far as Mark knew, they were strangers to each other, and had only seen each other in dim light. The man who had blundered out of the woods could not have seen the registration plates, and—now lying unconscious in a ditch—would not see them as Mark drove away. Mark may have concluded that David did not represent a risk.

Whatever his reasoning, he got into the car, the boy next to him, and drove away. As he headed back into town, the hospital kept its promise to let him know that his wife was going to die that evening. He changed his route towards the hospital, dumping his passenger at the edge of town.

David's face had fallen into a part of the drainage channel where there was a layer of twigs. They formed a nest that held his nose and mouth above the mud. In all likelihood he was only unconscious for a few minutes, but, when he stirred, Mark had gone. He was alone. He lay in the ditch until his brain had recalibrated which direction was *up*, and then pulled himself out far enough to be able to lean against a tree. His side, arm, and head all hurt. The full length of his front was covered in mud, though the wetness on the side of his head felt different. He guessed it was blood. When his mind had cleared, he recalled that the phone had rung, and dug it out of his pocket. He listened to the message I had left.

As David lay there, the fact most clear in his mind was that we had at last found the evidence we needed, and it was far more damning than we had ever imagined. It would not only ensure Mark could not have care of the children, but also end his career and probably put him in prison. That being the case, David judged, the justification for staying away from Kat had crumbled. My message told him that he had one last chance to be with her. He was not going to be denied.

David hurried back through the wood, stooping from the pain and wiping blood and mud from his face. This time he was able to use the phone freely as a torch. Soon he was back in the car and driving too fast towards the hospital. As he came into town he got held up by slow traffic, much to his annoyance. In a moment when he was stationary he managed to send me a text:

'We have evidence we need. Kids future safe with you.
On my way. Xx'

By that point I was with Kat, once more in my place at the side of the bed and holding her hand. Someone had thoughtfully turned off the sterile glare from the strip lights in the ceiling, leaving Kat pooled in the warmer light of a lamp over her bed. A nurse was in the room, staying in the background, and the young doctor I had met last time called by every few minutes. I didn't notice the small *ping* from my phone as David's text arrived.

360

Eulogy for Love

I was wondering whether I should say my farewells to Kat as she lay in her last sleep. Then her eyes opened, and after a moment she managed to focus on my face, close above hers. 'Hello, sister dear,' she said. I leaned forward and looked into her eyes, and I knew beyond any doubt that she was fully alert.

'I'm ready to go now,' she whispered. 'But I need to know my children are going to be safe with you always, with their Ayay.'

I looked back at her. I knew that I only had to say one sentence and she would die in peace. The sentence that would betray all the trust and honesty we had shared.

I nodded. 'Don't worry. It's all sorted out. I'm going to have the kids.'

Kat's face relaxed, and I felt her hand squeeze mine as much as her strength would allow. 'Thank you,' she said.

I could feel a wailing building up in me, and struggled to contain it. But then, as Kat continued to look up at me, I saw the peace that came over her face. I smiled and waited, thinking that was the last we would say together.

'And Annie,' she said, 'find David, and tell him that I love him. Always have, always will. Please look after him for me.' Then she closed her eyes. I knew we had said goodbye.

I sat up a little, but continued to hold her hand. At that moment I sensed someone walking into the room. It was Mark. I guessed he was expecting me to relinquish my place at the bedside, but I'd be damned if I would let him invade my last moments with Kat. He stood at the other side of the bed, and I ignored him. Yet he did disturb my thoughts. Where had he been? He was in jeans and a check shirt, entirely suitable for a Saturday evening at home. Could it be that the tracker had created another ghost journey? And if Mark had never taken that journey, where was David?

Mark stood looking down at Kat, expressionless. He leaned over and kissed her cheek. He was playing to the gallery, though the gallery consisted only of one nurse and a sister-in-law he despised.

We waited, certain that Kat would slip away at any moment. The bleep of the monitor said that her heart continued to slow, her breathing so shallow it hardly showed. Yet she held on. Mark got fidgety. He started to pace, then sat down on the chair at the end of the bed and slouched. After another five minutes he went out into the corridor, leaving the door ajar.

It was a long corridor. Mark looked down it and saw someone, a man, push open the doors at the far end, and start walking towards him. It was an odd, crooked walk, the legs moving forward unevenly in short steps, and even though the man seemed in a hurry, he only made slow progress down the corridor. As the man came through the open doors, he passed a nurses' station. The nurse behind the counter stood up, and looked as though she might challenge him, but then watched him pass.

Mark must have been puzzled at first. He had only met this man once before, and that had been in the darkness of a country night. The strange gait, consistent with a man who has been beaten with a wooden club, must have worried him, yet he would still have told himself that he was mistaken. But when the man came nearer, and Mark was able to see the man's condition, he could no longer have been in doubt.

The whole of David's front was filthy. There was one long mud stain that went up his jeans and continued up the front of his shirt. Dirt was still stuck to his trainers, in the crevices at the top of his jeans, behind his shirt buttons. It was falling off as it dried, leaving a trail of dirty crumbs along the corridor. On his face, the mud was streaked where he had tried to wipe it away. The wound to the side of his head was still red raw, and blood had dripped down onto his blue shirt collar, leaving a broad dark stain.

Mark stood motionless as David limped the last few feet. As they looked at each other, Mark voiced his confusion.

'How's that possible? How could you have found me so fast?'

'Because I know who you are,' David answered, 'and I now know *what* you are, you bastard. And I promise I'll be telling the police, just as soon as I leave here. Now get out of my way.'

David pushed him aside and came into the room. I looked up from the bedside and was horrified by his state. The nurse was also alarmed by the sight of someone who looked like a casualty of street living. I signalled she should not interfere.

If it had been an ordinary bed, David might have knelt by it like a child saying a bedtime prayer. But it was too high and bulky for that, so he perched on the edge of it, grasped Kat's hand, and looked down at her. Then—out of both grief and exhaustion, I suppose—he fell forward so that his upper body lay next to Kat's. The white pillows acquired dark streaks and a scattering of earth. He stretched an arm across Kat, as if to embrace her. His face was hidden in the pillow at Kat's neck, but I could tell from his shaking body that he was weeping. When, after several minutes, he had calmed a little, he whispered into her ear. I could not hear the words.

Then the monitor ceased its beeping. The nurse discreetly switched the machine off, closed and removed the oxygen supply. She left the room, presumably to call the doctor, and the two of us were alone with Kat. There was a sudden and complete stillness. Kat had gone on her way. She had died in the embrace of the man she loved, and with her sister by her side.

The nurse returned with the doctor. I sensed we had been at the bedside a long time. 'David,' I said, stroking his back, 'we must let these good people do what they have to do.' After a moment he sat up and looked for the last time at Kat's face.

He glanced over at me. The areas close to his eyes had been washed clean by his tears. 'Don't know what she was worrying about,' he said, smiling through his tears. 'She is still the most beautiful woman I have ever seen.'

He sat and looked at her a little longer, and then I came to him and put my arm round him. We moved together from the bed, allowing the doctor and nurse to get to the bedside.

'Are you alright?' the doctor asked him.

It took David some moments to realise he was being asked about his physical state. 'Yeah, guess I look an awful sight,' he said. 'I was in such a rush to get here that I fell badly.'

'Go down to the Minor Injuries Unit. They'll have a look at you.'

I couldn't face going out into the corridor, and into the indifferent world, without a moment with David. I stopped by the door and opened my arms to him.

He waved his hands at his muddy front. 'You sure?'

I found myself tearful again, and only nodded. We held each other.

As we hugged, David said, 'Did you tell Kat that the kids were going to be safe with you?'

'Oh, David, I did,' I said. 'She asked, and I felt I had no alternative. I feel so awful about it—betraying our relationship, lying to her right at the end.'

He pulled away, our hands sliding down each other's arms until they met. 'You didn't get my text? Annie, you didn't lie! They're safe with you.' He pulled at my arm. 'Come outside, where we can talk.'

Eulogy for Love

We went out into the corridor. I had expected to see Mark there, but there was no one around. David took my hands, and spoke quietly but firmly, as if I might misunderstand.

'Annie, you didn't tell her a lie. He really is a vile paedophile. I caught him in the middle of doing it. I'm in this mess because he thumped me over the head with half a tree and knocked me out. We just got one thing wrong. It's not little girls he abuses. It's boys.'

I stared at him. 'We've got him,' he said, and shook both my arms. 'We've got him. I'll tell you all about it, but please can we go and get me some treatment for my head?'

We walked, slowly, through the long corridors to the Minor Injuries Unit. It was all but closed for the night. A nurse made a call to the duty doctor, and brought the fluorescent ceiling lights flickering back to life in the waiting area. David lowered himself cautiously onto a chair.

'You look completely exhausted,' I said.

He nodded. 'I am. Physically and emotionally wiped out. It's been a rather difficult day.'

As we sat waiting for the doctor, he described what had happened with Mark. And when David was called, I went with him while he had stitches put in his head and the bruising on his side checked. He was sent on his way with some strong painkillers and a recommendation not to be alone overnight. I pleaded with him to let me drive him back to my place, but he wouldn't have it. He wanted, I guessed, to be in his bed at the farmhouse, as if he might find Kat's soul still lingering there.

I was barely home myself when he phoned.

'Safe back,' he said. 'But could you do something for me? That little pause you saw on the tracker screen at the supermarket. Could you check exactly where it stopped, and exactly what time it happened?'

I went to the laptop where I had abandoned it as I rushed to the hospital, and lifted the lid. The screen lit up, and for a moment I saw the tracker map as I had left it, the red line stopped at the clearing in the wood. But then the Wi-Fi reconnected, the map refreshed, and it unexpectedly zoomed out to make enough space to show a new red line. The line came back into town and continued to the hospital, as expected; but then it followed a path to the motorway and leapt perhaps forty miles north, past Birmingham and into Staffordshire. At that point the line stopped, apparently in the middle of the motorway. The tracker had run out of charge.

I passed on this news to David. 'The poor chap,' he commented, 'he's obviously gone crazy with grief for the wife he loved so dearly.'

'Seriously,' I said, 'it's very odd. I could just about understand if he'd headed south towards his father, but north makes no sense at all.'

I went back to the tracker record for earlier in the evening, gave David the details he wanted, and asked why he wanted to know.

I've realised we have a problem.' he said. 'Yes, you and I now know that Mark is even more vile than we imagined. But where's the evidence? It's only in my head. Think it through, Annie, and you'll see we've got ourselves in a bit of a bind.'

Chapter 28

David was sustained that night only by his intellect. His emotional capacities had been so overloaded that they had shut down to protect him from an unbearable sorrow. I, in contrast, had been grieving in advance through the weeks that I had sat by Kat's bed. I found it had only served to leave me unprotected in front of the wave of grief that hit me. I had clung to the raft, the unexpected comfort, that David had given me. Now he was taking it back.

But he was right. In our amateurish way we had been trying to create a fiction that would prevent Mark having care of the children. Then, last evening, David's encounter had hurled us into a horrible reality—the reality of Mark as a man who sexually abused boys. This was no device to get the kids out of his care. It presented an urgent need to keep him away from them, Jonathan most of all. On the other hand, we had no substantial evidence. Without it, nothing would change. Mark would return from his odd excursion and claim back his children. Neither they, nor countless other children, would be safe from him.

I only slept after I had seen dawn, and only until nine. I was barely out of bed when David phoned.

'Would you have a coffee to spare for me?'

'Of course,' I said. 'What time will you be here?'

'Actually, I'm parked outside your house.'

I looked down at myself. I was wearing a tattered blue dressing gown, and under it some old joggers and a t-shirt that had been white until it went in the wrong wash. I was decent, but not for public viewing.

'Hold on,' I said, 'I'll come and let you in.'

He seemed indifferent to my appearance. We hugged. He was looking and smelling cleaner than I had last seen him, though the wound on the side of his head, with its stitches, was ugly. I could tell he was still exhausted.

'I've just been to the supermarket car park,' he said, sitting down at the kitchen table. I put a mug of coffee in front of him. 'I thought there might be some CCTV cameras that could have recorded him picking up the boy.'

'And?'

'Had a very good look, and I don't think there are any.'

'That's disappointing.'

'Yes, but it does mean I can play the only card we have left.'

I brought my coffee over and sat down with him. 'Which is?'

'I'm going to the police to tell them what I saw.'

'Oh, David,' I sighed. 'It's a very noble idea, but you'd be sacrificing yourself for no benefit. Mark can simply deny everything. Worse, as soon as he knows your name, he'll know who you are, and then he'll claim you made it all up just to be nasty.'

He nodded. 'I realise all that.'

'And when the police hear about the tracker, and about how the two of us conspired against him, he'll be safe, and we'll be up on criminal charges.'

'OK,' he said, 'but don't worry about the tracker, or about you getting involved. I'm fairly sure we can prevent that. Let's stick to the basic question. Are we really going to do nothing to stop him? This is no longer about the future care of the kids.

Eulogy for Love

It isn't even about them anymore. It's about bringing down a man whose actions are harming children.'

He looked defiantly across the table at me. 'I know I couldn't live with myself if I did nothing. When something has to be done, and there is only one outcome that matters, the chances of success are an irrelevance.'

I was feeling impatient with him, and alarmed.

'I think you'd be sacrificing yourself pointlessly, I really do. The best outcome I can see if you take this course of action is that nothing will happen. The police will dismiss your allegations, and Mark will get the kids. The worst outcome is that you'll get taken to court—maybe me too—and Mark will deny me all contact with Jonathan and Rachel.'

The folly of his plan became more obvious even as I talked. 'The story could even get picked up by the newspapers. Just think of it, David. *Man makes false child abuse claims against husband of dead lover.* Is that how you want to be remembered? Surely there's got to be an alternative. Couldn't you find the boy, let him tell the police?'

'I've thought of that, of course. But I could be driving around town for weeks, hoping to spot him. We don't have that much time. And what if I found him? What then? If he'd wanted to spill the beans about Mark, he would have done it already. Something's making him stay silent. So, should I bundle him into my car and beat him up until he confesses that he's been abused? Or drive him to the police station and throw him out at the kerb, hoping he'll go inside and tell all? Somehow, I don't think that's how you're supposed to treat children who've been subjected to sexual abuse.'

I didn't know what more to say. Maybe he was right, but for me the priority was to preserve my links with the children, so that I could at least monitor Mark's care of them.

'Look,' David said, 'I'm pretty sure I can keep you out of the story. I'll tell the police that I happened to be in the car park and saw the boy get into his car. I know when it happened, and I know more or less where the car was parked. I'm guessing the boy came through the bushes from the housing estate on the other side. I can describe what I saw, and say I thought it was odd, and that I decided to follow him. From then on, I can tell the truth.

'If the police ask, you'll have to say that you left a message on my phone about Kat, and then saw me at the hospital, and that I told you I'd found Mark in the woods. But that's it. There was no tracker. You were never involved.'

He watched my face for a reaction.

'Will you tell them about you and Kat?'

'Not if I don't need to. If I have to, I'll say we had a bit of a fling last year. You can say we were friends, maybe even that you suspected that something was going on between us. But keep it light.'

I still wasn't convinced, and he could tell.

'Think about it, Annie. This way, you won't be involved. Mark will hate me, but you'll be fine. And there's just a chance the police will believe me. Who knows, Mark might even confess.'

'They'll have to pull his fingernails out first.'

'I have to do this, Annie. I'd like you to understand.'

I nodded unenthusiastically. 'I understand, David. But please, for the sake of the kids, keep me out of it.'

He said he wanted to get home and call the police as soon as possible. He downed his coffee and readied to leave. I hugged him before opening the front door, so the neighbours wouldn't see my slummy nightwear. 'Please take care of yourself,' I said. 'I get the impression you're running on empty. You can't keep going like this.'

370

He nodded without smiling, and left.

I was clearing away the coffee mugs when my phone rang. It was Tina. 'Hi Annie,' she said in her whiny Essex accent. 'Just thought I'd give you a little call to ask how Kat is. We haven't heard from Mark for a couple of days.'

***

David phoned the police on the number he found for non-emergencies, and was put through some police version of triage until his call landed at the desk of a woman police officer. He summarised the situation, putting the emphasis on witnessing child sexual abuse, and the officer quickly asked if someone could come to see him at home. It was Easter Sunday. Evidently the criminals were taking the day off.

Detective Constable Harris arrived at the farmhouse around eleven. She sat at the centre of his sofa in his living room. David took up position in an armchair that faced her, and made him a little higher. She was young, but knew her business. David wanted to concentrate on the lurid details of the incident in the woodland clearing, but she wanted to start at the beginning, and to understand what he was doing on Easter Saturday evening at a supermarket after it was closed. He explained that he had simply assumed it would stay open after eight, and didn't realise his mistake until he had swung into the parking area. Then he had pulled up to look on his phone for a supermarket that was still open.

'There aren't any supermarkets closer to here?' she asked. David explained that they were only small places, and he wanted a larger range of products.

'And anyway,' he said, smiling at her, 'I just felt like a bit of a drive out.'

They moved on to his account of what he had seen in the car park. He told her that he had first seen the expensive black SUV, and then the boy coming through the hedge and getting into the car. It didn't seem right to him. When they drove away, he saw it was Mark, and decided to follow.

'Do you know . . .' She checked back through her notebook. '. . . Mr Smallwood well?'

David's earth wobbled slightly. 'No, not well, but enough to recognise him.'

She kept looking at him, as if to let him know he wouldn't get away with that. He decided to throw her a little more, hoping she would then leave it alone.

'I've been friends with his wife for many years.'

'So, this must be Mrs Smallwood, I'm guessing,' she said, preparing to write in her book. 'And her first name is . . .?'

'Kat. Well, Kateryna, legally. With a 'K' and a 'Y'. But everyone called her Kat.'

DC Harris looked up sharply, and turned her head, a bird listening for the worm to surface. David said, 'She died. Last night. Cancer.' He heard the quiver in his voice, knew the officer had noticed.

'I'm sorry to hear that. Were you close?'

He paused, trying to calm himself. 'We'd been friends for many years.' She looked at him silently, watching his face. It was as if she were pinching him, waiting for him to cry out.

She wrote something down in her notebook, and then invited David to continue. Feeling that he was now on safer ground, he described how he had driven a little further, parked up, and walked through the wood. He described arriving at the clearing and seeing Mark abusing the boy. David explained how Mark had attacked him with the log. He pointed triumphantly at the wound on his head, though she must have seen it already.

DC Harris obliged by standing briefly to inspect it.

'Oh, yes, that does look nasty,' she said. 'Would be useful to have a doctor's report. Did you have it checked out?'

'Yes, when I was at the hospital.'

He silently cursed for another error.

'Just to be clear,' she said, 'Who started the fight? Did you hit him first?'

'Yes,' David retorted, offended, 'but I was trying to stop him doing what he was doing to the boy.'

'I'm sorry,' she said, straightening her back to look at him. 'I'm sure you'll understand that there are difficulties here. Not that I'm dismissing your story—far from it. All allegations of child abuse are taken very seriously. But there is no one to corroborate what you've told me. Mr Smallwood might say that he was alone, and that when you attacked him, he simply defended himself. He could even say you made the whole thing up. And I'm also getting the impression that your relationship with Mrs Smallwood might have been of a kind that would cause some friction between you and him. He might even suggest that you were conspiring to get him out of the way so that you could continue the relationship more freely.'

'But I'm telling you the truth.'

'I don't doubt that, Mr Barber. I'm only saying that Mr Smallwood could challenge your account.'

She curled back into her notebook once more, but continued with her questions. 'The boy—you got a good look? Can you give me any sort of description?'

'He was thin,' David said, talking to the top of the officer's head as she wrote in her notebook, 'with a boy's physique. Difficult to judge age, but he was certainly much shorter than Mr Smallwood. Maybe about twelve, perhaps a bit more. Oh, and he had that strange haircut that young men have started wearing—very short at the sides, but longer on top. Not a good choice for him, really. He had a long face anyway, and the haircut made it worse. Like those Easter Island statues.'

The police officer put her head up and looked at him. It was only for a second, but David thought he saw a look of recognition on her face. It was as if she had, at that moment, decided that he was telling the truth.

She asked a few more questions about what had happened after the fight in the wood, and wanted to know how he had heard the news that Kat was close to death. Thus my name and contact details were added to the notebook. She also took the landline number that David held for the Smallwood residence, though he had never used it. He told her, honestly, that he didn't have a mobile phone number for Mark.

At that point he thought they must be finished, but the officer leaned across to her brief case and pulled out a set of forms. 'I'd just like to have a formal statement from you, if you wouldn't mind, Mr Barber.'

David watched impatiently as the officer converted his story into stilted police language on carefully numerated continuation sheets, each of which he would have to sign. When she was finally done, the statement safely in the briefcase, DC Harris got up to go.

'There are well established inter-agency procedures that have to be invoked in cases of suspected child abuse,' she said, 'as I'm sure you can understand. But the next step must be to contact Mr Smallwood to see what he has to say.'

Good luck with that, he thought to himself, as he watched her drive away.

***

Eulogy for Love

David phoned me to report on his meeting with DC Harris, and to warn me she might be in touch. I told him to get some sleep.

That was immediately followed by another call from Tina to report on the children. She had been doing her best to prepare them for the loss of their mother, and had now broken the news to them. 'Poor little things,' she said. 'They have a little cry and then go back to doing ordinary things, as if nothing had happened.' *Just like the rest of us*, I thought. Then she said that Thomas wanted to talk to me, and passed over the phone.

Thomas went through the motions of offering his sympathies. He moved swiftly on to ask me to explain—as I had already to Tina—when I had last seen Mark.

'One minute he was in the hospital corridor, gone the next,' I said. 'That's all I can tell you.'

Thomas had already tried to reach Mark at home and on his mobile. We agreed it was hardly his style to disappear without explanation, even as a reaction to Kat's death.

'Anyway, Annie,' he said, 'there are some arrangements that need to be started. Fortunately, we'd already had some conversations when it became clear that Kat was, you know . . . when it became clear her illness was terminal.'

Kat had told me about the Smallwood Planning Committee. I should have realised that it would already have held preliminary meetings.

'Mark has been very clear that he wants Kat buried down here, in the churchyard, where there's an area that's more or less ours, if you know what I mean. And, on that basis, I'm going to go ahead and talk to some funeral directors, and arrange for her to be brought down. And I'll have a chat with the vicar about the funeral, just as soon as he's got through his Easter duties. I'm sure Mark will be OK with that, and find it a comfort not to be bothered too much with the practicalities when he gets back.'

That was it. One of the members might be *in absentia*, but the committee was still quorate and fully operational. It was going to steal Kat away from me and bury her in some churchyard too far away.

'Oh,' he said, 'and could you go to the hospital to pick up the death certificate, and sign a form for the release of the body to the undertakers? Mark is next of kin, of course, but I think you can do it.'

Fuck you, Thomas, I thought. He might seem pleasant, but he was built of the same stuff as the rest of them. He was making me the little woman who ran his errands. Then again, it seemed a bad day to start an argument. I agreed to drive to the hospital later.

***

I had hoped that I could get a little peace and quiet. It was, after all, Easter Sunday. But the phone kept ringing.

DC Harris could not have been back at the station for long when she called. She expressed her sympathies in a very professional manner, and checked that I knew about the story David had told her. She said she had driven a few minutes earlier to the Smallwood residence to see whether there was any sign of Mark. I had to admit to myself it was a sensible thing to do. For all we knew he might have gone out and got drunk after he left the hospital, and now be at home safely sleeping it off. But DC Harris had seen no sign of him, or his car.

'I take it,' she said, 'that you've got no idea where Mr Smallwood might have gone.'

'None at all, I'm afraid.'

Then she asked if I had a mobile number for Mark. I'd never known it, and I said so.

'Are you saying no one has tried calling Mr Smallwood on his mobile?'

I didn't like the implication that she was dealing with fools, and hastily assured her that Thomas had tried to phone Mark on his mobile. And then, inevitably, she asked for Thomas's number. I had to give it to her.

Unless the police simply ignored what David had told them, Thomas was going to hear about it, one way or another. But this felt too early. The police could not possibly be looking for Mark as a missing person when he had been absent for less than a day. Thomas would know there was something else going on. And then he would ask me if I knew about it.

DC Harris was still talking. 'I'm hoping we can make progress fairly quickly,' she said, 'and determine what's the right course of action to be taken here. Obviously, we need to locate Mr Smallwood, and then things may be much clearer. But it might be useful if I came to see you in the next day or two.'

***

Thomas phoned late afternoon, while I was at the hospital. I made him wait until I'd finished the paperwork. He had phoned with one very specific question: *Did I know anything about these other enquiries the police were making in connection with Mark?*

I had expected the question, and already considered my options. I wasn't going to lie to protect David. He had made his choice, and I wanted to preserve my chances of seeing the children when they were with Mark. That meant that I had to seem as straightforward and honest as possible, even if it harmed David.

'It's to do with an allegation of child abuse.'

'Against Mark?'

'Yes.'

'Good god. Do you know anything more about the allegation?'

'A bit more, but not every detail. Someone says they came across him last night, out in the countryside, molesting a young boy.'

'What do they mean by *molesting*?'

'Really, Thomas,' I queried, 'are you sure you want me to give you the full Anglo-Saxon detail?'

'Yes. I do.'

OK,' I said. 'They say he was committing sodomy with a minor. That's what they say your brother was doing. Fucking a child in the arse.'

Thomas said, 'Jesus Christ,' but it was in a low voice, not a shout of surprise or outrage. They'd both been to public school, I remembered, where such things are alleged to be almost normal. It flickered through my mind that perhaps Thomas already knew Mark had a penchant for buggery.

Thomas muttered his thanks, and rang off. The identity of Mark's accuser would remain secret a little longer.

I should have phoned David, but I was weary of phone calls and conspiracies. I went home, and spoke to no one. I had, somehow, completed a day in a world that no longer contained Kat.

Chapter 29

In the hope that the following day, Easter Monday, would be quieter, I went to the workshop for the morning. There were a couple of computers awaiting my attention. I made good progress until DC Harris called, asking to see me. I suggested she should come straightaway to the workshop.

We sat at a table I sometimes use for discussions with customers. As far as I could tell, and much to my relief, she seemed interested in me purely for my insights into Mark, Kat, and David. Mostly I needed only to offer dilutions of the truth.

She wanted to know whether Mark and Kat were happy together. I told her that Mark was work-obsessed, controlling and domineering towards Kat, short-tempered with the children, and unloving towards all three.

'So, a very troubled marriage,' DC Harris ventured.

'Actually, from my observations, I'd say it's fairly average.'

The officer honed in on *the marital relations*, as she put it. I told her that I knew from Kat that there were hardly any marital relations. They had, after all, been together for more than ten years.

'And what about the relationship between your sister and David Barber? What sort of relationship was that?'

'Oh, they'd been friendly for many years,' I said airily. 'In fact, she was a friend of the family years ago, when David was married. She was a kind of glorified babysitter, I think.'

'Were they close? An affectionate relationship?'

'Yes, good friends, for sure. But there was a big age difference between them.'

'Doesn't mean a relationship can't become intimate, in my experience.'

'No, you're right. I suppose they were sometimes a bit flirty together, but I think that was just the nature of the friendship.'

DC Harris nodded pensively and wrote in her notebook.

She asked me about my relationship with Kat. I said we had been very close. Then she asked me about my connection with David, and I said we had only got to know each other since Kat had been in hospital.

She was putting away her notebook in her briefcase, but I reckoned we hadn't quite finished.

'I get the impression that your focus is on deciding whether David's account can be trusted,' I said. 'For what it's worth, I've known him for some months now, and I've always found him highly reliable and completely trustworthy. Got the same impression from Kat. That makes me believe his account.

'I'm inclined to agree,' she said, holding her briefcase on her lap. 'But his account is all we've got. There are no other witnesses, no victim has come forward, and the alleged perpetrator has disappeared.

'Incidentally,' she continued, 'if we suppose there'd been no allegation, and that Mr Smallwood had simply walked out of the hospital and disappeared, would you be concerned?'

'I don't know about concerned,' I responded, 'but I'd certainly be puzzled. From what I know of him, it's very out of character.'

'That was my impression,' she said. 'He's not someone who would normally be considered a vulnerable person, but he has just lost his wife. You—or, better, his brother—can report him as a missing person any time you like, but I'd certainly recommend it if you haven't heard from him in the next forty-eight hours. That will give us a proper basis on which to start making enquiries.'

***

I finished the computer repairs and returned home at lunchtime. Thomas phoned towards the end of the afternoon. I expected him to ask more questions about the allegations, and who had made them. Instead, he told me that the funeral had been scheduled for the following Monday afternoon, and that he had not heard from Mark.

It was now a day since I had spoken to David. For no good reason, I phoned him. He said he was busy in his studio. I felt certain he had a bottle at his side. Not that he sounded drunk, exactly, but distant and uncommunicative. We exchanged the little news there was. He had not heard again from the police, and I had no news of Mark. I told him that the funeral was planned for Monday.

'Been thinking, Annie,' he said. 'I think I'll come to the funeral. I don't see why I shouldn't. If it's a gathering of people who loved Kat, I've got more right to be there than most of them.'

'It would be asking for trouble when people saw you there.'

'Why? They wouldn't even know who I am. I'd be there on my own—or as your friend, if you'll let me be that. They'd have no idea.'

'Mark would.'

'I'm not certain of that. He's only seen me twice. Once in the dark, and the other time covered in mud and blood. Anyway, what the fuck. If he saw me, he couldn't admit that

381

he knew me. And that's assuming, of course, that he even turns up.'

David was becoming uncharacteristically belligerent. I knew it was down to alcohol and grief. This was not the time to attempt a rational discussion.

'OK, David. Let's not talk about it now. Maybe I could come over tomorrow? Lunchtime? We could discuss it then.' He grunted agreement. 'OK, I'll see you then,' I said. 'And please don't drink too much more tonight.'

I left him to his grief, then spent the evening, and much of the night, absorbed in my own. It was ceasing to be a sharp pain, now that the drama was over, and turning into an ache that would ease, yet always be with me. My sense of Kat as a living being was drifting away from me, carried on the currents. The space in the world that had been hers was already closing.

***

I needed some news to cheer me up, and it came when Tina phoned the next morning. She said that she had been talking with Thomas, and they felt it would do the children good to return to normal school when term started the next Tuesday. Tina meandered around the point, but eventually said that they hoped I would have the children to stay until Mark returned.

Kat had once commented, I recalled, that though Tina was not very bright, she had a good heart. Tina was becoming my ally. I told her that I would, of course, be delighted to look after them, and thanked her for the decision.

'You don't need to thank us, Annie. Don't get me wrong, they're lovely kids, but a couple of weeks is long enough for both of us. With our two almost out of the nest, it comes quite hard to be doing it all over again.'

Encouraged by this acknowledgement of my status in their lives, I asked to talk to the children. Tina brought them in turns to the phone. Rachel chatted without prompting about their outings, activities at home, and the household dog. Then Jonathan came on the phone and talked in the same way. It was only as we were about to say goodbye that he asked the question.

'Ayay, now that Mummy's dead, will we be coming to live with you?'

He had to wait while I steadied myself. 'You can come and stay with me until your Daddy gets back. But then you'll go back home with him.'

'We'd rather go on staying with you.'

'I think your daddy would miss you. But you'll still see me, and come and stay in my house, just like always.'

Jonathan had nothing more to say. I tried to sound cheerful, but the call came to a bleak end.

***

I was not convinced David was taking care of himself, so I stopped on the way to the farmhouse to buy lunch for us both, with extras to leave in his fridge for later. As I pulled into the courtyard, I could see him working at his desk, and went to find him in the studio. He was busy making a large sketch in charcoal. His fingers were blackened from it, so he held his hands out of the way and let me give him a hug.

'I'm sorry I was grumpy last night,' he said, sitting back down at his desk, but still looking at me. 'Wine makes grief selfish. And you have more reason to grieve than me.'

'Let's not get competitive about it, David. I feel so lonely in my sorrow, as if I'm the only one that cares that Kat isn't here. With you, I know I'm not on my own. We're good companions in grief.'

I moved around the desk and stood next to him, so that I could see what he had been drawing. It also allowed me to put a hand on his shoulder. He was using a wide paper, and almost all that he had sketched was on the right-hand side, where the paper was heavily covered in charcoal. Two figures, wearing robes in a classical style, were standing on a ledge with a dark and almost featureless landscape below them. Vertical cliffs loomed a few feet behind them.

'Reminds me of old pictures of Hell,' I said.

David pointed a blackened finger up at me, and smiled. 'Good answer! Actually, I'm attempting to pastiche the work of Gustave Doré. He was the guy who did a set of illustrations for the Divine Comedy, Danté's journey through the Underworld. You've just proved that Doré pretty much cornered the market when it comes to images of the Underworld.'

He was making adjustment to the drawing as he spoke, alternately adding lines with the charcoal, then using a finger to soften them. 'These gloomy scenes have come to define what we think it looks like. Strictly speaking, my drawing is more like Dante's vision of Purgatory than Hell, because the people are stood on one of the seven ledges of Mount Purgatory. But you were close.'

'A miserable grey place. Can't see it as an upcoming tourist destination.'

'Yeah, a place of eternal twilight. That's how we all think of it—even how it's portrayed in Hollywood films. The irony is that the pictures are like that for technical reasons. Doré drew them as illustrations for a book. In the nineteenth century

384

that meant doing them as engravings, and engravings were printed in black or, sometimes, sepia. He might have imagined the scenes in technicolour, but he had to create them in greys.

'And now,' I said, anticipating him, 'we see the underworld in greys. Like we look at old black and white photos, and they fool us into thinking history was monochrome.'

'Precisely.'

'But why are you drawing a picture—or half a picture—of Purgatory? Could one of these people be you, by any chance?'

'Ah, well done again, Annie. I admit it—I'm drawing Purgatory because that's where I feel I am. Not so much this minute, with you here, but when I'm on my own. It feels like life has ended, and that I'm now a soul in the afterlife. The left half of the painting will be full of colour—blue skies, tall trees with green fronds, verdant hillsides. Think Hockney. Life as it so briefly was with Kat.'

He paused, staring at the paper as if he could see the whole scene. Then he said, 'Doré has two people in his engraving—Dante, and his companion, Virgil. At first, I just thought I'd better put two in mine. But I realise there is someone beside me. It's you. As you said, we're companions in grief. I hope you don't mind.'

'I'll stay with you awhile in Purgatory, David. But not forever. I'm hoping summer might come around again.'

I gave his shoulder a squeeze. 'Come on, you, enough of this. I brought some lunch. Let's go eat.'

We sat and ate, and for once we talked about good news. I told him about the kids coming to stay if Mark was still absent by the weekend.

David grunted. 'We can only hope he's run off to South America and never comes back.'

We repeated the discussion about David coming to the funeral. His mood was more reasonable than the previous evening, but he still wanted to be there.

***

Thomas phoned again that evening. It was, as he pointed out, now three days since Mark had gone missing. He had decided it was time to report Mark formally as a missing person, as DC Harris had recommended.

'Do you have keys to the house?' he asked unexpectedly. I nearly denied it, but then imagined Mark recounting how he had caught me using Kat's keys.

'Yes, now you mention it, I have. Kat's own keys. I used them a couple of times to get things for her while she was in hospital.'

'Good. If Mark hasn't come back by then, I'd like to come up on Thursday morning to have a look around the house. I was thinking you might bring the keys and meet me there.'

I offered to be available whenever it suited him that day. Thomas said he would text to confirm.

I got the text from Thomas the following morning, Wednesday.

Mark now officially a missing person. Will be at house at noon tomorrow. DC Harris also attending. See you there. Thomas.

***

Thursday was grey and damp. I arrived at noon and saw a car already in the drive. It was ostentatiously large, obviously the property of a male Smallwood. Thomas was sitting inside it. He got out and greeted me like a business acquaintance. We were walking to the front door when DC Harris appeared, presumably after parking her car on the road.

I tried the key in the deadlock bolt, and found it had been locked. Then I turned the Yale lock and waited for the alarm keypad to start its two-tone demand for attention.

There was silence. Mark had evidently not bothered to set the alarm as he hurried out to meet the child who would satisfy his needs. We walked into the stillness of the house and made a tour of it as a trio. The office door was locked. The dining room looked tidy. The kitchen had a clutter of dirty dishes on the worktop, the dishwasher full of clean crockery. In the living room there was a used dinner plate and fork left on the coffee table where Mark had obviously eaten in front of the television.

We continued our inspection in silence. Thomas led the way upstairs. I held back at the doorway of Kat's bedroom while the other two looked around it. I saw the bed she had once slept in, and a dress hung on the wardrobe door—one of her favourites, I remembered. I was also sure I could smell her, even as I leaned into the room. Not perfume alone, but the unique, sweet aroma of perfume that had rested on my sister's skin. When the others came out, I let them walk ahead while I wiped my tears away with a finger.

They briefly looked into the children's bedrooms, and then we went into the spare bedroom. DC Harris said nothing, but she would have seen from the man's clothes and the unmade bed that this was still where Mark slept, even though the main bedroom had been vacated. Maybe he had become too well established to bother to move. Or, perhaps, the main bedroom had become so imbued with the potent ambience of womanhood that he found it too intimidating.

That brought us back downstairs to the locked study door. 'I think it could be very helpful to have access,' DC Harris said.

'OK', Thomas said, and experimentally pushed against the door with his shoulder. 'Do you happen to know how difficult this is going to be?' He meant the door.

DC Harris tapped it. 'It's not a solid door,' she said, 'and I suspect it's only a cheap lock. Should give fairly easily.'

Thomas started hitting the door with his shoulder, each time more powerfully as he got the hang of it. On the fourth attempt the wood around the lock split apart and the door came open. Thomas staggered into the room.

We looked around. Nothing seemed unusual. I recalled sitting at the desk while David stayed on lookout at the window.

'What exactly are we looking for?' Thomas asked DC Harris.

'Documents giving bank accounts, credit cards, and phone accounts would be very useful,' DC Harris explained. 'We can find them out by other routes, but this would be far easier. If we can find his passport, then at least we'll know he's still in the UK. Diaries and anything else that might tell us about his appointments, though I imagine that sort of stuff will be on the PC. If I have your consent, Mr Smallwood, I'll take that away for further examination.'

There were a few documents on the desk to be checked, and then the contents of six desk drawers and a metal filing cabinet. DC Harris took the lead, picking out documents and placing them in piles, as if she were performing a card trick.

We soon found Mark's passport in a desk drawer. I saw Kat's next to it, and imagined her clutching it as she hurried towards the plane for Paris. Kat on the plane beside the man she had loved so long—the man she thought would bring the happiness so long denied to her.

Mark kept a tidy office, and we soon found documents covering all the kinds of account DC Harris had mentioned. She got Thomas to fill in some forms that would allow her to take away the computer and the documents. Then we left the house. I helped DC Harris carry the computer to her car, and she went on her way. I wondered whether I should invite Thomas back for a cup of tea, but I could not see the benefit, and did not want his company.

Instead, when Thomas had gone, I called David on my mobile.

'David,' I said, when he answered, 'can you spare me a little time?'

'Of course. All the time you want.'

'I had not realised how awful that was going to be. To be there in that house, the sense of her so strong that she felt present with me, and yet knowing she is gone. It was agony. Please be with me a little while, David. Even if I can't speak much more. Be my companion in grief.'

Chapter 30

When Sunday evening arrived, little had changed. There had been no word of Mark. The police had not been in contact. Thomas and Tina had been in touch, but only to agree some details of the funeral services, and to confirm the plan that Jonathan and Rachel would come back with me afterwards.

David and I had continued to debate the question of his attendance at the funeral. I understood why he would want to be there, and I had to agree that he could be explained away as a friend of mine. Thomas might find out later that my friend was the man who had exposed his brother as a paedophile, but we could cope with that. My greatest concern was that Mark would turn up at the funeral, leading to an unseemly row with David, or even another fight.

This led to a repeat of the discussion about where Mark had gone, and when he would come back. It was all fruitless speculation, inevitably—flimsy conjectures founded on nothing more than the altercation with David at the hospital, and the tracker report that showed Mark driving north. I had to agree, however, that Mark was very unlikely to appear at the funeral without warning, because he would not know where and when it was happening unless he had contacted one of us to ask. On that basis I could no longer see any good reason to discourage David from attending. I also wanted him there as a comfort to me.

Eulogy for Love

David's companionship meant that we could travel together in his car. I was waiting outside when he arrived. He was wearing a suit that looked as if it had been in a wardrobe for a very long time. The jacket had been placed neatly in the back for the journey, and he was sitting at the wheel in a white shirt and black tie.

'Well, David,' I said, as soon as I was in the car. 'You look. . . what shall I say? Tidy?'

He laughed ruefully. 'I think you mean that I look like a chimp in a tea advert. Never quite seems worth spending serious money on a new one. I hope I'm not going to be an embarrassment.'

'No, not at all. You're fine—it's just that it's not your natural style. I think Kat would be amused.'

'That's a good thought,' David said. He had started to drive, but glanced across at me. 'And you look. . .' he said, aware he had to say something in return. He paused, then glanced a second time, more carefully. 'Actually,' he said, looking ahead once more, 'you're looking lovely.'

I did have a suitable black dress, and had nearly worn it. But when I had tried it on, contemplating it in the mirror, I had a strong sense that Kat did not approve. I settled instead on a knee length dress, high necked and long sleeved, in a black and white print. Not quite sexy, I had judged, but smart.

'Thank you!' I said to David. 'I wanted to dress today for Kat, and I thought she'd like me in something cheerful. I don't think she would want us to be miserable.'

David said, 'No, I'm sure she wants us to be happy.'

***

We had driven for some miles in silence. Then David said, 'I don't know whether you'll understand, Annie, but I feel such a coward. I knew Kat—or at any rate, had a connection to her—for sixteen years. Sixteen years! But in all that time I never once stood with her, or stood up for her. I pretended to Helen that she wasn't important to me, and when Helen told me to stop seeing her I just went along with it. Then, when Kat and I found each other a second time, we never stood together as a couple. I never helped with the kids, never defended her against Mark. And then there's been these last months when I haven't even seen her. Every time, I've just skulked in the background.'

'But in each of those cases, you were doing the right thing. Circumstances made it necessary.'

'Oh yes, that's me. Mr Sensible. I know that technically you're right. But I so wish I could have been crazy enough, at least once, to let people see us together, see the love we had. To tell the whole damned world to fuck off and leave us alone.'

***

It was an immaculate Home Counties village, a base for wealthy London commuters. The Norman church, set amongst graves, stood on one side of a triangular green, with a primary school and a pub on the other two sides. There was a neat children's playground at the centre. I only realised as we arrived that this was the same church where I had come, thirteen years previously, for Kat's wedding.

We were in such good time that there was no one to greet us as we entered the church. Someone was shuffling about behind an organ screen, preparing to play. We walked down the centre aisle and claimed the front pew on the left.

There was a commotion behind our backs a few minutes later. I turned round and saw Tina and the children standing in the church doorway. Jonathan and Rachel came running down the aisle to me, and I bent down to receive them in my arms. When all three of us had calmed, I stood and walked towards Tina, the children still holding on to me.

She waited for me at the door. I noticed she was wearing a complicated, almost Victorian black dress. She might have looked stylish, but her hair was too blonde, and too extravagantly styled, for a woman of her age. She smiled, generously, at the fuss the children were making of me. 'They couldn't wait to see you,' she said.

'Nor I them. If it's OK, I'll take them outside for a few minutes.'

I looked back into the church and saw David standing at the pew where I had left him. I managed to indicate by gestures that I was going to take the children outside.

Tina tilted her head down and looked up at me past her expensively tweezed and threaded brows. 'New man in your life, Annie?'

'Just someone who was a friend of Kat's a long time ago. I've been letting him know how Kat was doing.'

Tina gave me a disbelieving look. I grasped the children's hands to free them from my legs, and we walked outside. Around the corner of the church, and sheltered from a cool breeze, we found a bench seat. I sat down so that I could talk to the children at their height. They stood in front of me, touching my knees, competing to spill out their news. Tina had taken them to buy new clothes for the funeral, and Rachel was very pleased with her blue dress and woolly tights. Jonathan had been bought a little grey suit.

When they had calmed, I asked, 'So, tell me, what have we come here to do?'

Tina had prepared them well. 'I know, Ayay,' Jonathan said, very seriously. 'We've come to say goodbye to Mummy.'

Rachel was sucking her thumb—a habit long abandoned, except when she was distressed. She nodded in agreement.

'Good,' I said, 'that's right. It's very sad for all of us, so this is a day when no one will mind if you cry. I'm sure I shall cry. And we're going to sit with my friend David, and he'll probably cry as well. But we can also smile and laugh, because we want to think about what a lovely person Mummy was.'

They were both silent, nodding. They seemed to be coping, so I went on.

'In a minute we'll go back into the church and sing some songs, and remember what Mummy was like. Do you know what happens after that?'

'We're going to put Mummy in the ground,' Rachel said.

'Not quite that,' I said. 'We're going to put Mummy's body in the ground, because she doesn't need it anymore.' I waited for a few moments, hoping we wouldn't have to discuss the afterlife. They stood and looked at me silently, so I continued. 'People like to come to churchyards where the people they love have been buried, and to think about them. But you can think about Mummy any time you want to, wherever you are.'

I looked at their solemn faces, and felt my heart vibrating, as if about to break under the strain and submerge these two children in my own tears.

'Come on,' I said as cheerfully as I could, 'let's go and sit in the church.'

As we came back to the front of the church I saw Thomas and his father stood near the lychgate. People, in an intermittent flow, were now making their way towards the church. Grey, balding men in dark suits and coats, accompanied by silent women in expensive dark dresses. It was the same crowd that had come to the wedding. Not people who were there because they loved Kat, or even knew her. Another gathering of the Smallwood clan. Charles and Thomas were bringing them in.

Tina's two sons were at the church entrance handing out Orders of Service. I introduced David to the children, in case they had forgotten meeting him that day at my house, and then we went to the front pew and settled in a row—the children on either side of me, and David next to Rachel. The organ was being played, tunelessly. When the service was due to start, Thomas and Tina came with their sons, with Peggy and Charles Smallwood after them, to sit on the front pew at the other side of the aisle.

What followed was, in almost every respect, a typical example of a modern Anglican funeral. The vicar appeared, and stood in front of the altar as the coffin was carried in by staff from the undertakers. He began the service with a formal statement and an informal greeting. We sang a hymn. I went to the lectern and read part of a psalm. I had not trusted myself to do more. I have never been a believer, and yet, like so many people, I still turned at times like these to find comfort in the old religious words.

The Lord is my light and my salvation; whom shall I fear? the Lord is the strength of my life; of whom shall I be afraid?

When the wicked, even mine enemies and my foes, came upon me to eat up my flesh, they stumbled and fell.

Though an host should encamp against me, my heart shall not fear: though war should rise against me, in this will I be confident.

The vicar gave a short address, wisely choosing not to make any personal statements about Kat, but instead taking the opportunity to make a sales pitch to a congregation of non-attenders. Tina had added a nice touch—I was warming to her, as Kat had predicted—by helping the children take two bouquets of roses and place them on the coffin.

As set out in the order of service, Thomas then went to the lectern. 'As some of you will know,' he began, 'Kat's husband Mark is unable to be here today. And so I'm going to say a few words that I hope and believe he would want to say himself on this occasion.'

Thomas proceeded to offer a picture of Kat composed of clichés, an enumeration of praises so faint it was damning. To that extent, he spoke more accurately on behalf of Mark than he had probably intended. It was joyless, loveless, uninspired, and impersonal. Thomas finished and left the lectern. This, it seemed, was to be the sole statement on Kat and her life.

I was jolted by David's touch to my arm when he leaned into me.

'Please forgive me, Annie.'

To my surprise, he got up. He took a folded sheet of paper from inside his jacket, and walked to the lectern. He did not look at me.

'Most of you do not know who I am,' he began. 'My name is David Barber. I knew Kateryna, at intervals, for around sixteen years. I speak today for the few here, and for the many more elsewhere, who loved her, and whose lives have been enriched by knowing her.'

David paused, and looked down at the paper he had laid on the lectern. He was choosing his own pace. Then he went on, often looking up at the pews filled with the Smallwood clan.

Eulogy for Love

'Countless others in recent years, standing where I am now, and searching to express their grief for the loss of a woman too early in her life, will have called upon a famous eulogy for a very famous woman. It was a eulogy given not in a pretty parish church, but in one of the great abbeys of our nation, and delivered by a far greater orator than I. Yet I still find echoes of it in the loss we are facing today.

'If you are expecting me to say that Kateryna was our princess, you are mistaken. That is not the comparison I want to make. She was not a princess, and there is no need belatedly to crown her as one. She was an ordinary woman. Ordinarily wonderful, ordinarily loving, ordinarily insightful, ordinarily longsuffering.

'Like so many other women, Kateryna, you not only brought children into this world but cared for them with limitless devotion. Once they had been born, it was the very purpose of your life. For the sake of your children, you were willing to abandon happiness for yourself. More than that, as you surrounded them with love, you—like so many other women—became a beacon of all the deepest forces in humanity that give it worth: Joy, wonder, laughter, love, devotion.

'These qualities are to be found in many women; but for you, Kat, they were always easily present. As a young woman you loved life and laughter. You loved to tease, but always with affection. You delighted in the company of children, but you did not need them to find the child in yourself—and yours was a joyful, loving, unselfconscious child. You had such pretty looks that passing strangers would turn back to see you again, but it is we, those privileged to have known you, who can truly attest to your beauty.

'In spite of all this you were oppressed—not only by the men in your life, but by the whole edifice of male power. Such oppression is the common and almost universal experience of women. It is an oppression that goes beyond the inequalities of rights and employment. It is an oppression that is not confined to other cultures, where patriarchy is sanctioned by state law and religious teaching. Nor is it, as the easy stereotypes would have us believe, limited in our country to poorly educated men. As Kat discovered, it is also the commonplace, though more subtle practice of educated, middle-class English men. It is baffling. I cannot believe that they do it merely out of convenience and laziness, to enslave the women they claim to love. My own explanation is that the life-giving, life-enhancing forces embodied in women are threatening to those people—predominantly those of the opposite gender—who are at the opposite end of the moral spectrum.

'I was not with Kat through the months of her last illness, but I know that even as she lay dying she remained gracious and generous in spirit, undemanding, and without bitterness. Her sole concern was that her children would be safe and happy after she had gone. She wanted to know that those who loved her would protect her beloved children, Jonathan and Rachel, and I pledge this here. We who have loved her are overwhelmed with sadness for the loss of a woman who was not even our mother. How great your suffering is, we cannot even imagine.

'I end this by giving thanks for Kateryna, a wonderful mother, sister, and friend. An ordinary woman, yet nonetheless remarkable, nonetheless irreplaceable. A woman who will never be extinguished from the minds of those who loved her.'

Silence echoed across the stone columns of the church as David came back to his seat by Rachel. I caught his eye, and tried to give him a look of horror. But I couldn't do it with sincerity. I understood.

David was plainly struggling to contain his emotions as he sat back in the pew. I think Rachel must have seen it, because her small hand reached out and grasped his.

The vicar, after waiting to see if there were to be more unscheduled eulogies, called the congregation to prayer. There was a final hymn, and we received a blessing from the vicar. The undertaker's staff returned to carry the coffin to the churchyard. I was unsure how well the children would cope with this last stage of the ceremony, and so had planned to stay behind the other mourners as they processed into the churchyard. David remained with us.

The four of us stood back from the main group around the grave, and watched as the coffin was lowered into the ground. The vicar spoke the words of the committal. The breeze sent playful gusts to lift the hems of the women's dresses and ruffled the grey hairs of the men. I felt the children leaning against me, sobbing, and I drew them in. David reached out behind the children and put his hand against my back.

Then it was over. The mourners dispersed, most heading toward the churchyard gate and across the common to the pub, where a room and refreshments had been hired. The four of us, our own private huddle, made our way to the graveside. I crouched between the children and looked down. Their bouquets were in place on top of the coffin. We wept together.

Eventually I looked up. David was holding out some paper tissues, and I used them to dry the children's tears, as well as my own.

'After that little speech of yours, David, I don't think we'll be mingling at the pub.'

'Did you want to? It's not really a gathering for children. They'll be patted on the head and then ignored. And anyway, those people are all too smug and self-regarding to take the slightest notice of what I said. Don't suppose they even listened.'

'No, you're right—the patriarchy continues undisturbed. But I do understand why you did it. And I also think you may have upset a few people.' I pointed discreetly up the slope. 'Like Thomas, for one.'

Thomas was alone near the church entrance, and talking on his phone. He ended the call, and stood staring as if in deep thought. We watched as Tina walked up to him from the gate.

'Might be better if you disappeared off with the children for a while,' I said.

'OK.' David reached his hands out to the children. 'Come on, you two. Let's see whether those swings are any good.'

I walked across to Thomas and Tina. Thomas saw me approaching. 'That was a call from the police,' he said. I'd told them I wanted to be called as soon as there was any news.

'They've found Mark. They were trying not to be too brutal with the facts, but it seems they've found his body in some woodland in Staffordshire. It looks like he hanged himself.'

'So suicide?' Tina asked, unnecessarily.

'Yes.'

'God,' I said. My reactions were so complex and contradictory that I didn't trust myself to say more.

'Does Charles know?' Tina asked.

'No,' Thomas answered. 'I'll have to take him to one side in a minute. And I'll have to make some sort of announcement when everyone's assembled at the pub.'

I was thinking about the effect of this on the children. 'Thomas,' I said, 'Rachel and Jonathan have had as much as they can handle. This is not what they need to hear now. I'm sure it would be best if we took them home straightaway.'

Thomas nodded. Tina said, 'I'll get their bags from the car.' Thomas gave her the car keys and she hurried off. I offered my sympathies to Thomas, and he excused himself.

Left standing on my own, I could see David with the children at the swings. As he told me later, the children had rushed ahead of him as they had gone over to the common. It seemed strange to him, at that moment, that they could so abruptly go from crying at their mother's graveside to running energetically towards the play area. He had stood back, watching them on the swings but absorbed in his own sorrow.

But the more he stood there, the more he felt aware of the churchyard behind him, and of Kat lying in her coffin. He had a sense that she was whispering in his ear, her hand at his back, pushing him forward. He recalled memories of her playing with Lauren and Hannah. She did not want this sadness. She wanted him fully alive and with her children—having fun with them, as she used to have.

By the time I reached the play area, all three of them were side by side on the swings, competing to see who could go the highest. I became the judge. While the last of the mourners processed untidily across the common, we laughed at our games.

When they had tired, I told the children that we needed to drive home, and sent them to find Tina with their bags. It gave me a chance to tell David the news.

'I know I once threatened to kill Mark,' he said, 'but in the last week I wasn't entirely sure it was OK to wish him dead. So I didn't like to say anything. But it had seemed to me that suicide was a strong possibility. It was always so important to him to be successful. Successful in the eyes of world, I mean. When I walked into the hospital that night, he didn't know who I was, but he assumed I was someone with the power to expose him. And exposure would have made him a failure in every way—a paedophile with no job, not even fit to have the care of his own children. He knew that this would be his future, and I guess he could see no other way out.'

We saw Thomas get out of a car and head towards us. 'I've just broken the news to my father. He's going to stay on his own in the car for a while, but insists on going over to the pub.

'Look,' he said. 'There's something we may as well deal with now, before you head off with the kids. I'm executor of Mark's will, and I already know what's in it.'

I thought this was cruel of him. We had been through enough for one day.

'Firstly, the will—which he wrote a while back, before Kat was ill—states that if he died after Kat, and while Jonathan and Rachel were minors, the estate was to be left in trust with me until they reached eighteen.

'Secondly, in those circumstances, his will places the children under my guardianship.'

It was some small comfort, I told myself. We had so long feared the children would end up with their father. They would be happier with Thomas and Tina. But it was not what Kat had wanted, nor I.

'However,' Thomas continued, 'that doesn't mean that Tina and I have to be the ones who look after them on a daily basis. As guardian, I have full and sole parental responsibility. This means there is nothing to prevent me determining that they will be resident with another member of their family. Tina has made it very clear to me that they should be with you. So, Annie, if you're agreeable, you're not just having them to stay for a while. They are going back with you to their new

home. And, of course, I can release money that I'll be holding
in trust to meet the costs of their care.'

Epilogue

The police believe that Mark had slept in his car on the Saturday night. Certainly, there was no record that he had paid for a hotel, and there were remnants of a takeaway meal on the back seat. He had needed to wait until ten o'clock the following morning, Easter Sunday, to buy some strong rope when the shops opened. Once he had done that, he headed into an area of woodland in rural Staffordshire. It was a managed pine forest with fire breaks, the trees planted in tidy rows. Mark drove along one of the firebreaks, then turned the car and forced it into the forest. The lower trunks of the trees had short, flimsy branches that broke easily as he urged the car through the gaps.

He may have chosen to stop when he thought he was far enough in, or perhaps reached a point where the car could not go further. Either way, the car halted when it was beside one of the trees. He took the rope and climbed on top of the car. At that height he could easily reach strong branches above his head. He tied one end of the rope over a branch at a point between the car and the trunk of the tree, and put the other end into a noose around his neck. He then only had to jump into the gap between car and tree.

It was efficiently done. The coroner heard that Mark's neck was broken as the rope went taut.

In a small last act of selfishness, Mark wrote no final note. He did not explain anything, express regret, or ask for forgiveness.

Thomas, in his role as executor, sold the car as quickly as possible. We do not know what happened to the tracker.

Eulogy for Love

Perhaps it fell off as Mark drove the car over the uneven forest floor. Or it may have been removed by a mechanic who took it to be an innocent component of a security system. Then again, someone may now be driving a large black SUV, unaware of the tracker that still clings to its underside, or of the man who stepped from its roof with a rope around his neck.

With Mark dead, there was no possibility of police action arising directly from David's report. However, David's description of a boy with an 'Easter Island face' immediately indicated a lad who lived on the housing estate next door to the supermarket. He had already come to the notice of child protection agencies for sexualised behaviours that indicated he might have been abused. He was interviewed in the week following David's report, but the boy would say nothing. That changed when he was told that Mark was dead. He no longer had anything to fear from Mark, nor any prospect of more money from him, and that was enough to make him talk. He was a former pupil at an educational establishment operated by Mark's company, and made allegations against two of the school staff. It led to prosecutions that damaged the reputation of the company, though the scandal was soon forgotten.

Mark's death was plainly suicide. In light of his bereavement the day before, there seemed no need for the inquest to speculate further on why he had wanted to take his own life. The children have thus been spared the additional psychological burden of having a convicted paedophile for a father.

That said, the sudden loss of both their parents has left Jonathan and Rachel terribly wounded. Although they are better off without an abusive father in their lives, they need a more positive model of men and fathers. David is already providing it. He and I do everything we can to help the children to recover, and to give them the joyful, secure life that Kat had wanted for them.

David abandoned his vision of Purgatory. He is often here at the house in the evenings after school, and for the whole of most weekends. We felt so sorry for Little Cat, too often left on her own at the farmhouse, that David brought her to live with us. She has been startled to be the object of so much fussing from the children, but is settling.

David and I first came together out of our shared love of Kat, and now we work together not only to fulfil our pledge to her, but also out of love for Rachel and Jonathan. Though we have not spoken of it, I think we both know that this growth of love has a third stem. Another flower is coming into bloom. This blossom is not brash, nor in the colour of passion. It is a love with a purity and quiet simplicity, and it promises to last the rest of our lives.

With the children using their bedrooms fulltime, David has been sleeping on a folding bed downstairs. It is a ridiculous arrangement. One day soon, when a little more time has passed, I will go to him as he sets up the bed for another night. I will take his hand, and kiss him, and lead him upstairs. And Kat, somewhere, will smile.

About the author

STEVE DOWSON began his career as a social worker, and by chance he soon encountered the injustices and awful treatment experienced by many people with learning disabilities. His campaigning work to improve policies and services for people with learning disabilities became the focus of his work for the next four decades, eventually leading to work as an international consultant.

In all this work, words have been his primary weapon—used by him in countless critiques of government policy, academic papers, inspirational descriptions of better futures, and sardonic editorials. But it is only since he retired that Steve has turned to fiction, with *Eulogy for Love* as his first novel.

Steve lives on the Malvern Hills in Worcestershire, UK.

More information about Steve and his writing can be found at **stevedowson.uk**

Printed in Great Britain
by Amazon

50480559R00228